NOVELS BY SEAN FLANNERY

The Kremlin Conspiracy
Eagles Fly
The Trinity Factor
The Hollow Men
Broken Idols
False Prophets
Gulag
Moscow Crossing
The Zebra Network
Crossed Swords
Counterstrike
Moving Targets
Winner Take All*
Kilo Option*
Achilles' Heel*
(*Bill Lane adventures)

WRITING AS DAVID HAGBERG

Twister
The Capsule
Last Come the Children
Heartland
Without Honor*
Countdown*
Crossfire*
Critical Mass*
Desert Fire
High Flight*
Assassin*
White House*
(*Kirk McGarvey adventures)

ACHILLES' HEEL

Sean Flannery

TOR ®

A TOM DOHERTY ASSOCIATES BOOK
NEW YORK

This is a work of fiction. All the characters and events portrayed in this book are either products of the author's imagination or are used fictitiously.

ACHILLES' HEEL

A Tor Book
Published by Tom Doherty Associates, LLC
175 Fifth Avenue
New York, NY 10010

www.tor.com

Tor® is a registered trademark of Tom Doherty Associates, LLC

ISBN: 0-812-55033-1
Library of Congress Card Catalog Number: 98-14325

First edition: August 1998
First mass market edition: August 1999

Printed in the United States of America

0 9 8 7 6 5 4 3 2 1

This book is for
Laurie

Prologue

Captain First Rank Aleksandr Rulov watched from the bridge of his destroyer *Uporny* as the submarine, riding low in the water and wallowing in the steep seas, made a wide turn to port, bringing its sail into the wind.

"Poor bastards," he said to his executive officer, Lieutenant Commander Selyutin.

"Makes me sick just looking at them," the sallow-faced man replied. "But they'll be aboard us soon enough."

The captain lowered his binoculars for a moment and gave his XO a hard stare. He was about to make a sharp reply but thought better of it. Even here aboard his destroyer, and in this day and age, the walls had ears. Silence was easier to explain than a misspoken word. The growler phone buzzed, and Rulov picked it up with a meaty paw.

"This is the captain."

"CIC, Captain. We're in position."

"*Da*," Rulov replied. He hung up the phone and looked at his XO. "We're there, and I don't want to stay long. Have the recovery crew stand by to launch on my order. See to it personally, would you, Yuri? Those are good men out there."

"Yes, sir," Selyutin said. He left the bridge.

In actuality Rulov had never met the scuttling crew of submarine 283 before. They were all new boys, sent up for this one job, and he didn't envy them their task.

Submarines in general gave him the willies; they were like sardine cans, no, like coffins. But 283 was even worse. It was an older Romeo-class diesel electric boat, cramped, smelly, and dangerous. Better to have the sea beneath your keel, and not over your mast.

He picked up the ship's comm. "Engineering."

"Engineering, *da*."

"We're there. Give me turns for dead slow."

"What's it like up there, Captain?" the chief engineer asked. He was a tough old bastard, every bit as crusty as the captain.

"Rough."

"Turn her into the wind, I don't want to bang around down here for nothing." The ChEng cut the connection. He was the only man aboard the ship who could talk to the captain like that and get away with it.

"Come left to two-seven-zero degrees," he told the helmsman.

The big destroyer began to slow down as her engine revolutions decreased, and she turned into the wind and five-meter waves. The motion aboard became easier, as it undoubtedly had for the submarine five hundred meters out when she turned into the wind.

Rulov radioed the submarine. "Two-eight-three, this is *Uporny*. Are you ready for us?"

"Stand by, *Uporny*."

Rulov could hear strain in the speaker's voice. "Do you have a problem?"

A second speaker came on. "This is Captain Lubiako, and you're damned right we have a problem. The high-pressure air system is wrecked, and we're taking on ballast water. The son of a bitch is going to sink out from under us."

"That's what we're here for," Rulov said. "Abandon ship now, and I'll send a launch for you."

"There's no guarantee she'll go down unless we blow the bottom out of her as planned."

Rulov switched the radio to the overhead speaker so that the helmsman, first officer, and others on the bridge could hear.

"Say again the nature of your problem, Captain?"

"Our ballast tanks are flooding!" Lubiako shouted. In the background someone else was shouting something.

"I'm sending over a launch. I suggest you abandon ship," Rulov said. He got on the ship's comm. "Launch the recovery crew now," he told Selyutin. "I'll patch over comms to you from two-eight-three. It sounds like they're in trouble."

"For real?"

"*Da,*" Rulov said, turning back to the radio. He flipped a switch which allowed the two-way conversation to be picked up aboard the recovery launch.

He walked to the port wing lookout station in time to see the thirty-foot rescue launch lowered into the sea, disengage, and peel away from the pitching destroyer. He went back to the radio.

"Two-eight-three, the launch is wet, and our rescue team is on the way."

"Tell them to stay clear!" Lubiako shouted. "I don't know how long I can hold this bastard!"

"I say again, abandon ship," Rulov radioed, careful to keep his voice calm, unlike Lubiako, who was clearly panicking. He was sorry that his crew had to bear witness to what he felt was a disgrace on the part of an officer.

The radio channel opened, but Lubiako was screaming something unintelligible, while in the background they could hear what sounded like water rushing in, and men screaming.

"Abandon ship! Abandon ship!" Rulov ordered.

"Too late . . ."

The submarine was hard down by the bow, her conning tower almost completely submerged, when an underwater explosion geysered the cold October seas.

The *Uporny*'s launch veered left, heading into the steep waves a hundred meters from the stricken submarine, and her six-man crew watched in horrified fascination as the boat sank as if her bottom had blown out.

A large oil slick came to the surface, and was blown off the tops of the waves and dissipated almost as quickly as it had appeared.

Several pieces of debris shot up, tumbling in the rugged seas.

"Bridge, sonar."

Captain Rulov picked up the growler phone. "This is the captain."

"Sir, I'm showing definite breakup noises. There've been two further explosions, and now the implosions as her pressure hull buckles."

"Is there any other underwater traffic in the area?"

"Nyet."

"Keep a sharp ear."

At fifty-four, Rulov had spent most of his life around ships or at sea. He'd seen it all—from the warm Caribbean waters off Cuba to raging storms and towering seas in the middle of the Pacific. But for this place he had the utmost respect. This was the Russian navy's graveyard, where her old, out-of-commission ships were sunk in a thousand meters of Arctic water. All sorts of naval debris littered the ocean bottom here, including a good number of nuclear submarines, and spent reactors cut from nuclear vessels. An unhealthy place to be.

God help the crew of any ship sunk here. Because if they somehow survived in an airtight compartment there would be no rescue attempts. Nuclear reactors began to leak sooner or later. Here and now this was the most dangerous piece of ocean in the world.

"Bridge, sonar."

The captain picked up the phone. *"Da."*

"I think she's on the bottom. I'm not picking up a thing now. She's dead."

"Any chance of survivors?"

"No, sir," the sonarman said. "I've never heard sounds like that before. She must have broken into a million pieces. There's nothing left now but junk."

"Very well," Captain Rulov said.

Selyutin came in. "They fished out a couple of life jackets."

"Are the jackets radioactive?" Rulov asked.

"Yes, sir. But not as hot as that scuttling crew." It was gallows humor.

"Take it easy, Yuri," Rulov said gently. "It's the risk all of us take."

"Especially submariners," Selyutin said. "They're all a bunch of crazy bastards."

"We'll hang around until it gets dark in case there are any survivors."

Selyutin looked out the windows. "Shall I inform Polyarnyy?"

"It's already been taken care of. Our orders are to make certain there are no survivors."

"Are they sending help?"

"*Nyet,*" Rulov said.

PART ONE

1

The evening was sparkling, traffic dense as the cab pulled into the circular drive in front of the elegant Hay Adams Hotel. Bill Lane, a husky, thick-shouldered man in his mid-forties, dressed in a dove gray Italian silk suit, an Hermès tie, matching pocket square, and hand-sewn Brazilian loafers, got out of the cab and paid the driver. As the bellman was getting his Louis Vuitton luggage out of the trunk, Lane stared at the White House through the trees across the far side of Lafayette Park, his deep blue eyes narrowing slightly as if he were measuring distances.

All of Washington was busy this Friday evening, with a reception for the prime ministers of all seven EC nations at the White House, and cocktail parties at every major hotel and many of the embassies. The United Nations General Assembly had just adjourned after one of the most contentious sessions in its history, and the diplomats and their staffs had come to Washington to celebrate. The trouble in the Balkans was finally over. The former Yugoslavia had been successfully partitioned into three independent nations, and although no one was overjoyed by the politics of the UN-brokered treaty, at least the killing had stopped.

The lobby was busy. A lot of people were dressed in evening clothes. A string quartet playing a Vivaldi piece was all but drowned out by the hum of conversation.

"You have a reservation for me. The name is Vandermeer," Lane told a young woman at the registration desk.

The night manager, wearing morning clothes, came over smoothly. "Welcome to Washington, Mr. Vandermeer," he said. His brass name tag read Mr. Wilson. "Indeed we do have a suite reserved in your name." He glanced down at a computer screen. "Three nights?"

"That's right," Lane said. He handed an American Express platinum card to the manager, who deftly slid it through the card reader and immediately returned it.

"I hope you had a pleasant trip."

"Tolerable."

The registration form popped out of the printer and the manager laid it and a gold pen from his pocket on the counter. Lane signed under the name William Vandermeer, the Kruger Investment Group, Cape Town, South Africa.

The manager pocketed his pen, handed one of the room keys to the bellman waiting with Lane's luggage, then came around the counter as the bellman headed toward the service elevator.

"I'll show you to your room, sir."

Lane followed the night manager to the bank of elevators on the left. Before the door closed he glanced across at a group of people dressed in evening clothes near the string quartet.

"The city seems busy tonight."

"Oh, yes, sir."

"Are you fully booked?"

"Completely," the manager said. "In fact you were lucky that there was a cancellation. Even the Presidential Suite is occupied."

"Russians?"

The manager was surprised. "Why, yes, sir."

"Bank of Moscow?"

"Yes, sir. They're having a reception this evening for their new North American branch manager."

"I would have thought they'd hold such a gathering at their own embassy."

"It's not big enough," the night manager said. "But you need not be concerned, sir. The reception is being held on the mezzanine, ten floors below you, so you shouldn't be bothered."

The suite was very large, and overlooked Lafayette Park and the White House beyond. One room was furnished with a larger than king-size bed, two walk-in closets, his and hers dressing areas, and a palatial master bathroom. The other room was furnished as a living room with sectional couches, chairs, an entertainment center, a second bathroom, and a fully stocked wet bar. There were vases of cut flowers here and there throughout the suite, and a thick terry-cloth robe was laid out on the bed.

The bellman was just finishing with the bags. When he came out, Lane handed him a fifty-dollar bill.

"Thank you, sir," he said and left.

"Shall I pour you a glass of champagne, sir?" the night manager asked.

"If it's any good."

"A vintage Dom Pérignon."

"Very well," Lane said. He lit a cigarette and went to the windows. He'd never stayed at the Hay Adams before. It was very nice; too bad Frannie wasn't here to share it with him. "The Russian reception tonight is a closed affair?"

"Yes, sir. By invitation only," the night manager said. He brought Lane a glass of champagne. "Will there be anything else?"

Lane handed him three hundred dollars. "I'd like an invitation to that reception."

The night manager hesitated only a moment before pocketing the money. "I'll see what I can do."

"What time does it begin?"

"Two hours from now. Nine o'clock."

"Right. I'll just change clothes and pop down to the lobby bar to wait."

"Very good, sir," the night manager said, and he left.

2

**NATIONAL SECURITY AGENCY
FORT MEADE, MARYLAND**

Tom Hughes was expecting the call, so when it came he snatched up the telephone in the middle of the first ring.

"The reception starts at nine, so you should have everyone in place no later than eleven."

"Where are you now?"

"At the bar," Lane said. "They just sent my invitation over. I'll go up around ten-thirty. But knowing Gregor, it's not going to take much of a nudge from me or anyone else to get him drunk."

"Just watch yourself, William."

"Okay, Mom," Lane said lightly, and broke the connection.

Hughes laughed to himself as he got an outside line and dialed a Washington number. Sometimes he *was* like a mother hen to Bill Lane, who was the closest friend he had ever had. They not only shared the NSA's Russian Division, but Lane was "Uncle Bill" and godfather to Hughes's six daughters, who loved him. He was family.

The call was answered. "Yes."

"It's on," Hughes said. "Be in place by eleven."

"How long are we supposed to hang around?"

"If it hasn't happened by two, we'll have to try something else. Just look sharp."

A homely, short, corpulent man, Hughes was brilliant and he was kind. He'd earned Ph.D.'s at Georgetown University with a 4.0 average in Far Eastern studies and languages (he read, wrote, and spoke eleven fluently). And Moira, his wife of twenty years, along with their six girls, two cats, one dog, and assorted gerbils, birds, and turtles, adored him.

At home he could not lift so much as a finger for himself, but here it was a different story.

He looked up at the series of photographs displayed on the six-hundred-square-foot situation screen in the NSA's Crisis Management Center. Russian navy captain Gregor Sergeyev, the military attaché to the Russian embassy in Washington, was an alcoholic and therefore unpredictable. But he was well connected in Moscow, which made him vulnerable to scandal. No one wanted to promote a man with a tarnished image. Especially one tarnished in the West.

Hughes got his jacket and started to leave, but then came back to his console overlooking the big screen. He unlocked the bottom drawer, took out the 10mm Beretta, checked to make certain it was loaded, and stuffed it in his pocket. He felt faintly ridiculous about it, but Bill had made him promise.

3

WASHINGTON, D.C.

Lane handed his invitation to the security guards and joined the party at the Bank of Moscow reception. It was already 10:30 and he estimated that there were at least five hundred people crowded into the main ballroom, and more were arriving.

A band at the head of the room played American show tunes and easy-listening music. A few couples danced, but most of the crowd had coalesced into knots of people who stood around, drinks in hand, discussing whatever the most influential member of that particular group wanted to discuss.

Gregor Sergeyev, dressed in a tuxedo with a wing collar and matching blue cummerbund and bow tie, was with a group of men near one of the service bars. At six feet he was a good four inches shorter than Lane, but he must have weighed a hundred pounds more. His neck and shoulders were massive, and if he moved too quickly he would probably burst his jacket at the seams.

But he never moved quickly. Lane knew that about him, just as he knew about the man's drinking, about his weakness for prostitutes, and about his financial troubles.

Lane walked over to the bar and ordered a Stoli on the rocks. While he waited for his drink, he lit a cigarette and scanned the room as if he were looking for someone. He was within earshot of Sergeyev's group, and it became quickly evident that the military attaché was already half-drunk.

Lane continued to pretend to search the room until the bartender came back to his end of the bar. "Say, you wouldn't happen to know Captain Sergeyev, would you?" he asked just loudly enough that he was sure Sergeyev had heard him.

The bartender shook his head. "I'm sorry, sir, I don't."

"Well, I'm trying to find him. He has a phone call."

Sergeyev detached himself from the group and came over, frowning. "I'm Captain Sergeyev."

"You have a phone call out in the hall, by the elevators," Lane said.

"Who is it?"

Lane shrugged. "She didn't give her name."

Sergeyev nodded, and headed unsteadily toward the doors. Lane waited a minute, then put down his drink and followed after the captain, catching up with him by the pay phones, none of which were off the hook.

"Sorry, Captain, that was just a ruse to get you out of there."

The Russian's eyes narrowed. "Who are you? What do you want?"

"I'm Bill Vandermeer. I'm with the Kruger Investment Group, Cape Town. We have an interest in doing business with you."

"I'm not a banker."

"Neither are most of them," Lane said, jerking his head in the direction of the ballroom. "And they're boring as hell. Anyway, a friend of mine, Toni Meyer, said I should look you up."

Sergeyev calmed down. "I don't know what you're talking about."

"Toni. Tall, blond, diamond choker. Said you knew where the good times were in D.C."

"I don't know what your game is, Mr. Kruger, but leave me alone."

"Vandermeer," Lane corrected. He spread his hands. "I thought we might do some business."

Sergeyev turned abruptly and walked over to the elevators. When a car came he stepped aboard, and did not look back. Lane waited until the indicator showed that the elevator had descended to the parking garage, then headed for the stairs.

4

WASHINGTON, D.C.

Hughes was waiting behind the wheel of a yellow cab in front of the hotel when Lane came out and got in the backseat. Sergeyev's dark blue Nissan Pathfinder came up from the parking garage and passed the front of the hotel, but instead of turning onto Sixteenth Street, which would have taken him to the Russian embassy, he headed the other way.

"He's heading north on Connecticut," Hughes radioed, pulling out into traffic and following the Pathfinder. He glanced at Lane's reflection in the rearview mirror. "How'd he react?"

"He's half in the bag, but he's suspicious," Lane said. "Something's going on that's got him bothered."

"A letter from Moscow?"

"Could be."

"Unit two has him," Hughes's handheld blared.

"Unit three, are you in position?" Hughes responded.

"Roger."

"Pick your spot," Hughes said.

5

WASHINGTON, D.C.

Gregor Sergeyev was more annoyed than worried, although he wouldn't put it past the SVR bastards to try to shake him up. There'd been talk that they wanted him out. If he resigned it would be easier than firing him. Vandermeer was obviously a fake, but he'd used Toni Meyer's name. That, Sergeyev could check.

A light blue Chevy Cavalier switched lanes directly in front of the Pathfinder without warning, and Sergeyev had no chance to react, slamming into the rear right quarter of the much smaller vehicle, sending it spinning half around before they stopped.

"Yeb vas," Sergeyev swore softly. He had diplomatic immunity, but the ambassador was sensitive to incidents like this. Especially involving drunk driving. It was *neokulturny*. Everybody in America thought everybody in Russia was a drunk. There was no use proving it.

Sergeyev got out of the Pathfinder, traffic flowing around them. One of the passing drivers honked and gave him the finger.

An older woman with gray hair, a little blood trickling down her chin from a cut lip, got shakily out of the Cavalier.

"Are you all right, madam?" Sergeyev asked. "Shall I call for a doctor?"

The woman's eyes opened wide, and she stepped back toward traffic. "You're drunk!" she cried. "You're drunk!"

"Nyet!" Sergeyev shouted, and he tried to reach her, but she was frightened and she stepped directly into the path of a yellow cab.

The driver slammed on his brakes, and the cab screeched to a halt inches from the woman, who reared back in shock, then collapsed in a heap on the pavement.

"Dear God," Sergeyev muttered, too stunned to do anything. It was happening so fast.

The cabbie jumped out, shot Sergeyev a dark look, and went to the woman, who was moaning and crying and thrashing around. He helped her sit up, but she was still out of it, and he had to hold her.

Traffic was slowing, people gawking out their windows looking for blood and gore. In the distance Sergeyev could hear a siren, and he could feel himself beginning to panic. The situation was getting completely out of control.

"Christ on the cross, what the hell is going on?" the passenger from the cab said.

Sergeyev turned as Vandermeer came over. "You," he said.

"I'm on my way to Toni's. What happened?" Lane asked.

"There was an accident, and the woman went crazy," Sergeyev said.

The siren was closer now, and Lane glanced at the woman. "Did she get a good look at your face?"

"I don't know. Probably yes." Sergeyev was confused. The siren and all the noise were bothersome.

"Is she going to be okay?" Lane called to Hughes.

"Looks like it."

Lane turned back to Sergeyev. "I need your help, otherwise I wouldn't stick my neck out like this. But you're drunk, and if you hang around until the cops show up you're going to be in trouble with your ambassador."

Sergeyev stared at him.

"Take my cab back to the Hay Adams. I'll meet you at the lobby bar."

"What about my car?"

"Just get the hell out of here, I'll take care of it. I'm not drunk so they won't arrest me. Nobody's been seriously hurt, and that woman won't remember a thing. I'll take care of it."

"What about the cabbie?"

"Give him a big tip—that's all they understand in this town," Lane said.

Sergeyev hesitated a moment, then climbed into the cab.

6

WASHINGTON, D.C.

"All right, get him out of here," Lane told Hughes.

"Did he buy it?" Joyce Katarian asked, her eyes fluttering.

"You'll get the Academy Award for sure," Lane said. "But you cut it close. Just about gave us a heart attack."

Joyce, who until three months ago was a special NSA operative in Kiev, winked at him. "Giving men heart attacks is a woman's prerogative," she said. "Now help me up."

Hughes went back to the cab as Lane helped Joyce to her feet and led her back to her car. Sergeyev looked out the window at them as the cab pulled away.

Seconds later, while the cab was still in sight at the end of the block, a District of Columbia Metro police car, its lights flashing, pulled up behind the Pathfinder, and two cops got out.

"How'd it go, Mr. Lane?" John Ribowski, the big black cop who'd been driving, asked.

"Like clockwork," Lane said. "The siren was a nice touch."

"How do you want us to write this up?" the other cop, Tom Morgan, asked, grinning.

"As an ordinary fender bender, no injuries, no drugs or alcohol." Lane handed them a printout with Vandermeer's vitals including driver's license and passport numbers.

"It's going to take a few days to run this through the system," Ribowski said.

"Take your time," Lane said.

He and the cops inspected Joyce's car. The rear fender was bashed in, and the bumper was bent, but the car was driveable.

"I'll run it through on my insurance. It's the third since I got back, so no one will think I did it on purpose."

"Except Ben Lewis."

Joyce chuckled. "That's your problem, sweetie, not mine." She got in her car, turned it around, and drove off.

"Don't ever get on her bad side," Lane said.

Ribowski laughed. "I hear you, man. I got one just like that at home."

WASHINGTON, D.C.

The Bank of Moscow reception was beginning to wind down when Lane got back to the Hay Adams. Several of the diplomats and businessmen had descended to the lobby, where they waited for their wives, who were upstairs in the powder rooms. Gregor Sergeyev was seated alone at a small table in the lobby bar. He was drinking coffee.

Lane went to the bar, ordered a Martell cognac, and took it back to Sergeyev's table. The Russian looked up, somewhat bleary-eyed but even more suspicious than before. The fact that he'd returned to the hotel as Lane had instructed, however, was a good sign that he would cooperate.

"Did you straighten it out with the police?"

"They're listing it as a minor fender bender. At some point you'll have to verify that you gave me permission to drive your car." Lane grinned. "Turns out the woman was half-drunk herself, so she was in no position to file a complaint."

"What do you want?" Sergeyev demanded harshly.

"A simple thanks would be appropriate," Lane shot back.

"All right, thank you. Now what do you want? You said you need my help. With what?"

"It'll keep," Lane said. He finished his cognac and got up. "Your car's out front. Go home and get some sleep."

Sergeyev watched him closely. "You have gone through a lot of trouble to meet me, Mr. Vandermeer."

"That I have."

"Here I am."

"In the morning," Lane said. "When you're sober."

"I'm sober now," Sergeyev said mildly, but with an underlying edge of irritation in his voice.

Lane glanced toward the lobby, then motioned to the bartender for another cognac. He walked over and got his drink, leaving Sergeyev to stew in his own juices, and perhaps blunt some of his suspicions.

Back at the table Lane sat down, and lit a cigarette. "I didn't think you were going to get into a car accident."

"You were following me."

"Of course. I figured you'd be going over to the club. I had a room and a couple of women set up for us. That's why I told you there was a call for you. I figured it would get you thinking through your gonads."

"Your timing was most fortunate," Sergeyev said dryly.

"It wouldn't have been if that stupid cabdriver had hit the woman."

"Will he keep his mouth shut?"

Lane shrugged. "He might if you tipped him well."

"He was a highwayman," Sergeyev snorted.

Lane suppressed a chuckle. "Toni gives you high marks."

"As she does you," the Russian said. "I telephoned while I waited. But now it's late, and my patience is running thin. Who are you, and what do you want from me?"

"I'm a middleman for a group of wealthy investors, venture capitalists, who are interested in high-risk investments because of the potential high returns."

"A nice speech. But what does it mean, and what does

it have to do with me? I've never been to South Africa in my life."

"My investors aren't South Africans," Lane said. "As to why it's you I've come to see, you're a Russian military attaché who holds the rank of captain in the navy, and colonel in the GRU."

"I see," Sergeyev said cautiously. "Are you going to tell me the rest, or am I going to have to guess?"

"Of all the military attachés in all the Russian embassies around the world, you are unique," Lane said. "Not only are you a military intelligence officer, you're an ex–submarine man. That and one other item were the combination we were looking for."

"What's that?"

"You're in debt right up to your ears," Lane said. "You've probably been warned to control your spending, but so far that's not happened."

Sergeyev's massive jaw was tight. "Are you asking me to sell military information?"

"We want to buy something, Gregor, but it's not information. And ultimately we won't be buying it from you. Like me, you will only be a middleman."

Sergeyev's anger and suspicion turned to puzzlement. "I don't have any idea what you're talking about. Start making some sense or I'll leave. Maybe I can interest some friends of mine to break your legs, just to impress you with my sincerity."

Lane took a plain white envelope out of his pocket and laid it on the table. "Copies of your Visa and MasterCard bills for the last three months. The banks are on the verge of starting legal action against you."

Sergeyev didn't touch the envelope. "If it's not information, what do you want, and what's in it for me?"

"Immediate financial relief for you. And for my people one of your surplus submarines. Specifically, she's a Romeo-class diesel electric boat with the sail number two-eight-three, that was supposedly scrapped in the Barents Sea five days ago."

"I don't know what you're talking about."

"Perhaps not. But you can put me in touch with the people who do know."

"How do you know it wasn't sunk?"

"I'm not authorized to tell you that yet, but I can tell you this much, that sub has probably been sold to someone my people don't want it sold to, and we're willing to pay a hefty premium to see that the boat doesn't fall into the wrong hands."

Sergeyev shook his head. "Not good enough."

"For now it'll have to do, Gregor," Lane said. He tapped the envelope. "This could be very important to you, and certainly even more important to Russia. You're selling off your surplus subs, that's common knowledge. So you might as well make as much money as you possibly can. That's the whole idea, isn't it?" Lane grinned. "We pay in gold bullion or Krugerrands. You can't miss."

"Who did you say you represent?"

"I didn't. But the consortium is involved on the African continent—the *entire* African continent, if you catch my meaning."

"I don't," Sergeyev said flatly.

Lane shrugged. "Then the hell with it. I'll tell them that I made a mistake, and we'll have to find someone else. Russians like you are a dime a dozen these days."

Sergeyev cracked a slight smile for the first time. "I thought you said I was unique. I think I prefer that, to 'dime a dozen.' "

"I'm talking about a lot of money."

"You'd better be," Sergeyev said darkly. "Wait here, I have to make a call."

Lane sat back as Sergeyev got up and used the phone at the bar. He spoke for several minutes, and when he was finished he ordered a vodka from the bartender, tossed it back, and returned to the table.

"You can drive," he said.

"Where are we going?" Lane asked, getting up.

"The embassy."

8

WASHINGTON, D.C.

The Russian embassy, on Sixteenth between L and M Streets, had once been the mansion of a wealthy businessman, and it still looked like one except for the brass plaque in front, and a rooftop bristling with antennae and satellite dishes. They were admitted through the iron gate and Lane parked at the back of the building. Just inside the rear entrance a pair of burly civilian guards ran an electronic wand over him, and patted him down for good measure.

"You may go right up, sir," one of the guards said to Sergeyev in Russian. "Mr. Zemin just arrived, and he's waiting for you."

Lane, who spoke fluent Russian, thought the guard's accent was odd. Far East, probably remote Siberia. A lot of the toughs used for enforcement came from out there. It was a holdover from the old KGB days. Some things never changed.

It was two in the morning and the embassy was quiet. They took an elevator to the fourth floor, where Lane followed Sergeyev to a small office at the front of the building looking down on Sixteenth Street. A man dressed in evening clothes, his bow tie undone, got up from behind his desk. Lane knew what to expect so he was not surprised; Gennadi Zemin, SVR Washington *rezident* and former KGB field operative in Western Europe, was at fifty-three a dead ringer for Robert Redford right down to the craggy but boyish features, blond hair, blue eyes, and charming smile.

"Here he is," Sergeyev said.

Zemin came around the desk. "The South African with the interesting proposition," he said, holding out his hand.

"Bill Vandermeer."

"Gennadi Zemin. I'm special assistant for economic affairs to the ambassador. May I offer you something? Champagne? Vodka?"

"Nothing for now," Lane said. "I don't want to waste your time."

"Let me be the judge of that."

"I want to speak to someone in authority."

"Do you mean the ambassador himself?"

"Of course not. I mean your *rezident*."

"I see," Zemin said. He and Sergeyev exchanged a glance, and it was clear they did not like each other. "Your name is Vandermeer. You're from South Africa. And you represent an investment group."

"That's right."

"May I see your passport, and something that might tie you to this group?"

"I'll wait for the *rezident*."

"First we'll verify that you are who you say you are," Zemin said.

Lane shrugged, and dug his passport and a buff envelope with the return address of the Kruger Investment Group, S.A., Cape Town, South Africa, out of his inside jacket pocket.

"That's a letter of credit on the Bank of South Africa in the amount of four hundred fifty million rand."

Zemin opened the envelope and his left eyebrow rose.

He looked up. "This is a considerable amount of money."

"It's a start," Lane said, setting the hook.

Zemin made a brief phone call, and a young man with wild hair and pimples came in, got the passport and letter of credit, and left.

"Why don't we have a seat and see what this is all about." Zemin motioned to chairs in front of his desk.

Sergeyev sat beside Lane across from Zemin, who folded his hands in front of him on the desk. There was a wary look on his face, but one of definite interest. The letter of credit had done its job.

"After Gregor's call I made a couple of preliminary checks on you," Zemin said. "At least on the surface you appear to be the genuine article. But before we get started, I'm curious about something. What makes you think that Gregor is anything other than our military attaché?"

"Are you denying that he's a colonel in the GRU?"

Zemin waited patiently.

Lane had to smile again. Russians were predictable. They always had been and they always would be. "*Jane's*," he said. "Get it at any library. I did."

"Captain Sergeyev hasn't been listed for the past three years."

"Not under naval forces. But two years ago he showed up under Moscow District Defense Command, with the army rank of colonel. When that happens it usually means a promotion to military intelligence."

"Very astute for a financial adviser," Zemin said.

"I said I represented a financial group. I didn't say that I was a banker."

"Just what are you then, Mr. Vandermeer?"

Lane nodded toward the door. "Your man will find out soon enough."

"Save us the anxious wait," Zemin said.

Lane shrugged. "I used to work for South African intelligence."

"Why did you get out?"

"Let's just say I came to the realization that there was more money to be made on the outside."

"Diamonds, gold?"

"Whatever."

"Information?"

"That too," Lane said. "What's your point?"

"Whether to trust you or not, of course."

Lane smiled. "That's rich, coming from a Russian."

"Did you resign or were you fired?" Zemin went on, ignoring the jibe.

"I quit by mutual agreement."

"For what reason?"

"I screwed the arse off a general's wife," Lane replied matter-of-factly. "If that offends your delicate sensibilities then I'm out of here."

"You came to us, not the other way around," Zemin pointed out, unimpressed. "With a proposition."

"That's right. The group I represent wants to buy a submarine from your government."

"A very specific submarine," Zemin said. "One that doesn't even exist."

"Ah, but it does, and I'll even tell your *rezident* where it is."

9

WASHINGTON, D.C.

Zemin took a bottle of vodka and three glasses from a desk drawer, and poured. Sergeyev's hand shook slightly when he picked up his glass and drained it. Zemin noticed but said nothing.

There was a lot of bad blood between the branches of the civilian and military intelligence services that went all the way back to Moscow. Yet because of the far-reaching nature of the intelligence-gathering business they were forced to work together.

The young man with wild hair and pimples brought the passport and letter of credit back, handing them to Zemin. Then he took Lane's fingerprints.

"This is going to take twenty-four hours, maybe longer," he said. "I'll push the request through Interpol's Special Branch, but if they want to drag their heels there won't be much we can do about it."

Zemin studied the brief report the young man brought. "Our friend checks out?"

"So far." The young man handed Lane a couple of sheets of paper towel to wipe the ink from his fingers. "We'll know for sure as soon as his prints are verified," he said, and he left.

"Tell me about this submarine then," Zemin said, handing Lane's papers back to him.

"I'll wait for the *rezident*."

"I am the *rezident*, Zemin said, amused.

"That's right," Sergeyev put in.

"You're checking me out. How do I know that you're the genuine article?"

"You'll just have to take my word on it, Mr. Vandermeer, because I have no way to prove it. But as I said, it was you who came to us. Not the other way around."

Lane paused for several seconds, but then shrugged. "I don't have much of a choice. My people expect results, not excuses."

"The Romeo-class submarine you speak of was scrapped in the Barents Sea last week. I'm told that she's a thousand meters down, and quite impossible to salvage."

"She was sunk up there all right. The message sent to Polyarnyy was that there was an accident. The salvage crew was lost. No survivors."

"I've heard nothing about that," Sergeyev said.

"Neither have I." Zemin studied Lane with a new wariness. "Question is, how has Mr. Vandermeer come by such information?"

"Very simple," Lane said. "One of the crewmen aboard two-eighty-three telephoned us from Polyarnyy and told us what was going to happen, and why."

"Who is this crewman?"

"I can't tell you that," Lane said.

"Did he call you personally? Here in Washington?"

"No, his contact was one of our people in Moscow." Lane held up a hand. "And I can't tell you his name either. The simple fact is I don't know their names, or how they come to be in contact with each other. But my people have some powerful financial connections in Moscow."

"Which is why you're here with this story," Zemin said skeptically. "Come on, Vandermeer, why don't you tell me what you really want? You have my undivided attention."

Lane sat back and lit a cigarette. "Something went

wrong. The crewman was going to make contact when two-eighty-three entered the English Channel, which was supposed to happen twenty-four hours ago. He didn't, and my people got worried.''

''Why did you place a man aboard the sub in the first place?'' Sergeyev asked.

''He was going to sabotage the boat, then send us a message. From there we would make direct contact with the skipper, and make him an offer he couldn't refuse. Take our money, and deliver the submarine where we want it delivered.''

''Or else your people would tell the British navy about the presence of a Russian submarine in their waters,'' Zemin said.

''Something like that,'' Lane said.

Zemin smiled. ''That's quite an inventive story. But frankly I'm at a loss. Let's say for the sake of argument that you are who you say you are, your letter of credit is good, and two-eight-three was not scrapped but in fact is in the English Channel or vicinity. What do you expect me to do about it?''

''My people want to buy the submarine, and they're willing to pay twice what it's already been sold for.''

''Why don't your Moscow people simply make the deal? They seem to have all the answers.''

''Easier said than done,'' Lane said. ''And there's no time.''

''Where is the submarine heading that has your people so concerned?''

''That's one bit of information I'm not going to share with you.''

''You said you were already here in Washington when you got the call,'' Sergeyev said. ''Doing what, following me?''

''That only took about forty minutes on the Internet,'' Lane said. ''The FBI has a master list of all your embassy personnel, and *Jane's* has a Web site where I picked up your name again. But I got lucky with the State Department's social calendar page. I wanted to see if you'd been invited to any parties that I might crash. Turns out you were at the Hay Adams the very night I needed you."

"So what were you doing here?" Zemin asked.

"If we missed two-eighty-three and the British couldn't find her either, I was going to tell the Americans where she was going."

"Maybe we'll just keep you here."

Lane smiled. "That would be a very large mistake."

"Oh?" Zemin asked. "Why?"

"Once your government got wind of the fact you blew an offer worth a great deal of money, you'd probably be sent to count the birches somewhere far, far away."

Zemin hesitated a moment. "Where are you staying?"

"The Hay Adams," Lane said. "Will you do it?"

Zemin shrugged. "I'm allergic to birches. Keep yourself available for the next day or two, and I'll see what I can do."

10

WASHINGTON, D.C.

Sergeyev went downstairs with Lane, and outside to the Pathfinder.

"When I called the club to check on you, Toni said that you'd been a regular off and on for the past couple of years," he said.

"I've been here before but there's no need to involve Zemin in things that are none of his business," Lane said. "But if I were you I'd get the dent in the fender fixed as soon as possible."

"Take my car over to your hotel. I'll have a body shop pick it up in the morning," Sergeyev said, giving Lane an odd, almost wistful look. Then he turned and went back inside.

11

WASHINGTON, D.C.

Lane drove back to the Hay Adams, where he instructed the parking valet that the Pathfinder would be picked up in the morning.

Upstairs he changed into a pair of dark slacks, a light cashmere pullover, and a Gucci leather jacket and matching loafers. He called down to the front desk and asked not to be disturbed until noon, then hung the DO NOT DISTURB sign on his doorknob and took the service elevator down to the laundry in the basement. From there he slipped unnoticed out the back way, walked to I Street, and caught a cruising cab over to his apartment in Georgetown, where he'd left his Jaguar sedan.

Tom Hughes was sound asleep in the passenger seat, his jacket bunched up under his head, his mouth wide open, the car windows fogged up.

Lane unlocked the driver's door and slipped behind the wheel as Hughes came awake with a start.

"If Moira finds out where you slept tonight, she'll have both our hides," Lane said.

Hughes's grin was lopsided. "Only if some rat finks on me. Did they go for it?"

"They're checking my bona fides now, but the worst that can happen is they'll say no."

Hughes shook his head. "Ben found out and he's on the warpath."

"How?"

"I don't know, but he's got spies everywhere. In the NSA, no less. It's un-American." Hughes smiled ruefully. "He wanted to pull you from the lap of luxury over at the Hay Adams, but I convinced him that you'd be showing up at the office sooner or later."

"When he comes in tomorrow morning, stall him. Twenty-four hours."

"He's camped out there right now waiting for you. I figured the least I could do is warn you."

"Exactly how much does he know?"

"Everything, I'm afraid, William."

"And he's mad?"

Hughes, his face drooping like a hound dog's, nodded.

"In that case you're coming with me," Lane said.

"Somehow I knew you were going to say something like that."

12

NATIONAL SECURITY AGENCY
FORT MEADE, MARYLAND

Instead of going up to Lewis's third-floor office, Lane and Hughes went directly to the Crisis Management Center in a subbasement, where Gregor Sergeyev's file photos were still projected on the main screen in the pit. Lane figured that with any luck it might take Lewis an hour or more to find out they were back and either come down here or send for them. In the meantime they could get some work done.

But Benjamin Lewis, the portly director of the NSA's Russian Division, was already seated at one of the electronic consoles facing the screen. He was a huge man, with thick black hair, a massive head that seemed too large even for his large body, and a barrel chest. His birth name was Lebedev and understood the Russian mentality better than anyone in the agency.

He didn't bother turning around as Lane and Hughes got off the elevator and walked over.

"Is Sergeyev as big a drunk as we've been led to believe, or is it all a sham?" he asked.

"He's a drunk," Lane said. He and Hughes pulled chairs over from other consoles. The center was deserted this evening, as were its counterparts in the White House, the CIA, and the Pentagon. "But Gennadi Zemin's not."

"Into the lions' den," Lewis said gently, which was a bad sign. He turned to them. "Tell me what has you two working nights, running up expense accounts at the Hay Adams, and involving the D.C. Metro Police . . . if you please."

"We're working on the CIA request for Russian navy traffic radio intercepts."

"The Sierra Leone thing?"

"That's right. The CIA wants help running down a rumor that Sierra Leone is trying to buy a submarine to counter increasing threats from their Liberian neighbor. It's getting pretty intense over there."

"You searched, and you found nothing," Lewis said.

"Not quite," Lane said.

Hughes slid over to one of the other consoles and logged into the NSA's mainframe. Sergeyev's photographs on the screen were replaced by a standard Robinson projection of the Northern Hemisphere from the

West Coast of North America to central Russia, with the African continent in the center.

"The Russians aren't about to sell submarines to just anybody because of the debacle in the Persian Gulf last year over Iran's Kilo-class subs," Lane said. "But they need the money now more than ever."

"We're keeping a satellite watch on every sub they own."

"That's right. So the only way they're going to get a sub to Sierra Leone, or anywhere for that matter, is to first destroy it, either by scuttling or by accident. Or at least make us *think* so."

Lewis studied the screen intently. "What'd you come up with?"

"An older nonnuclear Romeo-class submarine, sail number two-eighty-three, was scuttled in the Barents north of Polyarnyy five days ago. We stumbled on the radio traffic when we were running the program for the CIA. There was an explosion aboard, and the sub sank with all fourteen of its scuttling crew. No chance of rescue. In fact the Russian navy didn't even try to mount a rescue operation. The weather was bad, the submarine broke up on the way down, and that part of the ocean has been Russia's nuclear dumping ground for twenty years."

"Scratch one submarine."

"Maybe not," Lane said. "On the assumption the Romeo was meant to be sold to Sierra Leone, I worked out a probable track, and tapped into the navy's SOSUS network up there, as well as the ASW patrol ships from the Norwegian, Swedish, and German navies."

The track showed up in the green on the chart, and a series of four red slashes marked the vicinity of the course at irregular intervals heading south.

"Those were listed as underwater anomalies. Whale sounds. Subsea vents. Taken individually no one could argue with those conclusions. But the incidents were along the probable track, and at a speed the Romeo would normally cruise at.''

"Which may be coincidental," Lewis said.

Lane shot him a look. "Not likely."

Lewis spread his hands. "Nobody's arguing with your hunches, I'm just making sure that we understand all the possibilities. I'm assuming that your little operation against Sergeyev was designed to get you close to Zemin under a false ID.''

"We resurrected the Vandermeer legend."

"What did you and the *rezident* chat about?"

"I offered him a hundred million dollars for two-eighty-three."

Lewis's mouth dropped open.

"Actually I think it's quite a bargain," Hughes put in.

"What if he accepts?" Lewis asked, ignoring Hughes.

"Then I'll buy it. Of course I'll require an onboard inspection before money changes hands."

"They won't be happy if they find out that you're an imposter.''

"Once the sub has been pinpointed, they'll have to back off on their deal with Sierra Leone."

Lewis shook his head. "I gave you the assignment, so I suppose there's no use trying to take it away from you.''

"Not this close."

Lewis got ponderously to his feet. "Are you going back to the Hay Adams this morning?"

"Yes."

"I'd like a full report on my desk before you leave. Tommy will backstop you, of course, and if you need field people we'll arrange something with the CIA. It was their request in the first place. But watch yourself, Bill. You've had enough close calls to last a lifetime, and this isn't rocket science. Just a question of politics.''

13

WASHINGTON, D.C.

Hughes drove Lane back into the city and pulled over to the curb on I Street a block from the hotel. "Two-eighty-three is probably halfway to Gibraltar by now," he said.

"In that case it'll be a moot point. They'll probably offer me another boat. But I might get them to confirm that two-eighty-three didn't sink. It'd be something."

"Do you want me to call Frannie? She could pass this along to her boss. At least the Brits would have an idea what might be going on in their backyard."

"I'll let you know," Lane said, suddenly very tired.

"She's not going to simply give up on you and fade into the woodwork, William."

"Neither is Yernin," Lane replied sharply.

"He's done for."

"Don't count on it, Tommy. He's out there and he wants Frannie and me dead."

"What I'm saying is that the next move is his and it may never come. In the meantime life is what happens while you're looking the other way. She's a good woman. She loves you and I know that you love her. So get on with it. Marry her."

"Not yet."

Hughes shook his head. "You stubborn bastard. God help the sorry man if and when he ever does show up."

14

WASHINGTON, D.C.

The hotel was quiet when Lane entered through the laundry room and rode the freight elevator upstairs. There were no messages for him, nor had he expected any, but the lack heightened his sense of isolation. He took a shower, then poured a glass of champagne and sat by the window to wait for the dawn as he had many a morning over the past year.

Tommy was wrong. Death was what happened when you were looking the other way, and Valeri Yernin, a former KGB assassin, had vowed to kill him because of an operation that Lane had busted up more than a year ago.

"This time I won't fail, because I know his Achilles' heel," Yernin had promised his spymaster, Mikhail Maslennikov.

An NSA voiceprint of a telephone call from a phone booth in Karachi, Pakistan, was a 98 percent match with Yernin's. The voice at the other end of the line in Kiev was a 97 percent match to Yernin's agent runner, the wily old ex-submariner Maslennikov.

Those were the last words they heard from Yernin, who then dropped from the face of the earth, maybe killed by Pakistani bandits. Karachi was one of the most dangerous cities on earth. They'd held that hope for three days, until Maslennikov disappeared from Kiev. Like his star agent, he had dropped off the face of the earth. No one believed it was a coincidence.

It left Lane's pending marriage to Frances Shipley, a lieutenant commander in Her Majesty's Royal British Navy, and a liaison officer between the British and American intelligence communities on hold. Because the Achilles' heel that Yernin said he knew was Frannie. ·

It was an impossible burden for him—for anyone—to carry into a marriage. He drifted off to sleep thinking about Tommy's last words: "God help the sorry man if and when he ever does show up."

15

WASHINGTON, D.C.

After breakfast, Sergeyev went down to the *referentura*, where the embassy's innermost secrets were discussed in absolute security. One of Zemin's clerks buzzed him through, and he went back to the *rezident*'s cramped office.

"Don't tell me that we've already heard from Moscow," he said. ·

"I've been on the phone for the past three hours with my boss, your boss, and Lebed himself." Zemin's expression was neutral at best, but it was obvious that he found Sergeyev distasteful. "Four hundred fifty million rand—that's a hundred million dollars—has got them all interested."

"Could be an operation against us," Sergeyev said. "We'll just have to wait until Interpol gets back to us about his fingerprints."

"That'll have to be done on the run. They want him in London by tomorrow morning."

"Who does?"

"Moscow."

"Do you want me to get word to him?"

"You're going to do more than that," Zemin said. He passed a folder across to Sergeyev. "You're booked on an American Airlines flight that leaves at eight this evening."

Sergeyev hid his surprise. "Will we be met at the airport?"

"No. You're to go directly to the hotel, and someone will make contact with you there. It's all in the folder." Zemin sat back. "A word of advice, Colonel?"

Sergeyev shrugged. "If it pleases you."

"I know that you've been warned about your drinking, and your money troubles. But there is a lot at stake with this operation. Something else is going on besides the business with the money that has Moscow sitting up and taking notice. See that you don't make a mistake."

Sergeyev held his sudden flare of temper in check. "Am I to be told what this 'something else' is all about?"

"No, because even I don't know," Zemin said. "Now I suggest you get word to Vandermeer, and then pack."

Sergeyev nodded and turned to go, but Zemin stopped him at the door.

"I don't like you, Sergeyev. But I think that both of our careers may be riding on what happens in London. Keep it in mind."

PART TWO

1

LONDON

The FBI still monitored the comings and goings of Russian diplomats, so to avoid suspicion Lane and Sergeyev traveled separately, though on the same flight. They'd been booked coach class, but Lane checked in fifteen minutes before Sergeyev, upgrading his ticket to first class, and had been seated drinking a very good Merlot when Sergeyev boarded and spotted him. For a moment it seemed as if the Russian was going to come forward and say something, but he turned abruptly and filed aft.

It was 8:00 A.M. London time when they touched down at Heathrow, and well past 8:30 by the time Lane retrieved his four pieces of luggage, passed through passport control and customs, and reached the cab ranks. The redcap loaded the bags into the trunk of a taxi, and Lane handed him a twenty-pound note. He tipped his hat and when he was gone Sergeyev came over, his single carry-on bag in hand, a sour, slept-in look on his face.

"I don't know what the hell you're pulling, Vandermeer, but it won't work with me."

"You might as well understand up front that I don't travel coach."

"This isn't a game for your amusement."

"No it's not. My four hundred fifty million proves that. But it should also tell you that I intend having more control over this situation than your people may be completely comfortable with."

"We have something that you want," Sergeyev pointed out.

Lane patted his breast pocket. "And I have something that you want."

"Gentlemen?" the cabbie called politely.

Sergeyev gave Lane a dark look, tossed his bag in the cab, and climbed in, Lane following.

"Where will it be, sirs?"

"The Cumberland Hotel," Sergeyev said. "It's by Marble Arch."

"Indeed it is," the cabbie replied cheerfully, as he dropped the flag and pulled out.

"Where'd you get the British money?" Sergeyev demanded.

"At the machine outside customs. The rates are better than at the hotel," Lane said. "So we're here. Now what?"

Sergeyev looked pointedly at the driver on the other side of the split partition.

"You can talk almost as freely in a London taxi as you can in a confessional, or inside one of your *referenturas*."

"That'll be enough of that," Sergeyev warned.

"Let me guess. We've been sent to London because two-eighty-three is in the English Channel or somewhere thereabouts after all. But since the British aren't interested, the boat must be laid up. Maybe our crewman did what he was supposed to do, but got caught at it."

Sergeyev was aghast.

"Is it something like that?" Lane asked mildly. "Has your London *rezident* been in contact with the captain?"

"I don't know."

"Will someone contact us at the hotel? Or are they sending a messenger, or perhaps a car for us? Zemin must have told you something."

Sergeyev was at a loss.

Lane laughed. "He probably doesn't trust you, and I don't know if I do." He pulled another twenty-pound note from his pocket, and leaned forward. "We've had a change of plans," he told the driver. "Take us instead to Claridge's." He passed the note forward.

"Now that's a fine establishment, sir."

"You can't do that," Sergeyev said urgently.

"I just have," Lane replied lightly. "Let me give you some advice, Gregor. Three things. Control your drinking, control your finances, and every now and then do something unexpected. You'll be amazed at the respect you'll get."

Sergeyev was breathing heavily. He looked at the driver, then out the window at the heavy morning traffic on the motorway, and finally back at Lane. "You think we're fools."

"As a matter of fact I do," Lane said after a brief hesitation. "Most of the world does too. But dangerous fools. Loose cannons, with a lot of deadly toys lying around from the cold war. The sooner that stuff is spread around, the sooner we'll all breathe a sigh of relief."

"We're not all fools."

"No," Lane said seriously. "Which makes your situation all the more urgent."

Sergeyev said nothing, and Lane almost felt sorry for him. He was easy to maneuver. The others would be more difficult. But they were anxious, like all Russians, for Western capital, and to be thought of as equals. They had their pride, if not much else. And he intended poking at it every opportunity he got, because flustered people made mistakes. And mistakes were the stuff of golden opportunities.

"You can call your embassy as soon as we check in and get something to eat," he said. "We'll meet somewhere neutral. Somewhere open."

2

HYDE PARK

By afternoon the weather had turned cool, overcast, and drizzly in Hyde Park at the end of Brook Street from Claridge's. It was Sunday and traffic was light, though there were still some people out and about. The hotel had supplied Lane and Sergeyev with umbrellas but as they passed the U.S. embassy and entered the park, a sudden gust of wind drove the rain into their faces.

Speakers' Corner was at the northeast part of the park. A blind Islamic cleric was speaking to a group of about a dozen spectators who had stopped to listen, but nobody seemed particularly interested in what he was saying, and neither did he. Across the path three men sat on a park bench, one of them drinking something from a plastic cup, steam rising from the open lid.

"That's them," Sergeyev announced.

"I would never have guessed," Lane said dryly.

Two of them wore leather jackets and baseball caps, while the third was dressed in a dark raincoat and broad-brimmed hat. They didn't look like Londoners. The leather jackets were the muscle and the man in the middle was Konstantin Markov, SVR London *rezident,* Russia's third most powerful intelligence officer outside of Moscow after Washington and Mexico City.

Lane and Sergeyev headed across, and the two men in leather jackets got up and came over.

"Mr. Vandermeer?" one of them asked politely, his Russian accent almost nonexistent.

"That's right," Lane said.

"If you'll just give me a hug, sir," the bodyguard said seriously. "Like we're old friends."

The other bodyguard, his face scarred by teenage acne or some childhood illness, took Lane's umbrella and stood to one side, his eyes narrowed. Lane had the disconcerting feeling that he'd seen the man somewhere before, but he couldn't quite put his finger on a time or place.

The first bodyguard expertly patted Lane down as they hugged. When they parted he stepped away, with a dour look. "You may proceed, sir. Colonel Sergeyev will remain with us."

The *rezident* was a tall man, thin, all angles and planes, with a hawk nose and a prominent Adam's apple.

Lane walked over and sat down next to him. "So good of you to come out on a day like this. And on such short notice."

Markov shrugged indifferently. "You have created quite a stir in certain circles, Mr. Vandermeer. But now that you're here in my bailiwick I'll thank you to follow instructions."

"I don't do that very well," Lane said.

Markov shot him a dark look. "Don't play games with me."

"The people I represent want to buy a specific submarine from your government. If someone wasn't interested in our offer I wouldn't have been invited to meet with you. Am I correct?"

"What makes you think that submarine is in the English Channel?"

Lane had to smile. "The crewman we have aboard told us his sailing orders. But even if he was mistaken, calling me to London proves the point, wouldn't you say?"

Markov nodded. "Who is this mysterious crewman?"

"I'm not at liberty to say." Lane stared at the Russian. "Is two-eighty-three for sale or isn't it?"

"Why that specific boat?"

"Because it's headed to a country we don't want it to go to."

"What will you do with the boat if we sell it to you?" Markov asked.

"That's our business."

Markov thought about that for a second. "We could sell you two-eighty-three, and then turn around and sell another boat to the same country. What would your people say about that?"

"By then it wouldn't matter."

"Why?"

"Because that submarine would never be allowed to become operational."

Markov smiled faintly. "I see." He glanced over where Sergeyev stood smoking with the two bodyguards. "Have you known Gregor for a long time?"

Lane shook his head. "I met him for the first time Friday night in Washington."

"What made you pick him, of all people?"

"I needed to contact Russian intelligence as quickly and with as little fuss as possible. Most of your military attachés are GRU, and everybody pretty much knows it."

"Why not our military attaché here?"

"Because I happened to be in Washington. And we were running out of time. Our man aboard two-eighty-three should have contacted us by now. Do we have a deal or don't we?"

"What are you willing to pay?"

"Whatever is necessary," Lane said. "But if the deal sounds bad to me I'll walk away from it and my people will work something else out."

"Going to the British authorities, for example."

"Yes. And the Americans."

Markov put his cup aside. "If we agree on a deal, then what?"

"I'll need to inspect the boat."

"How will you take delivery?"

"The crew already aboard will be given a new destination." Lane took the letter of credit out of his breast pocket and handed it to Markov. "That represents our limit, based on what we already know was probably paid for the boat."

"I'll need to make certain arrangements," Markov said.

"Don't take too long."

"I assure you, I won't. In the meantime Sergeyev will remain with you as a liaison."

Lane laughed. "As you wish."

3

LONDON

The pockmark-faced guard was named Viktor Lychev. As Lane and Sergeyev headed out of the park he watched them until they were out of sight in the mist and rain, then went over to Markov.

"That guy Vandermeer is a fake, I think," he said.

"What are you talking about?" Markov demanded sharply. "Washington says his fingerprints check out. And the letter of credit is legitimate."

"He's supposed to be a South African, right, Mr. Markov?"

"That's right."

"Three years ago I was stationed at our embassy in Rio de Janeiro, when that joint war game was going on between our navy and the U.S. Navy. There were no South Africans down there.''

"Arms dealers were crawling all over the place from what I heard.''

"Not inside the command bunker. I was there, and unless I miss my mark so was Vandermeer. But he was wearing a U.S. Navy uniform.''

"He worked for South African intelligence. Maybe he was an infiltrator,'' Markov suggested.

"No, sir,'' Lychev said. "Security was tight. And I mean tight. Nobody got in that place who didn't belong there.'' He glanced toward the park entrance. "Be my guess that he's really an American intelligence officer.''

"Here to do what?''

"Find that submarine.''

Markov shook his head, although he wasn't as sure of himself as he wanted to be. "The Americans don't operate that way. This would be a major operation for them, and we would have gotten at least a hint of it.''

"We could be wrong about that, sir,'' Lychev said carefully. "Either that or they could have changed their methods.''

"Okay, if Vandermeer's not who he says he is, let's find out.''

"What if he's a fake?''

Markov's smile tightened. "Maybe we'd show him the submarine after all.''

4

THE CHANNEL ISLANDS

The call from London dropped like a ton of bricks on Mikhail Maslennikov. He'd been expecting trouble all along, and was surprised that their luck had lasted so long, but not like this, out of the blue. And not now, at this precise moment, just when the means of their guaranteed survival was scheduled to arrive.

He left his house on Guernsey's northeast coast at 8:00 P.M. and drove the van in the rain down to a private marina halfway to St. Peter Port. He parked in the shadows behind the big travel lift, and walked out to the end of A dock, where an eighty-foot Feadship motor yacht was tied to the bulkhead, her big diesels slowly turning over. There was no activity at the marina at this hour, but as he went aboard, one of the deck crew in a yellow slicker appeared out of nowhere.

"Good evening, sir," he said in Russian.

"Is Kovrygin here yet?" Maslennikov asked.

"*Da*. He's up on the bridge. He wants the gangway pulled as soon as you're aboard."

"Do it," Maslennikov said curtly, and he ducked inside and headed up the ladder to the sweeping bridge.

The boat, named *Charisma,* had been built to the specifications of a Pakistani arms dealer. Belowdecks it was laid out like a harem quarters, cushions and brocaded bulkhead covers, water fountains and mirrors everywhere. But the engines were no-nonsense super-turbocharged diesels that could push the boat to speeds approaching fifty knots, and on the bridge the electronics equipment was state-of-the-art, including satellite navigation, advanced radars, side-scan sonars, and communications equipment that rivaled anything afloat.

Maslennikov had purchased the boat three months ago and crewed it with some of his former submariners he'd brought out of Ukraine for one operation. When that was completed the boat would be scuttled.

Too bad, he thought, running a meaty hand along the highly polished mahogany rail. Such a waste. But the operation here was unraveling already. Time soon to leave. Richer now than when they started, but not as rich as they could have been.

Andrei Kovrygin, speaking softly into a walkie-talkie, could have been Maslennikov's younger brother, short, stocky with a peasant's square face and wide, dark eyes under thick eyebrows. He'd been a submarine captain in the Black Sea Fleet.

He looked up and caught the concerned expression on Maslennikov's face. "Are we ready?"

Maslennikov nodded.

Kovrygin keyed the walkie-talkie. "Now release the after spring," he ordered. Moments later he nodded at the helmsman. "Get us out of here."

"Yes, sir," the former Black Sea Fleet lieutenant said, easing the throttles forward and turning the wheel a few degrees to starboard. They slid away from the dock as smoothly as silk.

"When we reach the sea buoy, put her on course and let me know," Kovrygin said, and motioned Maslennikov to follow him aft to the captain's cabin.

"We may have to pull out sooner than we expected," Maslennikov said once the door was closed. "I got a call from Konstantin Markov."

"Who is he?"

"He's the SVR London *rezident*."

Kovrygin's jaw tightened. "Are they on to us finally?"

"I'm not sure. But someone in Moscow must have talked to him because he knows about the submarine. He even knows that it's here or at least he hinted at it."

"Impossible."

"That's what I thought, but he had the correct sail number, so it's not merely fancy guesswork."

"Then I suggest we let Lubiako know what's going on and then get the hell out of here right now," Kovrygin said. "If the British navy finds out what's about to be parked on their doorstep everything will come out. All our work will be for nothing."

"I agree," Maslennikov said. "But we're not going to leave the money behind. Africa is bad enough as it is, but trying to live there—anywhere for that matter—without money, and with half the Russian mafia after you isn't my idea of a comfortable retirement."

"How long would it take to get it all out?"

"That depends on the Swiss."

Kovrygin shook his head. "I'm not going to get caught here, Mikhail. I say we get out while it's still possible."

"I can buy us a few more days, maybe even a week, and Markov is going to help me do it."

"What do you mean?"

"The reason he called," Maslennikov said. "They want to buy two-eight-three back from us for twice what we paid for it."

"Fifty million dollars?"

"That's right. We'd make an easy profit of twenty-five million," Maslennikov said. "If we sold it, which of course we're not going to do. It's our guarantee for safe haven. But I'm going to negotiate with them, which is going to take time."

Kovrygin's lower lip curled into the semblance of a

smile. "They'll understand that," he said. "But why do they want the submarine back?"

"He didn't say that either. But I'm assuming it's political."

"When do you have to give them an answer?"

"In the next day or so," Maslennikov said. "I'll fly over to London tonight."

"Very well. Then let's get our crew before this weather gets any worse."

----------- **5** -----------

LONDON

Sergeyev hung up the telephone in his hotel room, a troubled expression on his face. What Markov had just told him made sense. It would certainly clear up some of the mystery about Vandermeer. But if they were wrong and he wasn't an imposter, they would be placing a one-hundred-million-dollar deal in jeopardy, not to mention his own financial salvation.

He walked across the hall to Vandermeer's room and knocked on the door.

Vandermeer opened it. His jacket was off, his tie loose, and his shirtsleeves rolled up. "Did we get word?"

"Not yet. But I'm hungry. Why don't we go down to the dining room and have some dinner. I'll pay."

"Did you get any sleep?"

"A couple hours," Sergeyev lied. He was too keyed up. "You?"

"The same," Vandermeer said. "Okay, dinner sounds good, let me get my jacket."

6

CLARIDGE'S

Viktor Lychev watched through the slit between the door and frame in a service closet at the end of the eighth-floor corridor across from the elevators. His monitoring and recording equipment was already set up in the basement telephone terminal room. Security at Claridge's, as at almost every hotel in the world, was a joke, so there was little danger of being discovered.

Right on schedule, Sergeyev and the man who identified himself as Vandermeer came down the corridor and buzzed for an elevator. So far they had nothing but speculation. The South African's credentials checked out. But Lychev knew he was a fake, and meant to prove it.

As soon as they were gone, Lychev slipped out of the service closet, hurried down the hall to Vandermeer's room, and opened the lock with a universal key card.

Flipping the security lock in place so that nobody could walk in on him, he went to the bedside telephone, removed its wall plug from behind the nightstand, and replaced the plug with an adapter. He did the same thing to the telephone on the desk by the window. The phone in the bathroom was hardwired into the wall, so there was nothing he could do about it. But his equipment in the basement would pick up whatever was said in the bedroom without lifting either phone. And if the telephones were used, both sides of the call would be monitored.

First making sure that the telephones still had a dial tone, and that he'd disturbed nothing obvious, Lychev let himself out and went across the corridor to bug Sergeyev's phones, before taking the service elevator back down to the basement.

7

CLARIDGE'S

Claridge's was one of London's premier hotels but its 1930s-style restaurant, done up in faded pastels, was mediocre at best, so Lane had always avoided the place. It was one of the reasons he'd brought Sergeyev here—he figured no one would recognize him. But his luck ran out when they were having their coffee and brandies after dinner.

"Mr. Lane, so good to see you again, sir," said one of the waiters coming over from another section of the restaurant.

Lane looked up, a neutral expression on his face. But Sergeyev had gone rigid.

"Anderson, sir. I used to serve you and Ms. Shipley over at the Connaught, though it's no matter if you don't remember. I have one of those faces."

"Nice to see you again," Lane told him.

"I hope you had an enjoyable dinner."

"Tolerable."

"Then I trust you'll have a good evening, sir," the waiter said, lowering his eyes and walking away. He knew he'd said or done something wrong, but not what it was.

"What was that all about?" Sergeyev demanded. "What's your real name?"

Lane took a moment to answer. "It's not Vandermeer. But it's not Lane either. That was another alias I used for a time about a year ago."

"What is it?" Sergeyev looked angry and frightened. He could see his financial salvation going down the drain. "You're going to have to tell me, because Markov will want to know."

"There's no reason for that," Lane said. "Because this changes nothing. That submarine is bound for Sierra Leone, and I was not lying when I told you that the people I represent don't want it to get there."

"Who are these people? Are you a goddamn American spy?"

"I can't tell you who they are. But if you're asking me if I work for the CIA, I don't, and that's a fact you can take to the bank." Lane grinned. "Believe me, if this were a CIA operation there'd be agents around every corner, in every doorway, and probably hanging from the chandeliers."

"What about the letter of credit? Is it real?"

"Of course it is," Lane said. And it was.

"And your crewman aboard the submarine, are you telling me that's true as well?"

"How else could I have known that boat would be here?" He sat forward. "Think it out, Gregor. Nothing has changed. I'm here and I want to buy that submarine. If your government wants to sell it to me for a decent price we'll have a deal. Simple as that."

"But first you have to see the boat with your own two eyes."

"Exactly."

"Any number could be painted on her sail. How will you know if the boat you're shown is actually two-eighty-three?"

Lane laughed out loud. "Good heavens, Gregor, how

many submarines do your people have floating around out there in the English Channel? I'll know it's the right boat by a certain set of serial numbers I have in my possession. The number on the attack periscope, for instance, on the upper ring at the collar.''

Sergeyev still wasn't convinced but he was wavering. "What about me?''

Lane dug an envelope out of his pocket and tossed it on the table. "I tried to give this to you in Washington, but you wouldn't take it. These are your Visa and MasterCard statements. Take a look. I think you'll be pleasantly surprised.''

Sergeyev opened the envelope, and took out two statements, and two new gold credit cards. The statements showed that the accounts were current with a zero balance due. And the cards were valid as of the first of the month.

Sergeyev looked up, an expression of relief on his face that changed to fear. "They know I'm in financial trouble. If they find out about this they'll want to know where I got the money.''

"It's a finder's fee,'' Lane said. "It was paid into your accounts yesterday from a South African bank. The money is clean. You earned it.''

Sergeyev shook his head. "This puts me in a difficult position,'' he said. "I don't know what the hell to do, because I don't know who or what you are for sure, and neither does Markov.''

Understanding dawned on Lane. "So that's what the American spy bit was all about. You really do think that I work for the CIA.''

"One of his people thought he recognized you from Rio de Janeiro. Markov wants to know what's going on before he takes this any farther.''

Lane nodded toward the waiter on the other side of the dining room. "That waiter calling me by a different name seems to confirm Markov's worst fears.'' He smiled. "What is he doing about it? My credentials are legitimate and so is my letter of credit. What next?"

Sergeyev hesitated.

"I've played straight with you, Gregor. Now it's your turn, or else my people will pull your credit cards and stick you with the old balance."

"There's a bug in your room." Sergeyev looked cornered. "When we go up after dinner I'm supposed to try to get you to open up."

"Is the receiving equipment in the basement?"

Sergeyev nodded.

"How many men down there?"

"Just the one from Rio. He was at the park this morning."

Lane was quiet, lost in his own thoughts.

"What are you going to do?" Sergeyev asked, finally, tense in the silence.

"Convince Markov of my sincerity of course. There's too much at stake here for me to do anything else." Lane smiled. "And you, Colonel Sergeyev, are going to do exactly what I tell you to do."

8

CLARIDGE'S

After they paid the bill they went up to Lane's room, where he opened the minibar, and rattled some of the bottles. "Do you want a drink?"

"Sure, some vodka," Sergeyev said.

"How the hell long is it going to take before Markov makes up his mind about our deal?" Lane demanded.

"I wasn't told."

"Well I'm not going to wait around very long." Lane slammed the minifridge shut. "There isn't anything worth shit in here. I'll order a bottle from room service." He picked up the phone and dialed the first number for room service. "Wait a minute," he said.

"What's wrong?" Sergeyev asked.

"Nothing," Lane said, replacing the phone on its cradle. "I don't think I want a drink after all. Get out of here, and tell Markov that I'm not going to wait any longer."

Sergeyev hesitated, not sure what he was supposed to do.

Lane motioned toward the door. "Get the fuck out of here. I have to make a call, and then I need to get some sleep. But I want to see Markov in the morning."

The moment Sergeyev was out of the room, Lane went to the closet and, working silently, opened the largest of his suitcases, removed the fake laptop computer, opened its base, and withdrew a lead-foil-wrapped package from inside. The package, which showed up on the scanners used for the check-on luggage as a collection of circuits and circuit boards, contained his Beretta, a compact silencer, and a spare magazine of ammunition. A small chip in the keyboard would light up the screen with a convincing display, but nothing more.

He pocketed these, then turned on the television and the shower, and let himself out without a sound.

It was still early but it was a Sunday night and the hotel had already settled down, the corridors deserted. He took the service elevator down to the second floor, which turned out to be the empty banquet kitchen, then used the stairs to get to the basement. If the Russian was cautious he'd be listening for the elevator, but he couldn't watch all the stairwells.

Lane slipped out of the stairwell into the shadows behind a large electrical cabinet, waited for a minute until his eyes adjusted to the dim light, then went over to a spot across from the service elevator. Several pieces of machinery were running somewhere, and the plumbing groaned and gurgled. The door to the maintenance office stood ajar, and there was no light from within. But fifty feet down the corridor a dim red light reflected off the gauge of a steam heating line.

He crept silently down the hall to a wire door that opened into a small caged room containing the hotel's telephone terminal board. A man was speaking softly in Russian.

"The water is still running, but he's made no attempt to use the telephone in the bathroom."

Lane took the pistol out of his pocket, screwed on the silencer, and thumbed the safety off.

"Sergeyev is in his own room. He ordered a couple of bottles of vodka from room service five minutes ago so I don't think he'll be going anywhere tonight."

Lane eased around the corner. The Russian, his back to the door, held a bright orange lineman's handset to his ear.

"If Vandermeer, or whoever the hell this guy is, is smart enough he wouldn't leave anything incriminating lying around his room, but when he's out tomorrow I'll check."

"No need for that," Lane said.

Lychev spun around and looked up, his eyes wide.

"If you want, you can come up right now and I'll show you everything."

Lychev's eyes strayed to the gun in Lane's hand. "It's him," he said into the phone. "And he's got a gun."

"Is that your boss?"

"Yes," Lychev said. "Do you want to talk to him?"

Lane nodded. "But not here. Tell him to be at the same spot where we met this afternoon."

Lychev relayed the message. He shook his head. "Impossible."

"Twenty minutes," Lane said loudly enough that Markov would hear, then reached around Lychev and yanked the handset's wires from the terminal.

"What now?" Lychev asked.

Lane shrugged. "Unplug your equipment and take it with you, and there'll be no problem. But if you come back down here, or if you try to go through my things without me, I'll kill you."

Lychev's eyes were flat and dangerous. "How'd you know there was a tap on your telephone?"

"The stuff you guys use puts an inductive load on the line. You can't miss it."

Lane pocketed his gun, then turned and walked back to the elevator.

9

HYDE PARK

The rain had stopped but the evening was very cool, and sitting on the park bench Lane wished he'd brought the liner for his raincoat. Markov showed up five minutes late, but he was alone. Or at least his bodyguards were not in plain sight.

"Well now, you're an amazing man," he said. "Maybe even more amazing than we first suspected." He stopped a few feet from the bench, his hands stuffed into the pockets of his coat. "I'm not armed, but I don't think you mean to shoot me. How did you know my name? I don't believe I mentioned it."

"Sergeyev let it slip," Lane said. "Is it important?"

"Not as important as who you really are."

"At the moment my name is Vandermeer. But as for who I am, I think that should be obvious. I'm an arms dealer."

"What were you doing in Rio de Janeiro a couple of years ago? In a U.S. Navy uniform."

Lane laughed. "So that's what this is all about," he said. "I thought I might have seen your man someplace. As for what I was doing in Rio, I wasn't alone. Every arms dealer in the world was down there."

"You were seen inside the command center. How'd you get there?"

"My client at the time arranged it."

"Who was it?"

Lane shook his head. "I don't discuss my clients with anybody. Nor do I believe you'd want me to."

Markov was frustrated. "I don't trust you."

"And you think I trust you?" Lane asked. "I came here to buy a submarine. Are you going to sell it to me, or are you going to run your stupid little surveillance operations on me?"

"We need to establish just who the hell you are before we do any business with you."

"I know that your name is Markov and that you're probably the London *rezident*, just as I know that Sergeyev works for the GRU, and that one of your Romeo-class submarines that was supposedly sunk last week in the Barents Sea is probably lurking around the English Channel. Possibly passing through on the way to her final destination, but still close." Lane sneered at him. "What does that make me, James Bond?"

"That makes you a disturbing man."

"So what?"

"How do I know that you don't work for the CIA?"

Lane laughed. "Jesus H. Christ. If the CIA found out that one of your submarines was here in the Channel what do you suppose they'd do about it? Send one of their agents and a drunken Russian military attaché to buy it?"

Markov said nothing.

"Are you people that stupid? Or did IQs disintegrate along with your empire?"

"Insulting me won't do you any good."

"Nor will bugging my hotel room do anything for you." Lane shook his head. "I hate to belabor the point, but is your government going to sell me that boat or not?"

"I don't know," Markov said after a moment.

Lane got to his feet. "I'm not going to wait around for you people to make up your minds."

"We can't allow you to go to the British authorities with this."

"How are you going to stop me?"

"You know," Markov told him.

"Then the next time I see you or any of your people I'll shoot first and let Scotland Yard figure it out. But I have friends here."

"I'll need a couple of days."

"For what?"

"To negotiate with the new owner of two-eighty-three."

"And who might that be?"

A faint smile crossed Markov's lips. "We'll leave you alone, Mr. Vandermeer, as you wish, if you'll promise to give me forty-eight hours."

"That suits me," Lane said. "What about Sergeyev?"

"He no longer matters."

"As you wish."

"Don't cross us," Markov said. "Despite what you think, there are still a number of endeavors that we Russians excel in."

"Two days," Lane said, and he brushed past Markov and headed back to the hotel.

10

THE ENGLISH CHANNEL

The yacht *Charisma* showed no lights as her helmsman expertly held her in position about ten miles from the tiny island of Sark. The night was pitch-black, though the rain had stopped, and the seas had calmed to a light chop of less than one meter.

A crewman at the starboard rail, amidships, lowered an aquaphone into the water. When fifty meters of cable had been paid out, he gave a signal to the darkened bridge, and Maslennikov keyed a handset.

"Igor, are you going to stay down there all night?"

"I was beginning to wonder if our navigation was off," Captain Lubiako replied. His voice *sounded* as if it were underwater. "Are you ready for us?"

"Standing by," Maslennikov replied. He turned to Captain Kovrygin. "They're on the way up. Turn on the underwater beacon."

Their only danger was for a low-flying aircraft to spot the glow from the underwater light. But with tonight's overcast they were perfectly safe.

Maslennikov went out on the port side bridge deck, the sea immediately around the *Charisma* lit by a soft aqua radiance. Minutes later a large bubble of air from the submarine's escape trunk boiled to the surface. And a couple minutes after that the first two crewmen appeared and swam the few meters to the lowered accommodations ladder.

The first aboard removed his Steinke hood, handed it

to one of the *Charisma*'s crewmen, glanced up at Maslennikov, then disappeared through the hatch.

Maslennikov went back inside as Valeri Yernin, seawater glistening on his wet suit, appeared in the doorway. He was strongly built, nearly two meters tall, with brown serious eyes and thick black hair. His features were sharply chiseled, and for all the years Maslennikov had known his star killer, he could count with the fingers of one hand the number of times that Yernin had ever smiled.

"I don't like submarines," Yernin said mildly.

Kovrygin handed him a glass of brandy. "You made good time."

Yernin took the drink, then looked at Maslennikov's face. "What is it?" he asked.

"A little bit of trouble," Maslennikov said. "So far it's nothing we can't handle, but we'll be leaving sooner than I thought."

"Good," Yernin said. "Because I don't like Guernsey either. And besides, I have something to take care of that's waited an entire year."

"You'll soon get your chance."

Yernin knocked back his drink. "Yes, I will," he said, his face devoid of expression.

PART THREE

1

LONDON

The British capital was as quiet as it ever gets. Lane walked back to Claridge's, where he caught a cab to Eaton Square in Chelsea. On the way over he glanced back a couple of times to make certain he wasn't being followed, and by the time the cabbie left him off behind the Royal Court Theatre he was sure he'd gotten away clean.

Frances Shipley had been born here, and after her parents had died and after her divorce, she'd moved into their palatial flat in one of London's more prestigious neighborhoods. It was comfortable, living in luxury, she said. And even more comfortable being surrounded by familiarity. Lane stopped in the shadows of a doorway across the street from her Georgian building and waited. Frances was a puzzle because she was an independent woman, yet she wanted to be loved and taken care of. But she would hate it when she found out that he'd arrived in London this morning and had not immediately called her, because it would make her feel her need for him.

After a full ten minutes, sure that her apartment was not under surveillance, Lane walked across the street and rang her doorbell. It was a few minutes after 10:00 and the night was utterly still.

They'd met several years ago when he'd been stationed in London on special assignment for the Agency. She was the SIS host officer assigned to help him, but also to keep him out of mischief. They'd hit if off immediately, and within the first two weeks were sleeping together. When he left to go back to the States, she wrangled an assignment to a United Nations intelligence unit so that she could be closer to him.

Lane had to smile thinking about Tom Hughes and his wife, Moira. From the moment they'd found out about Frannie, they'd made it their special project to get her and Lane married. They'd come close. Too close, he sometimes thought. He loved her, but the thought of getting married again after one disastrous marriage was enough to cause his legs to go weak.

She knew how he felt. And although she wanted him, she was too proud to chase after him.

Besides, he told himself, his jaw tightening, Yernin's threat to kill them still hung over their heads. And until that was resolved he wasn't marrying anybody.

A light came on, and Mrs. Houlten, Frances's elderly housekeeper, opened the door, her face lighting up in a smile. "My heavens, Mr. William, what a pleasant surprise."

"How's my girl?" Lane said, pecking her on the cheek.

"Still having trouble with my one wood."

"I didn't know you'd taken up golf."

"I haven't," the housekeeper said, standing aside to let him come in. "And that's why."

Frances, wearing a pink sweatsuit and fuzzy bunny slippers, a book in her hand, appeared at the head of the stairs. Her medium blonde hair was in disarray as if she'd already gone to bed, but her pretty oval face lit up when she saw who it was.

"William," she cried, and skipped down the stairs. She threw herself into his arms.

The housekeeper gave Lane a wink as she disappeared down the corridor in back.

"Hi, Fran," he said, looking into her eyes, when they parted.

"God, I've missed you."

"Me too," he said, and he drew her to him again and they kissed deeply. Her body felt familiar and yet exotic, as did her smell and the small sound she made in the back of her throat when she was content. She looked up and saw the expression on his face.

"I'm making that stupid noise again," she said.

"Don't ever stop. It's a part of you that I especially like."

"How long are you here for? Are we going to have some time together, or is it going to be all work and no play?"

Since Frances's job with British intelligence was acting as liaison with the American intelligence community, she would know if Lane had come to London on official business. Since he hadn't, her question was strange.

The housekeeper came to the end of the corridor. "Will you be needing anything else this evening?" she asked, grinning.

"No, nothing," Fran told her. "You can go to bed now. I'll make sure we're locked up."

"Very good, mum. Nice to see you again, Mr. William."

"You too, Mrs. Houlten," Lane told her.

"You didn't bring a bag, so I'm assuming you're not staying here tonight," Frances said, her voice suddenly flinty, her blue-gray eyes flat.

"I've got a room at Claridge's under an assumed name."

"I know, William. But a girl can still hope, can't she?"

Like many men of his era, Lane sometimes underestimated the women around him. His upbringing. But with Frances it was a dangerous failing.

"Did your people spot Sergeyev?"

"You, actually," Frances said, looking up into his eyes. "Keeping some very bad company."

She meant the Russian *rezident* of course. "I didn't know you kept that close a watch these days."

"We don't usually. But this one is special."

They went into the kitchen at the back, and Lane sat at the butcher-block counter while Frances opened a bottle of white wine.

"We hoped you'd show up here sooner or later," she said. "We didn't want to get in the middle of whatever you were up to."

"Have you talked to Tommy yet?"

"No. And I've taken some heat for it." She poured them both a glass of Chardonnay. "I don't think he would have told me anything in any event, and it would have just put him in a tough spot."

"He thinks that you're special."

"I feel the same about him," Frances said. "So why are you here, William?"

"I don't know if I want to make this official. I'm just going on a hunch. No hard evidence yet."

Frances smiled. "I know a lot of people who take your hunches as gospel." She shook her head. "It's moot anyway. You were spotted with Konstantin Markov, and some questions are being asked. For instance why did you enter Great Britain under a false passport? And what did you and Markov talk about in Hyde Park this afternoon, and again less than an hour ago?"

"Was I followed here?"

"No you weren't followed," she replied, vexed.

"What's your interest in Markov? What's he been up to that has anyone in Whitehall sitting up and taking notice?"

Frances smiled again. "I asked first."

Lane shrugged. "Has it anything to do with submarines? Maybe a specific boat?"

A puzzled expression crossed Frances's face. "No, not at all. Is that why you're here?"

"That's part of it. You're still acting as liaison, I presume, so who's running this operation?"

"My old boss, Brad Morgan from the Paris days. He's got the Eastern European Division. When you were spotted he suggested that I start liaising."

"At least give me a hint what has you interested in Markov."

"I don't know all of it, William. But the gist is that something is going on in the Russian expat community here that has Markov and his entire staff agitated. And when that happens it automatically piques our interest."

"Have you come up with anything?"

"Nothing so far," Frances said. "Are you going to tell me that you've heard something?"

Lane shook his head. "I wish I had. But I don't think there's any connection between your operation and what I came over to find out."

"Which is?"

"Would Brad be amenable to seeing me tonight?"

Frances nodded. "I can almost guarantee it."

"Good, let's do it that way. I want to keep this unofficial for as long as I can, otherwise it's going to put me in jeopardy."

Frances stiffened. "I suggest that you not make that kind of remark to Brad. Because he'll take it to mean that you believe that we've been penetrated again."

"It's a possibility, Frannie," Lane said heavily. "Nobody can guarantee that their shop is clean."

Frances pursed her lips. "I'll just pop upstairs and get dressed, then call Brad."

"Good," Lane said. "In the meantime I'd like to call Tommy. In private."

"If there's a tap on my phone, it won't be one of ours," Frances said, and she gave Lane a searching look.

"It won't always be like this," he said gently.

"I hope not, William. But I don't know how long I'll be able to wait around. Do you know what I mean?"

"Perfectly."

She put down her glass and left.

2

LONDON

Lane caught Hughes at home. It was late afternoon in Washington, and Moira and the girls had gone shopping so that Tom could watch the Redskins' game in peace.

"God bless their hearts, but they can't stand to see the 'Skins losing, even though they don't know a thing about the game," Hughes said. "Have you already made contact?"

Lane could hear the television in the background. By contrast to the quiet of Frannie's apartment it was like being in two worlds at the same moment.

"This afternoon, but I've run into a little bit of trouble. One of the waiters at Claridge's recognized me, and one of Markov's goons thought he knew me from Rio."

"The Vandermeer legend is airtight, it'll hold up," Hughes said. "Did they put a tap on your phone?"

"Just like we thought. But I didn't have to go looking for it. Sergeyev spilled the beans. He's in over his head, and he'll do just about anything to save his hide."

"Of course Markov knows this."

"He sure does," Lane said. "But they weren't overly surprised by my offer, which means we were right about two-eighty-three."

"Did he admit it was there in the Channel?" asked Hughes, a bit of excitement in his voice.

"He didn't go that far, but he asked for a couple of days to negotiate with the new owner," Lane said. "And he promised not to have me followed."

Hughes chuckled. "If you believe that, I've got a bridge in New York I'd like to sell you," he said. "What about Sergeyev?"

"Markov cut him loose now that the introductions have been made. I wouldn't be surprised if he was gone in the morning."

"Do you want to tighten the screws?"

"You mean renege on his credit cards?" Lane asked. "I don't think so. He did what we asked him to do. Let him go in peace. He's got enough troubles without us adding more."

"You're a good man, William," Hughes said warmly. "Now what about Frances? If you have a couple of days off, why don't you see her."

"As a matter of fact I'm calling from her house."

"Wonderful."

"Maybe not. I was spotted parleying with Markov, and Frannie's boss wants to know what's going on."

"Rightly so," Hughes said. "Do you want me to kick this upstairs?"

"Not yet. I'm going to try to keep this at an unofficial level for the moment in case Markov's reach is longer than we think it is."

Hughes sighed. "It's a tough world. But we don't have any solid proof that two-eighty-three is in the Channel. If she kept to her original course and speed she would be there by now, and out the other side by morning. We're talking about the open Atlantic, which is a pretty big pond. No guarantees we can keep up with her."

"I want you to keep looking," Lane said. "But something else might be in the works over here. The Brits have Markov under a pretty tight rein. It's apparently got something to do with the Russian expatriate community."

"Do you think there might be a connection?" Hughes asked with interest.

"I told Frannie no, but I'm not so sure. Coincidences aren't my long suit."

"Mine either," Hughes replied. "The miserable football game is over, maybe it's time I did a little shopping of my own. Maybe I can come up with something."

"Frannie and I are going over to see Brad Morgan tonight. Maybe he can shed some light."

"Our cousins won't take it lightly if they find out we're chasing after a Russian submarine in their backyard."

"It's all speculation to this point. But before we turn this over to Her Majesty's sub hunters, I'd like to see if I can finesse the situation."

"In other words you want me to keep Ben in the dark as much as possible."

Lane had to laugh. "You catch on quick. Must be because of your Ph.D.'s."

"The thanks I get," Hughes said. "Say hello to Frances for me, and take care."

"Will do."

LONDON

Frances had changed into a pair of blue jeans and a dark gray blazer over a cream-colored sweater. Her Range Rover was parked in the back, and she drove fast and competently, skirting Buckingham Palace and St. James's Park.

"Tom said to say hello," Lane said to break the awkward silence.

Frances smiled warmly. "How're Moira and the girls?"

"Fine," Lane said. "They ask about you all the time."

Frances laughed out loud. "More like pester, I'd guess."

"Sometimes."

About fifteen minutes later they came to an underground parking ramp beneath Bloomsbury Square, and Frances took a ticket and drove down to the lowest level. The ramp was less than a quarter full and there was absolutely nobody about. She drove to the far end of a back lane, pulled in beside a dark blue Ford Taurus, and shut off the headlights. A short, square-shouldered man who looked as if he'd played some rugby in his day stepped out of the shadows behind one of the support columns.

"That's Brad Morgan," Frances said.

"Why the cloak-and-dagger?"

"He agrees that for the moment we're going to treat

your visit here unofficially,'' Frances said. ''And it wouldn't do for the two of you to be seen together by the opposition.''

They got out of the Range Rover as Morgan came over, and he and Lane shook hands.

''At last we meet,'' Morgan said. ''I've heard a lot about you.''

''Frances has given you high marks.''

''Indeed,'' Morgan said, giving Frances an affectionate look. ''Actually I was referring to your reputation in the business. You've been quite a busy lad these past few years.''

''A bit.''

''And now you're here, traveling under an assumed identity, meeting with the chief Russian intelligence officer for these parts, and having dinner with the Russian military attaché from Washington, and tipping quite grandly—a lot better than your average South African— so I'm told.'' Morgan smiled knowingly. ''Quite extraordinary, what?''

Morgan was in his mid- to late fifties, and Lane figured the man had a thing for Frances. It was obvious by the way he acted around her. Not the best situation in the world.

''Let me level with you,'' Lane said. ''I'm here to buy a surplus submarine from the Russians who've sold it to Sierra Leone.''

''Right. It's sailed up the Thames then, and it's lying on the bottom beneath the Westminster Bridge.''

''It may be passing through the English Channel, if I'm right.''

That got Morgan's attention. His left eyebrow rose. ''That would be one route for them to take to Africa, though I suspect not the best. But then why did you come to London, why not Moscow?''

''I made the initial offer in Washington, and the Russians sent me here to meet with Markov.''

"And?"

"He said he needs a couple of days to talk to the new owner. Apparently it's someone here in London, or nearby."

Morgan glanced at Frances again. "Not your usual operation," he said. "We haven't been told anything about it. Why not?"

"Because until I met with Markov I wasn't sure it was the submarine we were looking for."

"Are you now?"

"Markov didn't turn me away."

"But he's had you followed," Morgan said. "Were you aware that one of his people was hanging about your hotel?"

"He bugged my room," Lane said. "So I told him to go away and stop bothering me."

Morgan had to smile despite himself. "And apparently he took your advice. Smart man." Morgan studied Lane for a moment. "The problem I'm facing is what to do with you. You come highly recommended, but entering England the way you did without informing anyone, not even Frances, is not cricket."

"Since we're both dealing with Markov, maybe we should start there," Lane suggested.

"Indeed," Morgan replied. "And why not?"

4

LONDON

They took Frances's car, Morgan riding in the front seat. "We made a quick check on your Vandermeer credentials," he said. "They're damned good. Did you do them?"

"A friend put it together."

"In the Agency?"

"Yes."

Lane caught Frances watching him in the rearview mirror, a secret little smile on her face. "Where are we going?"

"To meet someone," Morgan said.

They came to a residential area of tree-lined streets, three-story semidetached houses, and taller apartment buildings north of King's Cross. The rain had not quite started again, but a heavy mist hung in the air and drifted on the light breeze from the river.

Frances turned the corner off Copenhagen Street, and in the middle of the block passed a pleasant-looking cream-colored house, with a metal gate in front, and lights showing in a few of the upstairs windows. A big S-class Mercedes was parked in front but no one was around, and the house looked like it was locked up for the night.

Frances didn't vary her speed as they passed the house to avoid creating suspicion. But Lane caught a glimpse of a pale white face in a darkened downstairs window, peering out at them.

"Is this Markov's house?" he asked.

"Yes," Morgan said. "He lives well."

"No better than the *rezident* in Washington. Most of these guys have their own extra sources of income, otherwise Moscow couldn't afford to keep up."

"That's what we're thinking. Only Markov may be doing just a little bit too well."

"I assume you're watching his house, monitoring his telephones," Lane said.

"Right from here," Morgan said as Frances turned into the driveway of a fourteen-story apartment building on the corner, and parked in the rear. "We have a top-floor flat on this side which gives us a direct line of sight not only to his house, but to the corners at both ends of the block. It comes in handy if he takes off in a hurry. We get an idea which way he's initially heading. Makes it easier to catch up with him."

Morgan used a security card to gain entry to the building, and again to call the elevator. The vestibule was carpeted, and furnished with a Queen Anne hall table beneath a gilded mirror and flanked by armchairs. A well-framed Gainsborough print hung on the wall.

"This is nice," Lane said on the way up.

Morgan smiled. "We only pay half the rent and utilities, so nobody's complaining."

"Sounds like government efficiency, which is an oxymoron if ever I heard one."

"We get it right once in a while," Morgan replied blandly.

They reached the top floor, went to the end of the corridor, and Morgan knocked once, then let them into a large apartment, with floor-to-ceiling windows in the living room giving a stunning view of the city toward downtown. Most of the furniture was shoved aside, leaving room for an array of electronic eavesdropping equipment set up on card tables a few feet back from the windows. Two cameras with powerful telescopic lenses, one of them fitted out with a night-viewing attachment, were angled toward the Russian's house. And in one corner a very professional-looking Meade telescope with a CCD attachment that transmitted the images to a computer screen was also trained on the house. All in all it was a sophisticated setup, and Lane was impressed.

A compact man with a dark complexion and a wiry bantamweight boxer's build came from somewhere in back, a beer in his hand. He was dressed in a bulky turtleneck sweater, faded dungarees, and Nike running shoes. He looked sullen, almost street mean. But that impression faded the instant he flashed a boyish smile.

"One of your compatriots, Mr. Lane," Morgan said. "Meet Mario Garza, assistant chief of the CIA's London station."

Morgan checked the scope as Frances opened a bottle of white wine in the kitchen and brought back a glass for Lane and one for herself. They sat on the couch and chairs against the wall away from the windows.

"I've heard a lot about you, Mr. Lane," said Garza with a New York accent. "But when you showed up out of the blue it sorta knocked me for a loop."

"If it's any consolation, I didn't expect to stumble into a joint operation like this," Lane told him. "What's Markov doing that's got you interested?"

Garza smiled his boyish grin again, and Lane instantly saw that the smile was a cover. The man's eyes were dark and very hard. "You're into our operation now, so it's your turn first."

Lane nodded. "I assume that you've checked me out."

"Top to bottom," Garza replied. "The last Langley knew, you were working on a submarine deal for us. Something about Sierra Leone."

"Could be that the military government has bought an old Romeo-class sub from Russia," Lane said. "I'm posing as a South African arms dealer working for a group of Liberian junta generals who don't want to see that happen.''

"What are you supposed to be doing about it?" Morgan asked. "And what brought you here?"

"I've offered to buy it from them for up to a hundred million dollars. Which naturally has got the Russians' attention. They sent me over here to talk to Markov."

"He knows about the deal with Sierra Leone?" Garza asked.

"He's asked for forty-eight hours to contact the new owner."

Morgan's face lit up. "Did you say 'owner,' as in singular?"

"That's what he told me."

Garza started to snap his fingers as he stared at Lane. "Weren't you a little surprised when they sent you over here?"

"Nothing surprises me anymore," Lane said evenly.

Frances was looking at him, a troubled expression on her face. "Did you trace one of their submarines here?" she asked.

"I thought it was a possibility, Frannie," Lane said. "But without any real proof I wasn't about to blow any whistles."

Garza was laughing this time. "I'll bet you threw old Konstantin for a loop," he said, nodding toward the surveillance equipment. "Question is why didn't you tell Langley what you were doing?"

"Question is why weren't we notified if you suspect a Russian submarine is lurking about in our waters?" Morgan asked, almost petulantly.

"Never mind, Brad," Garza said. "He's here now. And it's our turn to lay the cards on the table, so to speak."

5

LONDON

A couple of wireless keyboards were linked to a superfast miniature CPU tower and several flat-screen color monitors. Lane recognized the Cray-inspired equipment, because the NSA's scientists had developed it for complex field operations. The CIA was one of the biggest users.

"I'm sure you know about this bit of hardware," Garza said. "Brad and his pals are sure impressed with it."

"What have you come up with," Lane asked.

"Just a minute," Frances interrupted. "This is all new to me. I thought we were running a simple surveillance operation. What do we need all this for?"

"We're in the computer age," Garza said. "Every camera, the telescope, and the infrared detector are digitalized, as are the recorders on the phone taps and the acoustical-mass detectors. Means no film in the cameras, no tape in the recorders, and no human eye in the telescope's eyepiece. Every bit of information is fed directly into the computer, which keeps track of absolutely everything for us. Any time Comrade Markov so much as breaks wind, it takes a few kilobytes of memory, but we get it."

"Are you watching the embassy this closely?" Lane asked.

Morgan's lips compressed. "This is superspy stuff, but the Russians have jamming equipment."

"Their gear is only partially effective," Garza said. "We still get a good deal of information from them. But not as good as the product we're getting here."

"And how long has this been going on?"

"Six months this coming Friday," Morgan said. "Ever since Igor Lobanov was gunned down in broad daylight in Soho, and his Swiss bank account worth in excess of three million pounds that we were closing in on vanished into thin air."

"It's a question of some thief or thieves killing other thieves and robbing what they've left behind," Garza said with relish.

"If it was as simple as all that we wouldn't care," Morgan put in. "But when their activities begin to have an effect on British citizens, then it's another matter."

"Are you talking about the Russian mafia?" Lane asked.

"In part," Garza said. "Simply put, for twenty years before the Soviet empire fell apart, some of its finer citizens stole anything they could get their hands on, mostly from the government, converted it into Western currencies, and stashed the loot away in offshore banks. Switzerland, the Channel Islands, the Caribbean. Wherever. Now somebody is systematically tracing these accounts back to their holders, killing them, and draining the money before anybody knows what's going on."

"When did it start?" Lane asked.

Garza spread his hands. "Unknown."

"Six months ago as far as we're concerned," Morgan said. "Lobanov was one of the Russian mafia kingpins here in London. He was using his money to set up a quasi-union organization that could have hamstrung half the service sector here in London and in a half dozen other major cities. We were closing in on him when he turned up dead, and within hours his Swiss account was gone." Morgan shook his head in disgust. "No witnesses to the shooting, and as far as the Swiss are concerned the account was closed by its legitimate holder, Lobanov. Which of course was impossible, he was already dead.''

"That's also the point at which we realized that Markov was interested in the same subject,'' Garza said.

—————— **6** ——————

LONDON

Lane brought up the light-intensified image from the telescope on one of the computer screens. The Mercedes was still parked in front, and the same lights as before illuminated some of the upstairs windows.

"Did he go after the same bank account?'' Lane asked.

"Yes. But we caught it by a fluke,'' Morgan explained. "His computer line was being routinely monitored, and a call was placed from his house to the bank in Zürich almost simultaneous with ours.''

"That's when Brad called us, because he knew we had the equipment and technical expertise to keep watch on Markov,'' Garza said.

"Has he made any inquiries since then?'' Lane asked.

"Several,'' Morgan told him. "Each time his bank queries have been associated with the death of a Russian, usually in Moscow. And each time he's been too late. The accounts were electronically drained within hours of the killings.''

"Then you should be able to trace the paths electronically,'' Lane said.

"No such luck," Garza said. "But you might be able to help. That is if you're willing."

"Let me get something straight," Lane said. "You say that you've monitored all Markov's calls from the house, including the one about me?"

"That's how we knew that you and Sergeyev were meeting him in Hyde Park this afternoon and again this evening," Garza said.

"But you've heard nothing about the submarine."

"Not a thing. He's got the nasty habit of stopping wherever he might be and making a call from a pay phone before we can get close enough to count the clicks."

"Well, he'll call me sooner or later," Lane said. "All we need is a switchover from my hotel room to a phone here. In that case it won't matter where he calls from."

Garza was grinning like a kid who'd found his own crab apple tree. "Already done."

"At this point it still looks like we're involved in two separate operations," Lane said. "So we have to force the issue and get Markov to make a mistake. About the same thing I was trying to accomplish on my own."

The street below seemed to have settled into a deeper darkness and a more complete silence. The upstairs lights in the Russian's house were out. Frances was in the kitchen making tea, and Morgan and Garza were fiddling with the computer.

"But there's a possibility that we can't ignore," he continued. "Whoever is raiding the stolen money accounts is quite rich by now. Rich enough to buy a submarine."

Garza looked up, startled. "Killing Russians and raiding bank accounts is one thing, but buying and selling submarines somewhere is another kettle of fish."

"Maybe," Lane admitted. "But let's assume, for the moment, that whoever is raiding the bank accounts knows that his good thing will have to come to an end sooner or later. The Russians themselves will get on to him, if no one else does. If he's smart he's planned ahead.''

"Bought the submarine for insurance, you mean?'' Frances asked, coming to the kitchen door.

"The ruling generals in Sierra Leone would be more than happy to give this guy asylum in exchange for a submarine,'' Lane said. "And I can think of a number of other countries that'd do the same.''

Lane stopped short, another thought dumping on him like a sudden cold shower. He shivered despite himself.

"What's wrong, William?'' Frances asked.

Lane glanced over at her and the others, who were staring at him. He didn't believe in coincidences. Never had. Yet he'd experienced more than his share, and he couldn't afford to ignore the possibility now.

He shook his head. "Jet lag,'' he said. "But I just had the thought that if our guy is somewhere here in London, or nearby, and if the submarine is also somewhere in the Channel, it might mean that he's already getting ready to jump. Doesn't give us much time.''

"If the two operators are one and the same,'' Morgan pointed out. "We still don't have proof of that.''

"No we don't. And we might never have unless we can arrange to be nearby when Markov makes contact with the owner.''

"Two days means he could be just about anywhere,'' Morgan pointed out.

"They wouldn't have directed me here to London if he was halfway around the world,'' Lane said. "Markov's two days was probably an arbitrary figure to make me think just that.''

"Well, so far Markov hasn't tried to make contact with your Mister X,'' Garza said. "At least not from his home or car phones.''

"What'd he do after my meeting with him this evening?'' Lane asked.

"He stopped at a phone booth, then came home," Morgan said.

"Then that's when he made contact," Lane said, and he had another thought. "You know what phone booth he used, and what time he made the call; have you checked with the phone company to see what number he dialed?"

"His own embassy," Garza said. "Probably for relay to an outside line. It's done all the time." His lower lip curled. "We're not idiots here, Lane. We know what we're doing."

"Then we're just going to have to wait until he makes his move, or calls me at Claridge's," Lane said.

7

LONDON

Maslennikov's Gulfstream jet touched down at London's Heathrow around midnight, and he picked up a rental car under a false ID from the sleepy agent at the Hertz counter. Within a half hour he was making his way into the city on a very empty motorway.

Yernin had hatched some insane scheme to lure Lane to London by striking at Frances Shipley. He wanted to fly with Maslennikov this evening, but in the end he had promised to stay put for the moment.

Ultimately, of course, he'd have to be allowed to take his revenge. But Maslennikov wanted to be well away before that happened. Because if Yernin came up against Bill Lane and lost, it could lead the British and American authorities back to Guernsey and the operation. That would never be allowed to happen, no matter how important a killer Yernin had become.

In Central London, Maslennikov took Harrow Road up to Regent's Park; then, past King's Cross, he parked the car on a narrow little side street that twisted away into a maze of alleys and lanes.

He telephoned Markov's house using his cell phone. The *rezident*'s sleepy voice answered after the fourth ring.

"Da?"

"I'll be there in five minutes," Maslennikov said, and he hung up. He locked up the car, hunched up his coat collar and pulled his hat low against the heavy mist, then walked back to Copenhagen Street, where he turned onto a residential street, a tall apartment building at the end of the block.

He paused a moment, his shadow cast by the streetlamp, then went the rest of the way. Even if Markov was under surveillance it wouldn't matter because the British counterintelligence people wouldn't learn much beyond the fact that the Russian had a mysterious late-night visitor. If they tried to follow him, he would lose them. Simple as that. All he was doing tonight was buying time.

One of Markov's bodyguards let Maslennikov in, and ran an electronic wand over his body before he was allowed to proceed to the study at the rear of the house, where he removed his hat and unbuttoned his coat.

Markov, wearing a robe and slippers, joined him a few moments later. "What are you doing here, you fool? The British are almost certainly monitoring my telephones and watching this house."

"It doesn't matter," Maslennikov said confidently. "I assume that your initial call to me was clean, or Moscow would have your soul for it."

Markov nodded uncertainly. "But I wasn't expecting you like this."

"No," Maslennikov replied dryly. "The item you want from me is for sale at fifty million *pounds* sterling, and that price is not negotiable. But it will not be available for another seven days because it's still in transit. Do you understand?"

Again Markov nodded hesitantly. "Where will it be delivered?"

"At a time and place acceptable to both of us. But first I need to know something. Why does Moscow want it back?"

"I don't know."

"But I think you do, Comrade Markov. And it has to be a very important reason for them to agree to such a steep price. More than twice what I paid for it."

"I'm sure that they have their reasons, and I'm just as sure that it's an important political matter. But this is as big a surprise to me as I'm sure it is to you."

"Do they have a timetable?"

"Not that I was told," Markov said, and it was clear that he was uncomfortable. "But I'm sure everybody concerned would like to get it done and over with."

"Everybody concerned?" Maslennikov asked. Something was wrong here, something with Markov's attitude. His nervousness.

"*Da*, Moscow."

"Who gave you my name?"

"General Korzhakov," Markov said.

Captain General Gennadi Korzhakov was director of the new Russian foreign intelligence service, the SVR. It was he with whom Maslennikov had made the deal for the submarine. And there were very few people who knew about it. Which meant something extraordinary was happening here. Probably to do with the raids on their bank accounts—raids that did not include any of the general's vast holdings.

"What did he tell you about me?"

"Only that you used to work together, and that you were retired now."

All of Maslennikov's senses were warning him that Markov was lying to him, and that this was a trap of some sort. It took no stretch of the imagination to believe that the SVR was suspicious of him, and that Markov had been directed to investigate the monetary raids.

"Seven days, and we'll set up a place for the hand-off," Maslennikov said.

"Here in the English Channel?"

Maslennikov laughed. "What do you take me for, a complete idiot? When I'm ready I'll let you know. In the meantime get the money."

"Whatever you say."

Maslennikov left the study, pulled on his hat, rebuttoned his raincoat, and let himself out past the watchful bodyguard. On the street he hesitated for just a moment, then headed back to Copenhagen Street in a dead run.

8

LONDON

Lane held the headset tight against his ears trying to make out the indistinct words they were picking up from the study when Garza gave a shout from the computer monitor attached to the telescope.

"He's on the move!"

Lane tossed the headphones aside, and went over to the monitor in time to see the dark figure racing down the street.

It was something about the voice they'd picked up on the incoming call that bothered Lane. Now this.

"Who've you got on the street?" he demanded.

"Nobody at this hour," Morgan told him.

"Did we get a clear shot of his face when he came out the door?"

"I don't know," Garza said, his fingers flying over the keyboard. "Maybe. But I just don't know yet."

"Give me your car keys," he told Frances.

"I'm coming with you," she said, and together they tore out of the apartment, and instead of waiting for the elevator, took the stairs down two at a time.

Frances got behind the wheel.

"Take it easy until we get around the corner," Lane cautioned her. "We don't want to make Markov suspicious."

She pulled out of the driveway and drove to the end of the block, where she turned left into Copenhagen Street. A police car passed going the other way. The cops looked at them, but did not turn around. No one else was in sight.

Cars were parked up on the curbs down all the narrow side streets, but only a few houses or apartments showed any lights, and no one was on foot.

Frances drove two more blocks, then turned left toward King's Cross, where there was some vehicular traffic, but no pedestrians.

"We've lost him," she said. "Unless you want me to keep circling."

"No, he's gone," Lane said. "Let's go back. But take a different route, one that doesn't pass in front of Markov's."

"Maybe something will show up on one of the cameras," Frances said.

"Maybe," Lane replied absently, hardly daring to think what he was thinking.

9

LONDON

Maslennikov sat in the darkness behind the wheel of his car, scarcely breathing. He'd just reached his car and got in when the Range Rover had passed in Copenhagen Street. Had he not looked up at that precise moment he'd never have seen the driver and her passenger briefly illuminated as they crossed under the streetlamp.

The woman was Frances Shipley and the man was Bill Lane. There was absolutely no doubt in Maslennikov's mind, and for the very first time in the year since he'd gotten out of Kiev, he was frightened.

He could see everything unraveling. All their work, all the money, all their plans, gone because of one man and his English bitch.

He remained parked where he was for a full half hour before he finally started the engine and cautiously crept away back to Heathrow, his brain seething with a dozen moves and countermoves. One thing was absolutely clear in his thinking, however: Bill Lane and his girlfriend would have to die, and die soon.

PART FOUR

1

LONDON

It took until four in the morning before the computer could generate a decent composite photograph of the man coming out of Markov's house. Because of the lighting, because of the speed at which the dark figure had been moving, and because his hat had been pulled low and his coat collar pulled up around the sides of his face, the final photograph had been built pixel by pixel, shade of gray by shade of gray. And even then at the end, the image was not much better than an old-fashioned police sketch artist could generate from descriptions. But it was enough for Lane.

He sat in front of the monitor eating a cheese sandwich and drinking one of Garza's beers as the picture came up. A cold fist closed around his heart and he looked over at Frances, who was working at another terminal trying to clean up the digitally recorded conversation from Markov's study.

Their eyes met briefly and she smiled tiredly, but then turned back to her work. Garza was talking on one of the phones to someone at the embassy, and Morgan was searching a passport control database for recent entries of Russians into Great Britain. But that was like looking for a needle in a haystack, and nobody expected him to come up with anything useful.

Lane turned back to the picture, stared at it for a moment, then picked up a phone and called Tom Hughes in Washington.

"Maslennikov is here, Tommy. I just missed him a couple of hours ago and I'm looking at his photograph right now."

"I knew it," Hughes said. "His name has come up in connection with what our friends are investigating."

"How so?"

"Someone is making raids on the offshore accounts of a number of well-heeled Russians, which is creating quite a stir in the Russian community there in London, and over here in Brighton Beach."

"Is Maslennikov behind it?"

"More like one of the victims from what I'm looking at," Hughes said. "He had a pair of bank accounts in Switzerland, and possibly some others elsewhere that I can't get a handle on yet. But Maslennikov's accounts were drained eleven months ago. Within weeks after he disappeared from Kiev."

"Unless he drained them himself."

"That's a thought," Hughes said. "What's he doing there in London, and where are you calling from? You're at a blind number."

"I'm at a CIA safe house across the street from the Russian *rezident*'s house. Looks like Maslennikov is the one who negotiated the submarine deal for Sierra Leone."

"He showed up there?"

"Yeah, but I didn't know it was him until just now," Lane said. "He's close, Tommy. And so is that sub. It's no coincidence that he came to see Markov."

"The sixty-four-dollar question remains, is Yernin with him?"

"And what have they been up to all this time," Lane said. "Have you come up with anything that might exclude Maslennikov from being the one raiding the bank accounts?"

"Nothing, other than the fact that two of his own accounts were drained."

"Could be Maslennikov then. Most of the accounts they raided belonged to Russians who were gunned down on the street. No witnesses. But it's not until *after* they're dead that their accounts are tapped."

"Yemin is the triggerman, and Maslennikov is the genius behind the scheme," Hughes said. "Is that what you're thinking?"

"The submarine is their insurance policy, because everybody—the English as well as the Russians—has taken notice. He sees that the end is in sight, and he's provided them with an escape route."

"There's still no guarantee that the sub is holed up somewhere in the Channel or along the coast. Might be passing right through on its way to Sierra Leone. That'd be the most logical assumption."

"What's the chance of convincing someone over at Navy to place a screen of ASW ships off Sierra Leone's coast?" Lane asked, although he already knew the answer.

"About the same as you convincing the Brits to go to war with Russia over using the Channel to transit a warship. Slim and none, and slim just left town. How about Frances, have you told her yet?"

"Not yet, but she's sitting across from me, so she's about to find out. And so are Brad Morgan and Mario Garza, Langley's number two man here."

"I knew there was something going on," Hughes said triumphantly. "I got the runaround when I tried to find out if Langley knew anything about the bank account thing. Are they starting to make the connection between that and Maslennikov and the sub?"

"Not yet, but I think it's going to dawn on them real soon," Lane said. "In the meantime I want you to take this to Ben and have him bounce it upstairs. I think we might need some help."

"One question, William," Hughes said gently. "Is there a possibility that Maslennikov spotted you?"

"I don't think so."

"Okay. But at the risk of sounding like a broken record, watch yourself."

"Thanks," Lane said, and he hung up.

Lane made a printout of Maslennikov's picture and laid it on Frances's table, then went into the kitchen for another beer. This was the day he had dreaded, and yet now that it was here he was glad. It would be closure between him and Valeri Yernin.

He went back to the living room, where Frances was still working with the digital filtering program, and watched her. He wanted to pick her up in his arms and take her away, far away, right now. Yet it was an unreasonable desire, because in the end it was quite impossible to protect anyone from a determined enemy. But he wanted to try.

Frances looked up at him, started to smile, but then did a double take and took the headset off. "What?" she asked.

"The computer came up with a composite picture of Markov's visitor."

Frances noticed it at her elbow. She picked it up and studied it for a few moments. "Do you know him?"

Lane nodded.

"Who is he?"

"Mikhail Maslennikov," Lane said. "Yernin's control officer."

"I see," she said softly, looking again at the imperfect image. "Are you quite sure?"

Morgan and Garza, both sensing that something was happening, looked up with interest.

"I'm sure," Lane said. "It doesn't mean that Yernin is here, but I think it's a real possibility, and I think I know why."

She thought about it and finally nodded. "As long as Maslennikov didn't see you, the advantage is ours." Her jaw tightened. "This time we won't miss him, William," she said, emphasizing the *we*.

2

GUERNSEY

The eastern horizon was just beginning to lighten by the time the Gulfstream jet touched down outside St. Peter Port and a worried Maslennikov took the car back to his house overlooking the coast road. The trip by air to London had taken longer than normal because they had swung out into the Atlantic, two hundred kilometers well below radar level, before popping up into the air traffic control system approaching from the west. They'd reversed the procedure on the way back.

Yernin, who never seemed to sleep, waited on the broad veranda overlooking the sea, smoking a cigarette and drinking a steaming glass of tea.

"How was London?" he asked from the darkness when Maslennikov mounted the steps.

"Bill Lane was there."

Yernin tossed his cigarette away, and languidly turned his gaze to his control officer. "Did he see you?"

"No," Maslennikov said. "But I think he was watching Markov's house. He came out of nowhere as soon as I left."

"Was he following you?"

"*Da.*"

"Why, if he didn't know it was you?" Yernin asked calmly.

"Because he saw someone going out of Markov's house and he wanted to know who it was and where they were going," Maslennikov shot back, irritated.

"The point is that he's in London now, and I don't know why."

Yernin shrugged. "Maybe he found out about two-eighty-three and came to negotiate for it."

Maslennikov snorted. "Not likely," he said. "But his girlfriend was with him. In fact she was driving."

Yernin's eyes were bright, but his expression was bland. "The fact that they're together makes it easier."

"I agree," Maslennikov said. "In fact I want you to leave for London as soon as you can come up with a sensible plan. But it'll have to be quick, because we're pulling out of here soon. We just need time to convert what assets we can into gold, and load the submarine."

"With Lane dead there'll be no reason for us to hurry our departure."

"We're going anyway," Maslennikov said. "Call it a gut feeling, but I think that if we stay here much longer the entire operation will crumble around us."

"As you wish," Yernin said indifferently. He pushed away from the rail where he'd been leaning looking out at the blackness of the night sea and the occasional pair of headlights passing on the road below. "I'll leave within the hour."

"I want you to work out a plan first," Maslennikov said. "We can't afford to have this backfire on you."

"I've had a plan for several months now."

"What are you talking about?"

"I've been watching Lieutenant Commander Shipley ever since we got here. I've been to her house. I've followed her to work, and to Harrod's and the shops she likes to go to. I've watched the way she drives, the way she walks, the way she sits, the way she eats." Yernin smiled gently. "I know a great deal about her."

"I want you to kill Bill Lane."

"I'll kill them both," Yernin said softly.

3

Frances let the computer continue on its own to try to make sense of the muddled recording from Markov's study, and Lane finished his beer in the kitchen doorway. Garza and Morgan had stopped what they were doing.

"Okay, Lane, you have our attention," Garza said. "You know this guy?"

"Until a year ago he was chief of the Ukrainian KGB's North American Division, with a lot of solid ties to the old Soviet KGB in Moscow."

"What happened last year?" Garza asked.

"I threw a monkey wrench in one of his plans, and nearly got his star agent killed in the process." Lane looked at Frances. "Nearly got both of us killed."

"Then what?"

"He disappeared from Kiev, a couple of his offshore bank accounts were closed, and no one heard from him until tonight."

"You're talking about the Iranian submarine investigation that you and Frances were involved with," said Morgan with obvious distaste. "The body count was beyond all reason."

Lane nodded tightly. "The point is that Maslennikov was a Black Sea Fleet submarine commander. So I don't think it's any coincidence him showing up here so soon after Markov and I had our little chat."

"You think he's the Mister X who bought the submarine from the Russians, and the one who'd been raiding the bank accounts?'' Morgan asked. ''That doesn't make any sense. Good Lord, the man would have been sticking his neck on the chopping block by going to the same people for help who he was stealing from.''

''He has the reputation for doing the unexpected,'' Lane said.

''It would mean that the Russians don't have a clue yet,'' Garza suggested.

''He might think so. Could be the reason he took delivery on the submarine just now. He might be getting set to jump to Africa.''

''Hell of a place to spend one's retirement,'' Morgan said.

''Even hell wouldn't be bad with enough money.''

''What about the crew? At some point they'll have to be sent back to Russia.''

''Maslennikov is a Ukrainian,'' Lane said. ''A lot of the men who used to be under his command are still loyal to him.''

''If he's the one who made the deal with the Russians he showed up too fast to have come very far,'' Morgan said. ''Means he's somewhere here in England, or maybe France. Close. You say that you traced the submarine as far as the Channel. If you have proof I'll turn this over to the navy and they can find it.''

Garza shook his head. ''Once they got wind of the search they'd just ditch the sub and take off, and we'd be no further ahead than before.''

''There's more,'' Lane said quietly.

''There always is,'' said Morgan, resigned.

''It's Maslennikov's number one, Valeri Yernin. If he's here too, which is a very real possibility, and it gets out that Frances and I are involved, he'll stop at nothing to come after us. He wants us dead.''

''For the Iranian thing last year?'' Morgan asked.

''Yes.''

"All the more reason to send the navy after the sub," Morgan told Garza. "At the very least it would break up Maslennikov's little operation."

"He'd just move it someplace else," Lane said. "And besides, I want him to come after me." He walked over to the window and looked down at Markov's house. The upstairs windows were turning red with the morning sun, and Monday morning traffic was picking up.

"Is that what this is all about? Some sort of a vendetta?"

Lane turned and looked at the Brit. "Yernin killed a lot of good people."

"For which you feel responsible."

"That's right."

Morgan shook his head. "Well it's not going to happen on British soil. You'll have to take your fight elsewhere."

"But you want Maslennikov's operation stopped."

"Only if it continues to take place here," Morgan said. "If he's operating elsewhere, then let him. He's killing Russians, doing us all a favor."

"What do you have in mind, William?" Frances asked.

"I'm going to give Maslennikov and Yernin the two things they want most."

"Which are?" Morgan asked.

"Me, and money."

4

LONDON

They sat around the computer that was filtering out the background noises from Markov's house so that his conversation with Maslennikov would become intelligible. In forty-five minutes they had most of it.

"Do you believe the seven-day timetable?" Garza asked.

"Not on your life," Lane said. "The submarine is close, which means Maslennikov is getting ready to jump, and he's buying himself some time so that he can clear out his own bank accounts. Probably convert it all to gold."

"That'll take more than a week. But if you're right about him going to Sierra Leone, and taking his crew with him, he'll need a lot of money."

"Another fifty million pounds' worth," Morgan said. "If he offered that to the Sierra Leone junta he wouldn't need to deliver the submarine. They'd welcome him with open arms."

"He doesn't believe the Russians will come up with that kind of money," Lane said. "But if they did, it might make him stop and think about a deal, even though he has no intention of giving up the submarine."

"Why wouldn't he?" Morgan asked. "The gold would be of greater value to him."

Lane shook his head. "What would prevent the generals from having them killed once they turned over the gold?''

Garza laughed. ''A submarine, on the other hand, needs a trained crew.''

''How about that,'' Lane said, and Morgan scowled.

5

LONDON

Morgan fixed them a breakfast of kippers, eggs, toast, and strong black tea that went down well after their all-night vigil. Garza volunteered to clean up. ''As soon as Markov leaves for work, we can get some sleep,'' he said.

''Between us we have four teams watching his movements,'' Morgan explained. ''Of course we've gotten more out of our efforts here than anywhere else.''

''Does he go directly to the embassy?'' Lane asked, watching the CCD monitor hooked to the telescope.

''Invariably. But at least twice a week he goes out for lunch, usually with somebody from the embassy. Sometimes he meets his wife and daughter, and they do a little shopping in the afternoon.''

The front door of the house opened, and Markov and two bodyguards came out, got in the car, and drove off. ''Does he always have his bodyguards with him?''

''Doesn't make a move without them,'' Morgan said. He glanced at his watch. ''He's right on time this morning.'' He keyed a walkie-talkie. ''Anvil is on the move.''

''Roger that,'' the reply came immediately.

Lane brought his dishes into the kitchen, where Frances

was helping with the cleanup. "I'm going back to the hotel and set up a meeting with Markov for this morning. It'll be in Hyde Park, and as soon as it's set I'll call you here. I want Brad's people to listen in with a parabolic microphone. Mario's team will have to get in as close as possible when Markov leaves, because he'll be making a call from a phone box afterward and I want to know what number he calls."

"What have you got in mind?" Morgan asked from the doorway.

"I'm going to make him that offer he can't refuse," Lane said, and Frances all of a sudden looked eager.

6

LONDON

After Lane left the safe house to catch a taxi in Copenhagen Street, Garza departed to get his people squared away, and Frances got her jacket and purse.

"I'm going home to change," she told Morgan, who had to wait for Lane's call. "I'll be back within the hour."

"Go to the office like you normally would this morning, Frances. If Maslennikov does take the bait, and if his henchman is around or about, you'd be putting yourself at risk."

"Taking risks is part of what I get paid for. And after all, this is London."

"People get killed in London too."

Frances's gray-blue eyes flashed in momentary anger.

"You can fire me if you want. It's within your power. But if not, I'll do my job as liaison to the American intelligence community as I see fit."

"As liaison to Mr. William Lane," Morgan flared.

"Yes, since he's a National Security Agency officer," Frances said. She hesitated a moment, then started to go.

"Wait," Morgan called after her, and she turned back. "I don't want us to go on like this."

"Like what, Brad?"

Morgan was embarrassed but he didn't avert his eyes. "At such odds with each other." He shook his head. "It's none of my business, of course, but are you in love with him?"

"Yes, I am."

"Are you willing to give up your career and your position for him? Because he certainly won't give up his for the sake of you."

A troubled look crossed her face, but Morgan was not glad that he had scored such an obvious point.

"I don't know what to do," she said at length. "But you have to understand that it's tied up with Maslennikov and Yernin. With them still at large my life is going to remain on hold."

"Unless you walk away from it."

Frances shook her head. "Sorry, Brad, but I can't do that. No matter the outcome, I have to stay with him at least until we're sure about this one issue."

"And then?" Morgan asked miserably.

She came over and laid a hand on his arm. "Then life will go on, and you and I will continue as friends, the same in the future as now." She looked into his eyes. "Nothing more than that, Brad."

When she was gone he watched from the window until her Range Rover pulled out of the parking lot and disappeared around the corner. Then he went into the kitchen and poured a large measure of cognac.

7

LONDON

Lane arrived at Claridge's just as a taxi carrying Sergeyev pulled out. The Russian didn't see him, but Lane caught a good look at a man clearly relieved to be away with fresh cash in his pocket and his immediate troubles behind him.

The clerk at the front desk confirmed that Sergeyev had checked out, but had left no messages.

Upstairs, Lane showered and shaved, and after he got dressed, telephoned Markov at the Russian embassy.

"I won't wait two days," he told the *rezident*. "But my people are willing to increase their offer."

"There may be nothing I can do," Markov said.

"Meet me in the park," Lane told him.

"When?"

"One hour." Lane hung up, waited a moment, then went down to the lobby, where he telephoned the safe house from a public phone.

"Has he agreed to meet with you?" Morgan asked.

"An hour from now, at the same place in Hyde Park."

"We'll be there."

8

LONDON

The weather had cleared somewhat but it had gotten sharply colder, and the air smelled like snow, which was highly unusual for this time of year. The same people seemed to be gathered around the same speakers when Lane showed up in Hyde Park, and no one seemed to mind the cold as long as it wasn't raining.

The same bodyguards met Lane as they had the first time, one of them patting him down, as they hugged, before he was allowed to proceed to where Markov was seated.

"You'd think that after everything that's happened in the past ten years, you people would have finally learned some manners," Lane said.

"It's for my protection," Markov explained. "They insist."

"I'm talking about Gregor. When I called his room this morning they told me he'd checked out. No good-byes, no thanks, no go to hell, nothing."

"Thanks for what?" Markov asked.

"For the introductions."

"Sergeyev is no different than the rest of us. He gets his orders, and he carries them out. What are your new orders?"

"Have you talked to the new owner of two-eighty-three?"

Markov hesitated for a fraction of a second, but then nodded. "Yes."

"What's he say to our offer?"

"He needs time. Seven days."

"To do what?"

"To be in a position to deliver the boat."

"That's not acceptable," Lane said. "In seven days the sub could already be in Sierra Leone. That, we won't allow."

"My hands are tied."

"Then tell me who he is, and where I can reach him. Maybe he'll listen to me, because I'm the one holding the purse strings."

"He wants seventy-five million pounds sterling," Markov said. He took out a cigarette and lit it. "Not quite within your letter of credit."

"Plus your cut," Lane said, watching the Russian's eyes.

"I'll take care of that out of his end."

"I'll give him sixty-five million," Lane said. "In gold bullion."

Markov was impressed. "He was quite adamant."

"He is here in London then? You met with him?"

Markov smiled. "I'll pass your offer along to him. But certainly it would take you the week to arrange for the delivery of so much gold."

"I could have it anywhere within the British Isles or even the Continent within twenty-four hours," Lane said. "Thirty-two and a half million by tomorrow, which you and I would deliver in person. You'd get the second half after I inspected the boat."

"The boat's not here."

"He's lying. According to our timetable two-eighty-three should have entered the English Channel yesterday."

"And if he refuses your offer?"

"I'll go to the British first thing in the morning. And if you try to stop me there'll be an all-out shooting war that'll do neither of us any good."

"The British might be less than enthused about listening to you, since by your own admission you've been trying to buy a Russian warship."

"Nothing wrong with doing an arms deal," Lane said. "Besides, I'm a South African and you're a Russian. Who do you suppose the British would believe?" Lane got to his feet. "Could be that your career would end."

Markov looked up at him harshly. "You're not armed at this moment. Maybe I'll signal my men and we'll end *your* career here and now."

Lane laughed. "And give up a big profit? Nobody would be happy about that. Especially not in Moscow."

The two bodyguards moved a little closer. The one from Rio had his hand inside his coat pocket.

Markov hesitated a moment, but then nodded. "I'll pass along your offer. It's all I can do for the moment."

Lane turned away and walked back to Claridge's. He sat in a corner of the lobby with the London *Times* and a cup of tea.

Fifteen minutes later a distinguished-looking man with gray hair, well dressed in a hand-tailored suit, sat down across from Lane.

"With Mr. Morgan's compliments, he'd like you to join him and the others at the safe house." His accent was slightly East End.

Lane glanced across the lobby, but no one seemed to be paying them any attention.

"Your back is clear, sir."

Lane got up. "Thanks," he said. "But the next time you dress up, don't forget to leave the bottom button of your vest undone. It's not proper otherwise, you know."

LONDON

Lane walked down to the Royal Academy and Piccadilly Circus, traffic heavy but reasonably polite compared to Washington or New York, to make sure he was coming away clear. Then he took a taxi to within a couple of blocks of the safe house off Copenhagen Street, and went the rest of the way in by foot.

Frances opened the door for him, though Garza had given him a security card. She was anxious. "We got every bit of it," she said.

"Good for you and Brad. Is Garza back yet? Do we know if Markov made his call?" Lane asked.

"He's on his way now."

Two of Morgan's men had come back with him from Hyde Park, and along with two others who manned the surveillance equipment on Markov's house, the apartment was getting crowded. Lane was introduced all around.

"What would you have done had the deal turned sour, sir?" one of the field officers asked. He looked like a banker, serious and proper.

"His bodyguards were too far away to be any good. By the time they'd drawn their guns, I would have had control of Markov and they would have had to withdraw." Lane shrugged. "Wouldn't have been elegant, but it would have worked."

One of the older men chuckled. "I just bet it would have at that, sir."

Morgan came in from another room. "Well, you sure leaned on him this time," he said. "We caught the words, but we were too far away to get an accurate read on his expressions. How'd he look to you?"

"In over his head, because this isn't his show," Lane said. "But he's on our side."

"It's up to Maslennikov if he wants to negotiate," Morgan said. "But if what you said about him is right, then sixty-five million pounds sterling in gold is going to make him sit up and take notice."

"But he won't give up the submarine," Frances put in.

"No, he won't," Lane agreed. "That's why I gave him an out. He can come for the first half thinking that when he has it he'll just turn around and run."

"At which time we'll have him," Morgan said.

Lane glanced at Frances. "At which time we'll be halfway home."

"If it comes to that we'll handle the situation my way," Morgan warned both of them. "In the meantime there's the problem of the gold. Markov will want to see it."

"We'll show it to him," Lane said. "My Vandermeer letter of credit is good. I think Barclays or Thomas Cook would let me borrow the gold for a few hours."

"Just like that?" said Morgan, vexed.

"Sure, why not?" Lane asked. The others were enjoying the exchange but Morgan was angry. "I'll trust you not to let the situation get so bad Maslennikov actually runs off with my gold. That is if you want to take responsibility."

At that moment Garza let himself in, but pulled up short when he realized that he'd barged in at a tense moment. "Have we got trouble?"

"Not unless Markov made no call, or you missed it if he did," Lane said mildly.

"Oh, he made a call, all right. But it doesn't do us

any good, because it was to the blind number at his embassy.''

"How long did he talk?''

"Eight and a half minutes,'' Garza said. "And he was smart enough to cover his mouth so we couldn't pick up so much as one word.''

"Then what'd he do?''

"Went back to his embassy. Which I don't understand. Why didn't he make the call from there?''

Lane laughed and said, "Because he wants to cut his own deal. He's telling Moscow one thing, telling me another, and Maslennikov still another.'' He pointed at the computer monitor on Markov's house. "He can't afford that lifestyle on the pay of a *rezident*.''

"Then we have the bastard,'' Morgan said, brightening. "He'll move mountains to get Maslênnikov here and make this deal work.''

"That he will,'' Lane agreed.

10

OXFORD

Yernin was aware that he'd been followed ever since he got off the ferry at Portsmouth and rented the Hertz Ford Taurus in Southampton. He was pretty sure that it wasn't the British authorities, but to make certain he'd given the two of them several opportunities to move in, which they had not taken.

By the time he pulled off the A34 outside of Oxford at a rest area, he knew who was following him and why.

They were driving a Chrysler minivan, and had parked thirty meters from where he was parked.

He got out of his Ford and walked down to the van, opened the side door, and climbed in. He thrust the muzzle of his Heckler & Koch 9mm autoloader between the seats before either of them could do anything.

"Why are you following me?" he asked in a reasonable tone of voice.

The driver tried to pull away, but Yernin jammed the pistol into his ribs.

"Be quick now. I don't want to have to kill you, but I will."

The other man reached inside his jacket, and Yernin reached over the top of the seat and batted his hand away.

"The captain sent us," the driver blurted. "He wants to make sure that you don't get into any trouble."

"He doesn't trust me, is that it?" Yernin asked, amused.

"No, sir. It's not that at all. He sent us in case you needed some help. We're pulling out in less than forty-eight hours and he doesn't want to leave you behind."

"At all costs," the other one said.

Yernin pulled back. "I imagine not. But I expect your orders are to kill me if I do get into trouble."

Neither one said anything, but it was clear from their expressions that Maslennikov had ordered them to do just that.

Yernin holstered his gun at the small of his back. "Were you on the ferry?"

"*Da,*" the driver said, looking at Yernin's reflection in the rearview mirror.

"I haven't seen either of you on the island before."

"We came in after you'd left for Polyarnyy," the one in the passenger seat said. He and the driver could have been twins; they were both darkly complected and slightly built.

"From Kiev?"

"Odessa, actually," the driver said. "We used to serve under Captain Maslennikov. But there's nothing back there now."

"Were you in the Black Sea Fleet?" Yernin asked, although he suspected he already knew the answer to that question as well. These two had the look.

"No, sir," the driver said. "We worked in the KGB. Department Viktor."

"You're shooters?"

"*Da.*"

"Good," Yernin said. "In that case I probably will have a use for you. What are you carrying?"

"Makarovs with silencers," the driver said. He turned around. "Maybe we should introduce ourselves, Comrade. I'm Ivan Yegorov."

"Besides pistols, did you bring anything else?"

"Silenced AK-47s, with light-intensifying scopes," the one in the passenger seat said. He had a long ragged scar across the top of his forehead. "I'm Nikolai Dondorev."

"Very well," Yernin said, thinking ahead to what might have to be done. "But you'll follow orders exactly as I give them, do you understand this?"

"Yes, sir," Dondorev assured him. "But what are we doing here? The captain thought you would go to London. That's where Lane and the woman are."

"And that's were Scotland Yard and half the decent cops in England are," Yernin said. "Within forty-eight hours Mr. Lane and his bride-to-be will be coming here quite alone."

"But why?" the driver asked.

"To attend to Sir Leonard Styles, who is Commander Shipley's uncle and only living relative."

11

OXFORD

The rambling house bordered the river Thames a few kilometers outside of Oxford. Yernin sat in the van parked across the road from the wrought-iron entry gate. The house, mostly dark, was just discernible through the trees at the bottom of a long, sloping hill. He broke the connection and lowered the cellular phone.

"Sir Leonard's man says he's in London," he told Yegorov.

"Then we're going there after all."

Yernin shook his head. "We're going fishing instead."

"Sir?"

Yernin looked at him, and the driver blanched. "Sir Leonard will be back tomorrow afternoon, and we'll be waiting for him, on the river."

PART FIVE

1

LONDON

The call from Markov came first thing in the morning. Lane had gone back to Claridge's around midnight to catch a few hours of much needed sleep on Frances's insistence, and when the bedside phone rang he thought it was her.

"Good morning," he mumbled. The gray morning was brightening the windows.

"Good morning, Mr. Vandermeer," Markov said. "Your offer has been accepted."

Lane tossed the covers back and sat up. "That's very good. When and where can we meet?"

"That depends upon how quickly you can come up with the gold. But we're ready to move today."

"You've spoken with the owner already?"

"Yes I have," Markov said. "But he's a cautious man, as you can well imagine. He wants certain safeguards."

"Name them."

"How soon could you make arrangements with the Creditbanque Suisse?"

"Where?"

"Zürich."

"Couldn't be easier," Lane said. He reached for a cigarette. "Five this afternoon, Swiss time. I'll meet you at Heathrow around two, and we can fly over together if you'll make the necessary arrangements." He lit the cigarette, but it tasted terrible—as they all did lately.

"We'll meet at the Swiss Air counter."

"Unless you'll be having your Swiss counterpart handle the deal."

"Two at Heathrow, Mr. Vandermeer," said Markov, not amused.

"Ta ta," Lane said, but Markov had already broken the connection.

Lane stubbed out the cigarette, ordered tea and toast from room service, then showered and shaved. He'd just finished dressing when his breakfast came, and a half hour later, his tie knotted properly and his smart English gray wool suit freshly sponged and pressed, he left the hotel.

He took a cab over to the Barclays Bank in the old city near Temple Bar, and spoke for twenty minutes with a polite, if somewhat indifferent, vice president about buying and selling foreign currencies in fairly substantial amounts. When they were finished, Lane shook the man's hand with enthusiasm, for the benefit of anyone watching, and outside, merged with the crowds.

Sure that he'd lost anyone following him, he caught a cab in Fenchurch Street and took it back to the vicinity of the safe house, which he cautiously approached on foot.

An irate Brad Morgan was waiting for him. "How did you know that you were being followed?" he demanded.

"I didn't know until now."

"Then why the hell did you go to the trouble of losing my people outside Barclays?" Morgan said, trailing off at the end because he realized what Lane meant.

"Standard procedure, Brad," Lane said. "On the chance the Russians were following me I didn't want to lead them back here. Anyway, they're going for the deal."

2

GUERNSEY

Maslennikov hung up the telephone in his study after talking to Markov for the second time this morning. Captains Kovrygin and Lubiako sat across the desk from him. They'd been discussing the reactivation of 283 tonight. Getting the crew back aboard would be much more difficult than getting them off, but the weather was with them, the seas fairly calm and the skies still overcast.

"The South African has agreed," he said. "He'll meet with me in Zürich this afternoon at five."

"With the gold?" Kovrygin asked.

"*Da*," Maslennikov said. "When it's transferred safely, I'll bring Vandermeer back here and we'll take him down to the boat."

"A one-way trip," said the submarine commander, Igor Lubiako, his narrow lips compressed.

"Yes. Have his body placed in one of the torpedo tubes and we can dispose of it in the middle of the Atlantic."

3

It was early morning in Washington, but Lane got the impression that Hughes had been awake and waiting for the call, because he answered on the first ring, and he understood exactly what he was supposed to do.

"I don't think Ben is going to be happy. But by the time he gets this one, it'll be too late to do anything."

"You do know that we're going to end up in jail one of these days," Lane said.

"At least the company will be tolerable," Hughes said lightly, but then he got serious. "Don't take any unnecessary chances, William."

"Are you worried about me or the gold?"

"Both," Hughes said. "But if Maslennikov suspects a trap, he might bring Yernin with him. And that man's insane enough to try anything no matter where he is. No matter what, though, the instant Maslennikov lays eyes on you the game will be over. Why don't you let me get the Swiss police involved? It'd cut the risks."

"I don't want you to do that," Lane said. "The bank was their call, which could mean that they've got someone on the inside. If we tried something it might tip them off and Maslennikov would never show up."

"I don't like it."

"Brad Morgan and Mario Garza are coming over with me, so I won't be alone. But if Maslennikov has been raiding bank accounts for the past year he's done a good job of it. He's careful, and he keeps his ear to the ground. If I went in there with the cavalry, I'd be wasting my time."

"The gold will be in place by five," said Hughes, resigned. "All two tons of it."

It was coming up on eleven and Lane had to get back to the hotel in case Markov's people were watching for him to head to the airport from there.

"As soon as Maslennikov sees it's me, he'll run," he told them. "If I can't stop him, you'll have to intercept him in the lobby or out front."

"If Yernin shows up we could all be in trouble," Frances said. "The Swiss won't understand why we haven't told them what's going on in their own country."

"We have help coming up from Bern," Garza said confidently. "No matter how good this guy is, he'll be seriously outnumbered if he sticks his ugly nose where it doesn't belong."

"I want you to stay in London," Lane told Frances. "We'll need someone to backstop the operation in case things go bad."

"For once I agree with Bill," Morgan said. He'd been in an ugly mood since last night, and he was going along with this crazy scheme only because Markov was involved. He didn't need the added complication of the relationship between Lane and Frances. "As I see it, our real problem is convincing the Swiss to let us transport Maslennikov out of the country."

"That may not be necessary," Lane said. "I may just offer him his freedom, and whatever money he's already collected."

"In exchange for what?"

"The submarine, and the whereabouts of Valeri Yernin."

Frances's eyes were bright. "Let's resolve the issue, William," she said with venom. "Once and for all."

"That's the idea, Frannie," Lane said gently. He

looked at the others. "Are we clear on what we're doing?"

They all nodded.

"Then I'll see you in Zürich," Lane said, and he left.

4

LONDON

Frances watched from the window until he emerged
from the rear exit and disappeared around the corner
toward Copenhagen Street, then got her jacket and purse.
Morgan was just finishing up on the telephone.

"I'm going home to change," she told him.

"I'll go with you, and you can drop me downtown
on the way," he said. He glanced at his wristwatch. "I'll
see you at the heliport at noon," he told Garza.

"Sounds good," Garza said. "I've got a couple more
calls to make, and then I'll head over from here."

Frances and Morgan went downstairs and climbed
into the Range Rover. The overcast had deepened and it
was so dark she had to switch on the headlights. Traffic
was heavy and erratic, which matched her jangly mood,
made more brittle by what she expected was coming
with Brad.

"I can tell you right now that, contrary to what Bill
Lane wants, I am not going to put myself or any of my
people in danger over this business," Morgan said out
of the blue. "My charter is to stick with Markov, nothing
more."

"I don't think he wants anything like that," Frances
assured him. "I think Maslennikov will be happy to

walk away with his freedom and money in exchange for the submarine.''

''And for this Valeri Yernin who has both of you so worried,'' Morgan said. ''And rightfully so, if half of what I've read about the lunatic is true.''

''It is.''

''That's why I'm pulling you off this operation as of this moment. What I need are clear heads, not people who are emotionally involved.''

Frances glanced over at him. He looked smug, an expression she'd not seen on his face before. ''You can't do that to me, Brad,'' she said evenly.

''It's for your own good, Frannie,'' he said, not facing her. ''As of this moment I'm placing you on administrative leave. But it won't reflect poorly in your evaluation jacket. I can promise you that much. But I want you on the sidelines until we finish.''

''You don't want me to run interference in case the Swiss authorities sit up and take notice?''

''No, I do not.''

''You want me to go home and stay there, is that right, Brad?''

''Look, I'm doing this for your good. The last time you ran off after Lane you almost got yourself killed. I simply can't allow you, or any of my people, to get themselves into that kind of a jam again. So it's final.''

''All right,'' Frances said calmly.

Morgan looked at her. ''What?''

''I said okay, Brad. I'll take a couple of days off. When you boys finish playing your games, I'll come back to help pick up the pieces.''

''You don't have to take it that way, Frannie.''

''What way is that, Brad?''

He didn't answer.

''I'm either a lieutenant commander in Her Majesty's Secret Service, or I'm the little lady on administrative leave." She glanced at him again. "You can't have both."

They had reached the Law Courts off Chancery Lane, and Morgan directed her to pull over to the curb. "You can drop me off here."

"And then what?"

"Go home, Frances. I'll call you after it's over."

Frances softened. "Take care of yourself, Brad. Because whatever you think you know about Yernin from what you've read, he's even worse than you can imagine. If he shows up in Zürich, William will have his hands full. All of you will."

"He'll be outnumbered," Morgan said. "But thanks for the advice."

When he was gone, Frances headed home after first doubling back twice to make sure she wasn't being followed. At this point she wouldn't put it past Morgan. The simple truth was that he was jealous.

Mrs. Houlten was off doing marketing, so Frances didn't have to answer the questions her housekeeper would have thrown at her for coming home in the middle of the day in such a snit.

Upstairs, she quickly changed into a traveling outfit of a dark woolen skirt, light cashmere pullover sweater with a shawl collar, low heels, and butter soft Italian leather three-quarter-length coat. She tossed a few items of underwear, a change of skirt and sweater, and her cosmetics into an overnight bag, in case they were detained in Switzerland.

Checking herself in the mirror a last time, she touched up her makeup and downstairs in the library got her .32-caliber Bernardelli automatic, a spare magazine of ammunition, and her diplomatic passport and stuffed these in her shoulder bag.

She might get a hassle at Heathrow because of the gun, but they wouldn't stop her. Nor would the Swiss require her to step through a scanner because of her diplomatic status. Morgan would go through the roof when he found out what she was up to, but by then the operation would already be over.

There was no way she was going to leave anything to chance, she told herself with resolve as she left her house and headed out to Heathrow.

5

GUERNSEY

Maslennikov was the last aboard the Gulfstream, behind his bodyguard, Anatoli Ivanov, and Captain Kovrygin. "If there's a trap we'll be in place early enough to detect it," he told them.

"I still say it's not worth the risk, Mikhail," Kovrygin grumbled.

"Fifty million pounds sterling will buy us that much more freedom," Maslennikov said.

"If it's there."

"Even if it's not, I want to see who knows about our submarine," Maslennikov said. He motioned for the pilot that they could get started. "Something doesn't quite add up, and I want to know why."

"If Vandermeer is legitimate, the group he represents is probably working for the Liberians," Kovrygin said. "It makes sense from a military standpoint. Two-eighty-three will put them at a disadvantage, even if he is an old toy."

"If that's the case, then well and good, but I don't like the timing. Just when we were getting ready to pull out, this offer comes up."

"What I don't understand is his intelligence source," Kovrygin said. "There aren't that many people who know what actually happened up there."

"What about the business with one of the crew being a spy?"

Kovrygin shook his head. "Those men were hand-picked. Igor swears that there's not one of them who is even questionable. Vandermeer is lying."

"We'll soon find out," Maslennikov said, glancing at the muscular Ivanov, as the Gulfstream's engines spooled up, and they headed down the taxiway to the active runway.

Günter Loos, their contact at the bank, said that as of noon no gold transfer had occurred from any account held under the name Vandermeer. Nor had any inquiries or special arrangements been made for such a transfer. Such a transaction, however, could be accomplished in a matter of minutes electronically at any hour of the day or night.

Anything was possible, Maslennikov thought. And that's what worried him the most.

6

OXFORD

The twenty-five-foot cabin cruiser pulled up at an unused wooden dock on the Thames a few kilometers south of Oxford, and Yernin scrambled aboard.

"Did you have any trouble at the marina?" he asked Dondorev.

"No, sir. I think they were happy to get the rental at

this time of the year. They didn't even ask if I knew how to start the engine."

Yegorov pushed them away from the dock, and they headed downriver. The minivan was at the marina's car park, and the Ford Taurus was left at their hotel in Abingdon a few kilometers away.

"Now we go fishing," Yernin said.

7

ZÜRICH

Swiss Air flight 153 from London touched down at Kloten Airport at 3:30 P.M. Lane got his gun through customs packed in his fake laptop computer. Markov and his two bodyguards traveled under diplomatic passports and were waved through without question.

They rented a dark green van from the Hertz counter and by 4:10 were on the way into the city, the afternoon bright and sunny, not a cloud in the sky, though it was considerably colder than in London.

"I'm assuming that you made all the arrangements this morning, and the gold will be in place," Markov said. He and Lane sat in one of the backseats.

"If your man shows up, the gold will be there," Lane said. He unbuttoned the computer's bottom panel, released four hidden catches to remove the fake motherboard and hard disk drive, and withdrew his Beretta and spare magazine.

"Clever," Markov said. "Is it South African?"

"I bought the computer in Singapore, actually," Lane

said, checking the pistol's action and holstering it. "It's an off-the-shelf item."

"I would have thought that a man in your position would carry a somewhat heavier weapon."

Lane looked Markov in the eye. "This one has served me very well in the past, and I think it'll do just fine in the future."

"Are you here to shoot somebody or buy a submarine?"

"Money sometimes makes people do unpredictable things," Lane said. "It's better to be safe than sorry."

8

ZÜRICH

Morgan and Garza waited at a sidewalk café across the street from the Creditbanque Suisse housed in a nondescript four-story faded yellow brick building on the Banhofstrasse near the main railroad depot. Two teams of two CIA field officers each had come up from Bern and were positioned in a brown Mercedes taxi parked three doors from the bank, and at a bus stop kiosk on the corner. Hughes had sent photographs of Maslennikov and Yernin, but neither had shown up, and it was nearing five.

A dark green van came around the corner and pulled up in front of the bank.

Garza sat forward and spoke into a lapel mike. "Bill is here. The green van."

"Got them," one of the men in the taxi said.

"Keep your eyes peeled."

"Will do."

9

ZÜRICH

The driver took the van around the corner, leaving Lane and an increasingly nervous Markov to enter the bank with Markov's other bodyguard. Lane had spotted Garza and Morgan seated at a sidewalk table across the street, and he expected there were others as well.

Inside the bank a haughty young man in a dark business suit showed them immediately to an office on the third floor. Markov's bodyguard waited in the anteroom.

A man so short he was almost a midget, his head impossibly large for his body, motioned them in from behind his palatial desk. Their escort withdrew and softly closed the door.

"Gentlemen, welcome to Zürich," the banker said. He held up a hand to Lane. "I'm Günter Loos, and you are Vandermeer?"

"That's right," Lane said, shaking hands. He introduced Markov.

"Yes, we have spoken on the telephone," Loos said. "Please have a seat." He produced a pen and a piece of bank stationery, which he passed across to Lane. "If you would sign this so we can verify your identity, we can begin."

Lane wrote down an eleven-digit number and slid the pen and paper back.

Loos opened a thin file folder and compared the handwritten numbers with the sample Hughes had faxed earlier.

"Everything is in order, Mr. Vandermeer," he said, looking up. "And at this time I am happy to confirm that a transfer of gold in the amount of slightly more than sixty-five million pounds sterling has arrived. My instructions are to make a payment on your behalf, less, of course, a slight fee for the transaction." He took another slip of paper from the file and passed it to Lane. "If that is satisfactory to you, sir, please sign the transfer order."

"First I want to meet the principal," Lane said, making no move to pick up the pen or examine the document.

"As you wish," Loos said, and he picked up the telephone.

10

ZÜRICH

Maslennikov was watching and listening from an office at the end of the corridor via closed-circuit television. He could scarcely believe his own senses. "The son of a bitch," he said softly.

"What's wrong?" Kovrygin demanded. "Do you know him?"

"That man in there isn't a South African. His name is Bill Lane, whom I sent Valeri to London to kill," Maslennikov said in a whisper.

The telephone on the desk rang, and in the other office Loos looked pointedly at the camera's lens. There was no mistaking that it was him making the call.

Maslennikov snatched up the phone. "The man across

the desk from you is an imposter. He's probably armed and he's come here to kill me. Stall him while I call the police.''

"Good afternoon, mein herr," said Loos calmly. "Mr. Vandermeer has arrived, and the documents are in order, but the gentleman wished to speak with you."

Maslennikov said nothing, but he carefully watched Lane, still hardly able to believe that the man was here.

"Yes, sir, I understand," Loos said. "Please join us in my office as soon as possible. We shall wait for you."

Maslennikov broke the connection and dialed the bank's operator. "There is a man with a gun in the office of Herr Loos. Call the police immediately."

"Who is this?" the operator demanded.

"Do it before someone is hurt," Maslennikov ordered, and he hung up. "We're leaving through the back, the same way we entered."

"He's just one man, sir," said Ivanov, confused. "Let me take care of him first and then you'll never have to worry about him again."

"If we can get out of here with our lives intact, you may consider yourself lucky!" Maslennikov told him. "Move it. Now."

11

ZÜRICH

Lane looked up at the ornate candle sconces on the wall that Loos had stared at while he was on the phone. The banker's manner had changed subtly, and now it was as if he was hiding something.

"Would you gentlemen like coffee?" Loos asked.

Lane got up and went to the sconces. The pewter center base was secured to the wall by three screws with decorative heads. But the center screw was a sham. It contained a miniature camera lens.

"He's somewhere here in the bank watching us," Lane said. "Where is he?"

Loos remained calm. "I suggest that you surrender your pistol and sit down. The authorities are on their way."

Lane ran out of the office just as a door marked *Sortie* at the end of the corridor closed. He pulled out his gun and followed, tearing open the door, then hesitating at the head of the stairs. Someone was on the stairs below.

"Mikhail," he called. "I don't want you. I want Valeri!"

Markov's bodyguard came down the corridor, his gun drawn, and Lane turned back to him.

"Stay out of this."

The guard hesitated with indecision.

Markov came out of the office and took in the situation. "Do as the man says, Viktor," he called.

Several people peered out of their office doors, but when they saw the guns they ducked back out of sight.

The bodyguard said, "Your name is Bill Lane, and you're an American, not a South African."

"This operation doesn't concern you or the SVR," Lane told him. "They are Ukrainians. KGB Department Viktor."

A door slammed somewhere below, and the bodyguard finally made his decision. There was no love between Russia and Ukraine. He stepped back and holstered his gun.

Lane raced downstairs to the ground-floor door, which opened into the small lobby where they'd been met earlier by the haughty clerk. A woman stood at one of the three teller windows, and the clerk was speaking to someone on a telephone. Already there were police sirens in the distance. If Maslennikov had just come this way, his passing had created no disturbance. In any event Morgan and Garza would intercept him out front and hopefully get him out of here before the police showed up.

Which left the rear exit from the bank, if there was such a thing. But if Maslennikov had taken that route it meant that he'd shown up here first, and had spotted Morgan, Garza, and the others. It was a possibility they'd considered, and they'd wasted precious time checking out the departures of every plane, private and commercial, from London to Zürich.

Lane turned and raced the rest of the way down the stairs, someone shouting something from above.

By the time he reached the back exit in the lower corridor, an alarm was blaring and a bright red light was flashing. He made sure the Beretta's safety catch was switched off, then shoved the door open and rolled outside to a narrow courtyard. A steel gate opened to the alley.

Someone was shooting what sounded like a small-caliber pistol.

Lane reached the open gate as a big Mercedes, running backward at a high rate of speed, roared past. He got the impression of two bulky men in the front, but his eyes were locked on the lone figure in the backseat. It was Maslennikov.

The front-seat passenger was hanging out the window shooting at someone down the alley. Whoever it was continued firing the small-caliber pistol one deliberate shot after the other.

Lane stepped around the corner as the car passed, and fired directly at the driver, his shots hitting the windshield and starring the glass in small pockmarks, but not penetrating.

He raced after the car, switching aim to its tires, hoping that whichever of Garza's men was firing from behind would have enough sense not to shoot him in the back.

The electric gate at the end of the alley opened and the Mercedes shot out into the side street, the driver slammed it into forward, and it raced off, big chunks of rubber flaying from the tire Lane hit.

Traffic had come to a standstill, and pedestrians were ducking into doorways or hunching down behind parked cars when Lane reached the end of the alley, and he spotted Morgan and Garza just coming around the corner.

The Mercedes was gone, and the sirens, which seemed to be coming from all directions, were right on top of them.

Lane ran over to them, holstering his gun. "Call for the car. They're in a black Mercedes. I managed to shoot one of its tires out."

"Was it Maslennikov?" Morgan asked, pulling Lane aside.

Garza got on the radio and called the team in the Mercedes taxi.

"He and two others," Lane said. "They were expecting trouble."

"We have to get off the street now," Morgan said.

"I'm going back in the bank. Get your man out of the alley and take off. Soon as you're clear, call Tom Hughes. He's going to have to get me out of this mess."

Morgan gave him a funny look. "We don't have anybody back there."

Their taxi came around the corner.

"Just get the hell out of here then. I'll see who it is. But unless I miss my guess Maslennikov will try to reach the airport. You have to get there first."

"Right. Watch yourself," Morgan said.

He and Garza started to get in the cab, when police cars came around the corners from both ends of the street, blocking off any escape route. Dozens of police officers leaped out and took up position, their weapons aimed at Lane and the others.

"I hope somebody has a plan B," Lane said, slowly raising his hands.

"We could try telling them the truth," Frances said, emerging from the alley with her hands up.

"I should have known," said Lane, amazed.

"I wasn't going to let you gentlemen have all the fun," she said. "But I wasn't counting on them driving an armored limo."

Morgan glared at her.

"Raise your hands and remain where you are," an amplified voice bellowed down the street.

"God, I love the Swiss efficiency," Garza said. "What the hell do they think we're doing?"

12

OXFORD

The afternoon was very dark. Because of the time of year, and the distance outside of Oxford, there was no one to see the cabin cruiser pull alongside the dock below Sir Leonard's house long enough for one person to jump off, and then head slowly downriver.

Yernin made his way from the gazebo above the faded boathouse, through the woods along the path, and across the croquet lawn to the rear of the house, where he let himself in through the dining-room French doors.

He'd been here twice before, the first time when he'd followed Commander Shipley up from London, and the second six weeks ago on a research trip, after which he'd formulated his simple plan.

He knew the layout of the house. It was registered with the National Trust as a historical site, and he'd studied the architectural plans on file. He knew that Sir Leonard and his man Albert were the only two people usually in residence. All other services, including gardening, were contracted.

Moving quietly to the stair hall, he stopped to listen. A television was playing somewhere beyond the kitchen. It was Albert relaxing in his quarters until Sir Leonard returned.

Yernin crossed the stair hall to Sir Leonard's game room, where he took down a Holland & Holland side-by-side 10-gauge shotgun from its rack beside the fireplace, found a box of magnum slugs in one of the drawers below, and loaded the custom-made gun. His touch was sure even though he wore gloves.

Back in the stair hall, he turned left down the corridor to the rear of the house, where he stopped at Albert's door. The television was still on, the accents Cockney, and at one point Albert laughed at something.

Yernin opened the door and, as Albert, who was seated in an easy chair in front of the television set, his feet on a hassock, looked up, fired one shot, catching the butler in the torso, the powerful slug destroying his chest and killing him instantly.

OXFORD

Yernin watched for forty-five minutes from an upstairs window until Sir Leonard's dark gray Range Rover, the same model as his niece drove, came down the gravel driveway. He waited until he could be absolutely sure that Sir Leonard was alone before he went back downstairs to Albert's room. On the way down he used his cellular phone to call the boat.

"Ten minutes," he said.

"Right."

Yernin turned up the television set in Albert's sitting room, then positioned himself with the shotgun behind the open door.

Even over the sounds of the blaring television he thought he could hear the mudroom door from outside slam.

A minute or so later Sir Leonard was in the corridor, his voice low-pitched and rough. "Right then, are you deaf or what, man?" he shouted over the television.

Yernin cocked the sterling-silver engraved hammer on the loaded barrel.

"Bloody hell," Sir Leonard swore from the doorway.

Yernin stepped from behind the door, and before Sir Leonard, who was a man in his late sixties with white hair and muttonchops, could react, he jammed the barrel of the shotgun under the old man's chin and pulled the trigger.

The back of Sir Leonard's head exploded, and he went down like a felled ox.

Working with a casual precision, Yernin placed the shotgun in Sir Leonard's hands, the thumb of his right hand on the trigger as if he'd committed suicide.

Taking care to step in none of the blood, Yernin went to the back door, where he set the house alarm system, then opened the door, tripping it, and let himself out.

The boat was pulling up to the dock when he reached the river. He stepped aboard and they pulled away.

14

OXFORD

Oxford police sergeant Tony Mallory came slowly down the long driveway and parked his blue and white behind the Range Rover at the rear of the house. For a few moments he simply sat and stared at the car, but then he got on the radio.

"Unit two-three. I'm at Sir Leonard's, but so far everything looks normal."

"Roger that."

"I'll check inside, and see what they're up to."

Sergeant Mallory put on his hat and walked around to the front of the Range Rover. The hood was still slightly warm to the touch. It had been driven less than an hour ago, which meant that Sir Leonard was home.

When the alarm had come in someone had tried to call the house, but there'd been no answer, which was odd. According to the alarm service, if Sir Leonard and his man were both away, and the alarm system was set, they switched on the answering machine. But not this time.

Mallory peered in the mudroom window, but there was nothing out of the ordinary inside, and he tried the door, which was unlocked.

As soon as he stepped inside he could hear what sounded like a radio or television turned very loud in another room.

There were no signs of forced entry, but the alarm panel just inside the door was blinking. Something wasn't kosher here. The hairs on the back of his neck were prickling.

He took out his service revolver, which they'd been ordered to start carrying a couple of years ago, and headed through the kitchen toward the source of the noise. He was going to be the big fool if he bumped into Sir Leonard, who would want to know what the coppers were doing, guns drawn, invading his house.

Even before he came around the corner Mallory could smell burnt gunpowder, and he wasn't completely surprised to see Sir Leonard's body sprawled on the rear-hall floor, his blood splattered on the ceiling and on the wall behind him, but his stomach did a slow roll.

Albert's body was slumped in a bloody heap beside an overturned chair.

It was pretty clear what had happened here. Mallory holstered his gun, turned the TV set down, and keyed his remote shoulder microphone.

"This is two-three, I'm going to need the BCI van and the coroner. Looks like a murder-suicide here."

"Roger," the dispatcher said, and Mallory could hear a note of resignation in her voice. "Turn off the alarm system, would you?"

"Will do."

15

ZÜRICH

They'd been separated at police headquarters downtown and after Lane's initial interrogation three hours ago he'd been left locked in a small windowless room furnished with nothing more than a steel table and two chairs. It was with some anticipation that he looked up when the door opened.

Police captain Rainer Schmidt, a heavyset man with thick white hair and jowls, tossed a file folder on the table and sat down across from Lane.

"Well sir, your story checks out so far as the National Security Agency is willing to cooperate with us," the Swiss cop said.

"Then you know that we're no threat to Swiss security," Lane told him. "Have you found the Mercedes limo?"

"Yes. It belongs to the bank. And the young man driving it still can't understand why anyone would shoot him for merely stealing a car."

"Let me guess. Herr Loos is confused by my actions. One minute I was discussing a business transaction in his office, and the next I was racing downstairs to catch a car thief."

"Something like that," said Schmidt, not amused. "But of course you and I know that you, the CIA, and the British Secret Intelligence Service were here, illegally, trying to find the identity of some Russian group that is apparently stealing money from some other Russian group or groups.''

"That's essentially correct," Lane said.

Schmidt looked at Lane over the tops of his glasses. "Essentially correct," he said dryly. "All of you entered Switzerland on one type of false passport or another, you brought illegal weapons with you, and you discharged those weapons down a street crowded with civilian traffic and pedestrians. It's a miracle someone wasn't severely injured by your reckless actions, Mr. Lane. For those offenses alone it is extremely likely that you will spend a great deal of time in one of our prisons."

"Believe me, I was aware of the civilian traffic, and I stopped shooting as soon as the limo left the alley," Lane said. "The point is that arresting us and placing us on public trial would create an international incident that nobody wants. As I see it, the only way out of the dilemma you've gotten yourself into is to allow us to leave Switzerland the same way we came in. Quietly and without fuss."

"Extraordinary," the cop said. "Is there anything else that you would like to say to me?"

"It's late. I haven't eaten since noon, and I'm starved."

"I was going to ask you to sign a statement, to make it easier on all of us. But I don't think that's possible now." Schmidt got the file folder and stood up. "I think perhaps that we will continue our conversation tomorrow."

"Did you at least check the airport to see where the man we came here to meet took off for?"

"There was no such person at the bank, in the limousine, or at the airport," the cop said. "But we'll get into that tomorrow as well."

16

ZÜRICH

Two hours later a uniformed cop came for Lane, but this time he wasn't handcuffed. They took the elevator up to the booking sergeant's counter on the ground floor. Because of the lateness of the hour the building was quiet.

The sergeant pushed a form and a pen across to Lane. "Please sign this, and your personal belongings will be returned to you, Herr Vandermeer."

The form was nothing more than an inventory of the items the police had taken from him when he was arrested. "I had a Beretta and holster. It's not listed."

"No, sir. It will be returned to you as sealed diplomatic material at the airport."

Lane signed the form and the sergeant passed a manila envelope across.

"This way, sir," the uniformed cop said, and he took Lane down the corridor and outside to a plain gray, windowless van waiting at the door.

Garza sat up front with the driver, while Morgan and Frances were in back with the four CIA field officers from Bern.

"They're deporting us," Morgan explained in an odd voice. "Someone must have pulled some strings."

Frances looked stricken with grief. "Oh, William," she said softly.

He slid in beside her. "What's wrong, Frannie?"

"It's Uncle Leonard. He's committed suicide," she

said in a small voice. "I have to go up there."

"I'll come with you," Lane said, holding her. "It'll be okay."

"No, it won't," she said. "Now there's no one left."

PART SIX

1

It was early morning but still dark by the time they got back to Heathrow and cleared customs, where the sealed packages were returned to them. The airport was practically deserted. The Swiss had flown them over as the only passengers aboard a special charter flight.

"Are you absolutely sure it was Maslennikov in the limo?" Morgan asked, on the way up to the terminal.

"I got a good look. It was him all right," Lane said, tight-lipped. Frances hadn't said a word on the flight over, and he was worried about her.

"Was Valeri Yernin with him?"

"No," Lane said. "But I don't think Maslennikov figured on running into any trouble. It was his bank, his setup all the way."

"He must have been worried about something," Garza put in. "He got there before us and he probably had a good laugh when he saw us pulling up out front."

"What a waste of time," Morgan said disparagingly. "I can just guess what Sir Hubert is going to say when the PM is told about this. It'll be a bloody wonder if any of us keep our jobs."

"You're going to have to convince the Royal Navy to hunt for two-eighty-three," Lane said.

"If they're still in British waters, and nobody's convinced me that they were here in the first place, I might be able to get it done. But I've changed my mind. It's a big ocean, and we're not going to spend the money looking for a boat that nobody's seen or even knows about, except you.''

"Then he's already won," Lane said.

Morgan stopped. "Won what?" he demanded. "Providing he leaves England, which you say is imminent, then well and good. Because frankly we don't give a good bloody damn if the Russians are stealing from each other. Our only involvement was with the SVR *rezident* here. Whatever he does on British soil is of great interest to us. But any advantage we might have had is gone because of your little operation in Zürich." He turned on Frances. "And your incredible bungling of a situation that could have gotten you killed."

Lane stopped himself from lashing out at the bastard, and Frances just looked miserably at her boss and shook her head.

Morgan immediately softened. "I'm sorry about Sir Leonard. The news is simply rotten. But it doesn't alter the fact that the ceiling is going to fall down because of what happened in Zürich. Heads are going to roll, and yours, I'm afraid, will be among the first to go."

"I don't care."

"Yes, you do. And I'll do everything possible to save your career, because as of now it's all you really have."

Frances flared finally. "You insensitive bastard!"

"I didn't mean it the way it sounded," Morgan told her, and he glanced nervously at Lane. "All I'm saying is what happened in Oxford is one thing, and the situation here is something else. Something that won't simply disappear."

"You can have my job," Frances said. "I quit."

"It's not going to be that easy. You'll have to answer some questions the Operational Oversight Committee is going to ask. We all will."

"When I get back from Oxford."

"I could stop you," Morgan warned.

"From doing what? Attending to my uncle's funeral?"

Garza and his people were clearly embarrassed by the exchange. "Look, we're going back to the embassy now," Garza said. "Langley is going to have a few questions of its own that we've got to have answers for."

"We'll need to get together sometime this afternoon, or tomorrow at the latest, for a joint debriefing," Morgan told him.

"I'll be there," Garza said. He turned to Frances. "Sorry about your uncle. I lost my brother the same way so I know what I'm talking about when I tell you not to judge him too harshly."

"Thanks," Frances said.

"How about you, Mr. Lane? Can we give you a lift into town?"

"No. I'm driving up to Oxford with Commander Shipley."

"No you're not," Morgan said. "You're coming with me, either by choice or under arrest. It makes no difference to me."

"I don't think that'd be such a good idea, Brad," Garza warned.

"Bugger off," Morgan shot back. "What's it going to be, Lane?"

"How do you propose arresting me?" Lane asked reasonably.

Morgan was furious. "If need be I'll turn it over to Scotland Yard."

"Then you'd have to answer some really tough questions. Like why you worked with me to begin with. And what were you doing in Switzerland with a bunch of CIA thugs, yourself traveling on a false diplomatic passport, and toting a gun around Switzerland? Are you ready for that?"

"Damn you."

"Yeah," Lane said cheerfully. "In the meantime sell it to the navy. Now that Maslennikov knows I'm around, he'll send Yernin after me and Frances, I guarantee it."

"Bastard."

"You've already said something to that effect," Lane said. "But if we're going to work together, you might try to be a bit more civil."

"I'll stop you," Morgan fumed.

"Oh, fuck off, Brad," Frances said flatly. "Just fuck off." She turned to Lane. "We'll take my car, it's in the ramp. I want to get this over with as soon as possible."

2

OXFORD

Frances asked Lane to drive, and by sunrise they had made it off the M25, which rings London, and onto the M40, which runs directly up to Oxford. Traffic was heavy, but most of it was funneling into the city, not out.

Lane had the radio tuned to an all-news station, but Frances shut it off. "I can't handle the noise right now," she said. They were her first words since leaving the airport, and Lane had not tried to draw her out. When she needed him, he figured she would ask; as she was now.

"It wasn't your fault, you know," he said.

She nodded. "I know that intellectually. But I can't stop thinking that he might have tried to reach me and I wasn't there for him." She looked at Lane in anguish. "Now it's too late."

"How long was he depressed?" Lane asked.

"He wasn't."

"Happy men don't destroy themselves."

"That's what's getting to me," Frances said. "There was no reason for him to do it."

"Something might have happened to him that he didn't want to trouble you with."

"Like what?"

"Maybe he was sick."

"Cancer?"

Lane nodded, and Frances slumped down in her seat, her head hanging. "I never thought about that. It would have been something he'd keep from me."

On the outskirts of Oxford, Frances directed him to the west on the ring road. Her uncle's house was on the river, south of the city toward Abingdon.

"When I was a little girl my mum and I used to spend summers up here," Frances said wistfully. "My dad would come up from London on weekends, and we'd go for boat rides, and play croquet and have lemonade in the gazebo."

"We'll create our own summers, Frannie."

She looked at him. "Will we?"

"We can't go backward."

Her expression softened. "It's a deal."

There was a police car by the gate at the head of the long driveway and two others parked down at the house. A uniformed cop got out of his cruiser and motioned for Lane to stop.

Lane pulled up and powered his window down, and Frances passed her ID across. "I'm Sir Leonard's niece. Can we go down to the house?"

The cop checked her ID and Lane's and handed them back. "Yes, ma'am. Sorry about your uncle and his man."

Lane drove down to the house, where he parked behind Sir Leonard's Range Rover. The morning was still deeply overcast and a chill wind came up from the river as they went inside through the mudroom.

The police were getting set to leave. Two of them, their evidence kits packed up, came through the kitchen, followed by a bulky plainclothes detective, a frown on his round face.

"Ah, Ms. Shipley," he said, shaking her hand. "Detective Brandwaite."

"I'm Bill Lane, a friend of the family," Lane told the cop. They shook hands.

"This is a bad business," Brandwaite said. "Nobody expected it."

"What exactly happened?" Frances asked.

Brandwaite hesitated a moment, then shook his head. "Sir Leonard came home sometime around four yesterday afternoon, got a shotgun from his study, shot and killed his man Albert, and then turned the shotgun on himself."

Frances turned white and she rocked back against Lane. "I don't believe it."

"Neither do we," the cop said heavily. He shook his head. "There'll be a coroner's inquest tomorrow afternoon. Could you be there?"

Frances nodded.

"How were the bodies discovered?" Lane asked.

"One of our people came out at the request of the security-alarm people. Evidently Sir Leonard forgot to reset the system when he returned—that's how the probable time of death was fixed. When the company tried to telephone Sir Leonard to switch off, there was no answer, so they called us."

Frances looked toward the hall. "Has everything been cleaned up?"

"For the most part," Brandwaite said gently. "But you'll have to call in a service. The rug will have to be replaced. And there'll be some painting needed."

"Then call the alarm people for me, please," Frances

said. "Tell them that I'll be here for the time being."

The detective glanced at Lane, but then nodded. "I'll do it. I'm sorry. Sir Leonard was a good man. If he was murdered we'll find the killer." He hunched up his coat collar and left.

"You don't have to stay here, Frannie," Lane said. "We can get a hotel in town."

"Just for a day or two, William," she said resolutely. "And then?"

She looked up into his eyes. "I'm going to sell the place and never come back. Never."

3

OXFORD

Looking through binoculars supplied with the boat, Yernin watched the two police cruisers go up the driveway, stop a few moments beside the cruiser by the highway, and then the three of them head back toward town. He swung the binoculars back down toward the house, and watched the mudroom door for several minutes. He'd accepted the possibility that Lane and Frances would not want to stay at the house, and he'd made his contingency plans in that case. But lifting his eyes from the binoculars a couple of minutes later he saw a curl of smoke lifting from the central chimney. They had laid a fire in the living-room fireplace, which meant they were planning on staying awhile. He'd never really felt any pleasure during a kill, but this time he thought he would.

4

OXFORD

Frances looked up from her reading when Lane came into Sir Leonard's study with a bottle of chilled Chardonnay and a couple of glasses. "I didn't realize it was this late," she said.

"You've been at it all day. Time for a break. Maybe we can go into town for dinner."

Frances shook her head. "I don't feel like going anywhere tonight, William. You don't mind do you?"

"Of course not." Lane poured them each a glass of wine.

She reached for his hand, gave it a squeeze, then sat back and closed her eyes for a few moments. "He didn't have any money left as far as I can tell."

"Maybe that's what made him despondent."

"There were no unpaid bills or anything like that," she said. "They weren't eating out of dog food tins. But I thought he was rich, with this house and everything. But it was all gone."

"Where?"

Frances flipped through one of Sir Leonard's files she'd been reading. "Maintenance of the property. It's on the historic register, and he kept up with the place. There were charities, his clubs here and down in London, and he'd put away four hundred thousand pounds over the years for Albert."

"He wasn't absentminded?"

"Not at all," Frances replied certainly. "He did his own books, managed this place, and even managed his investments all these years so that he could keep the place going for so long." She looked up from the file. "He wasn't on the verge of bankruptcy. There was enough money for him to keep going for as long as he wanted. But there was nothing extra." She looked away again and shook her head sadly. "It makes no sense, William. Why would he kill himself? And why in God's name would he kill Albert?"

Lane had spent a part of the day searching the house. Nothing was out of place, except for the disturbance in Albert's quarters and in the corridor outside his door where Sir Leonard's body had fallen.

"Nothing wrong with his health?"

"Not according to his doctor. My uncle was an old man, but his heart was sound and he was as strong as an ox." She smiled despite herself. "His only serious problem was that he cheated at bridge."

"So do I," Lane said absently. He put his glass of wine aside and went back through the kitchen to the mudroom, where he studied the alarm-system panel.

Frances saw the sudden look of interest on his face and she followed him. "What is it, William?"

"Your uncle was anything but absentminded. He wasn't disorganized or despondent, or even pre-Alzheimer's. He was so organized, in fact, that in case he might forget the alarm-system code, he wrote it on the wall."

The five-digit code had been penciled on the wall next to the panel's keypad.

"He *did* shut off the alarm when he came in," Frances said.

"Maybe. Call the police and see if they've come up with anything."

Frances went to the kitchen phone as Lane flipped off

the light and peered out the mudroom door window into the pitch-black night.

"The line is dead," Frances called softly to him.

"Where's your cell phone?"

"In the car."

5

OXFORD

Dondorev darted through the shadows across the driveway and joined Yernin at the dark, west side of the house. "They're not going anywhere in either car. I cut all the plug wires and destroyed the phone."

"Were the doors unlocked?" Yernin asked.

"*Da*. And the keys were in the woman's car."

Yegorov came around from the back, his AK-47 in hand. He was panting. "Okay, I think that they know something's going on out here. The back-hall light went out and I think Lane is watching in the darkness from the door."

"Did he see you?"

Yegorov shook his head. "I don't think so. Not where I was standing."

"Unless they tried to call out, there's no reason for them to suspect anything," Dondorev told him.

"Don't underestimate Bill Lane. It'll get you killed," Yernin warned them both. "We'll stick to our original plan, but watch yourself." He screwed the silencer on the barrel of his gun. "In five minutes Nikolai will start his attack at the front of the house."

"That should give me enough time to get into place in back," Yegorov said.

"If they try to get to the cars wait until you have a perfect shot because they're not going to get very far," Yernin said. "First Lane, the woman second. But don't underestimate her either. She's as highly trained as you are."

"If they put up a fight in front, I'll come in from the rear," Yegorov said.

Yernin checked his watch. "It's five-thirty-one now. We start at five-thirty-six." He gave both men a hard stare. "I don't like failure of any kind, for any reason."

They nodded.

"Go."

6

OXFORD

Lane met Frances in the dark stair hall after they finished locking up, and they went upstairs. "I'll take the front," Frances said.

They had their pistols, but the police had taken away all of Sir Leonard's firearms, which he'd been allowed to keep only under special permit.

"He might have brought some help, so watch yourself," Lane warned.

She nodded and went into a front bedroom which looked down on the driveway, and up the slope of the hill to the highway a quarter mile away. Standing to one side she carefully parted the curtains so that she could look out. She was in time to see a dark figure move between the privet hedges that lined the walkway.

She called across the upstairs corridor, "There's someone down there now."

Lane came to the doorway of the back bedroom across the stairs from her. "How many?"

"Just one. He's behind the hedges."

"Weapons?"

"I couldn't see."

"They're going to hit us from the front and try to drive us to the cars in back," Lane said.

"We can pick them off from here."

"Just keep out of sight, because that's one of the moves they want us to make."

"And let them come through the front door?" Frances asked.

"That's right," Lane said. He went to the back window and looked outside, but could see no movement. He came back to the head of the stairs and lay down on the floor so that he had a good sight line to the door. He screwed the silencer on his gun.

"He's up," Frances called excitedly. "Looks like a Kalashnikov. I can see the silencer."

More than a dozen rounds slammed into the front door, wood splinters flying everywhere, the lock shattering finally, and the door swung open on its hinges.

Lane switched the Beretta's safety catch off, and for several long seconds nothing happened. But then a figure appeared at the open doorway, swung a silenced AK-47 left to right, and rolled inside the stair hall. He was a large man who moved quickly and with competence, but he was not Yernin.

Lane fired just as the intruder started to swing his rifle toward the stairs, catching the man in the chest and staggering him backward. Then he fired a second silenced shot, hitting the man in the head, knocking him down.

"Is there anyone else out front?" Lane called softly to Frances.

"No. Did you get him?"

"He's down." Lane got up and took the first few stairs down so that he could see the back corridor, toward the kitchen.

Frances came to the bedroom door. "Be careful, William, the front door could have been a diversion. He might be inside the house already."

"I know," he said. "Stay here."

He crept the rest of the way down the stairs watching both the open front door and the back corridor. When he glanced up Frances was at the head of the stairs, and he waved her back, then darted into the drawing room.

A service corridor ran back to the kitchen, which was across from the mudroom door. Lane held up just inside the dish pantry, from where he could see the doorway to the mudroom. If the door had been shot open, there would be glass on the floor. But in the dim light filtering from the main corridor, he could see that the floor was unlittered.

Keeping low he dashed through the kitchen, held up at the doorway, and then slipped into the mudroom, keeping flat against the wall. From his position he could see the driveway out the window in the door. They might expect him and Frances to try for the cars after the attack in the front. So both had probably been sabotaged, and someone would be waiting out there.

But it wouldn't be Yernin. It wasn't the man's style. Nor would he expect that they would fall for such a ploy.

Yernin was already in the house, just as Frances had suspected! And Lane had a sinking feeling that he'd just done exactly what the man had wanted him to do.

7

OXFORD

Upstairs, Frances had come to the same conclusion. But since she and Lane had watched the front and back approaches to the house it meant that Yernin might have come in from the east or west sides. She rushed back to the head of the stairs, cocking her pistol.

She shouted, "William, he's already inside!"

"Stay where you are," Lane answered from somewhere downstairs at the rear of the house.

Frances was about to start down the stairs, when something cool and hard touched the nape of her neck, and her heart sank.

"If you cry out, I'll put a bullet in your brain," Yernin warned in a reasonable tone of voice.

Frances started to raise her gun hand, but Yernin jammed the barrel of his pistol harder into the base of her skull, and she stopped.

"You won't save him that way."

"You'll kill me in any event," Frances answered.

"That's true. But you can buy some time. Who knows what might happen?"

She considered it for a moment. "Very well," she said.

"Slowly raise your gun over your head."

Frances did as she was told, and Yernin took it from her.

"What now?"

"We wait for Mr. Lane to figure out how I got into

the house, and therefore come to the understanding that I am upstairs, at which point he'll appear on the steps below us, and I'll shoot him.''

"Did you kill my uncle and his man?"

"Yes."

"And now you have a gun on a woman. You're a filthy coward, nothing more."

"Monster, would be a more accurate description," Yernin said indifferently.

"You'll be hunted down like a mad dog."

"Probably."

"Like your man downstairs there in the front hall."

"But that was to be expected," Yernin said.

"Why don't you shoot me now?"

"Because I need you for the moment."

"William, he has me!" Frances suddenly shouted at the top of her lungs.

8

OXFORD

Lane reached the head of the service stairs that led up from the kitchen at the same moment Frances cried out her warning. Whatever advantage he had was gone.

"Yernin, I'm behind you," he shouted, poking his head around the corner.

Yernin spun around and fired a snap shot at Lane, who fell back into the stair hall.

"You missed," Lane called.

"I'll kill the woman." Yernin's voice was deadly calm.

"Then you'll die. It's as simple as that, because you can't fire in two directions at the same time."

The upstairs corridor was deathly still for several seconds. Lane had seen enough to know that Yernin was using Frances as a shield. For the moment he was in complete control of the situation. Or at least thought he was.

"You won't force me to kill her, Lane. She means too much to you. She's too important, too valuable. She's your Achilles' heel."

"Now she's your Achilles' heel. You can't shoot her, and you know it."

"Nor can I let her go. Interesting, wouldn't you say?"

"There is an alternative," Frances called to Lane. "You stay here and I'll go with him. He'll get away clean."

"Once you were outside with him, he'd kill you," Lane said. "I won't allow that to happen. Besides, I don't think he wants to do that."

"You're right," Yernin said. "We'll settle this one way or another, here and now."

"I'll do whatever it takes to save her."

"I'm listening," Yernin said.

"Let me work it out."

9

OXFORD

Waiting at the foot of the service stairs, Yegorov had heard enough of Lane's side of the conversation to know what was happening in the corridor above. Convinced that the attention inside the house had shifted to the front, he'd shot out the mudroom door lock with his silenced Makarov and entered just as the woman had shouted her warning.

Yernin was a clever bastard all right, but this time he'd backed himself into a corner. Yegorov grinned in anticipation. With Lane dead, shot and killed from behind, they all could get on with their new lives. He, for one, was ready to settle down in the good life Captain Maslennikov had promised. And just maybe with nothing for him to do, Yernin would disappear one night into a quiet desert grave.

It was a pleasant thought, Yegorov told himself as he started quietly up the stairs.

10

OXFORD

"Yernin, are you listening?" Lane called.

"We're still here."

"I have a question for you. Obviously you know just as much about me as I know about you. You must have studied my background, and you have to be a patient man to have waited all this time to get to me."

"What's your question?"

"The question is, do you trust me to keep my word?"

"What are you talking about?"

"If you let Frances go, I give you my word that I won't make a move until she has had a chance to get clear of the house. At that point it'll be just you and me. We'll toss our guns down, and settle this hand-to-hand. It's what you wanted all along, isn't it?"

"You must think that I'm stupid."

"As a matter of fact I do, but that's beside the point," Lane said brightly. "You're not leaving here alive without getting past me. If you shoot Frances I'll kill you immediately, guaranteed. If you let her go, you've got a chance of taking me, if you're man enough to handle it."

"Throw your gun down now, and I'll throw mine down," Yernin said.

"As soon as you let Frances go."

"William, he's got—," Frances shouted, but she was cut off.

Lane peered around the corner. Yernin had his hand clamped across her mouth, her struggles against him completely ineffectual. With his other hand he held a large pistol to her head below her right ear.

Yernin spotted Lane. "All right," he said.

------------------ **11** ------------------

OXFORD

A stair tread creaked softly, and Lane ducked back, switching aim down the stairs. It was the man he thought he'd spotted earlier. He had managed to come this far undetected, and it was only blind luck that he'd made a noise at the wrong moment.

"We'll do this on the count of three," Lane called out. He flattened himself against the wall and quietly moved down the four steps to where the narrow stairway switched left. He could hear the brush of fabric against fabric barely a foot away.

"I'm waiting," Yernin said.

Lane switched his gun to his left hand, and keeping his left shoulder to the wall, suddenly rolled around the corner.

A slightly built man, wearing a dark windbreaker, one hand trailing on the wall, the other holding a silenced Makarov pistol, reared back.

"Stop now or you're a dead man," Lane whispered urgently in Russian.

Lane could see the indecision in the man's eyes. Shoot or not shoot. His pistol was pointed a few inches to the right of Lane's head.

"Lane!" Yernin shouted.

The Ukrainian's eyes flitted to the head of the stairs, narrowed, and he started to bring his gun across as his finger tightened on the trigger.

Lane squeezed off one shot at point-blank range into the man's forehead, killing him instantly, his gun discharging harmlessly into the ceiling, and his body driven back down the stairs. Lane hurried noiselessly down after him.

12

OXFORD

Yernin's hand was still clamped across Frances's mouth, the gun still pressed against her head when Lane stepped out of the stairway.

"It's just us now," he said.

Frannie's eyes were wild—she was trying to tell him something.

Yernin was suspicious, but calm. He slowly moved the gun away from Frances's head, uncocked the hammer, switched on the safety catch, and tossed it nonchalantly onto the carpet runner. "I could break her neck before you could fire."

"I know," Lane said. He lowered his gun, uncocked the hammer, and switched on the safety catch. "I'll drop my gun as you release Frances and step away from her."

Yernin hesitated a moment, then released Frances and stepped back as Lane dropped his pistol.

"He's got my gun!" Frances cried.

She turned back toward Yernin as the killer reached for the second gun, intending to slow him down or at least throw off his aim. But he easily batted her away with a powerful swipe of his arm, and dragged out her Bernardelli automatic, as he stepped to the side.

Lane snatched the silenced Makarov he'd taken from the man he'd killed in the stairway, and got off a snap shot as he fell back through the doorway onto the landing, his aim distracted when he realized that Frances was pitching over the edge of the stairs, her arms flailing wildly in the air. She cried out as she tumbled down the stairs.

Yernin fired four times, the bullets smacking into the doorframe inches from where Lane stood. Lane reached around the corner and pulled off three shots down the corridor, and Yernin immediately fired back; this time the heavier slugs from his Heckler & Koch plowed through the wall, one of them hitting Lane in his right arm just below the elbow, causing him to drop the pistol out in the corridor.

"Did you have three guns, Mr. Lane?" Yernin called out playfully. "I don't think so."

"Why don't you come and find out," Lane called back, his arm numb and useless.

"With pleasure—"

"You bastard!" Frances screeched, and the distinctive

dull popping sounds of a silenced AK-47 on rapid fire came from the foot of the stairs.

Lane dove out into the corridor, snatched the Makarov with his left hand, and brought the pistol to bear as he rolled once, but the corridor was empty.

"Frannie, are you okay?" he shouted.

"I'm okay," she called back. "Did I get him?"

"No," Lane shouted. He jumped up and cautiously hurried down the corridor to the open door into the west bedroom, where he held up a moment.

There was no sound, but he could smell the outside air, and feel the coolness.

The French doors leading to the balcony were open, the curtains waffling on a light breeze. He reached them in time to see a dark figure disappear into the trees and toward the river.

"Yernin!" Lane shouted. "I know about the submarine. I'm coming for you!"

"William?" Frances said from the doorway.

In the distance they heard a boat motor start up and then fade away up the river.

"Are we going after him?"

Lane shook his head. "I can't swim that fast, and we don't have a working phone."

"Mine's in the car."

"If it's still there it won't be in working order," Lane said. "Now, are you as good at nursing as you are at tumbling?"

13

It was a little before six and very cold when they went out to check on the cars. Frances had bandaged Lane's arm and fashioned a sling for it, so he had to awkwardly lift the hood of her car with his left hand.

"The plug wires have all been cut," he said. "What about the phone?"

Frances slid out of her car and held up the shattered remnants of her cellular phone, which she'd left in the center console. "You were right. They didn't miss a trick."

Lane went to her uncle's car and opened its hood. All its plug wires had been cut as well.

"I'll walk up to the road and see if I can flag down a passing car," Frances told him. "We need to get you to the hospital."

"We can fix the house phones quicker. Get a small paring knife from the kitchen, and see if you can find a roll of tape."

Lane found where the phone line entered the house in back. The wire had been neatly severed a couple of feet off the ground. Frances joined him a minute later, and he directed her to pare back the insulation from the five color-coded wires on both sides of the break, then twist the bare ends together, and tape them.

The alarm system had kicked off, and Lane reset it as Frances called the Oxford police, and then Brad Morgan up in London.

"Do you want to call Garza?" she asked.

"I'll talk to him later. What did Brad have to say?"

"Plenty." Frances sounded weary. "But he's agreed to put out an all points for Yernin, and then chopper down here to take charge."

"I feel better already."

"He wants to know why we waited so long to call the police. There aren't that many boats on the water this time of year, and at this time of night."

"The boat will be found a couple of miles upriver. Even if your phone had been working and we'd called immediately, he would have gotten away."

"Why didn't he come back to finish us?"

"Because the advantage was no longer his."

"The question is, where did he go?"

Lane looked at Frances. "Not very far, Frannie."

She shivered. "He's not going to quit."

"No."

She looked up resolutely. "At least we know that the threat is real. No more speculation. No more waiting for the shoe to drop."

Lane took her awkwardly in his arm and held her. "There's at least that."

"You're amazing, William," she said after a few moments. "I'll never leave you as long as you want me."

"God help you, it's not going to be a quiet life," Lane said, and he glanced toward the mudroom door as the first of the sirens came from the distance.

14

**NATIONAL SECURITY AGENCY
FORT MEADE, MARYLAND**

It was four in the morning in Washington but Tom Hughes was still at the office, and Lane got the impression his old friend was expecting the call.

"If you keep spending so much time at work, Moira is going to start to wonder if you're keeping a mistress on the side."

"I am," Hughes said. "But it's not another woman, it's picking up after you."

"Are the Swiss still fuming?"

"You disturbed their sense of order, William. Shame on you. But they'll get over it."

"He was here," Lane said, lowering his voice. Morgan was upstairs with Frances and the police, and there were cops everywhere.

"Do you mean Yernin?"

"Yeah, and this time it was close."

"Are you and Frances unharmed?"

"I got a scratch, but Frannie's just fine," Lane said, and he told Hughes everything that had happened.

"The dirty bastard," Hughes said. "He killed the uncle just to lure her up there, knowing that you'd come along. And from the sound of it his plan nearly worked."

"He's not going to give up."

"Indeed not, William," Hughes said. "What about the two shooters he brought with him?"

"From the way they handled themselves, I'd say they

were not submariners. Probably former KGB.''

"But this was probably set up *before* Maslennikov got a look at you in Switzerland.''

"That's right.''

Hughes hesitated a moment. "They're close,'' he said. "But Maslennikov is no fool. He's going to pull out now for sure. Twice he's failed to stop you. I don't think he's going to want to remain for a third try, even though Yernin will demand it. Which makes for some interesting possibilities. Dissension among the troops, and all that.''

"That's what I thought,'' Lane said. "I'm hoping it will slow them down enough for the British to find two-eighty-three.''

"Do you think it's still in the Channel?''

"I do, and I think I know how to find it,'' Lane said. "But I'm going to need your help.''

"What can I do, William?'' Hughes asked.

Lane told him.

PART SEVEN

1

Valeri Yernin stepped off the morning ferry from Poole and walked across the quay with the handful of other departing passengers, his rage barely suppressed. The crossing had been long and rough, serving only to deepen his intense frustration.

Since the Channel Islands were a part of Great Britain, he'd crossed no borders, and therefore had not been required to pass through customs. Had someone tried to challenge him he would have killed that person without batting an eye, though outwardly he appeared calm, even pleasant.

Born in a small town near Kiev, he'd come to the attention of the KGB when he'd killed his army drill instructor in hand-to-hand combat training so quickly and easily that not one of the fifty soldiers watching had been able to tell investigators exactly what had happened. He'd refined his skills in the late seventies and early eighties, and his first assignments had taken him to the Middle East, where he'd engineered dozens of kidnappings, bus bombings, airplane hijackings, and assassinations. He carried out any assignment he was given, no matter how bloody, coldly, dispassionately, and efficiently. He was psychopathic. Killing a human being—man, woman, or child—was of no more consequence to him than swatting a fly.

After the breakup of the Soviet Union, he'd returned to his roots and gone to work for the Ukrainian KGB, where he became known as the "surgeon," because of his clinical precision.

Last year, after an assignment had gone bad—his only failure—he'd answered Maslennikov's call to arms, and had come here to work out of the islands, where his special talents had been put to good and constant use.

Now even this situation was coming to an end, as he'd known it would. But first he would finish what he had started out to do. And for that he was going to need Maslennikov's help one last time.

Former Ukrainian KGB major Fedor Nemchin, who was chief of Maslennikov's operational security force, was waiting with the Mercedes and a driver across from the cab rank. Dressed in a wool car coat, corduroy trousers, and gum boots, a dark hat pulled low over his eyes, he looked like a sheep farmer. But like all of Maslennikov's handpicked men, he was intelligent and efficient.

Yernin tossed his bag in the front seat beside the driver, then got in back with Nemchin.

"How did you know I would be showing up on this ferry?" Yernin asked as they pulled away. "Was someone else following me? Or has something gone wrong here?"

"Everything is going wrong, but not merely on this side of the Channel."

Yernin held back a sharp reply, his right hand resting casually near the pistol beneath his jacket on his left side.

"Mikhail was worried, so he had Markov send someone down to watch the ferry docks at Poole. He figured you'd be coming out the same way you went in."

Yernin's jaw tightened imperceptibly. He'd been too preoccupied last night to notice; another in a series of potentially deadly mistakes.

"What happened to Nikolai and Ivan?" Nemchin asked.

"They're dead. Lane killed them both."

Nemchin's left eyebrow rose. "Are you wounded?"

Yernin looked him in the eye. "No."

"Mikhail won't be happy," Nemchin said. He looked away momentarily. They were passing through the town of St. Peter Port, bustling with morning work traffic. In summer the town's population would double with tourists. Now the traffic was mostly local.

"Your men were supposed to kill me if the situation fell apart."

Nemchin looked guilty. "Those were my orders, but it wasn't my idea."

"Don't worry about it, Fedor. I approve of your orders. Only if there is a next time, send someone who is more efficient. A bullet in the back of my head when I'm not expecting it would be the most effective method."

Nemchin shuddered involuntarily. "You're a cold bastard."

"At this point I am a failure," Yernin replied matter-of-factly. "But that will be corrected."

"What happened over there?"

"Somehow Lane knew that we were coming, and he laid a trap. I barely got out with my life." Yernin held his temper in check, though he wanted to lash out. He wasn't used to failure.

"Is there any possibility, even a remote one, that you were followed here?"

Yernin shook his head. "Markov's people watching the ferry docks in Poole would have spotted them and warned you by now."

"True."

"He's motivated now that he knows I'm close."

"It's a moot point unless he does the impossible and finds the submarine," Nemchin said. "We're leaving within thirty-six hours."

Yernin looked sharply at him. "I thought we were leaving tonight."

"All that has changed. Mikhail needs the time to empty our bank accounts."

"It can be done electronically from anywhere in the world."

"That's what we all thought. But now he insists that we get the cash. Swiss francs, British pounds, American dollars, and gold."

Yernin thought about it. "By now the American government must be putting pressure on the Swiss."

"They are, but Loos is cooperating with us for the time being, and for a considerable handling fee."

"Is Mikhail going back to Zürich?" Yernin asked.

Nemchin nodded heavily. "*Da.* Later this morning. Captain Lubiako and some of the others want to leave, but Mikhail won't listen. Neither will our guest."

"What guest?"

"He came in yesterday afternoon from Madrid. I don't think Mikhail was expecting him, he didn't say anything to me about it. But he knows the man. He says his name is Roman Ortega, Colonel Ortega."

"I wasn't aware that we had any connections in Spain."

"Neither was I. But whoever he is he carries a lot of weight, because Mikhail is treating him with a great deal of respect."

"Have you talked to him?"

"Only a few words," Nemchin said. "But neither has anyone else except for Mikhail."

"Did you run a background check on him?" Yernin demanded.

"He doesn't show up on any of the databases that I have access to. Which might mean nothing."

"Or it might mean that he's in the business and has covered his tracks well. Where are they now?"

"When I left to pick you up, they were heading down to the marina with Kovrygin and Lubiako."

"Are they going out to the submarine?"

"All I know is that Mikhail wanted us aboard *Charisma* as soon as you showed up."

Yernin studied Nemchin's heavy-lidded Slavic eyes for some clue as to what might be happening. If it was a trap he wanted some warning, but although he could see irritation in the man's eyes, there was no guile. Nemchin was just as puzzled as he was.

The highway ran along the cliffs above the coast before switching down to the marina. From their vantage point Yernin could see some activity on the *Charisma*'s deck. Exhaust gases from the idling diesels came from the stack and were whipped by the wind. The yacht was being prepared to pull out, and Yernin felt a small measure of curiosity about what was coming next. But that feeling was nothing next to his anger.

"The yacht is going somewhere," he observed.

"So it would seem," Nemchin replied distantly.

2

ABOARD THE *CHARISMA*

Their lingua franca was English, and Ortega spoke it with only a very slight Spanish accent. He stood facing Maslennikov, submarine captain Lubiako, and the *Charisma*'s Captain Kovrygin on the bridge of the yacht, his lips curled into a slight smile, but his dark eyes were deadly serious. He was in his forties, with the dark good looks of a Latin aristocrat.

"Will there be any problem because of this change in plans?" he asked.

"Absolutely none," Maslennikov assured him.

"My crew will expect an explanation," Lubiako said.

Ortega studied him, his smile deepening. "You're the captain, and you give the orders," he said. "It's that way in my navy."

"We're no longer in any navy." Lubiako shook his head. "We've left that all behind. There's no going back, and my men know that. But they've agreed to follow orders so long as their orders make sense."

"There is a good reason for all of this, Igor," Maslennikov said, trying to be conciliatory.

"Pardon me, Mikhail, but I'm sure there is. I would like to hear it."

"You'll be rich men," Ortega said, but Lubiako brushed the comment aside.

"All the gold in Switzerland will do us no good if we wind up in a British jail," he said angrily.

"If we keep screwing around here, it could be worse," Kovrygin spoke up. "Listen to me, Mikhail, if the wrong people in Moscow put two and two together we could all end up dead."

"Criminals," Ortega spat.

"*Da,* mafia," Lubiako shot back. "Don't underestimate their power, because right now they're operating in every major Western city, including Paris, London, and New York. And Madrid."

Ortega shrugged. "Once we're away from here you and your crew will be safe."

"Where might that be, Colonel?" Lubiako asked, a dangerously soft edge in his voice.

"Morocco for now," Maslennikov said. "Once we've retrieved our money and loaded it aboard two-eighty-three."

Lubiako and Kovrygin exchanged a look of surprise. "Sierra Leone is only four days farther, why take the risk of being detected?" Lubiako demanded.

Maslennikov started to reply, but Ortega held him off.

"You were not going to be told about this until we

were well out to sea," he said. "When Captain Maslennikov informed me that there was a possibility, no matter how slight, that one of your crewmen was a double agent, it was my decision to keep you in the dark for the time being."

Lubiako was angry. "I told Captain Maslennikov, and now I'll tell you, Colonel, that Markov was mistaken. I know each of my crewmen like I know my brother. I trust each of them with my life." He pushed away from where he leaned against the chart table, his body language menacing. "*Yeb vas,* but you're beginning to try my patience."

Ortega's expression was bland. "Very well. We will lay off shore approximately seven hundred kilometers south of Rabat."

"What's there?"

"A deserted phosphate loading facility, with docks leading out to deep water."

"What are we loading?"

"Men," Ortega said. "Whom you will train in the operations of the submarine."

"Navy crewmen?" Lubiako asked.

"Yes."

"Submariners?"

"They have received training in the classroom for the past year, but this will be the first time they've ever been aboard an operational submarine." Ortega gave Lubiako a hard stare. "They are very dedicated men who know how to take orders."

"How many of them?" Lubiako asked, returning Ortega's stare.

"Thirty," Ortega said, and then he smiled. "The fact that you and a crew of thirteen officers managed to bring the boat this far is nothing short of astounding to them. As I understand it, the normal complement of such a submarine is fifty-four. I tell you that all of my men are very anxious to meet you and your crew. They'll have many questions."

Lubiako did his best to hide his discomfiture. "I'm sure they will."

"Did you bring the undersea charts for that stretch of coast up from two-eighty-three with you?" Ortega asked.

"Da."

"Get them. I would like to see what we're faced with."

Lubiako nodded. "They're in my quarters," he said, and he left as the ship's phone buzzed.

Kovrygin picked it up. "This is the captain," he said. "Send them up." He put down the phone. "Nemchin is here with Yernin."

3

ABOARD THE *CHARISMA*

Lubiako took several long waterproof titanium tubes from beneath his bunk, and finding the correct one, opened it and withdrew the rolled-up charts. These he separated, picking out two of them: one, a small-scale chart showing the entire northwest coast of Africa from the Strait of Gibraltar to Cape Palmas at the southern border of Liberia, and the second, the approach chart for navigable harbors along the Moroccan coast.

They were old Soviet navy subsea charts, and were very good, even better than the British or American charts for the region. For years the Soviet Union had sent more submarines to sea than any other nation. Besides combat training and missile drills, their crews constantly charted the seabed in their patrol areas.

He was expected back on the bridge immediately, but he took the time to light a cigarette and pour a small glass of vodka. The hell with them, and with the morning hour.

Maslennikov had changed in the last year. They all had, and not for the better. The money was fabulous, as was the adventure. Yet a lot of Russians had been killed to get the money, and they had finally become men without a country. They could never return to Ukraine. Nor was the prospect of spending the rest of their days in some African third-world nation very comforting.

The only time in his life at sea that he'd ever been truly afraid was in the Barents Sea off Polyarnyy when they'd faked the sinking and breakup of 283. They'd worn hazard suits until they were away from the graveyard, but their dosage badges had all turned milky. They'd taken enough rems to ensure that someday in the future most of them would develop leukemia or some other horrible cancer.

It was a future that they'd all managed to put out of their minds, because what was done was done. But several times in the past days he'd caught himself looking at his reflection in the mirror. Looking for bloodshot eyes, hair loss, skin lesions, coated tongue. He was sure some of the others were doing the same.

But he was even more frightened now. Even before Colonel Ortega had shown up out of the blue, Kovrygin had agreed that the situation had finally become untenable, and it wouldn't be any better once they reached Sierra Leone. Between them they'd decided that the *Charisma* would not be destroyed, as Maslennikov had planned, nor would 283 ever reach its destination.

Instead, somewhere at sea they would surface the submarine, transfer money and crew to the yacht, and scuttle 283. From there, Kovrygin thought they stood a very good chance of reaching the South Pacific, the Marquesas, or Tahiti, somewhere where they would divide the money and scatter.

Mutiny. The word itself was fearsome to Lubiako. If Maslennikov tried to resist he would have to be killed, as would any of the crew. Which left the problem of Yernin. The man was totally insane. No one believed any differently. Nor did any of them believe that he would be an easy man to kill. It was a problem that would have to be addressed as soon as possible, because if they waited too long, and Yernin sided with Maslennikov, which he almost certainly would, they'd find themselves in very deep trouble.

Compounding that problem was Colonel Ortega, and the thirty crewmen they were supposed to pick up. Once those bastards were aboard, mutiny would be impossible. And if, contrary to Ortega's assurances, the crew were trained submariners, then all hope would be lost.

Lubiako knocked back his drink, stubbed out his cigarette, and gathered up his charts as Kovrygin called him on the interphone.

"Yernin is here, and we're putting out to sea."

"On my way," Lubiako said.

4

ABOARD THE *CHARISMA*

Ortega was a man used to giving orders, not taking them, and the moment Yernin stepped aboard the bridge he sized up the Spaniard as someone with something to hide. Something very big, and very important.

"I can't say that I'm happy to see you back here like this, Valeri," Maslennikov told him. "At any rate, I'd like you to meet Colonel Roman Ortega. He's come from Madrid to help us."

Yernin and Ortega shook hands, warily.

"You encountered some trouble in England," Ortega said. "Were you followed here?"

"No," Yernin said. "With what are you here to help us, Colonel?"

"The delivery of two-eighty-three."

"Captain Lubiako and his crew brought it this far without assistance."

"For which he has my respect and admiration. But I require that he train the crew who will eventually take over once two-eighty-three reaches her home port."

"Where might that be? Not Freetown as we'd planned?"

"You have no need to know our destination at this point," Ortega said. He wasn't quite as nonchalant as he'd been with the others.

Yernin glanced over at Lubiako and Kovrygin, who stood at the chart table, two subsea charts of the African coast in front of them. "I thought we were leaving tonight."

"Tomorrow night," Maslennikov said. "As soon as we get Igor and a few of his crew back aboard two-eighty-three so they can start to reactivate him, I'm returning to Zürich."

"Is that wise?"

"It's necessary," Ortega said harshly.

Yernin didn't take his eyes off Maslennikov. "Mikhail?"

"Leave that part to me," Maslennikov said after a moment's hesitation. "You have your own problems. Problems that could affect all of us. I want to know what you intend doing about Mr. Lane."

"I'm going to kill him."

"What happened over there?"

"I failed," Yernin said, and he told Maslennikov everything that had happened, including the deaths of the two officers that Nemchin had sent over.

"Lane has a habit of doing this to you," Maslennikov said. "Maybe next time he'll finish the job and kill you instead."

Yernin's jaw tightened.

"Before this incident you were not a wanted man in England, is that right?" Ortega asked.

"That's correct." Yernin felt dangerous, and it was clear that everyone else aboard the bridge sensed it.

"Now you are."

"Yes."

"I'm not familiar with the name. Who is Lane?"

"He's an analyst working for the American National Security Agency's Russian Division."

"Where does the woman come into it?"

"She works for the British Secret Intelligence Service."

"She and Lane are friends?"

Yernin nodded.

"More than friends?" Ortega pressed.

"They're lovers."

"So in order to get to him you've gone after her."

"He's shown a willingness in the past to come to her rescue. It's his weak spot."

"His Achilles' heel," Maslennikov said.

"And apparently yours as well," Orgeta said, directing the remark to Yernin. He turned to Maslennikov. "I suggest we forget about Lane."

"That's not a good idea," Yernin said evenly.

"If you go after him and bungle it again, it could lead the British navy here. If you were captured they'd find out everything. There are methods that even the British aren't above using."

The tension aboard the bridge was suddenly thick. "If

I were taken alive something like you suggest is possible.''

"It's a risk I don't want to take, unless there is a very good reason," Ortega said. He smiled suddenly and spread his hands. "I'm not the enemy. I've been sent here to help bring the submarine to port. You'll see that when the time comes my presence will not only be desirable, but necessary."

"It's necessary to kill Lane," Yernin said.

"Why?"

"Because he won't stop until he finds me."

"Maybe you're not the man for the job," Ortega said.

Nemchin stepped back, his hand going inside his jacket.

Yernin didn't move.

"Or maybe we should give Señor Lane what he wants," Ortega said softly. "You."

Everyone on the bridge, including Ortega, knew what was about to happen, but nobody had a chance to move a muscle before Yernin had his Heckler & Koch out of its holster, the safety catch off, and had moved with catlike speed, shoving Ortega back against the bulkhead and jamming the muzzle of the pistol into his throat below his jaw.

"Vasha," Maslennikov warned sharply.

Ortega's lips were half-parted in a smile. "Pull the trigger and your comrades will become hunted men with nowhere to run."

Yernin increased the pressure on Ortega's throat, all his pent-up frustration focused on this one act.

"There is another way, Vasha," Maslennikov said at Yernin's side. "Without Colonel Ortega we're all in trouble. But you'll have Bill Lane. I promise you."

Yernin stared into Ortega's eyes, until suddenly he could see that the man finally understood just how close to death he was. The smile faded from Ortega's lips.

"I promise you," Maslennikov said.

Yernin eased his finger off the trigger, then stepped back, and holstered his gun. "I'm listening," he said, completely indifferent now to Ortega, who was pale with anger.

"I'll call Markov in London. He can hire a local team to kill them both. That way if there are problems the blame will fall on his shoulders."

"He won't do it."

"Yes he will," Maslennikov said. "He doesn't have any choice in the matter. If he fails, you can finish the job. You have my word."

5

ABOARD THE *CHARISMA*

The *Charisma*'s lines were slipped and as she headed out into the choppy seas past the sea buoy, Maslennikov went alone into his quarters, where he placed a call to London.

"Good morning, you have reached the embassy of the sovereign nation of Russia, how may I direct your call?" a woman with a cultured voice answered in English.

"Three-one-three," Maslennikov told her.

Konstantin Markov answered a few moments later. "This is Markov."

"This is Mikhail. Is your telephone secure? We must talk about something."

"*Yeb vas,*" Markov said. "You're the last person I thought I'd hear from. Are you here in London?"

"No. Is your telephone secure?"

"Yes, it is. But what do you want? After that fiasco

in Zürich I don't have anything to say to you."

"Perhaps not, but I have a great deal to say to you. All of it concerns Mr. Lane and his friend Frances Shipley, who if you don't know by now is a British intelligence officer."

"I've washed my hands of the entire affair. That Vandermeer had us all fooled. He's after you and your little toy. And frankly I don't care if he succeeds."

"If he does, Konstantin, you'll almost certainly be recalled to Moscow," Maslennikov told him. "Maybe you'll get your nine ounces after all." Nine ounces was an old Russian euphemism for a 9mm bullet to the back of the head.

"You're in no position to threaten me," Markov countered angrily.

"On the contrary, I am in just such a position now," Maslennikov said. Ortega had not only made everything clear, he'd brought them the way out. "Are you listening to me?"

"*Da.*" Markov was sullen.

"Within the hour your name will be placed on certain bank documents in Switzerland."

"What documents?" Markov sputtered.

"I think you know," Maslennikov said. "And I think you know what it will mean should those records fall into the wrong hands in Moscow, and elsewhere."

"I'm still listening."

"Bill Lane and Frances Shipley must be assassinated immediately. I don't care how or where it is done; suffice to say they must die now, or else all of us, you included, Konstantin, will be finished."

"You're insane," Markov said.

"I suggest that you call General Korzhakov immediately, and then make your plans accordingly. I'll telephone you again in one hour. I hope by then that you'll have something positive to tell me."

"Fuck you—," Markov said.

Maslennikov hung up on him, then looked again at the contents of the sealed envelope that had been delivered to him. The top page contained the shield-and-sword logo of the old Soviet KGB, and flipping to the second page Colonel Ortega's photograph stared up at him.

6

LONDON

Markov instructed his secretary to hold all his calls, then swiveled his chair to face the window that looked into a rear courtyard and parking area three stories below. It was drizzling, but one of the drivers was washing an embassy car anyway. Russian efficiency at work. Sometimes his own countrymen amazed him.

Maslennikov's call couldn't have come at a worse time. On his desk was the draft of his resignation letter. Everything in Moscow was falling apart, and he was afraid of getting caught in the collapse.

But now he was damned if he went along with Maslennikov, and damned if he didn't. If he simply ignored the insane proposal it would get back to General Korzhakov and his head would be on the block. The general ran a tight ship.

If, on the other hand, he did call the general, Korzhakov might brand him as a lunatic. Or worse than that, he might go along with the scheme.

Markov thought about that. Only in the old Spy Smasher films that had been so popular in Moscow did agents run around shooting up foreign nationals. In real life it was not done. For spying you could be arrested and deported. But for murder you could end up in jail for the rest of your life. Not a pleasant prospect.

After the incident in Zürich, he'd sent his report to Moscow, and the response had been immediate and unequivocal: Make no further contact with Bill Lane. Implied, but not in the reply, was that the fate of 283 would be determined in Moscow, and not in London.

But Maslennikov had sounded so sure of himself. And his reputation was nothing short of amazing. The only blemish on his record, besides switching allegiance from Moscow to Kiev at the breakup, was that he too had suffered financially in raids on two of his bank accounts.

What Markov was uncertain of was Maslennikov's allusion to certain bank records in Switzerland. It had got him thinking, and he did not like the conclusions that he was drawing. He didn't like them at all.

It was coming up on 10:00 A.M., which made it one in the afternoon in Moscow. By now the general would be back from lunch and at his desk as usual.

Markov had spent three years in New York, working in the UN, and during his tenure he'd picked up a lot of idiomatic English. As he got up and went to the door he smiled wryly, remembering one of the expressions that applied to him now. He was most definitely caught between a rock and a hard place.

His secretary looked up.

"Get General Korzhakov on the secure line, please. When you've done that, go downstairs and have a glass of tea. I'll call when you may return."

"Yes, sir," she said, not surprised. It was standard operating procedure. Secretaries had ears, and what they did not hear was for the best.

He left the connecting door ajar so that he could see her desk and telephone console, then took the red phone out of a drawer and sat down in front of it.

His palms were wet, because he was afraid of what

the general might say, and it made no sense to him. No sense whatsoever.

His secretary looked at him through the open door, and a moment later his red phone buzzed. He picked it up, and his secretary got her purse and left the office.

"General Korzhakov, I hope that I am not disturbing your lunch," Markov said.

"Not at all, Konstantin. How is everything in London?"

"Confusing."

General Korzhakov laughed. "You should be in Moscow. Everything changes every day. Nobody knows where we're going. Even I can make no predictions. My advice to you is to remain where you are. Whatever happens stay in place, and I'll do what I can to keep our foreign operations going."

"I'm getting homesick, but your advice is sound."

"It is," the general said. "Now what's confusing you in London? Is it the William Lane business?"

"Yes, sir," Markov said. "Mikhail Maslennikov telephoned me this morning."

"I'm not surprised. What did he want this time?"

"He wants me to assassinate Lane and a British intelligence officer by the name of Frances Shipley. A woman."

"Now that's something. Did he say why?"

"He told me that all of us, including me, would be finished otherwise."

General Korzhakov laughed. "He always had a touch of melodrama. I could tell you stories."

"Yes, sir."

"What did you tell him?"

"I told him to fuck himself, General."

Korzhakov laughed again. "An interesting proposition, Konstantin. The trouble is that he's right. You'll have to do it."

Even though Markov had felt at the pit of his gut that

Korzhakov would agree with the insane scheme, he was thunderstruck. "We don't do such things any longer, General. Especially not for Ukrainians."

"You're not going to have to do it personally. I'm not suggesting that. Nor am I suggesting that you use any of our people. But there are resources in London that you can use."

"I know of no such . . . resources."

"Nevertheless they are there in your files."

"I'm sorry to disagree, General, but I know all of our resources in London."

"Listen to me, Konstantin, it's just blind luck, but a block of files was downloaded into your system overnight. This information came to our attention from our embassy in Mexico City, and was sent to London on a purely routine basis."

Markov felt the trap snap shut. The general was lying to him. Maslennikov had lied to him. And so had Lane. They were three legs of a triangle effectively surrounding him. There was no way out.

He turned toward the window. The driver was still washing the car, soap suds dissipating in the rain, which was coming down harder now. He wondered if the man would dry off the car.

"You will have to make certain that the British-American surveillance unit watching you suspects nothing. Perhaps a diversion. But you can handle that."

"Is this necessary, General?"

"Yes. But it doesn't matter why, Konstantin. That decision has already been made for you, so you don't have to worry about it."

"Of course."

"Then, good luck," General Korzhakov said. "I may come to Paris next month. You can take the Chunnel over and we'll have dinner together."

"I would like that."

LONDON

Markov hung up the red phone, replaced the instrument in the desk drawer, and sat for several moments deep in thought. The general had said that the decision had *already* been made. The problem was Bill Lane. Were they simply reacting to his interference, had he come as a surprise? Or had they been expecting him to show up? Maslennikov definitely knew the man. There was no doubt about it.

He called the canteen downstairs and told his secretary that she could return to her desk when she was finished with her tea, then took the elevator down to the records section in the basement, where Dmitri Kedrov, the section chief, came out to greet him.

"Is your computer broken again, Mr. Markov?" he asked. He was a young kid in his late twenties, with wild red hair and wilder hazel eyes.

Markov had to smile, despite his worries. It was a joke between them. Markov was computer illiterate, and in fact didn't trust the machines. When he wanted something important he come to Kedrov, who, in his estimation, was a computer genius.

"I think it laughs at me."

"Shoot it, put it out of its misery."

"Believe me, Dmitri, I've considered it," Markov said. "Some information was sent to us from Mexico City last night. I'd like to take a look at it."

Kedrov gave him an odd look. "Yes, I saw it this

morning. Would you like a hard copy, or do you merely want me to pull it up on a monitor for you? I could send it upstairs to your office."

"I'll use one of your machines here if you'll set it up for me."

"No problem," Kedrov said.

Markov followed him back to a monitor and keyboard at the end of a bank of file cabinets. Kedrov entered a few commands, and the file came up on screen under the logo of their embassy in Mexico City, headed most secret.

"You'll have to enter your access code," Kedrov said, and again he gave Markov an odd look. "I'll just leave you to it. If you need anything I'll be in my office."

Markov sat down at the monitor as Kedrov withdrew, entered his seven-digit alphanumeric password, and began scrolling through the file marked "Special Units: British Isles and Western European Availability."

Six Cuban intelligence officers had been reassigned from their posting in Mexico City to a special branch here in London. For the past two years they had worked under the direct orders of the Russian *rezident* in Mexico, and were now London station's assets.

Department Viktor assets. Killers.

8

ABOARD THE *CHARISMA*

Yernin went down to the galley, where he fixed himself a cheese sandwich and opened a bottle of beer, which he took up to the main saloon. They were out of the lee of Guernsey, and the motion aboard the yacht was lively. Ortega came in and sat down across the table from him.

"I think we have gotten off on the wrong foot, señor," he said. "We will not become friends, but we will be working in close quarters so it would be better if we understood each other."

Yernin nodded. "Who do you work for?"

"That's not important right now."

"Where are we taking two-eighty-three?"

"You'll be told that once we pick up our crew in Morocco. But in the meantime there is this business with Bill Lane. I don't understand why he's so important to you and Mikhail that you are willing to risk not only this entire venture, but your lives as well."

"Either I stop him, or he'll stop us," Yernin said mildly. He hadn't had a chance to talk to Maslennikov about his plan yet, but talking with Ortega now he'd come up with a new idea.

"One man?"

"Yes, Colonel, one man. But he's very special, very dedicated, very good, and even very lucky."

"You've come up against him on several occasions and lost."

"That's right."

Ortega seemed to think about it for a moment. "We'll be gone in thirty-six hours. It's not likely he'll find us in such a short time."

"He probably has the help of the British navy by now, and he knows that we're close." Yernin shrugged. "Thirty-six hours is a very long time for a man like him, unless he's distracted."

"You're going to provide this distraction?"

"Yes."

"If he has the help of the navy, then certainly he has the help of the British intelligence service, and because of what you did, certainly Scotland Yard is on the case."

"Almost certainly."

Ortega was becoming vexed. "Are you going to share your scheme with me, or am I going to have to guess it?"

Yernin reached back and lifted the phone from its bracket on the bulkhead. "This is Yernin. Captain, when Maslennikov returns to the bridge ask him to join me and Colonel Ortega in the main saloon."

9

ABOARD THE *CHARISMA*

Maslennikov joined them a half hour later, a look of satisfaction on his face that turned to irritation when he saw that there was still a lot of tension between the two men.

"We'll be on station in five minutes," he said.

"Is radar still clear?" Ortega asked. "Will it be safe to send divers down to the submarine?"

"There is a freighter about two kilometers out, but it's heading away. The weather is too rotten for anyone else to be out here."

"How many are going down?"

"Just Captain Lubiako and four of his men, all of them engineers. They'll have the boat fully operational within a few hours."

"What about the others?"

"I'll be back from Zürich tonight, and we can start loading under cover of darkness. But with our limited manpower it'll take several trips. We can't keep on station very long. Someone is bound to notice us and become suspicious."

"But you're certain we'll be able to leave on schedule?" Ortega asked.

"We'll be finished by tomorrow night," Maslennikov assured him.

"Did you speak to Markov?" Yernin asked. "Is he going to do it?"

"I spoke to him twice, and he's agreed to do it within the next twenty-four hours. Possibly even tonight."

"That makes no sense. Why would he do such a thing for you? He has everything to lose and nothing to gain. He'd be a fool to try to kill Lane, even if he has the assets, which I doubt he does."

"General Korzhakov gave the orders," Maslennikov said. "And as for his assets, he has a small team of shooters at his disposal. Expendable shooters with no direct track back to the London embassy."

A look passed between Maslennikov and Ortega that Yernin caught.

"You must have been expecting trouble from the start," Yernin told Ortega.

"What makes you say that?" the colonel asked mildly.

"They're your people."

Ortega shook his head. "In this you are sadly mistaken. I don't know these men who Mikhail speaks of. I assure you they have never worked for me, and I have no knowledge of them.''

"You're a liar."

Ortega smiled and spread his hands. "Then the ball is in your court, Mr. Yernin. Because I am not going to waste my breath trying to prove differently to you." He shrugged. "Frankly, I don't care what you believe."

"Markov will take care of Lane," Maslennikov put in. "And if he fails I promise that you'll get your chance again."

That was when Yernin saw everything with a clarity that he'd not experienced for a long time. He'd been listening to what the others had been saying over the past week, and now what Ortega and Maslennikov were telling him, and he realized that they all would be betrayed. Maslennikov, with the help of Ortega and the crewmen they were picking up in Morocco, meant to kill them all. The submarine would go to Ortega's government and Maslennikov would keep the money. It was an elegant solution to a problem that had been bothering Yernin for a number of months now: What to do with so many Ukrainian naval officers, some of whom still had families back home? With so many men involved, there would be a leak sooner or later, and the Russian mafia would come after the people responsible for stealing their money.

All that occurred to Yernin in an instant, and without changing expression he nodded. "I hope he fails."

"I hope he doesn't," Maslennikov said. "But I understand what you're saying. Now, you called me down here, Vasha, what did you want to tell me?"

"He has another plan to kill Bill Lane," Ortega said. "Something about a distraction."

"It'll keep," Yernin said.

"And in the meantime?" Maslennikov asked.

"I'm going down to the submarine with Igor and the

others. They can use a hand, and I want to get the rest of my things off the boat.''

''What are you talking about?''

''I'm not going to Morocco with you. I want to make sure Lane is dead.''

''Then what?''

''I'll catch up with you there.''

''We won't wait for you,'' Maslennikov said.

''I'll be there.''

10

.– 283

The submarine's aft escape trunk hatch was in fifty meters of water. The boat's outline loomed out of the darkness as they descended, and the beam of Captain Lubiako's powerful flashlight played on the numbers painted on the boat's sail.

It took a little over ten minutes to lock all of them aboard. The boat was cold, and the air smelled stale and tasted of diesel oil.

After they shed their wet suits and tanks, the engineers went aft, and Yernin followed the captain forward to the control room beneath the conning tower, where he began switching on lights, the air scrubbers, recirculating fans, and some of the heaters.

Lubiako used the growler phone to call aft. ''How does it look back there?''

''We're dry,'' one of the engineers responded.

Next he used the aquaphone to call the *Charisma*. ''We're aboard and everything looks good.''

"We'll start loading in sixteen hours," Captain Kovrygin's muffled voice came back.

"We'll be ready."

Lubiako hung up, then turned to Yernin. "There is nothing of yours aboard except what you just brought down. So what are you doing down here?"

"I wanted to talk to you."

"About what?"

"Mutiny," Yernin said, and he was satisfied by the look that crossed the man's eyes.

PART EIGHT

1

OXFORD

Lane had been kept overnight in the hospital. Most of the bullet had passed through his arm, missing the bones and major blood vessels, but fragments of lead and wood from the doorframe had lodged in his flesh and had to be dug out. He'd already had his breakfast by nine o'clock when Frances returned with a new shirt and khaki trousers she'd picked up for him at a men's store.

"Not Armani, I'm afraid, but these'll do until we get back to London," she said, kissing him on the cheek.

"At least you got the sizes right," said Lane, sitting on the edge of the bed as he awkwardly got dressed.

His right hand was stiff, and his shoulder ached. The doctor had assured him that he was lucky and that there'd been no serious nerve or muscle damage, but he would have limited use of his hand and arm for several weeks.

"How does it feel?" Frances asked with concern.

"It hurts like hell, but I'll live." Lane looked at her. "How are you holding up, Frannie?"

"Uncle Leonard didn't have anything to do with this," she said angrily. "And there was no reason for that bastard to kill Albert. He's a coward."

"That he is. But he's a dedicated coward."

The young surgeon who'd worked on Lane's arm breezed in, a big grin on his boyish face. "How's the wing this morning? On the mend, I hope."

"I won't be doing handstands for the time being."

"I should say not," the doctor said. He removed the dressing and examined the wound, then rebandaged it. "The stitches will come out in a couple of weeks. In the meantime do keep it dry, change the bandages every couple of days, and try not to get shot again."

"I was hoping you'd offer me a discount on a second go-around."

"Right," the surgeon said. "You can take codeine for the pain, if you like. I'll write a prescription for you."

"I prefer Martell cognac, actually."

"Cordon bleu?"

"Naturally."

The smile left the doctor's face. "Seriously, don't count on that arm to do anything strenuous for the time being. It won't."

"I'll keep it in mind, thanks," Lane said.

"I was sorry to hear about your uncle and his man, Ms. Shipley," the doctor said. "I hope you catch the bloody bastard."

"We will," she said.

"Good."

The surgeon left, and a minute later a sour-faced Brad Morgan came in as Lane was slipping on his shoes.

"Are you ready to check out?" he asked gruffly.

"Yes. Any word on Yernin?"

"We found the boat a few kilometers upstream, and the van they used still parked at the marina, but so far there's been no sign whatsoever of him."

"What about the two shooters?"

"They carried no IDs, of course. But we think one of them was Nikolai Donderov, who, until he disappeared eleven months ago, worked for the Ukrainian KGB."

"The other one was probably KGB as well," Lane said. "They were professionals."

Morgan gave him an odd look.

"What about border crossings?"

"Sealed as tightly as possible with what manpower

we've got. In the meantime we're distributing the sketch artist drawings to every law enforcement agency in the country. But that's going to take time.''

''I can't ask for more,'' Lane said. He got shakily to his feet, and Frances took his left arm.

''Both Rovers have been impounded until the lab people can go over them with a fine-tooth comb. So you two will have to ride down to London with me in the chopper. Roger Stewart wants to have a word with both of you.'' Stewart was director of the Secret Intelligence Service's Clandestine Operations Division.

''I'll check with my boss,'' Lane said.

''It's already been cleared.''

''Okay. But first I'd like to get back to my hotel so I can clean up and change out of these dreadful clothes.''

''Not until you reimburse me,'' Frances said indignantly. ''I paid for them out of my own pocket, rather than see you walk out of here in a hospital gown open in the back.''

''Now that would have been a sight.''

''It sure would,'' she said enthusiastically, and Morgan shot her a sour look.

2

LONDON

Just after lunch a vexed Brad Morgan entered the office of Roger Stewart, overlooking the Thames. Stewart was a small, dapper man, no more than five feet six, with perfectly groomed hair, a sharp three-piece suit, and a penetrating gaze that never seemed to miss a thing. His job for the SIS was nearly the same as that of the CIA's deputy director of operations, and like his American counterpart, he was the Service's third most important man behind the director and deputy director. Though he was a hard man; he was intelligent and fair-minded. Morgan got along with him all right, but not as well as he wanted to.

"Did you bring Commander Shipley and Mr. Lane with you?" Stewart asked.

"They wanted to clean up and change clothes first. There wasn't much I could do about it, short of placing them both under arrest."

"Understandable after their ordeal down there." Stewart picked up his phone and gave instructions to his secretary that they were to be shown in the moment they arrived. "Has the Yard had any success finding Sir Leonard's murderer?"

"Not yet, sir. But if he's the man Lane says he is, then catching up with him won't be easy."

"Is there any reason to suspect that Lane is mistaken?" Stewart asked patiently.

"No."

"This man is somehow tied in with the submarine that the Americans are looking for?"

"According to Lane."

"He's a renegade."

Morgan allowed a smile to flicker across his face. "He's broken enough of our laws so that we would have no problem sending him home."

"Actually I was referring to Valeri Yernin," Stewart said, a look of annoyance on his face.

Morgan, realizing his mistake, was momentarily flustered. "Sorry, sir. But to be honest, if Lane hadn't come here, Yernin wouldn't have murdered Sir Leonard and his man. This is a vendetta for something that happened between them."

"Be that as it may, we've inherited the problem because it's now on British soil, and affecting the lives of British subjects, not the least of whom is Commander Shipley."

"His fight is with Lane, not Commander Shipley."

"He murdered her uncle."

"Because he believed that Commander Shipley would naturally drop everything to go up there. And Bill Lane would be with her. Which he was, of course. And he bungled the job."

"The second man was Ivan Yegorov. Former Ukrainian KGB. The two of them, plus Yernin, made for a formidable force. Yet Lane and Commander Shipley successfully defended themselves. I would have to say that it was Yernin and his men who bungled the operation."

"Lane was wounded."

"Defending one of our people," Stewart said. He looked at Morgan for an uncomfortable moment. "Is there a problem between you and Mr. Lane? Because if there is, I want to know about it now."

Morgan started to shake his head, but then thought better of it. Stewart was one man you didn't lie to. "It's a personality clash between us, sir."

"Mr. Lane and Commander Shipley have a relationship together, am I correct in this?"

Morgan nodded.

"Then let me ask you a delicate question, Brad. One that you don't have to answer if you choose not to. Has there ever been a relationship between you and Commander Shipley?"

It was as if a sharp knife had pierced his heart, but Morgan kept his reaction hidden. "No, sir. Never has, nor ever will be."

"Very well," Stewart said. "Then I suggest that you keep personalities out of all further dealings with Mr. Lane. Am I clear?"

"Perfectly, sir."

3

LONDON

Frances cabbed over to Claridge's, where Lane was waiting for her in front. He'd discarded his arm sling and changed into a fawn-colored hand-tailored Italian silk suit with an Hermès tie and Gucci loafers. In his early days with the NSA he'd been investigated by Internal Affairs because he was spending more money than he earned. It only took them an afternoon, however, to discover that Lane had inherited eight million dollars from an uncle, money which he never touched, content instead to let the interest income supplement his salary.

"My God, you're gorgeous," Frances said when he got in the cab with her, and they headed over to the foreign office. She was dressed in a tasteful Scottish tweed suit, ivory-colored silk blouse, and medium heels.

"I wouldn't kick you out of bed for eating crackers."

"Biscuits," she corrected brightly, though he could see that her mood was brittle.

He squeezed her hand.

"The worst part of it is that I'm already looking over my shoulder every five minutes," she told him. "I tried to convince Mrs. Houlten to leave London until this is all over with. She has relatives in Edinburgh whom she could visit. But she won't hear of it."

"Brad will have Scotland Yard watch your place. Yernin might be desperate to come after us, but he's no fool, he wants to get away clean."

"Brad doesn't like you."

''No.''

''It's because he has a crush on me.''

''I know, and I can't say that I blame him,'' Lane said. ''What about Roger Stewart?''

''His family and mine were close. His father, Sir Thomas, went to Oxford with Uncle Leonard, so he was raised old school, very proper. He knows what he's doing, he's good at it, and he's fair.'' She gave Lane a questioning look. ''Haven't you ever met him?''

''No.''

''Well, he knows all about you, William.''

Lane had to smile. ''Is that good or bad?''

''In this case I don't know. Brad reports directly to him, so there's no telling what tales he's filled Stewart's head with.''

''Then it's up to us to convince him.''

''Of what?''

''To look for the submarine. Because wherever it is, Maslennikov will be with it, and he's the one holding Yernin's leash.''

Frances shivered. ''I hope you're as good a salesman as I think you are.''

Lane smiled. ''I'll make him an offer he can't refuse.''

The cab entered Whitehall, passed the headquarters of New Scotland Yard, and just beyond Downing Street pulled up in front of one of the large government buildings. Lane paid the driver, and he and Frances went inside, where they were searched electronically before being allowed upstairs.

''Here goes nothing,'' he told Frances.

''Let's hope it's not nothing,'' she replied.

4

LONDON

On the fifth floor they passed through another security check, before Lane followed Frances to a suite of busy offices around the corner. The highly polished wooden floors were spotted with Oriental carpets. Original oils hung on the walls, and throughout this level a lot of people worked at what appeared to be a subdued frenzy. Except for the artworks and the age of the place, it seemed to Lane like the busy corridors of the CIA or NSA.

Stewart's secretary, an older woman with gray hair in a bun, announced them, and they went in. Morgan, seated in front of the desk, did not get up, but Stewart did, and he came around to them, a look of concern on his face.

He gave Frances a peck on the cheek. "I was so sorry to hear about Sir Leonard. It's simply terrible."

"Thank you, Mr. Director. It was quite a blow."

"But in the end you managed quite well up there."

"This is Mr. Lane, an analyst with the National Security Agency. Without him I wouldn't be here," she said.

"I've heard a great deal about you," Stewart said, shaking hands. "But I thought you were wounded."

"Just a scratch," Lane said.

"He took a bullet in his right arm," Frances said.

"I see," Stewart said, releasing Lane's hand. "And killed two former KGB agents in the process."

"But it was the worst one who got away. And without Commander Shipley's fast work I'd be lying in the Oxford morgue."

"Valeri Yernin," Stewart said, directing them to take a seat. "A decidedly bad man."

"No word from Scotland Yard yet?" Lane asked.

"Unfortunately not. But that's where you come in. Apparently you know more about him than anyone else, and I'd like you to help us catch him. I've spoken with your Mr. Lewis, who in turn mentioned it to the director, who agreed wholeheartedly." Stewart allowed a flicker of a smile to cross his face. "They actually said that if I could somehow convince you to help out, they'd okay it. But after speaking with an associate of yours, Mr. Hughes, I gather that might be no mean feat."

"In that case if I keep my mouth shut, the advantage will be mine," Lane said.

"Beg your pardon?"

"There's nothing I want more than to catch Yernin. As you say, Mr. Stewart, he is a decidedly bad man who has been directly responsible for the murders of a lot of people. Sir Leonard won't be the last unless we're successful."

"Then it's settled. You will be working directly for Brad—"

Lane interrupted. "*With* Brad."

"Ah, yes, *with* Brad," Stewart said. "All things considered, Commander Shipley, do you think you're up to this assignment?"

"I'd rather she not," Morgan said.

"I wouldn't miss it for the world, Mr. Director," she said. "Nor do I think there's any question why."

"Do you agree, Mr. Lane?"

"I'd just as soon she not be involved, but I don't think any of us could stop her if we wanted to." He smiled at her. "In any event I'd like to know that my fiancée isn't sitting at home alone worrying about me."

Morgan's mouth dropped open, but he quickly clamped it shut and shot them a dirty look.

"Well," Stewart said in surprise. "I believe congratulations are in order."

"Thank you, Mr. Director," Frances said without missing a beat. "But in the meantime there's a lot of work to be done, because I'm not willing to sit at home waiting for Yernin to try again."

"You came here looking for a Russian submarine, is that correct?" Stewart asked Lane.

"Yes, and Yernin is involved with it. So if we find the submarine, we'll find him."

"Are you certain of it?" Stewart asked.

"The navy has turned up nothing," Morgan put in. "If it was wandering around in our waters we would have spotted it."

"Not necessarily. But I think I have an idea how we can find it."

"Impossible," Morgan fumed, but Stewart motioned him to silence.

"Before I ask the navy to conduct an all-out search I'll need some solid proof that the submarine is actually in British waters. Do you have such proof, Mr. Lane?"

"Not yet."

"Very well, then for the time being, until you can come up with something solid, we'll confine our efforts to finding Yernin."

"With Brad's help, I think we can kill both birds with one stone," Lane said. He turned to Morgan. "Do you have a problem with that?"

"No he doesn't," Stewart said firmly.

5

LONDON

Frances's office was on the second floor, but Morgan assigned them an office on the third, next to his in Eastern Hemisphere Operations territory. He didn't say a word on the way down, but when they were inside the office he turned on them.

"It's not going to work, what you two are trying to do to me," he said angrily.

Lane picked up the telephone, and got the switchboard. "Could you put me through to Mr. Stewart? Tell him it's Bill Lane calling."

"Wait," Morgan said. His eyes were bulging. "I promised I'd work with you, and I will."

"Never mind," Lane told the operator. "I'll call him later." He hung up.

"I'll work with you for now," Morgan said. "But if you screw up I'll nail you, and that's a promise too."

"That's all I want," Lane said. "But we don't have to be enemies. That part is up to you. We have a job to do, and not much time to do it in."

Morgan gathered himself, the emotional strain showing on his face. "For now it's up to Scotland Yard and Customs to find out what happened to Yernin. If he's crossed the border, or if he's moving around inside England, he'll come to someone's attention."

"Who are we working with at the Yard, and at Customs?" Frances asked.

"I'll do the liaising," Morgan said. "In the meantime

it's up to you two to find sufficient evidence to convince Mr. Stewart that the Russian submarine is somewhere in British waters. Can you do that?''

"Not only that, but I'll show the navy how to find the sub.''

"Right,'' Morgan said, a smirk on his face, and he turned and walked out.

6

LONDON

The small office was furnished with two desks on both of which were computer terminals. Frances sat down at one of them and booted up. "I'll connect with NSA, and you can give me Tom's address. I assume you'll want him to download your files on the submarine,'' she said. "We can start with that.''

"First I want to get into your own system,'' Lane said, perching on the desk.

"What are you looking for, William? Scotland Yard and Customs are the ones searching for Yernin, and Brad has them covered.''

"He's probably got us blocked from making any direct inquiries,'' Lane said. "But if they come up with anything he'll bring it to us. I want to find out what the SIS is doing to find him.''

"I'm sure that our foreign stations have been sent a notice, especially in Kiev and Moscow.''

"I'm talking about domestically.''

"That's a fine line, William. Except for operations like the one against Markov that Brad is running with the CIA, we don't spy in our own country."

"Neither does the CIA or NSA. But your branch is called the Resources Advisory Section."

"Buggers."

Lane grinned. "You do have a way with words, darling. I hope that when it comes time to go to the altar you'll do better than that."

She gave him an odd look. "We'll get to that later, William." She glanced toward the open door. The corridor was busy but no one paid them any attention. "The RAS doesn't exist."

"Acronyms are not made of nonexistent entities."

"Well, where in bloody hell did you hear about it?"

"Around. But that's not important, Frannie. Can you get into the system from here?"

She turned away for a moment. "They'll probably hang both of us," she said. "But I think I know what you're getting at, and it'll probably save us some time if I can do it." With a few keystrokes she got into the SIS mainframe, and pulled up a directory of offices, which itself was classified, and required her to use her section's password.

"I'm assuming that the RAS has direct computer links with every official agency in England. So if Scotland Yard, Customs, or anyone else has come up with anything on Yernin the RAS will already have it."

"But if they don't have anything yet, it might not tell us a thing," Frances said, her fingers flashing across the keyboard.

"It'll tell us that Yernin most likely never left England. And if the same search for Maslennikov comes up empty, it'll mean he's most likely somewhere within the country. And so is the submarine."

Frances had to smile. "If we do come up with something, I don't think I'll want to be around when you explain to Mr. Stewart just how you came by the information."

"We'll cross that bridge when we get to it."

When the directory finally came up, Frances scrolled through it with the mouse. "We're not going to get in," she said. "That section is not listed."

"Bring up the organizational chart for the entire SIS," Lane told her.

She hit a few keys, and the chart appeared on the screen. "Okay, we've got two offices listed as nondesignated functions. One in Management and Services, and the other in Operations."

"It'll be in Operations," Lane said.

"But it won't do us any good. We can't get in from here."

"Bring up a list of every section head in the service, and match them with their offices."

"I see what you're getting at," Frances said, and she quickly brought up the personnel listing, eliminating the names office by office. Five minutes later they were left with two names high enough on the chart to head offices, but without office listings.

"Hartley Schilling and Daniel Monroe," Frances said.

"Now pull up the building directory, and find their phone numbers."

She did it. Monroe's number came up under Special Services in Management and Services, and Schilling's came up under Operations, with no title, but with an office on the fifth floor, though the bulk of operations activities took place on the second floor. It was the weakness in the system he was looking for.

"Hartley Schilling," Frances said, looking up. "So now what? He's not going to talk to us, let alone offer any help."

"You're probably right, but it was worth a try, even though it's a dead end for now," Lane said.

She shook her head. "Why is it I think that I've just been had."

"Nothing could be farther from the truth," Lane said.

He wrote down Tom Hughes's direct number at the NSA. "Call Tommy and have him download what we came up with on two-eighty-three."

"In the meantime?"

"I'm going over to my embassy to have a little chat with Mario Garza, and tonight I'm taking you to dinner at the Connaught, if you can get us a reservation." Lane telephoned Stewart's office. "This is Bill Lane. What time does Mr. Stewart usually leave for the day?"

"Five sharp," the woman said.

"Could you ask him to remain a little later tonight. I'd like to see him at five-thirty. I'll have something solid for him by then."

"Of course, sir."

"What are you up to, William?" Frances asked after Lane hung up.

"No good, Frannie, absolutely no good." He kissed her on the cheek. "I'll pick you up at your house at seven."

7

LONDON

Lane took a cab over to Frances's house to make sure that Morgan had stationed some people to watch the place. They were in a plain dark blue Toyota van in front, and another in the rear. Next, he had the cabbie drive him over to an ironmonger in Finchley Road, where he purchased two ice picks, a hacksaw, a pair of vise grips, and a small file.

Back at his hotel, he took off his jacket, loosened his

tie, and rolled up his sleeves. Clamping the wooden handle of the first ice-pick in the vise grips, he filed the metal case-hardened pick to the approximate thickness of a pencil lead, then cut it from the handle. He did the same with the second ice pick, then cleaned up the mess, disposing of the tools and debris at the end of the corridor one floor down in a service-alcove trash receptacle.

Calling from a pay phone across the street from the SIS a few minutes before five, he made sure that Frances had already left for the day to pick up her car, before he went over, signed in, and was allowed upstairs to their third-floor office. He had concealed the ice-pick blades in two ballpoint pens from which he had removed the cartridges so they did not show up on the scanner.

Picking up the downloaded file on the NSA's search for 283, he took the elevator up to the fifth floor, where the guards confirmed that he had an appointment with Roger Stewart in twenty minutes, and let him pass.

Stewart's office was around the corner from the elevator and guard station, as was 503, which was Hartley Schilling's suite of offices.

The corridor was deserted as he passed Stewart's office and removed the ice-pick blades from his pens. Suite 503 was locked, but the building was old, and the lock was relatively easy. He had it open in under fifteen seconds, slipped inside, and relocked the door.

The British, even more than Americans, were class-conscious. Bosses were separated from the worker bees. So while the work of the Resources Advisory Section was done around the clock, Hartley Schilling and his personal secretary kept regular office hours, trusting security to the guards on the first floor and those at the elevator on the fifth.

Schilling's suite was not quite as large as Stewart's, but the layout was similar, with a secretary in front, and his own office overlooking the river. In this case, however, since it was a corner office, there was a rear exit to a stairwell, alarmed from the outside, but not from within. It was a bit of insurance that Lane had not expected.

He sat down at Schilling's desk, laid the NSA file aside, and booted up the computer.

"Good evening, Mr. Schilling," the machine-generated voice said.

The British arrogance also included passwords. Upper-level directors didn't need them.

"Good evening," Lane entered on the keyboard. "I would like to initiate a current file search."

"Do you have a subject or file reference?" the computer asked.

"Former Ukrainian KGB officers Mikhail Maslennikov and Valeri Yernin. I would like to see the results of the current law enforcement and RAS search for them."

"Searching," the computer said, its machine-generated voice sounding slightly feminine.

A full minute later the computer continued.

"No current information."

"Has a customs and passport search been instituted?"

"Yes."

"What is its range and duration."

"Primarily London carriers, twelve hours and fifty-six minutes. Do you wish to see the entire record?"

"No," Lane entered on the keyboard. "In your estimation is either subject currently in Great Britain."

"Maslennikov, Mikhail, was identified in London. Yernin, Valeri, was reportedly involved in an incident near Oxford. Do you wish to see the entire record?"

"No. In your estimation has either subject entered or departed Great Britain in time of duration?"

"Unknown."

"Based on your current information, what is the probability that either subject would have been identified crossing a British border?"

"Eighty-seven percent. Do you wish to see a complete analysis?"

"No," Lane replied. "What is your current information on the search for a Russian Romeo-class submarine, sail number 283, possibly in British waters?"

The computer did not answer.

"Repeating the request," Lane typed.

The computer was silent.

Lane tried to back out of the program, but his keyboard no longer responded.

He got a piece of Scotch tape from Schilling's desk, opened the stairwell door, and taped the latch bolt so that the door would remain unlocked when it was closed.

He grabbed the NSA file and went to the outer door, opening it a crack. The corridor was still deserted. He let himself out, hurried down the hall, and entered Stewart's office just as a commotion arose around the corner at the elevator security station.

8

LONDON

"Ah, Mr. Lane. Mr. Stewart is waiting for you," Stewart's secretary said. "I'll just tell him that you're here."

When she went inside, Lane hurriedly put the lock picks inside the two ballpoint pens, and was just pocketing them when she came back out.

"You may go in now, sir," she said, gathering her coat and purse. "And I'll say good evening, because I'm off." She smiled warmly. "And let me offer my congratulations on your engagement. Frances is a lovely girl.''

"That she is," Lane said, and he kissed the woman on the cheek, causing her to blush, then went inside.

Stewart was also getting ready to leave, his topcoat and bowler lying on the arm of the couch, his desk clear except for a single, rather thick file folder. "I have an early appointment with the foreign secretary at his club, so thank you for being prompt, Mr. Lane," he said. "What do you have for me?"

Lane handed him the NSA report that Hughes had downloaded that afternoon. "The Russian submarine was in the English Channel as of a few days ago, and neither Yernin nor his control officer apparently crossed any British border, which means they, and therefore the submarine, are still here."

Stewart motioned Lane to take a chair, but he put the NSA report down without opening it, and gave him a rigid stare. "I don't quite know what to do about you."

"Sir?"

"I thought I knew all there was to know about you when we spoke this morning. Although your methods seem to be somewhat unorthodox, and apparently you have had a great deal of difficulty in following orders, you do get the job done. Though not without a great deal of bloodshed."

"I don't usually shoot first, Mr. Director."

"No, but shoot you do. Last year you assassinated Saddam Hussein."

"Self-defense—"

Stewart held up a hand. "But your mission was to penetrate Iraq's border, seek out the man, and kill him, was it not?"

Lane returned the man's stare. "Yes it was."

"A mission which Commander Shipley became involved with only after lying to her control officer, and probably sharing with you certain information that was quite sensitive to this government."

"It was a two-way street."

"Apparently," Stewart said dryly. "The question is what is Her Majesty's government to do about you now? Short of relieving Commander Shipley from her duties, and making you persona non grata, I see no other options."

"Valeri Yernin murdered two British citizens."

"For which Scotland Yard is in hot pursuit. Sir Leonard, if you didn't know, was a family friend, so I too have a keen interest in seeing the man brought to justice. But my point is, had you not entered England illegally in pursuit of this submarine, it would likely have sailed peaceably through the Channel, and down the coast to Sierra Leone, or whatever its ultimate destination is. None of which was of any concern to this government until your presence lured Yernin here." Stewart looked directly into Lane's eyes. "Do you catch my meaning?"

"Perfectly," Lane said. "But we can't back up the clock. Yernin and the submarine are here, and Frances and I are the bait to catch them."

"So long as you remain on British soil," Stewart said. "I'll ask you, as a gentleman, to return to your hotel, pack your bags, and leave England on the morning Concorde."

"What if I refuse?"

"That is not an option."

"What about Frances?"

"That will depend entirely on her. If indeed you two are to be married, I assume she will live in the United States with you, because you will not be allowed to return to England."

"Are you restricting my movements tonight?"

"Providing you break no further laws, no."

Lane got up, and Stewart held the NSA report out to him. "This is yours."

"Keep it, Mr. Director," Lane said. "I think you're going to need it more than I will."

The door to Schilling's offices was open, and one of the guards from the elevator security station stood looking inside, as Lane walked around the corner and signed out with the remaining guard.

"What's the fuss at the end of the hall?" he asked.

"I wouldn't know, sir," the guard said.

"Well, I'm off. Good night now."

9

LONDON

SIS Internal Security sergeant Fred Rudolph discovered the taped door latch almost immediately. He keyed his walkie-talkie. "This is Rudolph. Looks like he took the east stairwell from five-oh-three."

"I'm right there."

"Watch yourself."

Sergeant Rudolph's partner, Gerald Novak, settled his impressive bulk in front of Schilling's computer, which was locked into the last unauthorized query that had been made. "You'd better take a look at this, Fred."

Rudolph came over and looked at the screen. "I thought he was looking for what he had on that pair of Ukrainians."

"Apparently he's making a connection. I don't think he was merely fishing."

"I don't think so either. He was after something very specific. Question is how the hell did he get through the stairwell door. The alarm is still intact."

Novak used a special security override password which unlocked the computer terminal, and backed up the series of queries. "He got in at five-fifteen, and he was automatically locked out at five-twenty-one."

Rudolph checked his watch. It was 5:35. He keyed his walkie-talkie. "This is Rudolph. Any sign of him yet?"

"Nothing."

"He's had a fourteen-minute head start. Seal off all the exits. No one gets out without personal recognition, and I want all their names, no matter who it is. As soon as that's done, we'll start a floor-by-floor."

"He may already be out."

"Let's hope not."

"This is part of an Eastern Hemisphere Operation," Novak said.

Rudolph's long face looked resigned. He nodded. "Then we'd best call Mr. Morgan, as well as Mr. Schilling."

"You're the boss."

"Yeah," Rudolph said without enthusiasm.

10

LONDON

They caught Morgan on his cell phone on the way home, but it was nearly seven before he got back to SIS headquarters and up to the fifth floor, where Rudolph and Novak waited for him. They'd not been able to reach Schilling, though the RAS night duty officer, David Lundein, promised to keep trying. It was Lundein who'd blown the whistle on the computer hacker.

"What were they after?" Morgan asked.

Internal Security had dusted the office doors for fingerprints once they discovered that the lock had been picked. The building lockdown and floor-by-floor search had produced nothing. A guard, posted inside Schilling's office, thought it was akin to locking the barn door after the horse had escaped.

"That's why we called you, Mr. Morgan," Rudolph said. "They got into the program you're running on the two Ukrainians and the Russian submarine."

"Son of a bitch. How'd they get in?"

"Through the corridor door, and then probably made their getaway down the east stairs. We just weren't quick enough."

"I mean how did they get into the building in the first place, you idiot?"

Rudolph shook his head. "We haven't got that figured out yet, sir. Probably was someone on the inside. Someone from this floor."

Morgan turned and looked down the corridor toward the elevator security station. "Or came up in the elevator."

"They would have passed through my people."

Morgan's blood pressure was on the rise. He despised stupidity. But he held his temper in check. "Was Bill Lane up here this evening?"

"Yes, sir, and he was our first thought, because the times match."

"But?"

"He had an appointment with Mr. Stewart. I personally talked to his secretary, who said Mr. Lane was with Mr. Stewart the entire time."

"What time was his appointment with Stewart?"

"Five-thirty."

"What time was Schilling's computer in use?"

Rudolph consulted his notebook. "Five-fifteen to five-twenty-one."

Morgan strode down the corridor to the security station and snatched the in/out long. Lane had signed in at 5:10, and had signed back out at 5:31.

"Bloody hell," he said to himself. He picked up the telephone and dialed an outside number. It was answered on the first ring.

"Scotland Yard, Special Investigations Division."

"This is Morgan, let me talk to Benchley."

11

LONDON

Back at his hotel Lane changed his shirt and tie, grabbed a quick shave, and took a cab to within a block of Frances's apartment, arriving there a few minutes before seven. The rain had stopped, but the evening had turned bitterly cold. Those few pedestrians out and about did not linger.

He crossed the street and walked to her apartment. As he turned in at her gate, two men jumped out of the blue Toyota van and hurried up behind him, one of them with his gun drawn.

"Excuse me, sir," one of them said.

Lane turned. "Good to see you. Has she had any other visitors tonight? Anyone interested in her place?"

"Ah, Mr. Lane," he said, holstering his gun. "No, sir. It's been quiet. Are you and Commander Shipley going out this evening?"

"Dinner at the Connaught."

"Very good, sir. We'll have a team follow you."

"If anything is going to happen, it'll be soon. Probably within the next twenty-four to thirty-six hours. So watch yourself. This guy is good."

"Yes, sir."

12

LONDON

Each time Frances saw Lane her heart accelerated, and she felt a little thrill of pleasure in her stomach. And if that wasn't love she didn't know what was. But as she watched the exchange on the front stoop from her bedroom window, she also felt a stab of fear and anguish. She felt as if she were riding an out-of-control roller coaster that she was helpless to stop, and that William with all of his talent was equally helpless. There was no reason, she kept repeating to herself, for Yernin to have killed Uncle Leonard and Albert. Yet she understood perfectly well why he had done it, and that he'd very nearly succeeded in his plan to kill her and William.

She laid her forehead against the cool glass as the doorbell rang, and Mrs. Houlten let him in. She suddenly couldn't see her future with him, and that frightened her the most at this moment, because she knew that she wanted him with every fiber of her being, but she didn't know how to do it.

"Frances dear, Mr. William is here," Mrs. Houlten called from the bottom of the stairs.

"I'll be just a minute," she called down. She went into the bathroom and looked at her reflection in the mirror. She'd been crying without realizing it, and her eyes were red. Her father would have told her that she was just being an emotional woman, but then he would have held her. She daubed a cold washcloth on her face, then dried herself and touched up her makeup.

Lane was sitting at the counter in the kitchen drinking a glass of Chardonnay with Mrs. Houlten, who was beaming ear to ear.

"You wicked child, why didn't you tell me?" Mrs. Houlten asked, trying, but failing, to be stern.

"So the cat's out of the bag," Frances said, and she and her housekeeper hugged.

"With all that's been happening around here it's time for some happiness to come your way," the woman said in Frances's ear.

"It'd make me happy if you packed up and went to Edinburgh," Frances said.

"I'll not leave," Mrs. Houlten replied stubbornly. "And I won't hear such talk."

"I could fire you."

The housekeeper pursed her lips. "That you could." She stared directly at Frances, who finally shook her head.

"I don't think we'll be late, it's already been a long day."

"There are men in front and back watching the house," Lane assured her. "You'll be all right here."

Mrs. Houlten smiled faintly. "I have no doubt about that, Mr. William. None whatsoever. What would he want with an old woman like me?"

Lane and Frances exchanged a glance but said nothing to her.

In the front hall Lane helped Frances on with her coat, and they were about to leave when the doorbell rang. Lane reached inside his coat for his gun as Frances checked the peephole.

She looked back and shook her head, then opened the door. The two Scotland Yard surveillance officers from the blue van in front had been joined by another stern-faced pair.

"Good evening, Commander," one of them said. He held out his badge. "Sergeant Turner, Scotland Yard Counterespionage Division."

Frances's chest constricted. "What can I do for you this evening, Sergeant?"

"It's not you, Commander. It's Mr. Lane."

Lane stepped into view, and the cop's jaw tightened a little.

"Sir, are you armed at this moment?"

"I am."

"May I have your gun, sir?" the sergeant said. The others stood feet apart, their jackets open.

Lane withdrew his gun and handed it over. "What's this all about?"

"Sir, I have a warrant for your arrest."

"On what charge?" Frances demanded.

"Espionage, Commander," Sergeant Turner said evenly.

Lane held out his hands for the cuffs. "Give Tommy a call for me," he told Frances. He smiled. "Sorry about dinner. Will you take a rain check?"

PART NINE

1

It was a few minutes after three in the afternoon when Tom Hughes picked up Frances's telephone call from London, not knowing, but accurately guessing, why she was calling.

"What kind of trouble has he gotten himself into this time? Nothing too serious, I hope."

"Scotland Yard arrested him," she said. "They're going to charge him with espionage."

"What'd he do, steal the queen's jewels?"

"Worse. He broke into one of our computer databases."

"Which one?"

"The RAS," Frances said, not bothering to lower her voice. If the SIS was monitoring her telephone it wouldn't matter.

"He didn't try to resist, did he?"

"No."

"Thank God for small favors, at least," Hughes said. "I'll see if I can pull a few strings. It'll turn out okay, Frannie."

"It bloody well better," Frances said. "Because Yernin won't give up, and William thinks the submarine is still in British waters. On top of all that, the man has asked me to marry him."

"You have to admire his sense of timing." Hughes chuckled. "But now tell me everything that happened."

When he was finished with Frances, he telephoned

Ben Lewis. "Tell Mr. Roswell that you and I are on the way up."

"There's been no word from the White House," Lewis said. "Or has something else come up?"

"It'll be easier if I explain it just the one time, Ben."

"Very well."

Hughes put on his jacket, straightened his tie, and took the elevator up to the sixth-floor office of Thomas Roswell, director of the National Security Agency. Lewis, whose office was two floors above Hughes's, was already there, and they were ushered straight in.

"I haven't heard from Newby yet, and I don't think we should press them just now," Roswell said. Leslie Newby, the president's adviser on national security affairs, was a difficult but fair-minded man who saw both sides of any issue because he was a politician. Roswell, on the other hand, was more like a general, direct, straightforward, and end-game oriented.

"That's exactly what we must do, Mr. Director," Hughes said. "Because the Brits have arrested William and are going to charge him with espionage."

"This is getting completely out of hand. Newby was willing to intervene because that submarine was of some interest to the White House's new African policy. But it's just one submarine, after all, and an old one a hemisphere away."

"It's no longer simply about one submarine, Mr. Director. Now it's become an issue of Valeri Yernin. He won't stop until William is dead."

"It's a problem that won't go away on its own," Lewis put in.

Roswell gave them both one of his famous bulldog stares. "What's Lane done to upset the British?"

"He got into an SIS computer database," Hughes said. "The RAS."

"It's a wonder they didn't have him shot." Roswell

shook his head. "Newby is not going to take this to the president. I can guarantee it."

"He has to," Hughes said.

"And you're going to tell me why."

"Mikhail Maslennikov, Valeri Yernin, and a submarine. Makes for a powerful, dangerous combination. One which I think ultimately won't have anything to do with Sierra Leone."

"I'm listening."

"William thinks that Maslennikov may have amassed a substantial fortune for himself in the year since he and Yernin disappeared. Perhaps in excess of a hundred million dollars."

"Is there any proof?" Lewis asked.

"I don't know," Hughes admitted. "But William's hunches are usually close to the mark."

"Was that what he was fishing for inside the SIS?" Roswell asked.

"I don't know that either. But it's a safe bet that whatever he went looking for is important. Otherwise he wouldn't have taken the risk."

"All right, assuming that everything you say is true, that Lane's hunch this time is on the mark, what's your point?"

"With that kind of money, with an operational submarine and well-motivated crew, and with the skills of a killer like Yernin, Maslennikov would become a dangerous force. Because once he breaks out of the English Channel, he might be impossible to stop."

"You're telling me that he's become a pirate?"

"Why not?" Hughes replied. "If we move fast we might be able to stop him now, before it's too late. Think what kind of damage he could do with that submarine."

"For instance?"

"He might hold the Panama Canal for ransom by threatening to torpedo, let's say, an oil tanker in the middle of one of the locks. Maybe threaten the *QE II*, or some cruise boat filled with a couple of thousand American tourists in the Caribbean.''

''He'd have to have a base of operations,'' Lewis said.

Hughes shrugged. ''Maybe Sierra Leone. Maybe anywhere in the world. A Romeo-class submarine has a range of nineteen thousand miles.''

''I see your point.''

Roswell had his secretary put a call through to Newby at the White House. ''What's the president's schedule look like in the next half hour or so?''

''He's booked solid, but there's nothing we can't reschedule. What's up?''

''Something interesting, and potentially harmful.''

''How much time do you need?''

''Ten minutes. I'm bringing Tom Hughes with me. He can lay it out for the president.''

''This have to do with Bill Lane?'' Newby asked, suddenly on guard.

''Yes, it does. But something new has come up. It's important, Leslie.''

''Ten minutes,'' Newby said.

''We're on our way.''

2

THE WHITE HOUSE

The president of the United States spent a few minutes alone with his thoughts after Tom Roswell and Tom Hughes had finished their briefing and left the Oval Office. He stared out of the bowed windows at the Rose Garden, bare now in the winter. Nothing had gone the way he'd hoped it would after his reelection. His predecessor had warned him that the longer a president remained in office the more mired in chicken shit he would become.

Well, President Reasoner told himself, he was up to his neck in it now.

He picked up his phone and had his secretary call the British prime minister. While he waited for the call to go through he thought about Bill Lane, who in the last two years had twice nearly given his life for his country.

Lane had no family that the president knew about, only an uncle who'd made some money as a real estate developer, and on his death had left it all to his only nephew. By all rights Lane should have been a playboy, with his handsome good looks, his charm, his intelligence, and his flair for style. Instead he worked as an analyst for the NSA.

It was a waste of talent, the president thought, and he was wondering what better use could be made of Mr. Lane when the prime minister of England came on the line.

"Good evening, Mr. President."

"Good evening to you, Mr. Prime Minister," Reasoner said. "I called because I need your help with a ticklish matter."

"Of course. Anything I can do."

3
---

10 DOWNING STREET

Secret Intelligence Service director Sir Hubert Blaine and his director of clandestine operations, Roger Stewart, were directed into the prime minister's cabinet room a few minutes before 9:00 P.M. With his thick build and muttonchops Sir Hubert was the exact opposite of Stewart, but this evening he shared his DCO's mystification. Neither man knew why they had been summoned, Sir Hubert from home, Stewart from his club.

An aide poured them each a brandy, and moments later the prime minister, dressed in evening clothes, came in and motioned for them to take a seat.

"I won't keep you long, gentlemen. I myself have to get to a reception at the Japanese embassy before they think my absence odd."

"I understand completely, Mr. Prime Minister," Sir Hubert said. "What exactly is it that you wanted to speak to us about?"

"William Lane."

Sir Hubert's eyes narrowed, and he turned to Stewart. "Does this name mean anything to you?"

"He's an American intelligence analyst. Works for the National Security Agency."

"Scotland Yard's Counterespionage Division arrested him a couple of hours ago," the prime minister said. "He's to be charged with spying on us."

"I didn't know that," Stewart said, nonplussed.

The prime minister pushed a thin file across to them.

"This is a précis of a telephone conversation I had with President Reasoner this evening. It sums up the situation. Take it with you."

"Yes, Prime Minister," Sir Hubert said. "Do you wish for a special disposition of this matter?"

"Release him," the prime minister said.

"Sir?"

"I want a full investigation, naturally. And if Mr. Lane has indeed spied on us for his government, in a matter that has nothing to do with the reason he came here in the first place, then he will be rearrested and tried for his alleged crime. Is that quite clear?"

"Quite," Sir Hubert said. "In the interim?"

"President Reasoner asked that we help him." The prime minister glared at Stewart. "And I promised that we would."

"Yes, sir."

"Is it my understanding that there have already been deaths. British citizens?"

Stewart nodded. "Sir Leonard Styles, and his man."

The prime minister thought about that for a moment. "I would like this resolved at the soonest possible date. Put everything you have on it. Whatever Mr. Lane wants, he shall have."

"It may involve the navy," Stewart suggested.

"I don't care if it involves the queen mother. Get it done, at the soonest possible moment, with the minimum possible fuss."

"Yes, Prime Minister," Sir Hubert said. "You shan't be bothered with this again."

"I hope not."

4

SCOTLAND YARD

A car was waiting on Whitehall Street when Lane was released around 10:00 P.M. and he walked out the front door. A driver was behind the wheel, and Brad Morgan sat in the back, talking to someone on a cell phone. He looked up when Lane walked over and opened the door.

"Did you come to pick me up?" Lane asked.

Morgan cleared the phone. "We're going back to the office. Get in."

"Let's walk," Lane said. The SIS was less than two blocks away. He started away, and Morgan caught up with him.

"Well you've got us all by the short Hairs now," Morgan said bitterly.

"Who called whom?"

"I don't know. But before you ask, Frances is okay. She's on her way to the office now. All the stops are being pulled out for you, and it's not because of any admiration. We want to get rid of you as soon as possible."

Lane turned to him. "Good enough, Brad. But a word of advice. Get past what's eating at you. Okay?"

Morgan looked at him, his expression sour. "If I get the chance I'll cut you off at the knees, and piss on the bloody stumps."

Lane grinned. "It's what I admire most about you Brits. Your way with words." He walked off, leaving Morgan shaking with rage.

5

SIS HEADQUARTERS

Frances was waiting with Roger Stewart in the fifth-floor conference room when Lane and Morgan came up. The NSA file on the submarine was lying on the polished mahogany table.

"We're going to help you find the submarine, and run Maslennikov and Yernin to ground," Stewart said. "But you're going to have to help us too."

"That was the whole idea in the first place."

Frances gave him a secret smile of triumph. "You must be starved."

"Actually no," Lane said. "I had fish-and-chips. But they wouldn't let me have a beer so I had tea. How about you?"

"Mrs. Houlten fixed me a bite."

"I'm sure that's all well and good, Lane," Stewart said, vexed. "But would you mind telling us what we're up against? Give us something to go on?"

Lane opened the NSA file, extracted several eight-by-ten photographs, and spread them out on the table. "It's a Russian Romeo-class diesel-electric submarine, sail number two-eighty-three, built in Gorky around 1961 or 1962." He looked up at Stewart. "Have you read the file?"

"I glanced through it," he said. "That's a very old submarine. Not much of a threat, I'd think."

"These were updated in the late seventies and early eighties, with better electronics, weapons, and fire-control systems. In the end they even carried nuclear-tipped torpedoes. Whatever the age, that's a potent sting."

"They're quiet too," Frances said.

They looked at her.

"Diesel-electric boats can be rigged to make less noise than nuclear submarines. If they stay on the bottom they're hard to find."

"That's right," Lane said. "This one managed to pull off a disappearing act under the nose of the Russian navy up at Polyarnyy. A crew of fourteen men were supposed to scuttle her, and then get off. Supposedly there was an accident and they went down with the sub."

"All hands lost?" Stewart asked.

"That's right," Lane said.

"What's the normal complement of that class of submarine?" Morgan asked.

"Fifty-four."

"Fourteen men could scuttle it, but they couldn't sail this far."

"Don't be so sure about that," Lane said. "With the right fourteen men, all of them officers, well trained, highly motivated. The cream of the crop. Handpicked by Maslennikov. Anything is possible."

"The Russians wouldn't have loaded active weapons aboard a submarine they were planning on scuttling," Stewart said.

"I might agree if the actual plan was to sink the boat," Lane said. "After all, Maslennikov and the men loyal to him are all Ukrainians, not Russians."

"Are you trying to tell us that a Ukrainian crew stole a submarine from the Russians?" Morgan said with a smirk.

"Not at all. I'm saying Maslennikov bought the boat. And until I came along and offered the Russians a better deal Moscow didn't give a damn what the sub's ultimate destination would be."

"How did your shop find out about it?" Stewart asked. "I need to know, because we're not going to respond to mere guesswork."

Lane took out several pages of radio intercepts and spread them on the table along with a standard Robinson projection of the Northern Hemisphere, the African continent at the bottom.

"The CIA picked up a rumor that the government of Sierra Leone was in the market for a submarine. Any submarine, from any source. They need to change the balance of power if they're going to stand up to Liberia much longer."

"What'd you pick up?" Stewart asked.

"Nothing direct, at least nothing that told us the rumor was true. But I thought that if Russia were to try to sell a sub to a military junta like the one in power in Sierra Leone, there'd be a lot of objections. The sale would never go through. But Russia needs money, and they'd be willing to sell a surplus submarine if they could pull it off. So I went looking in the Barents Sea off the submarine base at Polyarnyy. The Russian navy's graveyard. If they could fake a sinking they might be able to deliver the sub after all."

"Then there was an accident with two-eighty-three," Frances prompted.

"Right," Lane said. "Which we picked up on Russian navy radio and data traffic." He pulled the map around. "The green line is the probable course that a submarine would have to take to get from Polyarnyy to Sierra Leone. The blue hash marks are the probable daily positions the submarine would reach on that track, at a normal cruising speed." He looked up at them. "The four red marks are the positions and times of subsea anomalies that were reported by our underwater listening posts out there, as well as a couple of other sources."

"What other sources?" Morgan demanded.

"Norwegian, Swedish, and German ASW patrol ships."

"Without their cooperation or knowledge, I suppose."

Lane shrugged, then turned back to the chart. "No coincidence," he said. "And no coincidence that the track points toward the English Channel, that there've been no sightings out the other side, and that Maslennikov and Yernin are here."

"I checked with a navy friend of mine down in Portsmouth," Morgan said. "He got excited when I started talking about Russian submarines, but he promised to keep his mouth shut for the time being. Point is that no Russian submarine has been spotted anywhere within British waters, including the Channel."

"If it came in quietly, and settled on the bottom in some secluded bay somewhere, it could have gotten through undetected," Lane said.

"That doesn't make much sense. According to my friend, if that submarine were heading for the west coast of Africa, it would have sailed north of the Faeroe Islands, well outside British waters, before turning south. There was no reason for them to risk being detected taking the route you suggest. The Channel is one of the busiest stretches of water anywhere in the world."

"That's a good assumption," Lane said. "Because no matter why Maslennikov and Yernin were here in England, they could have gotten to Sierra Leone very easily on their own. They didn't have to be picked up by a rogue submarine. Too risky."

Stewart was studying the chart on which 283's probable track and been laid out. "But that doesn't fit the facts as you see them," he said, looking up at Lane. "You've brought us this far, what's the next step?"

Lane went to the windows and looked down at the Thames and out across the huge city, fairly quiet because of the hour. He was aware that the others were staring at him, but he remained motionless at the windows, his deep blue eyes locked onto a truck crossing the Westminster Bridge. Stewart came over to him.

"We're going to cooperate with you, Mr. Lane. You have my word on it. But we can't go off in all directions, or worse yet, blind. We have to have something to go on. Something other than a hunch."

After a long moment Lane looked at him. "You're right."

"Well then?"

"I didn't come here to look for Maslennikov or Yernin. I didn't even come looking for two-eighty-three. It was the Russians who sent me here. It was their show, their boat that they wanted to sell me. And I didn't make the connection until Maslennikov showed up at Comrade Markov's house. The same Markov that your people and the CIA were watching because of the raids on the Russian offshore accounts. Are you starting to catch my drift?"

"I see what you're getting at."

"Your own computers confirmed the fact that Maslennikov and Yernin did not cross any border, which means they're here in England and have been the entire time."

"But you said Maslennikov was at the bank in Zürich," Morgan pointed out.

"That was before we were looking for him," Lane said. "Maslennikov and Yernin are here, along with the money and gold they've amassed, and they mean to load it aboard two-eighty-three and break out into the open Atlantic."

"For Sierra Leone?" Stewart asked. "Because if that's the case we'd know their probable course and we could intercept them."

"Maybe Sierra Leone, maybe not," Lane said. "Maybe they've changed their minds."

"Because of you?" Stewart asked.

Lane nodded.

"Then we'll have to find them before they get out of British waters."

Lane walked back to the conference table and pulled out a large-scale map of the English Channel from the North Sea approaches to the tip of Land's End, which opened to the Atlantic.

"There are a million places along our coast to hide a submarine," Morgan said. "Islands, back bays. It'd be impossible to find it if the captain is smart enough to stay put and make no noise."

"Not impossible, Brad," Lane said. "In fact if they do lay low they'll be even easier to find."

"I suppose you're going to show us how," Morgan said with a smirk.

Lane nodded. He glanced at his watch. "First I need to make a secured phone call to Washington. It'll probably take a few hours before I get the answers I need, but when I do we can go sub hunting."

"Are you going to explain to us what you're trying to do?" Morgan demanded.

"Later, because I don't know if I will be able to get the authorization," Lane said. "In the meantime maybe we can get some rest, because I think we're going to need it."

"You can use the phone in my office," Stewart said. "It'll be easier that way, instead of picking Schilling's lock again."

"Thanks." Lane grinned, and they all missed the look of abject hatred that flickered across Morgan's face.

6

LONDON

Lane had a feeling that Hughes would still be at the office even though it was quitting time over there, and he was right; answered on the first ring. Lane spoke for five minutes, during which time Hughes asked only one question to clear up a point. When he was finished Hughes promised to get back to him as soon as possible, even though what they were trying to do was a long shot. It was a big ocean out there, and one submerged boat little more than 250 feet long was a very small target.

"Thanks for pulling the right strings," Lane said.

Hughes laughed. "I have a feeling that I'm just getting started."

7

LONDON

Markov paused under the streetlamp in front of his house so that anybody watching would be certain to identify him, then crossed to his Mercedes and climbed in the backseat. One of his bodyguards was in the back with him, and the other was in front with the driver.

They passed the high-rise apartment building at the corner from where they were pretty sure the SIS was watching his house, and he resisted the urge to glance at it. They would be curious about his going to the embassy tonight, but not overly so. From time to time he went to his office to work, sometimes staying as late as one or two in the morning. Sometimes the ambassador would join him, and they would spend the night eating herring, caviar, and blinis while drinking vodka and reminiscing about the old days. On those occasions he would not leave the embassy until well after dawn.

In his long career Markov had never caused another man's death. He'd primarily been a paper shuffler, an administrator. But all that was about to change, and he was having a little trouble dealing with his emotions. On the one hand he thought that now would be as good a time as any to defect, although a few Russian defectors recently had been turned away by the United States, and sent back to Russia. So there was that risk. But there was an equally big risk that the operation against Bill Lane would blow up in his face. The Cubans would take the fall, of course, but so might he. So it might be a matter of whose prison system he spent time in—his own or the British.

The third alternative would be to flee to the Cayman Islands, where he'd stashed nearly three million dollars. He'd often dreamed of lying on the warm white sand beaches, sipping piña coladas while surrounding himself with beautiful young brown-skinned women in bikinis.

That might last a month or two, but he would get bored, the money would run out, or General Korzhakov would arrange for an incident. Perhaps a house fire, an automobile accident, or a boat sinking. Something. But paradise wouldn't last. He chuckled morosely.

"Sir?" his guard Viktor Lychev beside him asked.

"I was thinking out loud," Markov said. "Do you want to come with me tonight?"

"Of course." Lychev brightened.

"Don't be so quick to volunteer. The mission might fail, and we'd be sent home. But if we're successful we could end up in prison."

Lychev thought about that for a moment. "The Americans think they own the world."

"They do."

A slow frown spread across Lychev's pockmarked face. "Not all of it, Mr. Markov. Not all of the time."

"What's your problem with Bill Lane?"

"I saw his file."

"Da?"

"If he were to go down, the people responsible would do well."

"No reward was offered, Viktor."

Lychev looked at him. "For my own satisfaction then, because he thinks that we're all subhuman. Buffoons. *Neokulturny.*"

"And you're bored in London with nothing to do," Markov said. "Is that it? Do you want to flex your muscles?"

Lychev nodded.

"Good, Viktor. Very good."

They reached the embassy, and in the rear parking lot got out of the Mercedes and went inside.

Markov went upstairs to his office, where he changed into a pair of dark slacks and a dark turtleneck sweater. He took a 9mm Makarov and holster out of his desk and threaded it through his belt, settling the gun at the small of his back, like they'd taught him at School One. He'd used the gun so seldom he wondered if it would fire or was rusted shut. He hoped he wouldn't have to find out tonight. But reading the files on the Cuban hit team, he wasn't going anywhere near them without being armed.

The embassy was quiet a half hour later when he went

downstairs to the rear exit. Lychev was waiting for him in the dark corridor.

"Did you bring a gun, Mr. Markov?"

"Yes."

"A silencer?"

"No."

"It's just as well. If anything happens, the more noise we make the better off we'll be."

Markov patted his bodyguard on the shoulder. "Let me do the talking. They're supposed to be working for us. And they were sent here for just this kind of an assignment." Markov zippered up his dark nylon windbreaker. "Let's go."

8

LONDON

St. Katherine's Dock in the lee of the Tower Bridge had once been a vital part of the Port of London. Over the years the entire area had fallen into disrepair. Though some of the dock and warehouses had been refurbished into stylish marinas and apartment buildings, the fringes were still questionable.

A light drizzle had begun to fall by the time Lychev, his baseball cap still pulled low over his eyes, pulled behind an old riverfront warehouse under reconstruction. A tall chain-link fence surrounded the building.

Markov, who'd been lying on the floor in the back of the Toyota minivan since they'd left the embassy, rose up as Lychev shut off the headlights and engine and gave the all clear.

"Are you sure we weren't followed?"

Lychev glanced in the rearview mirror. *"Da."*

They got out and followed the fence down a shallow rubble-strewn gully to a section of wood-and-stone dock with big rusted iron bars and spikes jutting out at all angles. Fifty yards downriver, a derelict work barge, its stubby crane drooping over the flat bow, was tied to big iron rings, a wooden gangplank reaching down to the tilted deck. Dim lights shone in the dirty windows, and a thin wisp of smoke curled up from the tin chimney.

Something moved behind the tall concrete pilings across the dock from the work barge. Markov and Lychev stopped.

"You are trespassing here," someone called from somewhere on the barge. The English was heavily accented.

"We've come to see Carlos Palma," Markov said.

"Who is that?"

"A friend of Manuel Báez. I have immediate need of both of them," Markov said. "As well as the others."

A man appeared from behind the pilings, and the one on the boat stepped out from behind a donkey engine on the foredeck. "Señor Markov?"

"Yes."

"I am Báez. Who is your friend?"

"My bodyguard."

The one on the dock laughed, and spit into the river. "I'm Palma. Go aboard, then, *compar,* because I for one want to do something to get off this shit hole as soon as possible. Whatever it is."

They went up to the main saloon on the second level behind the bridge. Four Cubans sat around a large table. They'd been drinking beer and watching television. One of them reached for a pistol on the table.

"It's cool, Miguel," Palma told him. "These are friends."

They were slightly built, hard looking, like construction workers. Expendable, the file promised.

Markov walked over to the television set and turned it off. "Sit down. I have an assignment for you that has to be taken care of as soon as possible."

Palma and Báez exchanged a look of expectation, then sat down with their men. Lychev, his jacket unzipped, stood by the door watching them.

Markov took a pair of surgical rubber gloves out of his jacket pocket and pulled them on. The Cubans watched him nervously.

"The man's name is Bill Lane," Markov said. He took a plain white envelope from his pocket and tossed it on the table.

Palma understood that the envelope and whatever it contained would be free of fingerprints until he touched it. "What about after this assignment?" he asked.

"Back to Havana."

Again Palma exchanged a glance with Báez, but then shrugged and opened the envelope, which contained a map of downtown London, and a half dozen snapshots that Markov's people had taken.

"Who is this guy?"

"He's an American intelligence officer here in London," Markov said.

"And the woman?"

"Frances Shipley. She's a British intelligence officer working with Lane."

Palma studied the photos and passed them down the table one by one. "You want them dead, that right?"

"Tonight, if possible. But no later than tomorrow night."

"No time for planning. Even if we do catch up with them, it'll be messy, señor. Very loud and very messy. Is this what you want?"

"I want them dead, and you and your people out of London immediately afterward," Markov said. "How you accomplish that is totally up to you. But you won't get paid until the job is done, and until you're back home.''

Báez was shaking his head. "This is no good. We have the firepower, but what about transportation?''

"Steal it just before the hit," Markov said, before Palma could reply. "It'll be untraceable.''

"Not if we do one and then have to find the other one," Báez said.

"Lane is the primary target. If the woman is with him, then kill them both. Otherwise just kill Lane and then get out."

"How do we get out?" Báez tossed one of the photos down. "These are intelligence officers, which means there'll be a lot of heat.''

"You were sent to me as a self-sufficient team," Markov said. "Are you telling me otherwise? Because if you are, I'll send you back now, and get someone else.''

Palma raised a hand. "We can do this thing and get out, as you wish. But Manuel is right. After we kill them, we'll have to retire for a while. Perhaps for a long time. That costs real money.''

Markov couldn't blame them. In their place he would be raising the same objections, even more loudly.

He took out a second envelope, from which he withdrew a copy of a money transfer from the Bank of Ukraine in Kiev to a numbered account at the Banco Itaxxa in Mexico City, in the amount of three million pesos, about four hundred thousand U.S. dollars. He tossed it on the table in front of Báez.

"That much money will go a long way in Cuba.''

Palma looked at the wire transfer. "Kiev?''

"Do you care where the money came from?" Markov asked. "It's already there for the collecting. Once your work is finished, go and get it.''

"What if we fail?" Báez asked sullenly.

"Then I would suggest that you go nowhere near that bank, because all of you would be shot on sight.''

Báez shook his head, and was about to say something, but Palma held him off.

"Where can we find Lane and his woman?"

"They'll be at one of three places marked on the map. Claridge's near Hyde Park, the woman's apartment in Chelsea, or the Foreign Office in Whitehall."

"How will we know where, and when?"

Markov had saved the untraceable cell phone for last. He laid it on the table. "Someone will call you."

"Can we use this to contact you when we're done?"

"No."

"How will you know we succeeded?"

"I'll know," Markov said. "Twenty-four hours. No mistakes."

Palma nodded. "We'll wait for the call."

Markov and Lychev left the barge and on the way back up to the van Lychev glanced over his shoulder.

"Do you think they'll do it?" he asked.

"Would you for that kind of money?"

"No," Lychev said.

Markov had to smile. "Neither would I. But they will."

9

SIS HEADQUARTERS

After the close call they'd had in Oxford, it was considered safer for Lane and Frances to remain at the Foreign Office overnight. Cots had been set up in an operations office, and one of Frances's aides had gone over to Claridge's to pick up a few things for Lane, and to Frances's to get a few personal items that Mrs. Houlten packed. Morgan came in a few minutes after 3:00 A.M. and stood in the doorway, silhouetted in the light from the corridor.

"Lane?"

"Right," Lane said, sitting up. He looked over at Frannie; she was awake too.

"Your call from Washington came in. They want you to take it in Mr. Stewart's office. I'll escort you across when you're ready."

"Is Stewart still here?"

"No. But he said to call him if need be. He's at home. Where we all should be."

"Stay here," he told Frances, and he went across the corridor with Morgan to Stewart's office.

"I was instructed to stick with you. We don't want you roaming around inside our computers again," Morgan said. "The line is secure, and I'll stand out of earshot."

Lane sat down at Stewart's desk and picked up the phone. Morgan remained at the door.

"I've got the go-ahead, but we're going to have to answer a lot of questions when this is all over," Hughes said. "The unit and team are at Rota, Spain, now. They'll fly out first thing in the morning. Where do you want it delivered?"

"Portsmouth, I think, but I'll have to get back to you, Tommy. What about technicians?"

"They're part of the package. But they're not going to stay long, and I was told in no uncertain terms by a pissed-off admiral that no one, and he stressed *no one*, outside of our people will be involved in the actual operation of the equipment."

"Fair enough. How much of a refit will it take?"

"Not much, but the specs are critical. I'm sending you a fax with the data. Needless to say, William, it's classified top secret."

"I'll get things moving at this end, and get back to you about Portsmouth."

"Are you and Frannie keeping under cover?" Hughes asked, concerned.

"We're surrounded by Britain's finest, Tommy."

"All right, just watch yourself."

Morgan opened the computer to accept the NSA fax from Hughes, then stepped back out of range as the seven-page document came through. Included were orders assigning a lieutenant and a civilian from Sixth Fleet to temporary duty under Lane's care, as well as the platform and electrical requirements for the equipment. All of it was marked top secret Department of Defense. The last page authorized Lane to release any of the information at his discretion. The signature at the bottom was President Reasoner's. If there were any mistakes, it would be the president to whom Lane would have to answer.

10

SIS HEADQUARTERS

Lane had Stewart recalled, and while they waited for him to arrive they freshened up and had a cup of tea and sandwiches in the officers' commissary downstairs. He showed up forty minutes later, freshly shaved, and dressed in a three-piece suit and crisp shirt, as if his workday normally began at four in the morning.

"Presumably you've gotten word from your people," he said to Lane when they were all gathered back in the conference room. "So now you can clear up this mystery for us, and we can get on with it."

"Two-eighty-three was sunk in the Barents near Polyarnyy. That's been the Russian navy's dumping ground for a lot of years now. All sorts of hulls and other junk litters the bottom up there. Some of it leaking oil."

"I imagine those waters are very heavily polluted. So what?"

"That's not all they dump. When one of our nuclear-powered ships runs out of fuel, we pull out the old rods and replace them with new ones. When the Russians want to refuel, especially their older submarines, they simply cut the entire reactor out of the hull, and dump it, spent fuel rods and all."

"Near Polyarnyy," Morgan said impatiently. "We all know about that, Lane. The entire world has known about what they do up there for a long time. So what?"

"Over time some of those reactors have developed leaks. The fuel rods are no longer powerful enough to run a ship, but they still emit a lot of radiation."

"We know that too. And they say that they've all but stopped the practice," Morgan said. "But what does that have to do with two-eighty-three? She's a Romeo-class submarine. Diesel-electric, not nuclear."

"If they faked her sinking, she would have been forced to stay put until her escort ships and search vessels withdrew from the area before she could sneak off. It means her hull is radioactive."

"At very low levels, I would suspect," Stewart said. "Probably no more, let's say, than a large crude-oil carrier, which is slightly radioactive."

"Even if you had a ship equipped with a powerful radiation detector, you'd still have to be right on top of a weak source like that," Morgan said. "Sonar works better. In the end you'd probably be chasing after every stray bit of radiation out there."

"The Barents Sea radiation has a unique signature, because it comes from dozens of sources," Lane dropped the first bombshell.

Frances was the first to catch it.

"But that means your navy has actually been off Polyarnyy, and taken sea samples," she said.

Lane nodded.

"I say, that must have been a coup," Stewart said. He glanced at Morgan. "We never had any suspicions our cousins managed to get in that closely."

Morgan shook his head; his anger had turned to skepticism. "Have you any proof of that?"

"Not that I'm going to share with you, Brad."

"It's a moot point in any event," Stewart said, cutting Morgan's next comment off. "Unless you're going to tell us that your people have invented a radiation detector that's so sensitive it can pick up low levels of radiation at as great a distance as sonar can ping off a submerged..." Stewart trailed off as Lane nodded again.

"This I have to see to believe," Morgan said.

"Can it distinguish the Polyarnyy radiation signature?" Frances asked.

"Accurate enough for our purposes, so I'm told," Lane said.

"Even if such a gadget existed, and the Americans were willing to share it with us, it still wouldn't do much good," Morgan said. "We'd have to have a dozen of the things mounted on a fleet of fast patrol boats in order to cover the area in any reasonable length of time."

A light went off in Frances's eyes. "It can be towed through the water by an airplane, can't it," she said.

Lane grinned. "The device is lightweight. If you'll let one of our technicians ride second seat in a Harrier T-4, we could cover a lot of territory."

"How soon can you get the device here?" Stewart asked.

"It's in Rota. They'll bring it down as soon as I tell them. I suggested Portsmouth, but that's up to you."

"I'm sure that the Royal Navy can be convinced," Stewart said. "In fact I have no doubt of it. The base commander is my next-door neighbor, and he's home just now."

PART TEN

1

ZÜRICH

It was 4:30 A.M. and still dark when Maslennikov got up for the fifth time this evening and went outside on the hotel suite's balcony. They'd flown over last night.

"Can't sleep either?" Captain Kovrygin said from the rail of the adjoining balcony, where he smoked a cigarette.

Maslennikov joined him. "Loos is stalling us," he said weakly. "It has me worried. There's no reason for the delay."

"He's trying to cover himself, Mikhail. You're withdrawing a considerable sum of money from his bank, and he wants to make sure he won't get the blame. He's not a stupid man—he has some idea where it all came from, and the kinds of people he'd have to deal with if it got out that he had a hand in the operation."

"He's an old woman," Maslennikov complained.

"A cautious old woman who has done good by us to this point," Kovrygin pointed out. He offered Maslennikov a cigarette, and held the lighter for him.

"Is Yakov standing by at the airport?" Maslennikov took a deep drag on the American cigarette. It wasn't bad, though it was weak. He still preferred strong Russian cigarettes.

"Once we call him, he can have the Gulfstream ready to fly within fifteen minutes. It takes us longer than that to get out to the airport." Kovrygin shrugged. "But that's not all that has you worried, I think. This isn't like you.''

''We're close to having everything we've ever wanted, Andrei, but two men could ruin it all.''

''Who are you talking about, Günter Loos and Markov or Bill Lane and Valeri? All of them are a threat to us.''

''Not if Markov is successful.''

''But you have your doubts.''

Maslennikov drew on the cigarette. ''General Korzhakov assured me that he'd cooperate, but I'm not so sure that Bill Lane is going to be so easy to kill.'' He shook his head in consternation. ''Which brings us back to Valeri.''

''The man is a psychopath.''

''That he is, but up until now he's been a very useful madman. Without him we wouldn't have come this far.''

Kovrygin looked concerned. ''Shake yourself out of it, man. Your being like this won't do anybody any good. This has been your little show from start to finish. There isn't one of us who would have done anything or been anyone without you. Don't fold on us now.''

Maslennikov nodded finally. ''You're right, of course. But if this fails there are no alternatives. No going back. Kiev wouldn't welcome us with open arms.''

''We all know it.''

''Yet you and the others came when I called, and remain with me even now when so much can go wrong. I appreciate it.''

''It's called trust. We've known each other for a long time.''

Maslennikov contemplated the lights on the far side of the lake, his jaw tightening imperceptibly. ''Trust. Now that's a fine word, Andrei. Do you think the men trust me?''

''Of course.''

Maslennikov turned to Kovrygin. "Do you and Igor trust me? My two captains, without whom we couldn't succeed?"

"Yes, we trust you, Mikhail," Kovrygin said. "But not Ortega. Once he gets his thirty crewmen aboard in Morocco the odds won't be any good."

"I understand. But there are thirty of us now."

"Let's get rid of him. We don't need Morocco, and we certainly don't need Sierra Leone."

"I don't know." Maslennikov let a whining note creep into his voice. "Everybody knows our business. I don't think there's anyplace where we'd be safe."

"*Yeb vas,*" Kovrygin swore in Russian. He was disgusted. "Certainly not Africa."

"Is that why you've been talking about a mutiny?" Maslennikov suddenly asked, his voice hard.

Kovrygin reacted as if he'd been shot. "That's not true."

"*Da.* Two-eighty-three would be scuttled, and the *Charisma* would head south with the money," Maslennikov went on relentlessly.

Kovrygin looked away in shame. "How long have you suspected?"

"I've known for some time now. It's one of the reasons I entered negotiations with Colonel Ortega. Because I think that you and the men are correct. Africa is no place for us."

Kovrygin looked back, his eyes bright. "Where then?"

"You will have to trust me a little longer," Maslennikov said, laying a hand on the captain's shoulder. "That's all I've ever demanded of those who've served under me. Loyalty. It's very important, Andrei."

Kovrygin nodded contritely. "You have it."

"I sincerely hope so."

2

ZÜRICH

Only the earliest of morning traffic was on the streets when an assistant of Günter Loos showed up at Maslennikov's door. He was dressed in jogging clothes, a sweatband around his forehead. He identified himself as Dieter Mann.

"With the compliments of Herr Loos, we are ready for you," Mann said. "Pardon the hour."

"I don't care about the hour," Maslennikov replied irritably. He'd just gotten back to sleep. "Are we to meet at the bank?"

"At the airport, mein herr."

"What about the cargo?"

"It is being loaded even as we speak," Mann said. "If you will get ready, I'll wake Captain Kovrygin, and then check you out. Leave your key in the room. Let's say, the lobby in ten minutes?"

Maslennikov wanted to throttle the smug little bastard. But he nodded. "Ten minutes."

Kovrygin came out of his room at the same time as Maslennikov. "Hell of an hour for the Swiss to conduct business. But I don't suppose they want any witnesses."

"Neither do we," Maslennikov said.

"I called Yakov, but he was already at the plane. Seems as if Herr Loos beat me to it. And air traffic has already accepted our flight plan, no questions asked."

"We're cleared for Tripoli?"

"Just like before. Nobody down there gives a damn, and nobody up here checks to make sure we made it to our final destination."

Mann was waiting for them in the deserted lobby. No one was behind the front desk at the moment, and even the night elevator operator was missing.

"We have a car waiting for you."

Outside they climbed into the back of a Mercedes limo like the one they'd taken the last trip. Mann did not join them, but Günter Loos was seated drinking a cup of coffee and reading the *Wall Street Journal*. He looked up and smiled.

"Good morning, gentlemen. I trust you spent a good evening."

"You have made it difficult for us, by your delay," Maslennikov said crossly. "We wanted to be gone before this."

"Unavoidable, I'm afraid. Given the unusual circumstances of your account."

"What circumstances?" Maslennikov demanded.

Loos tapped on the glass partition, and the driver headed out. "The nature and the timing of the deposits, the amounts, the trouble with Herr Vandermeer, and now this sudden and unexpected withdrawal of the entire account in gold and Western currencies." Loos shrugged his tiny shoulders, which seemed barely able to support his huge head.

"Make your point."

"This is what we term a high-maintenance account. That is, our bank entered into a business arrangement with you that has created an extraordinary amount of work above and beyond the norm for such accounts. Delicate work. At times troubling to some of our directors, who prefer reliable associations and small steady profits to dangerous, possibly damaging partnerships."

Kovrygin started to object, but Maslennikov held him off.

"What do you want?"

"A greater share of the funds which you mean to take out of Switzerland this morning. I believe if you think about the situation, you will come to see my side of the issue."

"You seem sure of yourself, Herr Loos." Maslennikov smiled grimly. "Perhaps I will arrange to have you assassinated."

"I think there's no real danger in that happening."

"You think not?"

"No, because it would be a foolish mistake that in the end would profit you nothing but grief. Better to walk away with most of your considerable fortune intact, than to run away with all of it knowing that someone was following you. Money, Herr Maslennikov, is a powerful aphrodisiac."

"I would advise you to watch your step. Very carefully, because you may not know all the facts."

"I know more than you think I do. For instance, Herr Vandermeer is in fact a man named William Lane, who works for an American intelligence agency. I know, for instance, that he is hunting you and a man named Valeri Yernin, and would be very interested in learning what I know."

"You may not reach the airport this morning," Kovrygin warned.

"In that case you and your money would not leave Switzerland," Loos shot back. "The Americans and Russians and Ukrainians aren't the only ones with intelligence-gathering organizations. Ours, serving the Swiss banking community, goes back further than your governments' very existence."

"You son of a bitch," Kovrygin said.

"Don't be tiresome, Captain. Although you have not directly broken any laws here or in Britain or America, there is a certain group of people in Moscow who would be extremely grateful to learn of your whereabouts once they were told what part you played in the operation."

Kovrygin was shaking with rage.

"But of course I have no intention of doing anything like that, providing we can come to a gentleman's agreement," Loos said. "One that can profit us all."

Again Maslennikov held Kovrygin off. "I think we can come to some agreement, Herr Loos. I don't think that will present an insurmountable problem."

"I'm glad you see it that way."

They had passed through the city and were heading out into the countryside, traffic to the airport picking up slightly.

"You are a vice president of the bank, nothing more," Maslennikov said. "Who else will know about our arrangement?"

"No one. Not in the bank, and certainly not in the federal banking commission. Of course I have certain safeguards in place. So in effect I am not working alone, although factually this agreement is strictly between us."

"What's the upshot, how much do you want?"

A crafty expression came into the banker's eyes. "I could demand fifty percent, and you would be in no position to deny me."

Kovrygin laughed disparagingly. "For that kind of money I'd slit your throat myself."

"Nor would I blame you. So that is why I am asking for only thirty percent. It still leaves you a considerable fortune. An untraceable fortune."

"Would this be in addition to the bank's usual handling fees?" Maslennikov asked.

"Of course not. Those fees would come out of my share." Loos spread his tiny, well-manicured hands. "I am not a common thief."

"You're anything but common, you little prick," Kovrygin said.

"Let's not put too fine a point on who is calling whom

a thief,'' Loos replied calmly. ''At least I am man enough to steal from you face-to-face.''

''You're a fucking dead man,'' Kovrygin said, white faced.

''Let's not be hasty, Andrei,'' Maslennikov said, his tone conciliatory. ''What Herr Loos is offering does have merit. But what about afterward? When we're gone? What's to prevent me from sending someone back here to kill you?''

''Because I have safeguards.''

''Yes, you've told us. But what if we don't believe you? What if we're willing to take the risk?'' Maslennikov glanced at Kovrygin, who looked fierce. ''What if we worry that once you have your share, you might have an accident, and your safeguards might be activated? Or perhaps someone from Moscow, tracing us this far, finds you, and convinces you—as only they know how in Moscow—to coöperate with them? What are *my* safeguards, Herr Loos?''

''You won't need them once you leave Switzerland.''

''What do you mean?'' Maslennikov asked gently.

''Once you fly off I'll have no way of knowing where you're going.''

''We've come from Guernsey. You know that.''

''I'm assuming now that you've cleared out your accounts you won't remain there.''

''That's possibly correct.''

''Well then, unless you tell me where you intend going I will have no idea. Even if I'm tortured, I would not know what to tell them.'' He inclined his huge head. ''So, leave no traces, and you will be safe.''

They passed the sign for Kloten Airport, and in the distance Maslennikov could see the control tower and rotating beacon.

''Have our funds been loaded aboard the Gulfstream yet?'' he asked.

''Yes. And I assume that you will take the usual precautions for entering British airspace with all that undeclared wealth.''

"Do you have an accounting of our share?" Maslennikov asked.

Loos handed over a plain white envelope. "Because of considerations of weight, I converted only ten percent to gold. The remainder has been divided into American dollars, German marks, British pounds, and French francs.''

"No Swiss currency?"

"No."

"What is the total amount?" Maslennikov asked.

"Slightly more than an equivalent of eighty-one million U.S. dollars," Loos said. "And if that seems too little for all your efforts over the past year, remember that you are in possession of an operable submarine that should bring serious money in the right market.''

"I would suggest for your sake, Herr Loos, that you try very hard to forget us," Maslennikov said.

"I will, in this you can have complete and utter faith.''

-------- 3 --------

KLOTEN AIRPORT

The Gulfstream was backed into a hangar, and Yakov Nikitin, a tall, thick-waisted man, was doing his walk-around when the Mercedes limo pulled up. The first commercial flights of the morning were at their gates readied for departure, but here there was no activity. No ground crew. No witnesses. No customs. Loos had taken care of all that.

Maslennikov and Kovrygin got out, but Loos remained seated, a look of triumph on his face.

"It would be unfortunate if you have double-crossed us," Maslennikov told the banker.

"I haven't. There'd be no profit in it for me."

"Because no matter what happened to me, no matter how long it took, I would have my revenge. You, and everyone close to you, would die."

"You have to trust me."

"I don't," Maslennikov said. "But I'm beginning to believe you." He shut the door, and the limo sped away. He and Kovrygin walked inside to the Gulfstream as Nikitin finished his preflight inspection.

"Are we ready to take off?" Maslennikov asked.

"Any time you are, Captain. We're cleared for Tripoli."

"Has the money been loaded aboard?"

"The gold's in aluminum cases in the cargo hold. Better than six hundred kilos. The currency is packed in ten duffel bags. I strapped them in the back."

"Did you look at it?" Kovrygin asked. "Did you verify that it was all there?"

"*Da*. They made me open every case and every duffel bag, then sign for it."

"What name did you use?"

Nikitin grinned. "Boris Yeltsin."

Maslennikov clapped him on the shoulder. "Well done, Yakov. Now let's get the hell out of here. The sooner we're airborne the better I'll feel."

"I agree," Kovrygin said. "We have a lot of work ahead of us before this day is done."

"*Da*," Maslennikov said. "But we're almost home free, Andrei. And then there'll be plenty of time for rest." He looked at the young pilot. "And play, Yakov. Lots of play."

4

GUERNSEY

The Gulfstream came in low from the northwest, Nikitin announcing to the tower that they were inbound from a private airfield outside Exeter that they had supposedly flown to yesterday. Since it was an entirely domestic flight no customs inspection was needed.

Although visibility was limited in a light drizzle, they came through the overcast a couple of miles out on final, and spotted the *Charisma* at her berth, two crewmen in yellow foul-weather gear on deck. Ortega had gotten their message and was making ready for their departure even though they would not be pulling away from the dock until early this evening, after dark. Going out to the submarine's location again was just too risky in the daylight, even if the overcast held, which it was supposed to do. If it took the entire night, Maslennikov was determined that the money and his entire crew would be aboard 283, and the *Charisma* scuttled before dawn. Frankly, he didn't think he could hold them together much longer. And he was truly worried about Bill Lane. They hadn't heard the last of that man.

When they touched down, Maslennikov looked at his watch. It was a few minutes after eight. They were nearly twenty-four hours behind schedule.

As soon as they turned onto the taxiway from the active runway, he picked up the phone. ''Has the crew arrived yet?''

"Yes, sir," Yakov answered. "They're standing by for us."

"Pull into the hangar and shut it down. We're done with her."

"Too bad, she's a nice bird."

"*Da,* too bad," Maslennikov said, and he put the phone down.

Kovrygin was watching him. "I'll be glad to get out of here, Mikhail. But Morocco has me worried."

"Don't be. It's going to work out, Andrei. You'll see."

The doors of the private hangar they'd leased for the past year were open. Nikitin eased the Gulfstream inside, and as the engines spooled down, the big doors started to close.

Kovrygin unlatched the airplane's hatch and started to swing it open, but Maslennikov laid a hand on his arm.

"I want you to do something for me," he said.

Kovrygin nodded. "What is it?"

"Make sure that Igor and the others understand that despite what they may be thinking, Colonel Ortega is not our enemy. In fact, he's our way out."

"That's going to be a hard sell."

"I know, which is why I want you to convince them. Without Ortega we're lost."

"There's always Sierra Leone."

"*Nyet.* The Americans know about it, and Moscow no longer wants two-eighty-three or any other boat to reach Freetown. There are diplomatic pressures being brought to bear."

"I understand," Kovrygin said softly.

"Nor will trying to take off aboard the *Charisma* work. They'd find us. We'd be hunted like animals. Two-eighty-three and Colonel Ortega are our only way out now. Make the others understand."

5

LONDON

At SIS headquarters Lane phoned Hughes with instructions for the radiation detector to be sent to the Royal Naval air station attached to the naval base at Portsmouth. He left Stewart's office and went back to operations, where he and Frances had bunked for the night. Someone had taken the cots away and straightened up the room. Frances had gathered her and Lane's things and was heading to their third-floor office.

"Did you reach Tommy?" she asked.

"I just talked to him. The equipment will be delivered to Portsmouth later today," Lane said.

"Then we can finally do something, other than sitting around."

Lane took his overnight bag from her. "Let's get out of here for a couple hours. We can go over to Claridge's and I'll buy you breakfast. We can use the fresh air."

She nodded. "Another commissary meal will kill me," she said. "Afterward we can stop by my place and check on Mrs. Houlten."

They took the elevator down to the underground parking garage, signing out with security. Tossing their things in the backseat of Frances's Range Rover, they exited the garage and headed over to the hotel. The morning had dawned gray and dismal, with a light but steady rain that seemed to have little if any effect on the heavy rush-hour traffic. Londoners were a special breed, Lane thought. Tough and resilient.

As she drove, Frances frequently glanced up at her rearview mirror. Lane could see the troubled look on her face, but there was little he could do for her that he wasn't already doing, short of stashing her away in some safe house. But she'd never put up with that. And he knew that he would probably lose respect for her if she would.

She made a couple of unnecessary turns. They'd not heard the last of Yernin. And it was possible that he was behind them now. She was taking sensible precautions.

"We probably should have told Brad where we were going," Lane said.

She glanced at him. "Do you mean that, or are you just being politic?"

"He's going to have a bird when he finds out that we're gone."

She grinned viciously. "Good." She glanced in the mirror again. "I read your final report on Kilo Option. The last you saw of Yernin he was going down on that submarine in the Arabian Sea, yet NSA had a ninety-eight percent match on a voiceprint several days later from Karachi."

"Makes him one tough man."

"A survivor," Frances agreed. "But intelligent. He didn't come back to Uncle Leonard's because he knew that he was outgunned, and that the Oxford police might respond to the fact that the security alarm wires had been cut. He wanted enough time to get away, to regroup, to think out his next moves. Because there will be a next time."

"That's what he wants. But he's tied up with Maslennikov and the submarine. If we can pin them down, bring the fight to them first, he won't have a chance."

"Unless he's already back."

Lane nodded. "Are you armed?"

"I have the Bernardelli."

"Extra ammunition?"

"Two spare magazines. I don't leave home without them anymore."

"Then we keep our eyes open."

She looked sharply at him. "You *want* him to show up."

Lane could see the image of a young navy Wave shot to death by Yernin, lying in the corridor of Atlantic Submarine Headquarters in Norfolk, Virginia. He'd booby-trapped her body so that when the medics tried to check for signs of a pulse, the brick of Semtex exploded, killing them, and spreading her body over the walls. Her pregnant body.

He nodded. "Yes, I do, Frannie. One-on-one. As soon as possible, before he kills someone else."

6

LONDON

At that moment the Cuban team was waiting on a side street near Green Park in a dark blue Ford panel van they'd rented from the Hertz Commercial Division at the airport. Báez was behind the wheel. He and Palma had decided that too much could go wrong stealing a car. In any event, they didn't think it would matter very much to the Russians how they did the job as long as they did it.

The cell phone chirped and Palma answered it. *"Sí."*

"They're at the hotel," a man said. "Driving the Rover." The connection was broken.

*   *   *

Like Palma, Manuel Báez was a captain in the Cuban intelligence service. At thirty-two he'd been working on special assignment for the Russians from their embassy in Mexico City for three years. Uncle Fidel had cut a deal with Yeltsin to do some of his dirty work in exchange for secret military assistance. It was just fine with Báez, because at home he had trouble taking care of his wife and two children on his meager pay. But working for the Russians he was given bonuses sometimes amounting to ten times his base salary. And now this assignment would put him on easy street, because foreign currencies went a long way in Havana.

They drove over to Claridge's, and he circled the block twice until they spotted the woman's Range Rover in the hotel's valet lot.

"Park in front," Palma said.

It took another five minutes before a parking place became available a half block from the hotel's front entrance, and Báez pulled the van in. They were in luck because from here they could see the valet parking lot exit.

"This is perfect," Palma said. He turned to the others in the back. "As soon as the Rover comes out of the parking lot, we'll make the hit."

One of the men had cracked the side door slightly, and he looked back toward the hotel. "From here?"

"*No, estúpido*," Palma said. "Manuel will drive past the hotel and we'll kill them both where they stand, before their car arrives, and before anyone knows what's happening. *¿Comprende?*"

"*Sí.*"

Palma turned back to Báez. "No matter what happens, keep driving. We'll ditch the car on the way to the ship."

The ship was the Cuban motor vessel *Santa Clara*,

unloading sugar in London. She was due to depart this evening. The timing was perfect.

"*Sí*," Báez replied, his nerves already starting to get jumpy.

7

LONDON

After breakfast, Lane left Frances in the restaurant while he went up to his room to take a quick shower and shave, and change into a pair of tan slacks, a light blue cashmere sweater, and a pair of hand-sewn half boots he always carried with him. The leather was butter soft but tough, and the boots were incredibly sturdy.

The message light on his telephone was flashing, but he ignored it. Morgan had probably found out they'd left, and was trying to track them down. They'd check in when they got over to Frances's place.

By habit he checked the action on his Beretta, which Scotland Yard had grudgingly returned to him, cycled a couple of rounds through the breech, reloaded it, and reholstered it at the small of his back. Then he pulled on a Gucci leather jacket, threw a few more things in his overnight bag, and went back downstairs.

Frances was just finishing her tea, and she looked up and smiled. "It's a good thing that we both have money."

"Why's that?"

"It's going to take both of our incomes just to keep you in clothes."

"Not to mention feeding you," Lane said.

She was suddenly serious. "Did you mean what you said in Stewart's office the other day? About us?"

"Yes."

"You're not going to give up your career, and I don't know if I'm ready to give up mine. So I don't know how it's going to work out, because even if I can wrangle another assignment to the States, it'll still be nearly impossible for us."

Lane took her hand. "It'll work out, Frannie, if we want it to."

"You're an impossible chauvinist pig, sometimes."

Lane grinned. "That's what Tommy and Moira say."

She looked into his eyes. "But I love you, William."

"I know," Lane said with feeling. "And I love you, Frannie. Everything else is superfluous."

The waiter came with their check and Lane signed for it, leaving a more than generous tip even though he was troubled. He didn't know how it could possibly work out for them, short of both of them getting out of the business.

8

LONDON

It started to rain harder, reducing visibility so that Báez and Palma almost missed the Range Rover coming out of the valet parking lot at the end of the block. It pulled out into traffic and followed a bakery truck. From where they sat they could not make out the Rover's driver, nor could they see the area beneath the canopy at the front door of the hotel. But it was a reasonable assumption to think that if the Ranger Rover had been called for, then the woman and possibly Lane would be waiting for it.

Báez waited for a taxi to pass by, then pulled smartly out into traffic and accelerated down the block toward the hotel entrance, the Range Rover coming head-on from the opposite direction.

He was excited, and he reached for his pistol.

"No, Manuel," Palma said. "Concentrate on driving. We'll do the shooting."

"Don't miss, Carlos. I don't want to do this again."

"We won't miss," Palma replied tightly.

Bill Lane and Frances Shipley came out of the front door. He was carrying some kind of a shoulder bag, and he turned to the doorman. The woman stood slightly behind him and to his left. She had spotted the approaching Range Rover and her concentration was focused in that direction.

Palma pulled the bolt back on his PM-63 machine pistol. "Get ready."

The other four Cubans in back drew back the bolts of their Polish-built 9mm submachine guns, and at the last second Báez cut in front of another taxi, and shot across the street directly toward the hotel's front entrance.

"Okay, brace yourself now!" Palma shouted.

One of the men crashed the side door open as the van slewed sharply right.

The woman turned slowly, but Lane's reaction was faster, incredibly faster, Báez thought fleetingly as he found himself staring down the barrel of a pistol that had suddenly materialized in the American's hand.

Palma was the first to open fire, and then the others began shooting, but their aim was off because Báez turned the wheel sharply to the left as Lane's first shot starred the windshield in front of his face.

The doorman was pushed backward through the glass doors, blood flying everywhere. Lane shoved the woman to the left, and rolled right, firing directly at the driver's side of the windshield as he moved like a ballet dancer.

Báez continued to haul the van in a tight U-turn, the rear end skidding on the slippery pavement.

Incredibly, the woman pulled out a pistol, and, standing in a shooter's crouch, calmly fired at the side of the van as if she were at a shooting gallery where no one was trying to kill her. He felt a grudging admiration for her.

Miguel shouted something hysterical in back, and Palma hung out the window and continued to fire until his weapon ran out of ammunition. By then they were back in the street, heading the way they had come, and Báez put his foot in it, the van shooting forward, passing several cars, a truck, and a taxi.

"Did we get them?" he shouted excitedly. "Jesus Christ, did you hit them?"

"Slow down!" Palma ordered. "We don't want to crash!"

Báez glanced in the rearview mirror. So far no one was coming after them. There were no flashing blue lights.

Then he focused on what was happening in the back of the van, which was covered with blood, and he almost ran into a parked car. Miguel was gone.

"Get us to the boat, Manuel," Palma shouted. "Pay attention!"

LONDON

Lane ran out into the street hoping to get off a couple more shots at the retreating van, but it was already out of range and there was too much traffic.

One of the shooters had been tossed out of the vehicle and lay in a heap in the middle of the street. All traffic in front of the hotel had stopped.

Frances ran up. "Was it Yernin?"

"I don't think so," Lane said. He looked at her. "Are you hurt?"

"I'm fine, how about you?"

"I'm okay. Call an ambulance for the doorman and then call Scotland Yard and give them a description of the van. Tell Brad what happened. They won't get far driving around London in a van full of bullet holes."

Frances looked over at the downed shooter. "Be careful, William."

"Yeah," Lane said, and keeping his gun pointed at the body, trotted over to it. This was not Yernin's style. Somebody else was gunning for them.

The man's gun lay several feet away from his body, and Lane recognized it as a PM-63. Odd, he thought. There weren't many professional shooters using that weapon these days.

He turned the body over. The slightly built man was dead. He'd taken a bullet in his forehead just above his left eye, and another in his neck, destroying his windpipe.

Lane holstered his gun and went through the man's pockets. There were a few pound notes and some coins in a pants pocket, two extra magazines of 9mm ammunition stuck in his belt, but no wallet or identification, except for a letter in Spanish in his jacket pocket.

The envelope was addressed to Miguel Sanchez at an address in Mexico City. But Lane's eyes went to the postmark. Havana.

"How about that," he said to himself, pocketing the letter.

10

GUERNSEY

Maslennikov put down the telephone, his heart pounding, his mouth dry. It was time to leave. Most of the others had filtered down to the *Charisma* during the afternoon after they'd finished closing down the house, removing all traces of who had been here. It had been a joke when they'd first come to the islands. No one on Guernsey knew or cared who was here as long as the bills were paid on time. Everyone in the Channel Islands minded his own business.

But now trouble was coming as Maslennikov knew it would from the moment he'd seen Bill Lane in the office of Günter Loos.

He wiped down the telephone handset, looked around his study one last time to make certain he was leaving nothing incriminating, and went out into the front hall as his chief of security, Fedor Nemchin, came downstairs.

"Is everything secure?" he asked.

"*Da*. How about your office?"

"It's clean," Maslennikov said. "Who else is left up here?"

"Just me," Colonel Ortega said, coming from the back. He carried a small canvas bag with a shoulder strap. "This was left in the garage."

Maslennikov recognized the bag for what it contained. "It's Valeri's."

"Yes. Five kilos of Semtex. Your star pupil may be dedicated, but he's sloppy."

"Did you find any more out there? Or was that it?" Nemchin asked.

"This was it."

"There were at least four other bags this morning." Ortega shrugged. "They're gone now."

"If there's nothing else, it's time to go," Maslennikov said.

Ortega looked sharply at him. "Something is troubling you."

"We must leave now."

"What's wrong, Captain?" Nemchin asked. "Who telephoned just now?"

Maslennikov hated to admit mistakes. But they deserved to know. "It was Markov. He failed."

Ortega's eyes were bright. "The team missed?"

Maslennikov nodded.

"Did they get back to the *Santa Clara*?"

"All but one of them. He was killed and they had to leave his body behind."

Ortega looked away in anger, and said something in Spanish under his breath. "As you suggest, Captain, it's time to leave."

"You knew about the team," Maslennikov accused.

Ortega shook his head. "Only what Markov told us.

But it won't matter if we can put to sea by morning, because within twenty-four hours we'll be in the open Atlantic and undetectable.''

Maslennikov was sure that Ortega was lying. But it no longer mattered, because they were committed to him now. There was no other way out.

─────────── 11 ───────────

ABOARD THE *CHARISMA*

The marina was deserted except for the night watchman, who would remain in his shack for the remainder of the evening as he usually did. The *Charisma*'s powerful diesels were idling, and the yacht showed only a few lights, the bridge illuminated in red. Nemchin parked the Mercedes across from the berth, and they went aboard.

Two crewmen in yellow foul-weather gear stood by the gangplank.

"Are we all aboard now?" Maslennikov asked.

"I think so, sir," one of the crewmen said.

"Pull in the gangplank and stand by the lines. We're leaving immediately."

Nemchin went below to see to his people while Maslennikov and Ortega went immediately up to the bridge, where Kovrygin, his first mate, and his helmsman were waiting.

"Are we all set, Mikhail?" Kovrygin asked.

"Time to go at last, Andrei."

Kovrygin glanced at Ortega, who'd walked over to the port-side windows and was looking down at the dock, and nodded toward him with a questioning glance.

Maslennikov returned the nod. Everything was all right. But something was obviously troubling Kovrygin.

"Is everyone aboard?"

"I didn't make a head count," Kovrygin said, a slight hesitation in his answer.

"I suggest we get out of here while we still have time," Ortega said. "We have a long night of work ahead of us, and the sooner we get started the better I'll feel." He glanced out the port window. "The gangplank is secured."

Kovrygin keyed his walkie-talkie. "Release all lines." The wind was blowing away from the dock.

The *Charisma* drifted off, and the helmsman expertly maneuvered them slowly through the marina and out past the seawall, where her bows rose to meet the seas.

Maslennikov stepped out on the port bridge deck and looked back at the lights of the island city of St. Peter Port. When he'd first arrived here he was full of hope. Now that he was leaving, he was filled with apprehension even though he'd accomplished everything he'd set out to accomplish.

One man had nearly ruined it all for them. And even now that they were away from the island, he could not shake the feeling that they'd not heard the last of him.

A two-meter swell was running, and the night was frigid and pitch-black when the *Charisma* arrived in position above the submarine two hours later. Radar showed that they were clear to twenty miles.

A crewman lowered the aquaphone, and Maslennikov keyed the handset. "This is Mikhail. We're here."

"Did you run into trouble? You're late," Lubiako's distorted voice came back.

"There was a delay in Zürich, but everything is fine. We're ready to begin loading. Is everything in order below?"

"Yes. We'll stand by both escape trunks."

"Negative," Maslennikov said. "There is a change of plans." He glanced over at the radar, which showed they were still clear to the twenty-mile ring. "I want you to surface the boat. We can load much faster that way. And the risk will be minimal. It's overcast up here."

"You're asking for trouble."

"The seas are getting up, and sending twenty-five men and cargo down through the escape trunks will be dangerous."

Lubiako hesitated a moment, but when he came back he sounded resigned. "That makes sense. But back off a couple of hundred meters, the five of us are going to have our hands full bringing this old bastard up."

"Valeri is there with you. He can help."

Again Lubiako hesitated. This time when he came back his voice was cautious. "He's not aboard, Mikhail."

"What are you talking about?" Maslennikov demanded. He looked over at Ortega, who was watching him. "Where is he?"

"I'm telling you that I don't know. The after escape trunk cycled after midnight, and he was gone."

"Did you search the boat?"

"Every square meter."

"He said nothing to you, or anyone else?"

"*Nyet.*"

"He didn't communicate with anyone?"

"The message buoys are still in their racks," Lubiako said. "It's a safe bet he didn't swim to shore. Someone was waiting for him. We thought that you knew about it."

"I didn't," Maslennikov said. "Surface the boat. We'll give you plenty of room."

"As you wish, Captain."

Maslennikov put down the telephone. "Where is he?" he asked Ortega.

"If you mean your madman, I don't know where he is. But I would guess he's in London by now, or on his way, to finish the job Markov bungled."

"You brought the *Charisma* out here to pick him up?"

"I wasn't alone."

"But you and he arranged it before he went down to the sub."

"He thought that you would be back from Switzerland by then. But in case you weren't, he wanted to come back to the house." Ortega shrugged. "When we docked he took off, and that's the last we saw of him. So I assumed he went to London."

"They have his description," Maslennikov said. "They'll be watching for him. You knew that."

Again Ortega shrugged indifferently. "We didn't think it was prudent to get in his way."

"Did you know about this?" Maslennikov asked Kovrygin.

"*Nyet.*"

Maslennikov nodded. "Igor wants us to stand off a couple hundred meters while he surfaces the boat."

Kovrygin gave the orders to the helmsman, and as the *Charisma* got under way the aquaphone was brought back aboard.

Maslennikov suddenly had another thought. He called Nemchin on the ship's interphone. "This is Mikhail. Send Nikitin up to the bridge."

"He's not here, Captain," Nemchin said.

"Search the yacht."

"He never came aboard," Nemchin said.

"Why wasn't I told?" Maslennikov shouted.

"I didn't find out about it until a few minutes ago."

"Why didn't someone say something?"

"Captain, they thought he was with you, or doing something for you. We just didn't know."

Maslennikov crashed the phone down.

"Well at least we know how he meant to get to London," Ortega said. "Maybe he'll catch up with us in Morocco."

Maslennikov looked over at Kovrygin and he knew exactly what his captain was thinking, because he was thinking the same thing.

Trouble was coming their way. Big trouble.

12

OFF SARK ISLAND

Bernard St. Germaine was a smuggler, and at the age of fifty-four he was finally beginning to make a decent living at his trade. His ten-meter wooden lapstrake gaff-rigged sloop was heeled over in the twenty-knot winds, but she was heavy and took the big seas very well. He reckoned he was still about fifteen or sixteen kilometers off his drop point on a deserted beach on Sark. He was running ahead of schedule. He'd drop the six bundles of cash to be laundered in the Channel Island banking system, and return the thirty-five kilometers to Flamanville in plenty of time to be at home drinking his first bowl of coffee before the sun rose. Once a month he picked up his cargo at the airport in Cherbourg, drove down to his boat, loaded it aboard, and made the run. No questions asked. Within days, he got notice that his private account on Jersey was credited with amounts that varied between twenty thousand and fifty thousand francs. He wasn't a wealthy man, but he was comfortable, and in a position to be able to retire in a few more years, at which time he would leave his wife, and set up in a beach house in Tahiti. He smiled just thinking about it.

13

ABOARD THE *CHARISMA*

The submarine broke the surface a couple hundred meters out, settled back at an angle, its deck awash, then straightened up, and rose the last few meters as its bows were turned into the wind and seas. No lights showed, nor were the *Charisma*'s running lights on.

It was a sloppy job, Maslennikov thought. But with only Igor and four crewmen it was a credible job made of an impossible task.

Lubiako appeared on the bridge a minute later, his image a ghostly green in the light-intensifying scope Maslennikov used.

"Here," Lubiako radioed.

Maslennikov keyed his low-powered walkie-talkie. "Stand by your forward loading hatch."

"Da."

Maslennikov had stationed lookouts on the bow and stern as well as both bridge decks. The bow lookout radioed up excitedly.

"Captain, I have a target less than a hundred meters out, thirty degrees off our port bow."

Maslennikov swung the scope to port, and picked up the target almost immediately. It was a small sailboat under a full press of sail, with no running lights. The numbers were French registry.

"Nothing on radar," Kovrygin reported.

"It's a sailboat. Looks like wood construction." Maslennikov trained the scope on the cockpit as the boat suddenly straightened up, its sail luffing. One man was at the tiller, and he was looking toward the submarine.

"She's sending a signal," Kovrygin said.

Maslennikov looked up. "What kind of a signal? Voice?"

"No. Sounds like a beacon. Above four hundred megahertz."

"An emergency beacon?"

"Unknown."

"Has there been any response to it?"

"We're picking up nothing."

Maslennikov went back to the scope. The sailboat skipper had put the tiller hard over and the sails were filling on the opposite tack. Whoever he was, he'd seen the submarine, realized he was in a place he shouldn't be, and was trying to get away.

"There's a sailboat off my starboard bow," Lubiako radioed.

"Stand by, we'll take care of it," Maslennikov responded. He turned back to Kovrygin. "Jam the signal, and then sink him."

"If we shoot at him, it'll be noisy."

"Run him down," Maslennikov said. "Now."

14

OFF SARK ISLAND

St. Germaine had been around long enough to know trouble when he saw it. And looking back over his shoulder as the fancy yacht turned toward him, he understood that he was in the biggest jam in his life.

He didn't recognize the make of submarine, but it looked like an old model, and somehow he didn't think it was British. It would have shown lights, and it wouldn't be making a rendezvous with a civilian yacht that also showed no lights. Something was amiss here, and he'd had the bad luck to stumble into the middle of it.

"Merde," he swore.

He thought about turning on his diesel, but that would only give him an extra knot or two. Nor could he use his radio to call for help, because even if it came it would be too late, and afterward he'd have no reasonable answers for the questions that would surely follow.

The big yacht was gaining on him, and there wasn't the slightest chance of escape, so he reached over and released the mainsheet, letting the big sail run free. The sailboat immediately slowed down as if it had run into a pool of tar.

All his life he had lived by his wits. His only hope, now he figured, was talking his way out.

He sat back and lit a cigarette as his boat rounded up just off the wind, and he waited for the big yacht to circle around to his leeward side. They'd shine a spot-light on him, and seeing that he was the only one aboard, they might just go away.

He gave a Gallic shrug. Stranger things had happened.

The yacht was less than twenty meters away, and still not turning. In fact it was nearly out of room to turn now.

St. Germaine tossed his cigarette overboard, snatched a powerful flashlight from the coaming locker, and shined it up at the yacht's bridge.

At the last moment, realizing that the bastard meant to run him down, he dropped the flashlight, grabbed a life jacket, and scrambled up on the cabin roof.

He turned as the yacht's bow wave swamped his cockpit, then screamed as the big boat slammed into his, and he jumped, his only thoughts, survival and then revenge.

15

ABOARD THE *CHARISMA*

They circled the debris for five minutes and, finally sat-isfied that there were no survivors, headed back to the lee of the submarine. Kovrygin and the others on the bridge were subdued. The radar showed that they were still clear.

"Has the beacon stopped transmitting?" Maslennikov asked.

Kovrygin put down the headphones and nodded. "*Da.*"

"We had no other choice," Maslennikov said.

"I know. But I wonder what the poor bastard was doing out here in the middle of the night."

"He wasn't fishing," Maslennikov shot back. He keyed the walkie-talkie. "Stand by to take our lines."

"Da," Lubiako radioed.

Maslennikov phoned his security chief. "Are you ready below?"

"Yes, Captain. We placed six kickers along the length of the boat, low in the bilges. When it's time they'll take the bottom out of her and she'll go straight down."

"Very well. Get everybody on deck. We'll be alongside in a couple of minutes."

"I have a spare firing transmitter in case yours goes bad," Nemchin said. He and Maslennikov had discussed the possibility that some of the crew still might want to save the *Charisma*, and might have tampered with one of the transmitters. The second was for insurance, though they both sincerely hoped there'd be no need for it.

The seas were increasing, and the helmsman had trouble bringing the yacht alongside the submarine, and then keeping it there. But he was very good, and within minutes the two vessels were secured side by side, with less than a meter of roiled water between them.

Maslennikov watched from the bridge. The first over were the rest of Lubiako's delivery crew. Next, the aluminum cases containing the gold were passed across, followed by the ten duffel bags of currency, which were quickly passed hand over hand to the open loading hatch, where they disappeared into the submarine.

"Our annuity is aboard," he said, turning to the others. "It's time to abandon ship."

Kovrygin nodded tightly. "Too bad we have to leave her, she's a hell of a boat."

"That she is," Maslennikov said.

"Cut your engines," Kovrygin ordered.

The helmsman killed the engines, patted the top of the compass box, and left the bridge.

"After you," Maslennikov told Kovrygin and Ortega.

The motion aboard the yacht became lively, as she was no longer being held in position by her engines and bow thrusters. Maslennikov followed the other two down to the deck.

"Stand by to cut your lines," he radioed to Lubiako.

The last of the crewmen went across and Ortega followed, Kovrygin jumping across just behind him.

Maslennikov hesitated a moment to look up at Lubiako on the submarine's bridge; then he too jumped across.

Crewmen cut the bow and stern lines, as well as the two spring lines holding the boats together, and immediately the *Charisma,* wallowing in the seas, drifted away.

16

ABOARD 283

On the bridge Maslennikov and Lubiako studied the *Charisma*'s distant form with binoculars. There continued to be a lot of shipping traffic up in the English Channel, but their radar showed they were still clear to at least thirty kilometers.

"This is far enough," Maslennikov said.

"Then let's get it over with," Lubiako said nervously. "The sooner we're submerged and on our way the better I'll feel." He keyed the growler phone. "Sonar, stand by for an underwater explosion."

Maslennikov opened the firing lock on his handheld transmitter, glanced at Lubiako, and pushed the button.

A subdued thump came to them on the wind, and the *Charisma* seemed to slightly rise up in the water, then almost immediately went straight down. Within seconds she was gone, and Maslennikov tossed the transmitter overboard.

"What a waste," Lubiako said softly.

"She served her purpose," Maslennikov said. "Time to go."

They leveled off at sixty meters and started their run west southwest, Guernsey to the north and Jersey to the south. At a best speed submerged of thirteen knots, they would be in the open Atlantic within fifteen hours.

Kovrygin and the men not actually running the boat were still settling in. Maslennikov and Ortega were in the cramped control room with Lubiako and his command crew.

"We'll surface once we're in the clear," Lubiako said.

"Is that wise this close to England?" Ortega asked from the plotting table, where he'd been studying a chart of the eastern Atlantic.

"Necessary," Maslennikov answered. "This boat has a limited battery capacity. We have to surface to run the diesels in order to recharge them."

"How is our fuel?"

Lubiako shrugged. "Enough to reach Morocco. But after that, what?" He turned to Maslennikov without waiting for Ortega to answer. "Are we going to be kept in the dark, Mikhail? We've come this far together. Nobody's going to back out now. It's too late for that."

"You'll be told after Morocco," Maslennikov replied uncomfortably.

"Andrei said you talked to him about trust. It works both ways." Lubiako gave Ortega a withering glance. "I don't trust him. None of us do. And when his crew is aboard the decisions might be out of our hands. Have you thought about that?"

"I'm not the enemy," Ortega said.

"I don't know that," Lubiako shot back. "Where is he taking us, Mikhail? And what will we be expected to do when we get there?"

"Follow orders," Ortega said harshly.

"Not yours."

"My orders, Igor," Maslennikov said softly.

Lubiako's eyes were round. But he nodded at last. "*Da*, Captain."

17

GUERNSEY

A slight noise woke Yakov Nikitin. In the dim light from the windows in the side of the hangar he saw a dark figure standing at the foot of his cot.

"We'll leave now."

Nikitin recognized Yernin's voice. He sat up and switched on the lamp. But the man standing there was old, his hair short cropped and gray, his complexion sallow, his body stooped.

"*Yeb vas*. Who the hell are you?"

Yernin straightened up. "Scotland Yard knows what I look like."

Nikitin shivered. When he had agreed to help Yernin, he'd done so partly for the money, but partly because he was afraid of the man. Now he was even more afraid, because it was obvious from the look in Yernin's eyes that he was not sane.

"Let's go. Now."

"Where?"

"Exeter, where you'll keep the Gulfstream ready for me," Yernin said, his voice soft. "You'll do that for me, Yakov?"

"Yes, of course I will," Nikitin said, and although he hated submarines, he sincerely wished he were aboard 283 at this moment.

PART ELEVEN

1

BERKELEY SQUARE

Sir Roger Stewart answered his own door shortly after midnight and ushered George Lennon back to his study. Lennon was director of counterespionage at Scotland Yard.

"We're finished with the van, but aside from a lot of blood, a bunch of nine-millimeter shell casings, and a few so far unidentified fingerprints, we've come up with nothing usable. What about your American?"

"We're keeping him under cover for the moment lest someone else decides to shoot up the streets trying to kill him," Stewart said. He poured his friend a whiskey. They sat in front of the fireplace.

Lennon looked into the flames. "A bad business, this. The old man was called on the carpet this afternoon by the prime minister for not adequately carrying out his charter."

"Sir Hubert was at the same meeting, and I was given my share, this afternoon, as I'm sure you were."

Lennon nodded, his long narrow face hound dog–like with bags under his eyes and much too large ears. "There's still no telling if the attack this morning had anything to do with the other trouble Lane has brought with him." Lennon looked up. "Could be some old flame gunning for him."

"That's what we thought. Even Lane admitted that neither Yernin nor Maslennikov was apparently involved. But Mario Garza thinks that Markov might be behind it.''

"The Russians?" Lennon asked. "Why not? Maybe Maslennikov ordered him to come up with a hit squad and eliminate Lane. Wouldn't be the first time they used foreign nationals.''

"Do we know who they were?"

"No ID on the body. He wasn't carrying anything but a few pounds. And his fingerprints aren't on file. But he's Hispanic. So were the driver and shooter in the passenger seat. There were enough eyewitnesses to give us that. And the clerk at Hertz said the man who rented the van spoke with a Spanish accent. The driver's license and credit card he used were false, of course.''

"Another dead end," Stewart said. It had been a day of dead ends. Everywhere they turned, their leads dried up on them. And now even the navy wanted to back out, and he couldn't say that he blamed them. Bill Lane was definitely a dangerous man to have around.

"What's the Yard's official position?" Stewart asked.

"We're to stick with it, and give Lane anything he needs. At the moment it would seem that keeping him alive is the first priority. But in actuality it's an SIS-directed operation which puts you in front of the wicket. Though Lane is a good shot in his own right.''

"He's been on a few assignments," Stewart said. "But this business between him and Yernin will not go away of its own accord.''

"Then you're taking the stance that this morning's attack was not connected with the investigation?"

"We have to treat it that way, or else we'll be led down a path that no one wants to get back to. We fought this sort of game with the Russians for too many years to start up again. If Markov directed the hit squad, for whatever reason, I don't know if I want to know about it.''

Lennon knocked back his whiskey and put the glass down. "Let's try to put it all in perspective. What's at stake here for us? So far as I can see nothing, except that whoever is gunning for Lane is also shooting up our streets. Not to mention the deaths in Oxford. So the sooner we get rid of Lane the better off we'll all be."

"We're not really interested in the submarine."

"No, but the navy can handle that. And once it's gone, do we really care where it goes?"

"If it shows up in the Med it becomes a NATO issue. But if it heads down the African coast I don't think the PM will want to pursue it."

"So we chase it out into the Atlantic and kiss it goodbye."

"The Americans might want more help than that."

Lennon shrugged. "Again, that's more your bailiwick than mine, Roger. But I say that if the Americans want to play policemen to the world, then let them. In the meantime we're looking for Sir Leonard's murderer. It's a simple manhunt. We have a good drawing which has been distributed to every policeman in the country, so if he pops up anywhere we'll find him."

"Have you read his file?"

"I've seen it," Lennon said. "But one man can't fight an entire country. We'll get him all right. That's my job."

"While all the while trying to keep Lane out of trouble."

Lennon nodded. "That's the biggest problem of all. But I've read his file too. Makes me glad of at least one thing."

"What's that?"

"That Mr. Lane is on our side. I'd hate to go up against him."

"In the meantime you're still investigating this morning's incident."

"Of course," Lennon said. "They'll turn up sooner or later."

"Unless they're aboard the submarine."

Lennon shook his head. "Now there's a thought."

2

PORT OF LONDON

Lane stood in the deep shadows between two warehouses across the dock from the cargo vessel *Santa Clara* watching a deck gang battening down the hatches. She was the only ship of Cuban registry currently in London and she was scheduled to sail within the hour. He had come up with that using one of the computers in the safe house, and had managed to slip away and get down here just in the nick of time.

One piece of information was all he needed to nail down Maslennikov's ultimate plan. He had to be certain that the men who'd attacked him and Frances this morning were Cubans. Finding them aboard this ship would all but clinch it.

Hunching up his jacket collar against the steady drizzle, he stepped out into the lights, strode across the quay, and went up the boarding ladder as if he had every right to be there.

Someone came out of a hatch. "Who the hell are you?"

"I want to see Captain Torrado," Lane said in English, but with a Russian accent. "I have something important for him before you sail."

The short, sturdily built man studied Lane's face for a second or two. "I'm Captain Torrado."

Lane pulled the letter from his pocket that he'd taken from the body in front of Claridge's this morning and handed it to the captain. "That fool Sanchez was carrying this when he was gunned down. One of our people managed to take it from the body before the police arrived."

Torrado looked at the letter.

"Give it to the others, unless they're all dead."

The captain shook his head. "There was one other casualty, but Palma is okay." His eyes narrowed. "Were they followed here?"

"*Nyet,*" Lane said.

"Do you want to talk to them?"

"No. As it is I took a chance coming here. Now I must go." He started to turn.

The captain was suspicious. "Wait a minute." He pulled a pistol out of his jacket pocket. "You're going to stay here."

Lane reached back with his left hand and batted the pistol away, while with his right he drew his own gun. He stepped inside the captain's guard and jammed the muzzle of his Baretta into the man's neck below his jaw.

"Follow your orders, Captain. Precisely."

The captain raised his head slightly.

Lane took the man's gun, backed up a step, and handed it back to him. "Good sailing," he said, then turned and went down the boarding ladder into the night.

3

THE SAFE HOUSE

Brad Morgan took the telephone from a tired and frustrated Mario Garza. They were all strung out from lack of sleep and an investigation that seemed to be going nowhere, although every time they turned around someone ended up getting shot at or killed. It was Roger Stewart.

"Has Markov made a move?"

"Not yet," Morgan said. "But the lights are still on over there."

"Has he made any calls?"

"None."

"Scotland Yard is still scouring the city, but it looks as if the team has gone to ground somewhere."

"No identification yet on the body?"

"No," Stewart said. "We can only assume that they're not going to try anything like that again. So I want Lane taken down to Portsmouth this morning. As soon as possible. The Americans are there with the equipment, but they're not even going to unpack it until they talk to Lane."

"I'll see to it myself, sir," Morgan said. "Garza and Commander Shipley will probably insist on tagging along."

"I don't care. Just get Lane down there in one piece as soon as possible. No screwups this time. I don't want you losing sight of him again."

"Yes, sir. He's here sleeping."

Garza watched him as he hung up. "Are we finally going to Portsmouth?"

"That was Roger Stewart. He wants us to get Lane down there right now. Go wake him."

"That won't be necessary," Lane said coming from the front vestibule.

Morgan was thunderstruck. He looked from Lane to the corridor that led back to the bedrooms. "Where the hell have you been?"

"I'll tell you later."

A sleepy-eyed Frances came out. "Did Scotland Yard find them?"

"No," Lane told her. "Get your things, we're going to Portsmouth. We have work to do."

"Good," she said, and went back into the bedroom, leaving Morgan and Garza staring at Lane, one with hatred, the other with a vexed admiration.

------------------------------ 4 ------------------------------

ON THE ROAD TO PORTSMOUTH

Over Morgan's objections they used Frances's Range Rover for the sixty-mile trip down a fairly deserted A3 motorway to the navy base.

"Half of London has seen you two in this car," Morgan said. "If they start coming out of the woodwork again, we'll be sitting ducks."

"That's right," Lane said from the front passenger seat. "So I suggest you keep your eyes open. We might just end it all out here tonight, because I think it's a safe bet no one is going to attack us at the base."

Garza sat back grinning. "If one of Morgan's people came to Washington and did what you've done here in London we'd probably shoot the son of a bitch."

"The thought has occurred to us," Morgan said tightly.

5

PORTSMOUTH ROYAL NAVAL AIR STATION

The air station was off by itself away from the main navy base where the aircraft carrier *Hermes* was home-ported, and where one third of the navy's Harriers were based. Morgan presented his credentials to the gate guards, but it was a full fifteen minutes before they got authorization to proceed.

A staff car came out and led them across the base to a hangar on the flight line. A full commander in battle dress climbed out of the backseat, and came over to them as they got out. He was almost as big as Lane, and he did not seem happy.

"I'm James Moore. One of you is William Lane?"

"Yours truly," Lane said.

"Your people have been notified that you're here, sir," he said. "They're inside with my staff." He took the measure of Lane. "Frankly, we thought you would have shown up a lot sooner considering all the fuss that's been made."

"We were unavoidably delayed, Commander," Lane said. "Somebody tried to kill Commander Shipley and me. Slowed the program down just a bit."

Moore didn't know if his leg was being pulled, and

he couldn't tell from the expression on Lane's face. "This way, then," he said.

They trooped inside, where a Harrier vertical takeoff and landing jet was parked on the floor, and made their way to the back of the building as Tom Hughes came down the stairs from the offices on the second level, a big smile on his face.

"There you are finally," he said. He and Frances hugged, and he whispered in her ear. "Moira and the girls are beside themselves with excitement."

"You're as bad as he is." Frances laughed.

"True."

Lane introduced him to Morgan and Garza.

"I wasn't aware that you knew Commander Shipley," Morgan said prissily.

Hughes gave him a frank look. "Any friend of William's is a friend of mine."

"If we can get started now," Moore prompted.

Four of Moore's people, including the Harrier squadron CO, sat across the conference table from the two Americans from Rota. One of them was Lieutenant Arthur Ramsey, and the other was Tony Sayers, a civilian rep from Burroughs, which made the equipment. There was a lot of tension between them.

"Gentlemen, Bill Lane," Hughes said.

Lane handed copies of the fax to them. "How long will it take to install your gear in the Harrier?"

"About an hour now that you're here," Sayers said. "And providing we're given complete access, and I do mean *complete* access to that bird downstairs."

"That's the problem," the squadron commander, whose name tag read BARNES, broke in. "There is certain sensitive equipment aboard that aircraft."

"We're not here to steal your secrets, Captain, nor give ours away," Lieutenant Ramsey replied crossly. He looked as if he hadn't slept in a week. They all did, and tempers were running high.

"We don't have time to argue," Lane said. "We have a job to do. It's a joint operation and we're all going to cooperate with each other. Since Lieutenant Ramsey will be riding backseat during the search, it's only fair that a Royal Navy technician watch over the installation of the detector."

"Not a chance," Lieutenant Ramsey said, but Lane cut him off.

"Did you happen to notice the signature at the bottom of your orders?" It was President Reasoner's. "I'm calling the shots. If you don't like it, we'll put you on the next aircraft back to Rota, and Mr. Sayers can instruct a British technician to operate the detector."

An angry Ramsey nodded. "It's your call, but I'll make my report."

"Please do," Lane said just as crossly. "All this could have been avoided if the Royal Navy had agreed to an all-out search pattern."

"Not without proof," Morgan said. "We've gone over that before. To this point it's only your theory that this submarine was not sunk in the Barents Sea. Full-scale exercises cost a lot of money and are not conducted because of someone's hunch."

"You have the Harrier and our cooperation, Mr. Lane," Commander Moore said. "We'll give you that much, and as many daylight sorties as it takes to cover the Channel. But no more than that. Those are my orders. And I too noticed the signature at the bottom."

"I'm going to have to ask for one more favor," Lane said. "I need to borrow a ship."

Moore's mouth dropped open. "A ship?"

"A frigate or a destroyer, something that can hunt subs," Lane said. "And I'll need to talk to the captain as soon as possible."

6

PORTSMOUTH ROYAL NAVAL AIR STATION

"You're crazy if you think I'm going to ask Sir Hubert to take this back to the prime minister," Stewart said on the telephone.

"Nor do I want to bounce this to Washington," Lane said. "I'm not asking for the entire Royal Navy." He was calling from the maintenance office in the hangar.

"I had trouble convincing the navy to go this far, even under the PM's okay. They think that you're crazy, still fighting the cold war and all that."

"That's exactly what I'm doing, Mr. Stewart. Trying to prevent it from happening again. A lot of very good people lost their lives. British as well as Americans."

"I don't need a lecture. We're well aware of what's at stake. Your life as well as Commander Shipley's. But Scotland Yard is looking for Yernin, and for the madmen who tried to kill you yesterday morning."

"They won't find them, because they don't know who they're looking for, or where."

"But you do?"

"Yes, I do," Lane said. "And if you'll go along with me it'll only be a matter of days, maybe sooner, and I'll be out of your hair."

Morgan came to the door, a smirk on his face. "You're clutching at straws."

"I'm afraid that we've gone as far as we can with you, Mr. Lane," Stewart said.

"Is that your final word?"

"Yes, it is."

"Okay, you win, Stewart. I'll have my technicians out of here within the hour, and I'll take that Concorde back to Washington as you suggested. Then we can all write our reports, and wait to see what happens. At the very least it'll be interesting."

"You won't walk away knowing that Yernin is out there somewhere."

"Yes I will. Because wherever I go, Yernin will follow. He'll kill more people in the process, but he'll come after me, guaranteed. So besides three British citizens killed by murderers you'll never catch, who knows when the next submarine will sail right up to your front door. Maybe up the Thames as Brad suggested."

"You're a bastard, Lane. And I'll give you a guarantee of my own. Once this has been resolved, you'll never set foot in England again. Am I coming over loud and clear?"

"Does this mean we're no longer friends?"

Stewart blurted, "Bloody hell."

"Will you call the navy?"

"I'll turn this over to Sir Hubert. Maybe we can keep it off the PM's plate."

"Don't be long," Lane said, and he put the phone down. "I should have been a salesman."

Morgan was gazing wonderingly at him. "Like I said, Lane, at the first chance I'll cut you off at the knees and piss on the bloody stumps."

7

PORTSMOUTH ROYAL NAVAL AIR STATION

Commander Moore had been recalled to base headquarters, and Lane sent the others, including Frances, over to the BOQ to get a couple of hours' sleep. He stood on the balcony looking down at the Harrier. Two British marines stood guard.

"Whose arm did you twist this time, and what outrageous lies did you tell?" Hughes said from behind him.

"Roger Stewart's, but they were just white lies. We need that ship."

"Because even if we find the sub we won't be able to do a thing about it without firepower," Hughes said. "But you don't honestly think that the British navy will actually put a shot across her bows? Short of that Maslennikov will just thumb his nose at all of us."

"That's right, Tommy. But I want him to know that we're on to him."

"He figured that out last week," Hughes said. "What else have you come up with? What deep thoughts are you thinking, William?"

"You didn't hear what happened to us in London."

"What?" Hughes asked softly, as if he expected bad news.

"Frannie and I were attacked in front of Claridge's. This time it almost worked. By all rights they should have succeeded."

"I was in transit, I didn't catch any news broadcasts.

But Ben should have called. Was it Yernin?''

"No. At least he wasn't with them. It was a hit squad. Four or five of them, at least. In a van. Something made me look up at the last second, and I knew what was about to happen, so I shoved Frannie aside and started shooting."

"You're okay?"

"We're fine, but the doorman wasn't so lucky."

"Did they find them?"

"I did. They sailed last night on the *Santa Clara*. For Havana."

"Cubans," Hughes said in wonder.

Lane looked at him and nodded. "It opens up all sorts of possibilities."

"Are you thinking that Sierra Leone was just a ruse to throw everybody off track?"

"No. I think that when I showed up in Zürich, Maslennikov finally realized that he was in trouble. He couldn't go to Africa, there wouldn't be enough security for him. He'd no longer be anonymous there. But he wasn't just going to walk away from a fifty-million-dollar investment. So he scouted around for another likely buyer. A country where he and his men would be safe and comfortable. Wherever they ended up he knew they'd be boxed in. Better to have your cage velvet-lined. Makes it more palatable."

"There isn't one chance in a million that we could convince the president to order a blockade. Not merely on a hunch. If it was a nuclear submarine, armed with nuclear weapons, it would be a different story. So our only chance now is finding the submarine while it's still in British waters and challenging it with a warship to turn back."

"We'll find it, Tommy," Lane said. "It's just a matter of keeping the British interested long enough to get the job done."

"If anyone can convince them, you can."

Lane smiled tiredly. "Thanks for the vote of confidence. I hope it isn't misplaced."

"But why didn't you tell the Brits you'd found the hit team?"

"Because I don't want to spoil Maslennikov's plan yet. Not until I'm sure."

8

PORTSMOUTH ROYAL NAVAL AIR STATION

Two hours later Commander Moore returned. Lane and Hughes were studying the subsea charts for the English Channel and its approaches east and west, and they looked up when he walked in. He was resigned.

"You've got your ship. The HMS *Beaver*. A Broadsword-class frigate, and a damned fine sub hunter." He shook his head. "I don't know how you did it, but I have to give you high marks for brass."

"I'm trying to save lives, Commander," Lane said. "Same job as you. If we can stop them now, we'll prevent a lot of bloodshed later."

"I was warned about you."

A lightbulb went off in Lane's head. "Brad Morgan said that when he first told you about the submarine you were interested."

"That was then," Moore said tersely, not denying his connection with Morgan.

"When can we get started?"

"It'll take a couple of hours to get the captain back, and several more hours to make the ship ready for sea.

She just came off patrol, and most of her crew have already gone home.''

"Don't you have another cruiser or frigate we could use?" Hughes asked.

"Not for this operation."

"In the meantime let's get our people started installing the radiation detector in the Harrier," Lane said.

"They're on their way," Moore said. A small look of satisfaction crossed his features. "Mr. Morgan, Commander Shipley, and Mr. Garza will not be joining you. They've been recalled to London. And don't you try to argue with me. Those are my orders."

"Fair enough," Lane said mildly. "But I'd like you to get a message to Brad before he gets back to London."

Moore waited.

"Tell him to keep an eye on Commander Shipley."

"Very well."

"And Commander, tell him that when it comes to bloody stumps, turnabout is fair play." Lane smiled grimly. "He'll understand."

9

EN ROUTE TO LONDON

Morgan had wanted to drive but Frances wouldn't let him. "We could have seen them before we left."

"I told you, Frances, that they were taken by helicopter over to the *Beaver*. They're on a tight schedule. It's what you wanted wasn't it?"

"We all have plenty of work to do in London," Garza

said from the backseat, not sure why he'd been recalled, except that the Brits suddenly no longer wanted him on their military installation.

"Roger Stewart wants this resolved every bit as much as you do," Morgan said. "As I do."

"Right," Frances said to herself.

10

SIS HEADQUARTERS

It was still before dawn when they dropped Garza off at the U.S. embassy in Grosvenor Square and made it back to Whitehall. "Stay away from me, Brad," she told Morgan in the parking garage, and she went directly up to her office, leaving him standing alone.

She made herself a cup of tea, then powered up her computer, connected with Scotland Yard, and started with the data they had posted on the investigation into her uncle's murder in Oxford, the search for Valeri Yernin, and the more recent investigation into the shooting incident yesterday morning in front of Claridge's.

A half hour later she had learned nothing new. Scotland Yard's investigation was at a virtual standstill. Yernin had not been spotted anywhere in England, and the hit team that had tried to kill her and William had disappeared without a trace.

Next, she started a search program within the Customs Office, with the same results. Valeri Yernin had not entered or left England in the last ninety days, which was as far back as she was going to take it for now.

Her staff came in at eight o'clock, but nobody bothered her until Morgan showed up a half hour later, tapped on her door, and walked in.

"I thought you were going home," he said.

"No." She didn't look up from her screen.

"What are you doing?"

"My job."

"Well, you need a break. How about lunch? I'll pick you up at noon."

She looked up. "Get out of here," she said without inflection.

His lips compressed. "They'll spend a couple of days out there until the navy finally pulls the plug. But it's wasted effort, because that submarine was never here. Think about it. If it had sailed in and settled on the bottom, the crew would not have remained aboard all this time. Not in that vintage boat. Which means her crew had to have come ashore somewhere. Someone would have seen something. It's impossible to hide that kind of an operation anywhere near the Channel coast. Maybe up north, but not here. Too many people."

"What did you say?"

"I said the navy will pull the plug in a couple days."

"I meant about people. Too many people."

He nodded, warming to her interest. "The Channel coast is too populated. If the submarine was here someone would have seen something."

She thought about it. "You're right, Brad."

"What about lunch?"

"Get out of here," she said, turning back to her computer. "And close the door."

He hesitated at the doorway. "It's never going to work between you and him. He doesn't have your heritage, and that will come to bear sooner or later."

She ignored him.

After a moment he went out and closed the door.

She looked up, her despair deeper than it had been for a long time.

SIS HEADQUARTERS

Working on the assumption that both William and Brad were correct, that the submarine was somewhere in the Channel and that someone would have seen something, she pulled up detailed coastal survey maps from Ramsgate on the Strait of Dover in the east, to Land's End in the west. Eliminating the major population centers such as Portsmouth, Bournemouth, Torbay, and Plymouth, she concentrated on back bays, small islands, and isolated inlets that were sparsely populated.

Pulling up the subsea charts for those areas, she eliminated places where the water was less than one hundred feet deep, therefore too shallow to hide a submarine. She also eliminated areas very near shipping lanes, fishing beds, spoils where dredged material was dumped, and coast guard patrol routes.

She eliminated ferry routes, local yacht club racing courses, and areas where shipwreck locations were shown as approximate on the charts. Maslennikov would not have sent his submarine to wait on the bottom where there was a possibility of crashing into something.

Two hours later she had eliminated 80 percent of the entire Channel coast, and she dropped into Scotland Yard's system, and the coast guard's search-and-rescue records for the past week.

Aside from the usual small boats in distress calls, and one incident three days ago with the Newhaven-to-Dieppe ferry in which the captain reported he was taking on water, the most common report was interdiction of smugglers.

A few minutes before noon, however, she thought she'd found what she was looking for in the files of Scotland Yard's Special Branch.

Two nights ago a Frenchman from Flamanville, suspected of smuggling cash from the Continent to the islands, where it would be laundered through the banking system, suddenly disappeared without a trace. It was off Sark Island.

In the morning a police patrol boat had been dispatched to the area, and found a debris field that contained not only pieces of the wooden sailboat, but a large oil slick. The preliminary police report suggested that the smuggler's boat may have collided with a larger boat, and both of them sunk. The investigation was continuing, but since no other boat had been reported missing or overdue, it would be several days before divers would go down to search the sea bottom. The smuggler was a small-time operator and he was a Frenchman whose government didn't seem to care about him, so the incident was getting a low priority.

She pulled up the subsea charts for the area, which showed there was plenty of water to hide a submarine. And the thought suddenly occurred to her that Jersey or Guernsey would have been the perfect place for Maslennikov to operate from. The Channel Islands people considered themselves apart from England, and almost never cooperated with London. An entire foreign division could be hiding over there, and no one would say a thing as long as the money held out.

It was possible that the submarine had lain in wait off the thinly populated Sark Island until Maslennikov and his crew made ready to take off. The smuggler from Flamanville had the bad luck of getting in the way, possibly crushed by the surfacing submarine, which itself may have been damaged, or more likely by the boat that brought Maslennikov and his people and the money out to the rendezvous. In fact they may have sunk their own delivery boat on purpose, because it would no longer have been any use to them once they were aboard the submarine.

But the evidence was thin. William might buy it, but the navy wouldn't without more information. They could save time by beginning their search around Sark Island. But first they would have to be convinced.

Frances backed out of the program, and pulled up the airline reservations system. She hesitated. No one on Sark had seen anything, or it would have shown up in the police report. In any event Maslennikov and his people wouldn't have taken up residence there. They would have stood out too plainly. So it was either Jersey, the largest of the Channel Islands, or Guernsey, the most rural. Both islands had all the international banks, but Jersey was more touristy, something she didn't think Maslennikov would care for.

She brought up flight information for Guernsey, figuring if she was going to go on a hunch, she might as well push her luck to the limit. At this point there was nothing to lose.

12

GUERNSEY

Frances rented a small Peugeot at the St. Peter Port Airport and even though it was noon, and she was famished, she was too excited to eat. Before she left the car park she studied a map of the island. Covering an area of only twenty-four miles there was a surprising number of highways and roads, but she would concentrate her search along the coast road. If Maslennikov and his crew had left from here by boat to rendezvous with the submarine, it would not have been a rental. That would have been missed. Nor could it have been a very small boat, because someone would have noticed it hadn't come back overnight, and the coast guard would have been notified. It would have to be a larger boat, a cruiser, expected to stay away for long periods. And when a boat that size left a marina, it left a hole.

She got lucky in the first half hour at a marina a few miles outside of town, not far from the airport. Posing as a newspaper reporter for the *Portsmouth Times,* she told the dockmaster, a young, good-looking Frenchman, that she was doing a story on the yachts of the rich and famous during the off-season.

"We don't get much business this time of year," the dockmaster said, eyeing her legs.

"But you must get some," she said. They were sitting in his office overlooking the marina. "Maybe year-round people? Foreigners?"

The dockmaster laughed. "Some of them are crazy." He circled a forefinger at his temple. "They have money but no brains."

"I know what you mean," Frances said. "Maybe that's my story. Any examples?"

"The *Charisma* left two nights ago and hasn't come back. They're crazy foreigners. Lots of money, but nuts. They're Russians. Probably mafia, you know. No class."

Frances had to control herself. "You must be talking about Yuri Didenko and his people. I heard about him somewhere. Small guy, mustache, likes to party."

The dockmaster shook his head. "The captain is Andrei Kovrygin. He's okay. But the others keep to themselves. They've practically got an army, but they pay on time and mind their own business. But they go out only when the weather is bad. Like I said, they're crazy.''

Frances tried to keep the amazement off her face. All this time Maslennikov and his crew were operating here under their noses. "You said they left two nights ago. Did they say where they were going?''

The dockmaster smiled wishfully. "South,'' he said. "They didn't say anything to me, but I know about the charts they bought last week. Be my guess they're heading for the South Atlantic.''

Back at the airport, waiting for the next flight to London, she telephoned a stupefied Brad Morgan at SIS headquarters.

"You're calling from where?'' he demanded.

"Guernsey. You have to get word to William. As of two nights ago the submarine was off the coast of Sark Island. But it's already gone.''

"Stay right where you are. I'll have someone from Special Branch pick you up and bring you home.''

"You're not listening to me, Brad. I have proof that Maslennikov and his people were living here. They left two nights ago.''

"It's you who aren't listening!'' Morgan shouted. "Yernin is still out there gunning for you. Bloody hell, you're in danger.''

"Just get word to William, would you? Before it's too late.''

"If you promise to stay right where you are until I can get someone to you.''

She sighed. "I promise,'' she said. "But hurry.''

PART TWELVE

1

PORTSMOUTH ROYAL NAVAL AIR STATION

The installation of the radiation detector aboard the Harrier jet was completed at 2:00 P.M., almost twenty-four hours behind schedule. Lane, Hughes, the Harrier squadron commander Captain Talbot Barnes, the Harrier pilot Lieutenant Charles Decker, and the two Americans, Lieutenant Ramsey and Tony Sayers, stood together on the tarmac outside the hangar.

In the distance a helicopter was incoming.

Commander Moore came out of the hangar. "We're ready to get started," he said. "As a matter of fact, here comes your ride now."

"This new equipment is all very impressive, and it might work in the open Atlantic, but not here in the Channel," the navy pilot said. He was a serious-looking young man with bright red hair.

"Why's that?" asked Lieutenant Ramsey, who would be operating the equipment from the backseat.

"In the first place, there're bound to be snags. Fishing nets, buoys, small boats we might not see in time. They'll rip us apart."

"When that happens we'll return here and replace the sensor head and first fifty feet of cable. That's the simplest part of the system, meant to break away without damaging the rest of the cable or the reel."

The detector head was connected by up to three miles of ultrathin ceramic fiber-optic cable encased in a titanium sheath which was deployed from a pod about the size of a thousand-pound smart bomb carried beneath the starboard wing. The heart of the system was the ultrasensitive, ultrafast computer and display LEDs mounted just aft of the Harrier's front seat.

"The currents are vicious. Even if the submarine was there, any traces of radiation would be dissipated almost immediately."

"If we come within fifteen or twenty miles of it, we'll pick up a usable signal," Ramsey said, and he looked to the Burroughs rep for confirmation.

"That might be stretching it a little," Sayers said. "But the real problem you'll be fighting is the time element. The half-life of some of those isotopes might be a thousand years or more, but once the currents disperse them they'll become diluted below the sensor's threshold. We designed a good system, but it can't work miracles."

"If it's resting on the bottom somewhere along the coast its signature will stick out like a sore thumb," Ramsey said.

"Assuming it was here in the first place," Moore objected.

"If it was, it'll be heading west," Lane said. "If you start in the Strait of Dover and run a grid pattern five miles on a leg, you'll come across it sooner or later."

"That's if it's on the move and not still holed up somewhere," Lieutenant Ramsey said.

"At the end of each leg search the five miles of coast down to the next leg," Lane said.

Squadron commander Barnes nodded. "That might work. But it'll take a lot of time. And we'll still have to get lucky."

Lane smiled. "At this point it's the only game in town."

The Westland Lynx ASW helicopter set down noisily thirty yards from the Harrier.

"Mr. Hughes will be with me in base ops, but the

Harrier will be in direct contact with the *Beaver*," Commander Moore said.

"Do they understand the drill?" Lane asked.

"They've been briefed."

Lane shook hands with Ramsey and the pilot. "Good hunting."

"Thanks," Ramsey said.

"If you pick up anything, no matter how slight, even if you're not a hundred percent sure it's anything, let us know."

"If my equipment gives so much as a twitch, I'll shout bloody murder. Count on it. But we probably won't get very far today. There's not much daylight left."

Ramsey and the pilot went over to the Harrier, where they did a final walk-around, then mounted the boarding ladder, and the ground crewmen helped them strap in. Almost immediately the Rolls-Royce Pegasus turbofan began to spool up.

"They're waiting for you aboard the *Beaver*," Moore said.

"Did you pass my message along to Morgan?" Lane asked.

A smirk curled Moore's lips. "As a matter of fact I talked to him ten minutes ago."

"What'd he say?"

"He made an appropriate reply, Mr. Lane."

Lane laughed out loud. "I'll bet he did."

2

ABOARD 283

Unlike modern submarines with three or four decks for the control room, accommodations, machinery, and weapons, the Romeo only had one pressure cylinder, which allowed for only one deck. The conn, sonar, radio, crews quarters, all of it was on one very cramped level, with batteries beneath. For now there was plenty of room, but once they picked up Ortega's crew in Morocco they would be packed in like sardines, and already resentment was beginning to build.

Captain Lubiako came forward when he was finished inspecting the after torpedo room, and stopped in the tiny galley to get a glass of tea. The cook, Anatoli Tulayev, was carving meat and cheese for sandwiches.

"Do you want something to eat, Captain?"

"Not now. How about the men?"

Tulayev shrugged, his thick black hair falling over his forehead. "I can't force it down them. But I'll make a lamb stew for tonight."

"I'll redirect the air circulators. Once we get that smell throughout the boat, they'll come around."

At thirty-five, Tulayev was a veteran. He'd sailed with Lubiako for a long time. "Permission to speak frankly, Captain."

"Granted."

"Put Colonel Ortega in a torpedo tube and get rid of him. That'd do more to cheer up the men than lamb stew."

"The thought has occurred to me. But for now let's stick with your excellent cooking."

Tulayev nodded glumly, and Lubiako poured a second glass of tea, added some lemon and sugar, and took it forward to the officers' quarters, stepping carefully over the tall sills in the waterproof hatches. They were running submerged at sixty meters, and the boat was very quiet. Two-thirds of the crew was off duty and supposedly in their bunks sleeping. But he'd heard no snores on his inspection tour and saw only anxious faces looking up at him as he passed.

Maslennikov was sitting on the edge of his bunk smoking a cigarette. Unlike the crew he did not seem troubled. He looked tired but content.

Lubiako stepped into his compartment. "Here, I brought you some tea, Mikhail."

Maslennikov smiled and took the glass. "How are we holding up?"

"The boat is doing fine, but the men are worried."

"The difficult part is behind us. Have you made them understand that?"

"Not very well," Lubiako said. "It's you they want to hear from."

"Where is Colonel Ortega?"

Lubiako's mood darkened. "The last time I saw him he was in the control room as if he owned this boat. I think you should talk to him as well. Tulayev thinks that we should get rid of him and just get the hell out of here."

"To where? Sierra Leone is out," Maslennikov said. "Iran, perhaps, if we could get past the American submarines on patrol in the Gulf. Maybe South America, but we'd have to refuel somewhere." He shook his head. "Maybe you're right. It's time I talked to the men. What's Tulayev making for our dinner tonight?"

"Lamb stew."

"Good. That's perfect. With their bellies full they

won't be so quick to jump to the wrong conclusions.''

Maslennikov set his tea aside, pulled down the tiny sink, and splashed some cold water on his face. ''Are the men getting their rest?''

''No.''

''That's no good, Igor. If something should come up, some emergency, they'd need all their wits. They're not boys, they're all seasoned veterans.''

''They'll hold up if it comes to that,'' Lubiako said.

Maslennikov finished drying, hung the towel up, and squared his peasant shoulders. ''The situation will improve after tonight. There's no going back now.''

Lubiako shrugged. ''We haven't discussed all the alternatives.''

Maslennikov gave him a look of irritation. ''I told you that I need your trust a bit longer.'' He shook his head. ''You, of all people, have to understand that I have our best interests at heart. If I don't have you behind me, I won't have the crew. I've brought us this far.''

''Da,'' Lubiako said, lowering his eyes momentarily. He looked up. ''We'll fight for you, Mikhail. And die for you if necessary. We ask only to be told what we're getting ourselves into.''

''Fair enough.'' Maslennikov pulled on a bulky turtleneck sweater and picked up his tea, and they went forward to the control room.

The only crew on duty were the helmsman Nikolai Bykov, his brother Yuri, who was the diving officer, and Vasili Drankov, the officer of the boat. The sonar man, Vladimir Papyrin, was in his compartment around the corner. Ortega was not present.

''Captain's on the conn,'' said Drankov, looking up from his position behind the helmsman.

''As you were,'' Lubiako said.

Maslennikov stepped around the corner. ''How does it look, Vladi?''

''Very busy, Captain,'' Papyrin said, looking up.

''About what you would expect in the English Channel.''

''Have you heard any active sonars?''

Papyrin shook his head. ''No, sir.''

''No subsea traffic?''

''Nyet.''

''Keep a sharp ear.'' Back in the control room Maslennikov instructed Drankov to call Colonel Ortega. ''Have him join us in the officers' wardroom.''

3

ABOARD 283

Lubiako had the cook bring more tea and a carafe of strong coffee to the wardroom. A few minutes later the colonel arrived, zipping up his dark blue jacket. He'd brought a chart with him.

''Is there no heat in this boat?'' he demanded angrily.

''If we keep it warm it produces condensation,'' Lubiako said. ''The newer boats are better.''

Ortega slipped into a seat. ''I know why you called. I see the looks on the men's faces. On your faces.''

They cleared the glasses from the table and he spread out the small-scale chart of the eastern Atlantic extending five hundred nautical miles beyond the west coast of the Iberian Peninsula. Morocco was at the lower left corner.

''How is our battery power?''

''It's holding. But we'll have to surface again after dark to recharge,'' Lubiako answered.

''And our fuel?''

"Enough to reach Morocco and as far as Sierra Leone with a reserve, if that's still our plan."

"We'll make a rendezvous here," Ortega said, pointing to a spot on the chart.

Maslennikov and Lubiako bent over to look. The position was well out into the Atlantic, north of the Spanish coast, and somewhat north of the normal sea-lanes.

"Are we picking up your crew here? Has there been a change in plans?" Maslennikov asked.

"We're still picking up the crew in Morocco. But we'll take on fuel out here, away from prying eyes."

Maslennikov was uncomfortable. "You had this planned from the beginning."

"Of course, Captain. I don't like taking unnecessary risks. This boat is too important."

"What ship are we meeting?"

"She's a cargo vessel. Left London early this morning."

"What's her registry?" Lubiako asked.

"That doesn't matter for now. When the time comes I'll give you the exact coordinates and the code word. She'll send the all clear if it's safe for us to surface. Afterward we'll continue to the pickup point."

Lubiako got a set of dividers, parallel rules, and a pencil from a drawer, and laid out the course to the approximate position, then stepped off the distance. He made a few calculations at the edge of the chart. "Thirty hours."

Ortega nodded. "That's about right."

"How much fuel are we taking on?"

"A full load."

"If we slowed to nine knots surfaced, we could make thirty thousand kilometers. Anywhere in the world."

Ortega said nothing.

"Just what do you have planned for us, Colonel? Where are you taking us? And for what purpose?"

Ortega gave him a hard look, then took his time pouring a cup of coffee. "You are a very capable man, as are your crew. Captain Maslennikov has the highest confidence in you. And yet your crew are unhappy. They've even .spoken about mutiny."

"I'll take care of my crew," Lubiako said angrily. "But they cannot work in a vacuum."

Ortega pulled a notebook from his pocket, wrote something, and pulled the slip of paper out. "This is a small boat. There is no place safe from prying eyes or ears."

Lubiako stared at him.

Ortega handed him the slip of paper. "This is our final destination," he said. "Keep it to yourself until after Morocco."

A smile spread across Lubiako's lips. He looked up at Maslennikov. "I see," he said.

4

IN THE ENGLISH CHANNEL

At 471 feet on deck, with a crew of 273 men and officers, and bristling with radars, sonars, and sophisticated weapons, the frigate HMS *Beaver* was a powerful warship that could hold her own in a head-to-head battle with any submarine afloat. The problem was detecting the submarine before it detected you.

Lane was called up to the bridge once they had cleared the Portsmouth sea buoy, the Isle of Wight to starboard, and the ship's crew had settled into the routine.

Captain Gordon Guthrie, a slender handsome man

with curly gray hair, was waiting with his XO, Steven Ohlson, who looked big and tough enough to have played professional rugby.

"Some of my crew were just settling in with their wives and girlfriends when the recall came," Captain Guthrie said dryly. "So I hope you can convince me that we're not on a wild-goose chase."

"I hope we're not," Lane said. "Because it would mean that I don't know what I'm talking about, in which case a lot of people could get killed."

The captain exchanged a glance with his XO. "You have my attention, Mr. Lane. But first the ground rules. This is my ship. The moment I think we're wasting our time and Her Majesty's money, I'll give the order to return to port. There will be no questioning of that order, no matter how you perceive the situation."

"Fair enough."

"Very well, what are we looking for?"

"She's a Russian Romeo-class submarine that was supposedly scrapped in the Barents a couple weeks ago. I think that she was brought down here and laid up somewhere in the Channel. In some back bay, behind some island. Somewhere out of the way."

"Like looking for a needle in a haystack," Guthrie said. "Have we heard any hint of this?" he asked his XO.

"No," Ohlson said without taking his eyes off Lane. "What are the Russians doing down here?"

"The crew is Ukrainian. Former Black Sea Fleet. They bought the sub from the Russians for resale to the military government in Sierra Leone."

"Why'd they come through the Channel? Why not over the top?" Ohlson asked.

"Because the rest of the crew were waiting somewhere in the British Isles for them."

"Okay, assuming that you know what you're talking about, do you think the submarine is still somewhere around here, or is it possible that the crew is aboard and they've already made it to the open Atlantic?''

"That's possible," Lane admitted. "In which case I'd like you to follow them."

"Providing we pick up their scent first," Ohlson said. "There are a lot of places to hide. Once a submarine is gone, it doesn't leave much of a wake for very long."

"This one will," Lane said. "Her hull is radioactive."

Guthrie shrugged. "From the Polyarnyy graveyard. Are you saying you've brought a radiation detector along that can pick them up?"

"It's aboard the Harrier," Lane said. "I was told you'd been briefed."

"I wanted to hear it from the horse's mouth," Guthrie said. "What you want us to do is circle around out here until the Harrier picks up the trail, if it does, and then chase after it. Still a lot of water to cover, so I'd say we're going to have to get very lucky to pull it off."

"The submarine is going east to west, heading out of the Channel, if it's already on the move. If the Harrier pilot makes north-to-south sweeps they'll pick up traces."

"*If* it's on the move, and *if* it was ever here," Ohlson said.

"That's right." Lane was getting tired of telling the same story with the same results, but he couldn't blame them for their skepticism.

"Then what?" Guthrie asked. "Let's say we do get lucky. The Harrier picks up the track, and we follow it and catch up with the sub. What do you want us to do, kill her?"

"Force her to surface and arrest the crew."

A thin smile spread across the captain's face. "In the open ocean?"

"That's right."

"On what charge?" Ohlson asked.

"Murder," Lane said. "Piracy. Conspiracy to commit

acts of international terrorism. Fraud. Theft. The possibility of carrying illegal nuclear weapons.''

Captain Guthrie's thick eyebrows rose a notch. "You spies do think deep thoughts, I'll say that much for you.''

5

IN THE ENGLISH CHANNEL

On the captain's reluctant orders, Lane was allowed into the Combat Information Center just aft and one deck below the bridge. The suite of four cramped compartments filled with electronic equipment, some of it covered for security reasons, was lit ghostly red. Ohlson introduced him to the CIC watch officer, Lieutenant Commander Roger VanDyke, a slightly paunchy man with a sunny disposition.

"So, we're going hunting for a submarine, and nobody gives us much chance of success," he said. "In the first place that boat was probably never here, but if it did come through Dover it probably went straight on through. Nothing illegal in that. These are international waters. But assuming it not only entered the Channel, but hung around on the bottom somewhere, finding it will be a bit tricky, considering the area we have to work with, and the limited resources at hand. That about sum it up?''

"Close enough," Lane said. "But we have a specially equipped Harrier up flying to help us out.''

VanDyke, a smile on his face, gave Lane a skeptical

look. "Has anyone talked to you about the currents in the Channel?"

"If it's on the bottom, the Harrier will find it, because the boat will emit a constant radiation signature, I don't care what the currents are."

"Okay. But what if it's already gone? Its track would be like a jet contrail broken up by strong winds aloft."

Lane walked over to the plotting table, on which a chart of the entire English Channel was laid out. "The Harrier is going to start up here in Dover, and run a grid back and forth to the French coast. Five miles on each base leg."

"You're assuming that if the submarine is on the move, it'll be heading west, out into the open Atlantic."

"That's right."

"You're gambling that it won't have doubled back and headed toward Scotland. Or that it wasn't holed up along our east coast in the first place."

"As you pointed out, Commander, I was given limited resources. Searching the Channel makes the most sense to me. If two-eighty-three is on the move, the Harrier will catch up to it and cross its track."

VanDyke studied the chart. "Do you know where the submarine is heading?"

"I have a fair idea."

VanDyke looked up. "Then why not just beat it to the punch, and wait for it to show up?"

"Not possible for political reasons. Or at least it'd be a lot easier if we could catch it now."

VanDyke looked at the chart again. "Well, Mr. Lane, in that case you're faced with another problem. Dover to Land's End is a distance of about three hundred fifty miles. That's seventy legs with a base five miles each. The distance across the Channel for each leg is anywhere from a little over twenty miles, to more than one hundred thirty west of Portsmouth. If you want them to adequately search all the likely hidey-holes along the coast, and around islands, they'll have to slow down, and of course operate only during the day. Combined with the sad fact that a Harrier flying that slowly burns up a lot of kerojet, meaning she'll have to refuel often, this little project of yours could take several weeks.''

Lane nodded.

"Her Majesty's navy might not give you all that time.''

"Then we'd better hustle, wouldn't you say so, Commander?''

VanDyke laughed. "Name's Roger,'' he said. "And we're going to need more than hustle.''

6

ABOARD THE HARRIER

The ferry to Calais was just passing the Dover sea buoy, her bows rising into the choppy seas, whitecaps for as far as the eye could see, when Lieutenant Charles Decker dropped to three hundred feet and reduced his speed to eighty knots. They were just below the overcast, which was much thicker than at Portsmouth. He switched to the HMS *Beaver*'s frequency.

"Red Base, this is Red One, ready to make our first turn.''

"Roger Red One. Watch your traffic and good hunting.''

Decker switched to intercom. "Are you ready back there?''

"Yes,'' Lieutenant Ramsey said. "Are we clear?''

"Affirmative.''

Once they were airborne, Ramsey had partially deployed the cable, at the end of which was an eighteen-inch sensor shaped like a fish with slightly angled fins. When the device hit the water, it would dive, its depth computer-controlled at five feet. Ramsey released the final three hundred feet of cable. Moments later the *sensor wet* indicator lit, and the computer took over.

"Start your run, we're wet," Ramsey spoke into his helmet mike, his eyes on the CRT displays.

"Red Base, we're commencing our first leg," Decker radioed, and he turned sharply to starboard, toward the coast of France, on a parallel track two miles northeast of the ferry.

"Oops."

"Are you getting a reading?"

"That was almost my lunch all over the back of your seat," Ramsey said.

"Sorry about that, Lieutenant. I'll take it easy next time."

Ramsey swallowed several times. "That's okay, I'll hang in back here. They say you're the best pilot in the squadron, so just do your thing, ace, and we can get this over with ASAP."

"If it gets too bad let me know."

"Don't worry, you'll know about it."

It was nearly dark and getting difficult to see when they finished their third leg.

"Time to pull the pin, Decker," Ramsey said.

"We didn't get very far, but we'll do better tomorrow. We'll have the whole day."

"We'll need it," Ramsey told him. He flipped the switch to reel in the cable. "The Channel is getting a lot wider, more water to cover. But at least the shipping won't be so concentrated."

Decker switched to the *Beaver*'s frequency. "Red Base, this is Red One. We're securing from operations."

"Roger Red One. No indications?"

"Nothing."

"How's your passenger holding up?"

"Okay, Red Base. Actually quite good."

"Glad to hear it."

Decker switched back to intercom. "Let me know as soon as your sensor is back in the barn, and we'll get out of here."

"About sixty seconds," Ramsey said. "Say, ace, when you've accomplished your mission you usually do a victory roll, right?"

"Depends on who's looking."

"What about when you aren't successful?"

"In that case we return to base for our debriefing, and then head over to the officers' club for a stiff whiskey. Or two."

"Thank God for small favors."

"Lieutenant?"

"We didn't find anything, so there'll be no victory roll. I don't think my stomach could handle it."

Decker laughed.

"But I'm buying the whiskey. Maybe two."

7

HMS BEAVER

After supper in the officers' mess, Lane stepped out on deck and stood smoking a cigarette by the rail. The night was pitch-black, the Channel rough, the air very cold. They would spend the night doing sonar sweeps back and forth, gradually working their way east. If anything was moving beneath the surface they would find it, if they got close enough. He figured their best bet—a long shot at that—was still with the Harrier. But what they were doing tonight would not hurt. And they might get lucky.

Captain Guthrie came up behind him. "Nothing's turned up yet," he said.

Lane shook his head. "I think they're west of here."

"Then why not start at Land's End and work this way? Unless you're even less sure than I think you are, and you're covering all your bets."

"Something like that."

Guthrie leaned against the rail next to Lane and stared out at the lights of a number of cargo vessels in the distance. "It's more than just the submarine, isn't it?"

"It's not simply political, if that's what you mean."

"I was told some of it before we left port. You've been chasing after these people for more than a year. Bad people. Killers. Assassins."

"All of that," Lane said. "We either stop them here and now, or they'll keep doing it. And believe me, Captain, they're very good at what they do."

Guthrie looked at him. "Why? What's the point? The cold war is over, or are they simply terrorists? What are they after? Revenge?"

"They were spies for their country but now they're terrorists."

"What battles are they fighting?"

"Their own," Lane said. "They were highly trained, and when they weren't needed any longer, they couldn't quit."

Guthrie was silent in his thoughts for a minute. "Is it that simple?"

"For them it is."

A hard look came in Guthrie's face. "If you're right about them being here, we'll find them." He pushed away from the rail. "And I hope you are right, Lane."

8

ABOARD THE HARRIER

It was still dark when the specially equipped Harrier lifted off the tarmac at Portsmouth Royal Naval Air Station and headed north to resume the search. Ramsey was bleary-eyed from a night at the officers' club, but he'd come to the conclusion that Decker, and in fact most of the British officers he'd met, were okay.

"The sun should be up by the time we get on station," Decker said from the front seat. He didn't sound any better.

"If you make crazy turns like you did yesterday, I'll guarantee that you'll be wearing my breakfast."

Decker laughed. "I was ready for a decent burial myself this morning. Especially when I got a gander at those eggs. I don't know how you did it."

"I was trying to keep up with Tom Hughes. Dumb move."

"Good heavens, I thought my CO could drink, but I heard that Hughes had to carry him back to his quarters last night. Or should I say this morning. And did you see the gargantuan breakfast the man ate? It was inhuman."

Ramsey shook his head, and instantly regretted it. "He and Lane are quite the pair."

"That they are, Arthur."

HMS *BEAVER*

Back in the CIC after a few hours' sleep, Lane telephoned Hughes. "Nothing so far. But this is a good crew, and they're pushing it."

"If two-eighty-three is already in the open Atlantic, they're not going to follow it. We just got that word from London. But they're giving us the entire Channel."

"That's something," Lane said. "Have you talked to Frannie?"

"Her housekeeper said she didn't come home last night, so I called Morgan. He said they've placed her in a safe house."

"Where?"

"He wouldn't say."

"See if you can find her, Tommy. I'd like to know that she's okay."

"So would I," Hughes said.

PORTSMOUTH ROYAL NAVAL AIR STATION

Hughes had charmed the Harrier squadron commander, and everyone in operations, so he was given his own desk and computer terminal. He telephoned Mario Garza at the American embassy, a niggling fear in his gut that all was not as it should be with Morgan or with Frances.

"How's it going down there?" Garza asked. "Have you come up with anything yet?"

"Nothing yet," Hughes said. "Are you going over to the safe house today?"

"After lunch."

"Would you tell Commander Shipley to telephone me?"

Garza was suddenly guarded. "She's not there. Have you tried her office?"

"Brad Morgan says they have her at a safe house."

"Not one of ours. I could snoop around."

"Would you please? I'd like to talk to her."

"I'll see what I can do, but Morgan has definitely got an ax to grind."

"Let's hope he doesn't swing too wildly, he might cut off his own foot," Hughes said.

"Or somebody else's," Garza replied darkly.

11

ABOARD 283

The passage between Little Sole and Great Sole Banks marked the edge of the continental shelf. With that position well behind them, everybody aboard the submarine breathed a sigh of relief. They were in the open Atlantic, where it would take a miracle for anyone to find them. Combined with the good food they were getting, and Maslennikov's assurances that he was not leading them into harm's way, the crew had settled down, and no longer were there the anxious looks, or grumbling.

Kovrygin was acting as navigation officer. He looked up from the chart on which he was plotting their position. "Sunset is in thirty minutes. I recommend that we make a sonar sweep and then come to periscope depth."

"Very well," Lubiako said, and he stepped around the corner to sonar. "How does it look, Vasha?"

"Our only contact is Sierra eighteen, and she's fading. Twenty-one thousand meters, relative bearing one-nine-five." Papyrin looked up. "All the shipping lanes are to the south. We're clear."

"No subsea traffic?"

"None."

Back in the control room Lubiako gave the order to Vasili Drankov, the officer of the boat, to bring them slowly to twenty meters, periscope depth, then went to the plotting table. "How close are we to our rendezvous?"

"Fifty kilometers," Kovrygin said, and he glanced aft toward the officers' wardroom. "But the bastard only gave us an approximate position. We could be right on top of it."

"There's nothing within twenty kilometers," Lubiako said. "In any event we need to surface as soon as it gets dark."

"I agree."

Five minutes later they leveled off at twenty meters. Lubiako raised the search periscope and did a slow 360-degree sweep. It was twilight and the weather was closing in, but there was nothing within visual range on the surface.

"Raise the snoop plate, and give me a radar sweep to thirty kilometers."

"Roger," the Electronic Support Measures (ESM) officer said, and two minutes later he was back. "Two airborne targets at our extreme range, bearing one-eight-seven and two-three-four. The range is opening."

"Anything on the surface?"

"*Nyet.*" Because of the low height of the mast, the radar's surface range was less than ten kilometers.

"Are we being illuminated by any radars?" Lubiako asked.

"Negative."

Lubiako made another sweep, then straightened up and retracted the periscope. "Very well. Surface the boat, and prepare to switch to diesel operation."

Ortega came forward in a rush as the submarine surfaced, his face screwed up in anger. "Who gave the order to surface?" he screamed.

Everyone in the control room looked up, startled.

"I did," Lubiako said calmly.

"Those weren't my orders! Submerge this boat, now!"

Lubiako turned to Drankov. "Vent the boat, then secure from battery operation and start the diesels."

"Yes, sir."

"I forbid this," Ortega said, regaining control of himself. "You're putting us all in jeopardy."

"On the contrary, Colonel. There is no traffic nearby in the air, on the surface, or beneath the surface. We're quite alone out here, and our batteries need recharging."

Maslennikov came from his compartment at that moment. "What's the problem?"

Ortega turned to him imperiously. "Captain Lubiako has seen fit to come to the surface without my authorization."

"I wasn't aware that you were in command," Maslennikov said. "Is there anything out there?" he asked Lubiako.

"Nothing within twenty kilometers, but we're coming up on the rendezvous point."

Ortega walked over to Kovrygin at the plotting table. "What is our present position?"

Kovrygin showed him.

"Where is your ship?" Maslennikov asked.

"Within radio range," Ortega said.

"The weather looks like it's starting to go to hell," Lubiako said. "If we're going to refuel, let's get on with it before conditions make it impossible."

"Do you have a problem with that, Colonel?" Maslennikov demanded. "If not, call your ship, give them the proper code, and let them know that we're ready to take on fuel."

"There is nothing behind us?" Ortega asked.

"Nothing," Lubiako assured him. "We'll keep a tight watch, something that is difficult to do when we're at periscope depth and even more difficult to do when we're running deep."

"If you'll give me the frequency and the initial code, I'll try to make contact," said the young officer at the communications console.

Ortega shot Maslennikov a hard look, but then nodded. "Very well." He gave the communications officer the proper frequency. "They'll answer to *Dos Centavos*. But use the lowest power possible."

"Good," Lubiako said. "Mr. Drankov, muster the line handlers and refueling crew. Have them standing by. I'll conn the boat from the bridge."

12

ABOARD 283

The name on the bow of the cargo boat had been covered up, and she showed no flag or lights. Lubiako stood on the bridge with a radioman and the pilot lines that they would use to drag the fuel hoses across were shot over.

In the days before the Soviet Union disintegrated, and the effectiveness of the Russian federal navy came to an end, this operation would have been impossible to do in secret, he thought. In those days these waters were continuously patrolled. Along with the SOSUS network of underwater sensors, nothing could have gotten out of the English Channel undetected. These days security was lax.

"Lines secured, steady up," he said.

The radioman relayed his order.

Next, two fuel hoses came across, and within minutes the crew had them secured to the intakes.

"Positive connection on one and two," the radioman said.

"Proceed," Lubiako said. He looked up at the bridge

of the ship towering above them, and thought he saw a movement at the windows.

Maybe it would work out in the end, he told himself. But if they were cornered, he knew that his men would not hesitate to fight. To the death if need be.

13

HMS *BEAVER*

The day had somehow gotten away from Lane, and when the message came from the Harrier pilot that they were securing from operations he could scarcely believe it.

He sat back in his chair and pressed his eyes, which were bleary from staring at sonar screens. Maybe he was wrong. He didn't believe that. He thought that they were just late, but he was going to have to answer some tough questions that Her Majesty's navy was going to shove his way. No one liked to spend money and effort and come up empty-handed. Made them look like incompetents.

Captain Guthrie came into the CIC. "When's the last time you got some sleep?"

Lane looked up. "This morning."

Guthrie perched on the console next to Lane's. "We're not giving up just yet, but you're not doing any good down here in your condition."

"You're probably right," Lane said tiredly.

"What's a man like you doing out here in the first place? You're wealthy. You should be tending after your investments. Or is this some kind of a hobby?"

Lane had to laugh. "I can think of a lot safer hobbies. It's my job."

"What happens if we come up empty-handed? Are you going to quit and return to Washington, or are you going to make a lot of noise on somebody else's doorstep until they give in?"

"If they're in the Channel we'll find them."

"If they're already gone, we won't go after them. Those are my orders. If that's the case, what will you do?"

"Continue following them."

"Will you swim out to sea? Right across the Atlantic? That's a long way."

Lane had drifted, but he suddenly focused on the captain. "A very long way," he said. "Thousands of miles. After already having come thousands of miles. And they were pushing it."

"I'm not following you."

Lane jumped up and went to the chart table, where the navigation officer found a chart of the entire North Atlantic, from the Barents and Norwegian Seas all the way south to the equator. Using a pair of dividers Lane stepped off the distance from Polyarnyy, down to the English Channel, and then out the other side into the open ocean.

"When they faked two-eighty-three's scuttling, they had to dump fuel to convince everyone on the surface that she'd really broken apart. It means she came down here light. Almost empty, as a matter of fact. She has to refuel."

"The Romeo is a long-range submarine. She'd have enough fuel to make it to Sierra Leone."

"If that's where she's headed," Lane said.

"Where else?" Guthrie asked.

Lane sat down at his console and telephoned Hughes back at the base. The call went through immediately on the special channel the navy had set up for them.

"Morgan is holding her incommunicado for the time being," Hughes said.

"As long as she's out of harm's way it's okay for now, but keep trying to reach her," Lane said. "Are you at a computer terminal?"

"Yes."

"Find out from customs when the *Santa Clara* sailed, and what she declared for her next port of call."

"Stand by."

Guthrie was looking at him. "Are you thinking that the submarine took on fuel at sea?"

"If the times match, it's possible."

Hughes came back a couple of minutes later. "She sailed the night before last. Nearly forty hours ago. Headed for La Rochelle, France."

"She'd be there by now."

"Just a minute," Hughes said.

"If they're refueling it means they probably aren't going to Sierra Leone," Guthrie said.

Lane nodded.

Hughes was back. "La Rochelle Port Authority has no record of the *Santa Clara*."

"That's it," Lane said. "Two-eighty-three will probably meet up with her, if she hasn't already done so, to take on fuel. Find out if we've got a satellite covering this part of the Atlantic. I'd like to know just where the *Santa Clara* has gotten herself to."

"The weather's been bad for the past forty-eight hours, William. Overcast. But we can project her probable track, and keep looking, if we've got a bird in position."

"We need proof, Tommy, if we're going to take this to the president."

"The location of one ship isn't proof."

"No, but it's a start. If we can tie the ship and the submarine together, we'll have at least one of the answers."

"I'm on it," Hughes said.

"That's providing the submarine was here in the Channel in the first place," Guthrie said when Lane put the phone down. "To this point there's not one shred of proof."

"Then it's up to us to find it," Lane said. "We can sleep later."

PART
THIRTEEN

1

GREENWICH

Scotland Yard's Special Branch maintained a debriefing facility on the grounds of the old Royal Observatory a half hour from Central London. The agent in charge of the two-man, two-woman detail was Harry Weiss, a hulk with thick white hair and arms like ham hocks. He'd been a tough man until his petite wife of seventeen years died of cancer. In the eight years since, he'd mellowed considerably, but in the past twenty-four hours his patience had been tested.

The closely guarded compound was used to interrogate high-ranking spies or very important criminals, but Weiss was puzzled by their only guest, who was neither.

Brad Morgan showed up just before 8:00 P.M., and came up to the main house. "Is she still giving you trouble, Harry?"

Weiss was drinking tea alone in the kitchen. He shook his head. "She understands that she's here for her own protection. But she doesn't understand why that means she can't use the telephone."

"Because if she calls the wrong numbers, she could be traced," Morgan said crossly. He was getting tired of explaining himself to every Tom, Dick, and Harry.

"Well, maybe you'd better explain it to her, because she sure as hell won't listen to us. Especially not after we took to locking her in her quarters."

"That's why I'm here," Morgan said, and Weiss

started to get up, but Morgan motioned him back.
"Don't bother, I know the way."

"If you can't convince her to settle down, maybe you
can find another place to take her. Frankly, I don't know
what to put on my report."

"She's in protective custody, that's what."

Weiss looked at him skeptically. "Find another place
for her, Mr. Morgan, if you please. I'm afraid I'm going
to have to insist. Either that or send an official request
for investigation through channels."

"Very well."

Weiss handed him a master key. "Care for a cup of
tea first?"

"No," Morgan said, and he stormed out of the
kitchen and charged upstairs past a startled matron who
was on her way down. He knocked once and let himself
into the suite where Frances had been kept since Special
Branch picked her up at the airport on Guernsey.

She was watching CNN, and when she saw who it
was a look of relief crossed her face, which almost immediately changed to irritation. She jumped up.

"You better have a good explanation for this, Bradley,
or I swear to God I'll have your head on a pike."

"This is for your own good," Morgan said, but she
brushed that aside.

"Rubbish. I want to use the telephone."

"No calls."

"I want to talk to Roger."

Morgan shook his head. "No calls are allowed out of
here, Frances." He spread his hands in a gesture of
peace. "Even Bill agrees with me on this one."

Her face lit up. "Have they found something at
Sark?"

"Nothing yet. And it doesn't look like they will, because that submarine was never there. Our only problem
right now is keeping you alive until we can find Yernin."

"But they went to Sark and searched for the wreck," she insisted.

"I don't know."

"What do you mean, you don't know?" she demanded. "Tom Hughes should still be at Portsmouth. What'd he say?"

"That son of a bitch thinks he owns the place. If I had my way he and Lane would be on the first airplane out of here." Morgan was beside himself with anger. "It'll happen a lot sooner than either of them suspect."

Frances stared at him. "My God, you never told him about Sark."

"It's a wild-goose chase. You have no proof—"

Frances brushed past him, and before he could stop her she was out in the corridor and heading for the stairs.

"Get back here," he shouted, racing after her. "That's an order, Commander!"

Weiss and one of the matrons came out of the kitchen as Frances reached the front hall. She charged past them and went to the phone.

"Just a minute, Commander," Weiss said.

Frances turned to him as Morgan reached the hall, his face red with exertion. "I won't remain here any longer, Bradley, unless you can produce a warrant for my arrest. And the charges better be good."

"You're putting yourself in danger, you little fool."

"What's it to be?" she demanded.

Morgan shook his head after a moment. "Go on, then. Chase after him. But if you get cornered, don't expect me or the service to come running."

"I've not expected anything from you for years," Frances said. She turned to the matron. "If you'll be kind enough to get my things, I'll be gone." She telephoned base operations at Portsmouth, where she got through to an anxious Hughes.

"I've been looking all over for you," he said.

"I'm in Greenwich. Has William come up with anything yet?"

"Nothing, but the search goes on."

"They're looking in the wrong places. Maslennikov and his people were living on Guernsey. Two days ago they all left aboard the motor yacht *Charisma* and nobody's heard from them since."

"If it was a big enough boat they could have rendezvoused anywhere."

"The submarine was hiding about ten miles off Sark Island. They had to sink a small sailboat that a French smuggler was using. He probably stumbled on to them transferring the crew. Once they were aboard the sub they scuttled the yacht."

"How did you find this out?"

"I went there, talked with the people at the marina. It was Maslennikov and his men, there's no doubt about it." Frances shot Morgan a withering glance. "Get that to William as soon as you can." She gave him the exact position.

"Will do," Hughes said. "But listen, my dear, maybe you should remain there. After all we don't know if Yernin is aboard the submarine. He might still be lurking about waiting for you and William."

"I'm going home. But I hope the bastard does show up. I'll put a bullet between his eyes, and we'll be done with it. Besides, the Yard still has people on my doorstep. I'll be fine."

"Be careful, Frannie."

"Just get the message off to William," she said, and she hung up and went to retrieve her things, including her pistol.

LONDON

Yernin had a late supper in a small pub around the corner from his hotel in Piccadilly Circus, then walked two blocks to where he'd parked his rental Ford. Frances Shipley had not returned home last night, nor was her Rover parked in back this morning or noon when he drove over to check.

On his first pass yesterday he'd spotted men in the two dark blue Toyota vans, one parked in front and the other in back. No doubt they were from Scotland Yard assigned to protect her, and he decided that when the woman finally returned home he would have to kill them. Preferably in the early-morning hours when they would be least alert.

Traffic was heavy and it took him fifteen minutes to drive over to the apartment for his first pass. He expected to see the blue van parked in front, but it wasn't there, nor was the Rover. He continued to the end of the block, and turned left, then made three more turns which brought him back to her apartment from the opposite direction.

The Toyota was gone from the alley as well, and the house was dark.

He found a parking spot, lit a cigarette and adjusted the rearview mirror so that he could watch the building. Nothing seemed out of the ordinary. The vans had not been replaced with other vehicles. Every parked car was empty, and there was nothing in back. He considered the possibilities. It could mean that she wasn't coming back. They might have moved her to a safe house. Or possibly they thought that she was no longer in danger, and no longer needed to be guarded.

But there was no way of knowing which was true, or if some other possibility was in fact the case.

But she would have to return sooner or later. It would be several days before 283 reached Morocco, and much longer before it reached its final destination, if he was correct in his assumption. He had plenty of time to wait. All the time in the world.

Stubbing out his cigarette, he got out of the car, and, bent over in an old man's stoop, shuffled down the street to the corner, waited patiently for a break in traffic so that he could cross, then headed for the alley that ran behind her apartment.

3

ABOARD 283

The submarine ran on the surface at sixteen knots south by southwest after a following sea with a stiff wind at their backs. Maslennikov climbed up to the bridge where Lubiako and two lookouts studied the lights of a ship far to the southeast.

"He's well north of the shipping lanes," Maslennikov said. He took a pair of binoculars from one of the lookouts and studied the lights. "He's a container ship."

"Heading for Gibraltar," Lubiako agreed. He lowered his binoculars. "A hundred roubles the watch officer is drunk and doesn't know his position within fifty miles, satellite navigators and all.''

"They wouldn't be Japanese."

"Or British," Lubiako said. "They're better than that. Lookouts go below and get something to eat."

"Yes, sir," they said, and they disappeared through the hatch. The sky was overcast and it was very cold.

"What do you think about Ortega now?"

Lubiako glanced toward the open hatch and shrugged. "If we actually get this boat where he wants us to take it, the fat will be in the fire."

"Does that worry you?"

"Everything about this mission worries me, Mikhail." He sniffed the air. "That's death out there I'm smelling. For the right cause it's a risk I'm willing to take. We all are." He shook his head. "But this is no longer our fight."

"It's just a business deal," Maslennikov told him. "Unless you believe it would be preferable to take up residence in North Africa."

Lubiako laughed. "Taking up residence necessitates getting there in the first place. That's what has me worried. Because if the crew we're going to take on in Morocco doesn't slit our throats in our sleep, our problems will just be starting. It won't be like the English Channel."

"Which is why we took him aboard in the first place."

Lubiako shook his head again, but said nothing. He leaned out well over the coaming and studied their wake, and the bilge pumps spewing water over the side.

"There's only one navy that counts anymore, is that what you're thinking?" Maslennikov asked.

"*Da*," Lubiako said seriously. "That and Yernin. If he fucks up again and gets himself arrested, there'll be a reception committee waiting for us."

"It won't happen."

Lubiako looked at his old friend. "Let's hope not."

4

HMS _BEAVER_

They headed at their top speed of thirty-two knots toward Sark Island, the captain on the bridge, Lane with VanDyke in the CIC. The position of the wrecked smuggler's boat and oil slick that Hughes had given them was slightly more than two hours away.

"If that was them they've had a helluva head start," VanDyke said. "But if Commander Shipley is correct and they scuttled their motor yacht we'll find it. Side-scan sonar, and underwater television cameras."

"I need proof before I can take this to my president," Lane said. He studied the French coastal charts, which included the British-owned islands.

"The weather is too rotten for the satellites to see anything. But in the morning the Harrier can make a pass."

"Tonight," Lane said, looking at the CIC officer. "It'll be risky for them, but every hour that passes makes it less likely the detector will find anything."

VanDyke looked serious. "Nobody is going to give that order. I for one won't recommend it to the old man."

"I agree," Lane said, reaching for the phone. "But maybe they'll do it as a favor."

Hughes was on the way out. "Trouble?"

"No, we're heading to Sark. But it's going to take another two hours. The Harrier could make it faster, if Decker's CO is willing to take the risk."

"I was just on my way over to the officers' club to ask that very question."

"Tell them to be careful."

"Will do," Hughes said. "If you can snap a picture of the sunken yacht, and we can get a positive trace on the radiation signature, we'll have enough to take to Newby at the White House."

"Then let's do it, Tommy. Be convincing."

5

LONDON

A police car, its blue lights flashing, hurried by on the street in front. Yernin stepped farther back into the shadows and waited a full five minutes to make certain it was not coming back.

When it didn't, he made his way in the darkness to the rear door that led into the apartment's kitchen. A light was on over the stove, but otherwise the apartment was in darkness.

Directly across from the door the alarm system's keypad was mounted on a wall next to the pantry. A small green light was lit, and the word READY showed in the small display, which meant the system was armed and ready to be switched on. But apparently the old fool of a housekeeper had forgotten to switch it on when she left.

The door was locked, but he opened it with a pick set in under a half minute, and slipped inside and relocked it.

Moving quietly to the front stair hall, he took out his

Heckler & Koch, and screwed the Carswell silencer on the end of the barrel.

The house had a faintly musty smell of books, but was utterly silent, except for the faint noise of the occasional car or truck passing on the street.

He went to the window in the vestibule, parted the curtains a crack, and looked outside. The police car had not returned, nor had the blue Toyota van come back.

Turning away, he looked up to the head of the stairs, then went in search of the housekeeper's quarters. Like uncle, like niece, the thought occurred to him.

A telephone rang in the front hall, and Yernin stepped out of Mrs. Houlten's sitting room. After the third ring, Frances's voice came from the answering machine, explaining that the call was important to her, after the tone please leave a message.

"This is Tom. It's just nine o'clock. As soon as you get home call me. I'll be in Operations. William is off to Sark Island aboard the *Beaver,* and the Harrier is up. If there's anything out there we'll find it. Nobody's reported the *Charisma* docking anywhere in England or France, so she just may be lying on the bottom as you suggested."

Yernin was thunderstruck. The bastards were even better than he'd given them credit for being.

"Call me, please," Hughes said. "There's still been no word about Yernin, and I think you might be better off returning to Greenwich. Moira would never forgive me if I didn't insist."

Yernin was so intent on listening to what Hughes was saying that he did not hear the back door open and close.

"This will all work out, you'll see," Hughes said.

Mrs. Houlten, still dressed for the outside, rushed down the hall from the kitchen, switched on the light, and snatched the telephone, her back to Yernin.

"This is Mrs. Houlten."

Yernin's reflection was in the mirror above the telephone stand. He could clearly see the housekeeper's face, her eyes directed toward the front door. If she looked up she would see him.

"No, she's not home, Mr. Hughes, but the moment she arrives I'll have her telephone you."

Yernin thumbed the safety catch to the off position.

"Scotland Yard?" Mrs. Houlten said, puzzled. "I'm sure I saw them when I came in. They were here this afternoon when I left."

If he killed the woman while she was still on the telephone Hughes would figure out what was happening, and any chance of getting to Frances Shipley would be lost.

"It's a waste of good money, if you ask me, standing guard over an old lady. But I'll let them know that Frances is on her way and to keep a close watch."

The woman laughed.

"You're a shameless charmer, Mr. Hughes," she said girlishly. "But I promise to be careful."

Mrs. Houlten hung up, then turned as she took off her hat. Her eyes met Yernin's in the mirror. For a second she did nothing, but then she slowly reached for the telephone.

"I have no reason to kill you, Mrs. Houlten. Nor will I if you do exactly what I tell you to do."

"You mean to murder Frances, just like you did Sir Leonard," said Mrs. Houlten in a surprisingly strong voice.

"On the contrary, I need her alive. I'm going to hold her hostage."

"Why?"

"That needn't concern you," Yernin said, stepping away from the sitting-room door. "You're going to lie down on your bed, and I'm going to tie you up and gag you so you can't cry out, just like they do in the movies. Nothing more than that." He didn't want blood in the

front hall. If Frances came in through the front door she
would see it and possibly get out before he could take
her.

"Bloody hell—"

"I'll kill you where you stand," Yernin warned.

Mrs. Houlten turned slowly to face him, then shook
her head in resignation. "You'll rot in hell with no one
to pray for your soul," she said, and she went into her
sitting room.

Yernin shot her in the back of the head at point-blank
range, her body pitching forward the rest of the way
inside.

"I don't have a soul, Mrs. Houlten," he said matter-
of-factly. He closed the door, turned off the hall light,
and went in search of a pencil and piece of paper.

6

LONDON

Frances's Rover was parked in the SIS garage downtown, so she had to ride in with Brad Morgan. Since
leaving Greenwich he'd not said a word, a permanent
scowl on his face. As they entered the outskirts of London, she touched his arm.

"You've been angry for too long," she said. "Have
you forgotten how to smile?"

"There's nothing to smile about," he replied without
looking at her. "If you don't want us to protect you,
then I'm washing my hands of the entire affair. I'm putting you on administrative leave. And I think Roger will
back me."

"There's no need for this, Brad."

"No, there's not, if only you'd come to your senses." He glanced at her. "You're a damned fine intelligence officer, but you're besotted with Lane, and it's affected your judgment."

"I'm not the only one afflicted," she said, and she instantly regretted the remark.

A momentary look of hurt crossed Morgan's features. "What a cocked-up mess," he said softly.

"You're right."

"You almost got yourself killed the last time."

Frances nodded. "If being safe means I can't be with him, then I don't care what danger I'm in."

"Bullshit, Frances. Pure, unadulterated bullshit. You're not thinking straight."

"What do you want me to do?" she cried in anguish.

"Let me take you back to Greenwich. You can wait it out there."

"Until when?"

"Either Lane is going to find the submarine in our waters, or he's not. Either way, it's all over after that, and you can come back to work. Or chase after him to Washington, or wherever he's going."

"All for love?" Frances asked.

"You have to answer that."

"You do, Brad. Everything you've said and done was to protect me. In your mind Lane is the enemy, not Yernin and the others."

He looked at her again, this time his face bleak. "I do love you, Frances. Nothing you do or say will change it."

"I'm sorry, Brad," she said gently.

"So am I," he replied.

Morgan dropped her off by her car in the underground ramp, then drove back up one level to his slot. She tossed her purse and overnight bag in the passenger seat, then got behind the wheel, where she sat for a moment before starting the engine. She opened her purse and got out her Bernardelli, 9mm semiautomatic, checked the load, and stuffed it back in her purse.

On the way out she passed Morgan's car. He stood at the elevator and waved. She waved back.

"Dammit to hell," she muttered, the words choking at the back of her suddenly thick throat.

7

ABOARD THE HARRIER

Sark was the least populated of the major islands, and except for a couple of hotels and restaurants, and a few farmhouses, there was little else there. Cars were banned on the island; only horse-drawn carriages and bicycles were used. Very few lights were visible from the air as the Harrier dropped out of the clouds beneath the overcast.

"Red Base, this is Red One on station," Lieutenant Decker radioed the *Beaver*.

"Roger, Red One. Is there any surface traffic in your vicinity?"

"Negative."

"Okay, cover your area and then get out of there, Charlie."

"I hear you," Decker said. He switched to intercom. "We're on station, Art. Are you ready?"

"Thirty seconds," Ramsey replied.

Decker spotted the sea buoy marking the entrance to Sark's only harbor well to the south. The only other lights were those of cargo ships, but they were up north in the shipping lanes and would cause them no trouble.

"The sensor is wet," Ramsey said.

"Are you picking up anything?"

"Nothing."

Decker started the first sweep at eighty knots, two hundred feet above the waves. The Harrier was extremely noisy, especially at such slow speeds, and was hard to hold on an accurate course. The jet seemed to be stressed to its absolute limits.

"Wait!" Ramsey shouted.

"Did you find it?"

"Yes," said Ramsey excitedly. "It was narrow. I had it and then it was gone. Make your next turn to the south."

Decker gently banked the jet to the left while he switched back to the *Beaver*'s frequency. "Red Base, this is Red One. We have a positive read right where you said it might be. We're going back for a second run."

"Roger that, Red One," the controller in the CIC responded dryly.

Straightening the jet out on a track a half mile south of the first one, Decker made his run, reducing his speed to fifty knots, the jet straining even harder.

"There," Ramsey said. "I have a positive read. Definitely a Polyarnyy signature. But dispersed. It's old."

"Red Base, this is Red One, we have a positive on that signal. It's an old one, but definite," Decker radioed.

A huge bang came from just aft of the cockpit, shaking the jet as if it were a toy, and they immediately began to fall, all the engine indicators dropping out of the green, to zero.

"We're going down, bail out!" Decker shouted over the back of his seat. He was still on the *Beaver*'s frequency. "Mayday, Mayday, Mayday! We have an engine failure, we're going down! Say again, Mayday, Mayday, Mayday!''

He ejected the canopy, the explosive bolts peeling it up and backward, then brought his feet back away from the rudder pedals.

Too late. The thought passed through his brain as he reached for the ejection handles at the same time they hit the sea.

8

ABOARD 283

The control room, bathed in red light, was quiet when Maslennikov went below. Only the helmsman and chief of the watch were on duty in addition to the sonar operator forward, and the communications and radar man in the radio shack. The others were asleep in their bunks, or aft in the crew's mess. Lubiako and his two lookouts would remain on duty on the bridge until midnight, when Kovrygin would take over.

Maslennikov walked over to the plotting table and studied the course Kovrygin had worked out for them, shaping their track well outside the normal shipping lanes to a point west and south of the Canary Islands. From there they would submerge and make a dash directly for the Moroccan coast in another two days.

After that it was anyone's guess, Maslennikov told himself tiredly. But they were out of viable options, in part because of Bill Lane.

He shook his head, and went forward past the officers'

wardroom to his own compartment, where he took off his jacket, and lay down on his bunk.

In the old days, when he was a young man, the Soviet navy was the preeminent navy in the world. The U.S. had its carriers, but they were nothing by comparison with the USSR's fleet of submarines, which outnumbered the Americans' by three to one.

But no longer, he thought. Those glory days were gone, and they would never return.

He fell asleep finally to that morose thought.

9

LONDON

The lights were out in the house when Frances parked the Rover in back. Mrs. Houlten had either retired early to her own rooms, or she'd gone to a movie, which she sometimes did when she was home alone. But the Scotland Yard surveillance vans were gone. She hadn't expected that from Brad, and it deepened her sad mood.

She let herself in through the kitchen door and automatically went to reset the alarm, but it hadn't been switched on. A little warning went off at the back of her head, thinking of the situation they'd run into in Oxford, but she immediately dismissed it. Mrs. Houlten didn't believe in alarm systems. A stout Yale lock was safety enough in her mind, and simple.

"Mrs. Houlten," Frances called, locking the door. She turned on the kitchen lights, dropped her overnight bag and purse on the counter, and put on the kettle.

She laid out the tea things, then went into the front

hall, where she checked her phone messages. There were several calls from friends, three from an anxious-sounding Hughes, and then a final call, which Mrs. Houlten had picked up.

That had been less than an hour ago. The old dear was probably sound asleep in front of the telly, something she did regularly.

Frances went back to Mrs. Houlten's door, knocked softly, and opened it. Mrs. Houlten lay facedown in a pool of blood, obviously dead.

Her heart went to her throat, and she stifled a scream. "The bastard," she said. "The dirty, fucking bastard!"

She turned on her heel and headed back to the kitchen, where she'd left her gun in her purse on the counter, when Yernin stepped into view, her purse in his hand.

"Is this what you want?" he asked mildly.

She was struck dumb for a split instant, but then sprinted across the hall and grabbed the telephone. The line was dead.

Yernin set her purse aside and came toward her, a bland expression on his face. "You're coming with me."

"Like bloody hell I am," Frances snarled. She ripped the handset from the base and, holding it by the end of the three-foot elastic cord like a mace, stepped into Yernin's charge and swung with every ounce of her strength. The handset hit him in the side of the head with a satisfying crack.

He grunted in pain and fell back against the stair banister.

Frances stepped around him and started for the kitchen, but he grabbed her arm and yanked her back with such force it nearly dislocated her shoulder.

Blood welled up above his ear, and his eyes seemed glazed, but his expression and manner remained frighteningly bland. He slapped her on one cheek, and back-handed her on the other, her head snapping back each time.

"You will cooperate with me, or you will die, Commander," Yernin said.

"You're going to kill me anyway," Frances said thickly.

"Not until Lane comes for you. In the meantime something might come up." A hint of a smile creased the sides of his mouth. "I might suffer a heart attack."

"You bastard."

"Yes," he said indifferently. He slapped her again.

"Wait," Frances cried as he raised the back of his hand to her. "Whatever you say," she said.

"Good."

She looked up into his eyes and tried to find something there. But it was like looking into the glass eyes of a stuffed animal. "Don't make a mistake," she said. "When you do, I'll kill you."

This time Yernin did smile. "That should be interesting," he said. He took a piece of notepaper from his pocket, led Frances over to the hall table, laid it down, then brought her back to the kitchen.

"We'll take your car," he said. "You'll drive. But first we need to get your passport."

"Where are we going?"

"Exeter, to begin with."

10

ABOARD 283

The midnight change of watch went quietly, the new crew respectful of those still asleep in their bunks, and the old crew too tired to do much more than stumble aft to their bunks. They were all handpicked professionals, Lubiako thought. Good men. He got a sandwich and glass of tea from the galley and went forward to his compartment.

Passing Maslennikov's quarters he looked in. The old man was asleep on top of his bunk, his shoes still on. Lubiako put down his sandwich and tea, and gently removed Maslennikov's shoes and covered him with a spare blanket.

Maslennikov stirred, but didn't wake up, and Lubiako took his midnight supper back to his compartment.

Good men, from the captain down. Dedicated, loyal, competent. When the subject of a mutiny had come up none of them liked it.

Lubiako put his sandwich down and reached for a package of cigarettes on the top shelf above his tiny desk, his fingers brushing against a plastic packet of radiation badges that had broken open.

He put down his tea and pulled the split packet out, then stopped. The badges that had popped out were milky. He set them aside, tore the packet open, and fanned the remaining two dozen badges on his desk, his stomach doing a slow roll.

All of them were milky, indicating radiation levels inside the submarine well above acceptable limits.

11

HMS *BEAVER*

"I had the feeling from the start that this mission could get completely out of hand," Captain Guthrie said angrily. "Well, it has, and it looks likely that we have one dead pilot, and one dead American navy lieutenant out there."

They were on the bridge, the warship plowing through the seas as fast as engineering could push her. They were still a half hour out.

"They proved that the submarine was there," Lane said, not backing away from the captain's wrath.

"Two men dead, and that's your take on it?"

"Several people have already lost their lives, and there'll be a hell of a lot more casualties unless we stop them."

"I want you to get something straight. As of this moment this mission is no longer about looking for a renegade submarine, it's about search and rescue for a downed aircrew."

"Skipper, it's Air Ops," the XO said, holding out a phone.

Guthrie gave Lane a searching look, then walked over and took the phone. "This is the captain."

Commander Ohlson came over to Lane. "Look, this wasn't your fault," he said, lowering his voice. "They understood the risks when they volunteered."

Lane nodded. "I wouldn't have asked them if I hadn't thought it was important."

"They wouldn't have gone if they thought you were wrong."

The captain finished on the phone. "Air Sea Rescue has two choppers on site. They've found wreckage."

"Any survivors?" Lane asked.

"Not yet," Guthrie said. "If you'll return to your quarters we'll get on with our jobs."

A marine guard at the door came to attention. "I'll show you the way, Mr. Lane."

"As soon as possible I'd like to hitch a ride back to Portsmouth," Lane said.

"See to it, would you, XO," Guthrie said.

"Yes, sir," Commander Ohlson said.

"Good luck," Lane told the captain, who gave him a hard stare.

"You too, Mr. Lane."

Lane followed the marine aft and down one level, where VanDyke was at the door to the CIC.

"I'll take it from here, Sergeant," he said. "There's something I need to discuss with our guest first."

"Do you want me to wait, sir?"

"Won't be necessary," VanDyke said. "Carry on."

12

ON THE ROAD TO EXETER

It was a five-hour drive, and traffic did not thin out until they were well outside London, nearly to Basingstoke. Yernin leaned over to see the fuel gauge, which showed less than a half tank. "Stop at the next gas station," he told her.

"Aren't you afraid that I'll scream for help?"

"I'd kill the attendant and whoever else happened to be there." He looked at her looking at him. "Later I would break one of your bones."

Frances turned her attention back to the highway. "What's in Exeter?"

"You'll see."

Outwardly Frances let her expression sag in resignation, but inwardly her resolve hardened, a picture of Mrs. Houlten lying dead indelibly etched in her brain.

—————— **13** ——————

HMS *BEAVER*

They arrived on the scene twenty-five minutes later, where they picked up the rescue beacon that had activated when the Harrier hit the water. Most of the jet had sunk in 150 feet of water. They were picking it up on the side-scan sonar.

"Drop the locator buoy now," VanDyke radioed the bridge.

"Roger," Ohlson said tightly.

"How does it look?"

"Not good. I don't think they had the chance to bail out."

"Are we sending divers down?"

"They'll deploy the moment the marker beacon is in the water."

"Maybe we'll get lucky."

"Maybe," Ohlson said.

VanDyke glanced over at Lane seated beside the side-scan sonar operator. The Harrier had sunk within fifty yards of a much larger target they'd picked up on the way in.

"Ask the skipper to keep circling, we're picking up another target."

"Stand by," Ohlson said.

The captain came on. "What is it, Roger?"

"Looks like Mr. Lane's cruiser. About the right size, fifty yards north of the Harrier."

The captain paused a moment. "Once we find the bodies, I'll have the divers take a look at the other target."

"Yes, sir," VanDyke said, and he gave Lane a nod.

"Tell Mr. Lane that the chopper will be standing by to return him to Portsmouth as soon as we have confirmation."

--------------- **14** ---------------

ON THE ROAD TO EXETER

A few minutes after midnight Yernin telephoned the hotel in Exeter using his satellite phone. Nikitin answered after four rings. He'd been sleeping.

"Yes?"

"We're three hours out. Have everything ready."

"I refueled yesterday, so it'll take me less than an hour."

"Has anyone taken an interest in you?"

"No, sir. You're a businessman from Guernsey and I'm your pilot. Just like you told me to say."

"Will there be any problems because of the early hour?"

"I checked that out, and everything will be fine. The airport is shut down for the night, but I can bring up the runway lights on unicom, and file a flight plan once we're in the air."

"Very well," Yernin said, and he broke the connection. He looked at Frances. "How much does Lane know?"

"Everything."

"Good. In that case it won't take him very long to figure out what has happened to you."

"Kidnapped by a coward."

"Yes," Yernin said indifferently, as he continued to stare at her with his lifeless eyes.

15

HMS *BEAVER*

The bodies of Lieutenants Decker and Ramsey, still strapped in their ejection seats, were recovered by divers around three-thirty. Once they were aboard, the captain released the mission to VanDyke, who directed them to the much larger target. Within ten minutes they were on top of it, and divers were sent down again.

Lane got on the comms link to the lead diver, who carried a low-lux underwater television camera connected to the ship by wire. "This is Lane in CIC. I'm going to need a clear picture of the name on the bow."

"We're coming to it now."

The overhead television screen showed an indistinct

shape that gradually cleared and became recognizable as a ship as the divers got closer and their lights came into effective range.

"Doesn't look like there's anything wrong with her," VanDyke said over Lane's shoulder.

"They probably blew the bottom out of her so that she'd go fast and straight." Lane keyed the mike. "We're getting good images now. Anything in the debris field?"

"Not a thing so far," the head diver replied. "But that French sailboat could be a mile from here."

"We don't see any visible damage."

"Neither do we," the diver said. "Whoever sunk her knew what they were doing."

As the camera moved forward from amidships, the superstructure appeared to be in perfect condition except that some of the windows were blown out. It was difficult to gauge the size of the ship, but then one of the other divers swam into view, giving them a perspective.

"Twenty meters, at least," VanDyke guessed.

"Twenty-five," Lane said. "She's a Feadship."

"Expensive boat."

The camera came into opposition above the flaring bows, then dropped as the lead diver swam deeper. The name painted on the hull was *Charisma*.

"I'll be damned," VanDyke said.

"May I have a copy of this tape?" Lane asked.

VanDyke nodded.

"Do you want us to go aboard and check for bodies or evidence?" the lead diver asked.

"It's not necessary," Lane said. "There won't be any."

16

The airport was dark, but before they pulled into the hangar and she saw the Gulfstream she'd still held some hope that Yernin was human and would make a mistake, giving her an opening. Scotland Yard and every cop in Britain were looking for him. But with the jet they could go anywhere in the world.

"Where are you taking me?" she asked.

"Africa," he said. He took the Rover's keys from her, then made her climb over the center console and follow him out the passenger door.

Nikitin appeared at the head of the boarding stairs.

"Is everything ready?" Yernin asked.

"Yes, sir."

"Are you taking me to Sierra Leone?" Frances asked, desperately looking for an opening. Anything.

"Either get aboard the airplane now, or I'll put a bullet in your brain. It won't matter, because once Lane reads my note, he'll come to me. He won't know that you're dead."

Frances nodded after a moment, and went aboard, Yernin right behind her.

PORTSMOUTH ROYAL NAVAL AIR STATION

The Westland Lynx helicopter touched down on the tarmac outside Base Operations shortly after dawn. Lane thanked the crew, then went inside, where Hughes was waiting for him in the dayroom with an angry Commander Moore. By the looks of things Moore and Hughes had been arguing.

"Did you get the tape?" Hughes asked.

Lane nodded. "What about Frannie?"

"I talked to her housekeeper last night, but there's been no answer since." Hughes was clearly concerned.

"A car and driver are standing by to take you gentlemen back to your embassy in London," Moore told them.

"First I'd like to make a couple of phone calls," Lane said.

"No," Moore said flatly. "I want both of you out of here immediately. The driver's been instructed not to deviate from his orders under any circumstances."

"I'm sorry about Lieutenant Decker and—"

"Get out while you can," Moore warned. "The Royal Navy has done all it's going to do for you. You'll be leaving the country later this morning."

Lane nodded. "Very well, Commander. For what it's worth to you, Decker's and Ramsey's actions may have saved more lives than you can imagine. Keep that in mind before you condemn their deaths as useless."

Outside, he and Hughes climbed in the backseat of a

British Ford, and without a word the driver headed toward the main gate.

Lane handed Hughes the tape. "It was the *Charisma*, just where Frannie said it would be."

"What about data from the Harrier?"

"Nothing other than the two brief radio transmissions. They wouldn't give me that tape."

"Then there's no proof that two-eighty-three was there after all. At least nothing we can take to Newby."

Lane laid his head back and closed his eyes. "It'll have to rest on the videotape, and our word, Tommy."

18

LONDON

Lane left Hughes at the U.S. embassy and took a cab over to Frances's apartment in Chelsea. Scotland Yard's surveillance vans were nowhere in sight.

With shaking hands he opened the front door with the key Frances had given him, and stepped inside the hallway, all of his senses alert. There had been trouble here.

He took out his gun and, leaving the door open, went the rest of the way inside.

The telephone handset had been ripped off the hook, and lay in the middle of the hallway. A note was lying on the phone stand.

"I have her . . . ," it began, in a very neat, precise hand, and at the bottom, after the exact instructions, it was signed: *"Yernin."*

PART FOURTEEN

1

Lane felt for a pulse in Mrs. Houlten's neck, but her body was cold. She'd been dead for several hours, possibly since last night.

The situation was so eerily like Oxford that the hairs prickled at the back of his neck.

A car pulled up out front, and Lane went to the front hall in time to see Mario Garza coming across the sidewalk in a dead run. He spotted Lane at the door.

"You have to come back to the embassy with me. Scotland Yard is on the way over."

"They've taken Frannie," Lane said. "And they've killed her housekeeper."

"Who's taken her?"

"Yernin."

"How do you know it's him?" Garza asked, following Lane back to Mrs. Houlten's body.

Lane gave him a fierce look. "Who else?"

2

ABOARD THE GULFSTREAM

The coast of Africa cut a hazy brown streak across the horizon as they began their descent toward landing at Rabat's international airport. Frances was looking out a window when Yernin sat down across from her and opened a brown canvas satchel.

"Remove your skirt," he said. He took a small brick of Semtex, a tiny radio-controlled fuse, and a roll of duct tape from the bag.

"You're out of your mind," she said.

Yernin set a code into what appeared to be a small scientific calculator, pocketed the device, then embedded the fuse in the plastic explosive, which he shaped into a gently curved mass about four inches in diameter and a half inch thick.

"I want no trouble from you when customs boards us for inspection. If you cooperate no one will get hurt. Take off your skirt."

Frances looked from the Semtex to Yernin's eyes, then unbuckled her seat belt, stood up, unzippered her skirt, and slowly pulled it down around her hips and stepped out of it. Her panty hose were back at Greenwich hanging on the towel bar in the bathroom, and her black panties were very brief. But when he looked at her near nakedness she could see his expression was nothing but clinical.

He peeled a long strip of tape from the roll and handed

it and the explosive to her. "Tape it to your thigh, just below your crotch."

"Is this how you get your jollies?"

Yernin waited patiently, his face and manner bland.

Frances positioned the plastique against her inner thigh, and taped it in place. She looked into his lifeless eyes again, then put on her skirt, sat down, and buckled her seat belt.

"I'll be sure to stay very close to you," she said. "If you push the button you're coming with me."

3

LONDON

Lane replayed the phone messages on Frances's answering machine. He needed a better sense of the timing. If Yernin had much of a head start he was already out of the country. Garza stood at the front door watching the street. The last message from Hughes that Mrs. Houlten had picked up had come at nine last night, nearly ten hours ago.

"Shit," Garza swore as several cars and vans screeched to a halt on the street.

Lane hit the erase button, then stepped away from the phone. "You can't let them arrest me," he told Garza. "I need to get out of here."

"I'll do what I can."

Morgan was the first up the walk, followed by a half dozen Scotland Yard detectives in blue windbreakers, and several uniformed cops. He bulled his way past Garza.

"You're under arrest, Lane," he shouted triumphantly.

"Who called off the surveillance team?" Lane demanded.

The door to Mrs. Houlten's rooms was open, her body in plain sight. Morgan's gaze went to it, and the color drained from his face.

"Where's Frances?" he asked.

"She's gone," Lane said. "Did you call off the team?"

"She didn't want them—"

Lane reached him in three strides, grabbed his lapels and slammed him against the wall. "You son of a bitch. One good woman is dead because of you, and I swear to Christ if anything happens to Frances I'll take you apart in such a way that you'll wish you'd never been born."

The detectives tried to pull Lane away, but he slammed Morgan against the wall again.

"What time did you see her last? What time did she get here?"

He elbowed one of the detectives in the sternum, drove his heel into a second cop's instep, and shoved Morgan against the wall a third time.

"What time did she get home?"

"I don't know," Morgan cried. "I dropped her off at her car downtown around nine last night. Maybe a few minutes before."

Lane let go of him and turned to the cops. "She's been gone all night, and Yernin has her. So you can either waste time arresting me, or you can start living up to the Yard's reputation and find them."

4

RABAT, MOROCCO

Yernin, Nikitin, and Frances sat together in the Gulf-stream's main cabin as one customs officer examined their passports while a second searched their luggage.

"What is the purpose of your visit to Morocco?" the passport officer asked.

"Tourism," Yernin said graciously. "It's our honeymoon."

The officer grinned. "How long do you plan to be in Morocco?"

"A week, perhaps a little longer," Yernin said. He smiled affectionately at Frances. "Isn't that right, dear?"

She glanced at his right hand in his pocket, and nodded stiffly.

The remaining Semtex and their weapons were hidden in a secret compartment aft. Finding nothing, the second customs officer came forward and gave them a curt nod.

"Well, congratulations," the officer said. He stamped their passports. "You will need to refuel before you park your aircraft. And there is a landing fee."

"Of course," Yernin said agreeably.

5

LONDON

Brad Morgan, still shaken, but even angrier than before, stepped aside as the ambulance attendants wheeled Mrs. Houlten's body out. Lane was staring at him.

"This was not my fault, and I refuse to take responsibility for the actions of some madman running around England with a vendetta against you," he said.

"Let's at least work together to find him and Frances," Lane said. "Can we do that much?"

"We'll do it, but without any help from you. And that's on direct orders from Mr. Stewart. You're going to face charges here, and then be deported as soon as possible."

Garza, who'd been speaking to someone on his cell phone, broke the connection and came over. "The ambassador agrees," he said.

Morgan nodded smugly. "Finally."

"But first we'd like to ask a little favor, Brad," Garza added. "The ambassador asks that Lane be temporarily turned over to our custody. We'd like to debrief him. It's a matter of our own national security. Yernin did spy on us, and he was responsible for a number of deaths in the States."

Morgan shook his head.

"Come on, Brad. It'll only be for a few hours. Maybe overnight."

"I'd have to clear it with Mr. Stewart first."

Garza nodded. "That's fine with me. But the sooner

we get this done, the sooner Lane will be out of your hair.''

Morgan glared at Lane. ''Nothing will give me greater pleasure.''

6

U.S. EMBASSY

Hughes was waiting in the third-floor library. The embassy was busy this morning and no one gave Lane or Garza a second look when they came up on the rickety elevator and marched down the corridor.

''I'm going to call Langley, because frankly I don't know what the hell to do next,'' Garza told them. ''And I know it'll be hard, but try to stay out of trouble for the time being.''

''Word of honor,'' Lane said.

Hughes was distressed. When Garza left, he said, ''I just heard about poor Mrs. Houlten. Was there no sign of Frances?''

Lane handed him the note. ''He left it for me on the hall table.''

Hughes quickly read it, then looked up, his expression dark. ''Did you share this with anyone?''

''No. By the time the British got themselves organized he'd kill her.''

''With his head start they're already in Morocco. And that's a very big country, William. Lots of places to hide. Why don't we give this to Garza; at least our people in Rabat can be notified.''

''He has this all planned out, Tommy,'' Lane said.

"If he gets so much as a hint that anyone else other than me is coming after him, he'll kill her."

Hughes shook his head. "I would sincerely like to dispute the wisdom of your logic, but I can't. So the next step is to get you to Rabat as soon as possible. But why did he choose Morocco?"

"That's simple," Lane said. "He's going to meet the submarine there."

Lane went over to a large world globe and turned it so the coast of Africa was on the right, the spread of the Atlantic Ocean to the left.

"The sub came out of the English Channel, took on fuel from the *Santa Clara,* and is headed toward some deserted spot on the Moroccan coast."

"Those are some big assumptions."

Lane looked up, his deep blue eyes narrowing. "Why else did he choose Morocco?" He looked again at the globe. "This time the advantage will be mine, because I know *his* Achilles' heel."

"What is it?"

Lane smiled cruelly. "Me."

7

RABAT, MOROCCO

Nikitin rented a Land Rover and they drove in from the airport to the Hotel Royal across from the gardens on the Avenue Algal ben Abullah. They parked a half block from the hotel, and Yernin, seated in back with Frances, watched the comings and goings on the street for fifteen minutes.

"It's clear," he said. He handed Nikitin an envelope addressed to Bill Lane. "Leave this at the desk." He gave Nikitin a twenty-pound note. "Give them this too, for their trouble."

Nikitin left without a word, and they watched him walk down the street and enter the hotel. A couple of minutes later he emerged and came directly back to the car.

"Any problem?" Yernin asked.

"*Nyet.*"

"Then let's go. We have a long drive ahead of us."

8

LONDON

Hughes, carrying Lane's hanging bag and laptop computer, emerged from Claridge's, and circled the block on foot to make sure that he wasn't being followed. When he was certain that he was clear, he walked over to a pub in New Bond Street where Lane was waiting in a dark back booth. It was lunchtime and the place was crowded.

"Garza is mad, but I don't think he's very surprised. I told him we had something to take care of, and that I'd come back to the embassy later this afternoon."

Lane had to smile, even though worry was eating at his gut. "Is my Vandermeer legend still holding up?"

Hughes nodded. "You're booked first-class on a British Air flight to Casablanca at three-eighteen this afternoon." Hughes looked at his watch. "Gives you plenty of time to get out to Heathrow. A car will be waiting for you at the Hertz counter. From there you're on your own.''

"See if Ben can get through to Newby and convince him of what's going on.''

"I wish you'd let me call the CIA's chief of Rabat station. They wouldn't have to do anything except provide you some backup.''

Lane shook his head. "This is my fight, Tommy. But if something goes wrong you know what to do.''

Hughes looked away. "Not that it would make much difference.''

"That's not true, and you know it,'' Lane said sharply.

Hughes turned back, his pudgy face even more mottled red than usual. "I don't know what would be worse. My conscience or Moira's wrath.''

"I don't know if I'd care to trade places with you,'' Lane said.

"Take care of yourself, William,'' Hughes said. "And when you see Frances, give her a hug for me.''

9

MOROCCO

It was eight in the evening by the time Lane cleared passport control and customs at Casablanca's busy Mohammed V International Airport. He had to open his laptop and turn it on to prove that it worked, but his bag was not checked. Walking through the terminal he scanned the faces in the crowd. He wouldn't put it past

Yernin to be waiting for him. But if he was waiting he was well hidden.

The Hertz counter had a Renault reserved for him, but he upgraded to a Toyota Land Cruiser. On the flight over he'd given some thought to Yernin's plan. If the submarine was heading to some spot along the Moroccan coast, it would not be showing up for at least another twenty-four hours. Perhaps longer. And it would approach the southern coast, which was far less populated, and therefore more secure.

Yernin would want to set up the final confrontation somewhere near where the submarine was due to show up, so that if he ran into trouble he might count on some help from the crew, or at the very least be able to make a quick getaway to sea.

The backcountry and beach roads were poor. In many cases they were simply vague tracks in the sand, for which a four-wheel-drive vehicle like the Toyota, with its high undercarriage and powerful engine and transmission, was designed.

The logic was thin, but he had nothing else to go on. Yernin would make it easy, because he wanted this meeting as much as Lane did.

"Enjoy your stay, Mr. Vandermeer," the girl at the Hertz counter said pleasantly, misunderstanding his smile.

"I will," Lane replied.

Rabat was about seventy miles south on the main coastal highway, and traffic was extremely heavy, so that by the time he'd cleared the airport and headed south it was well past nine. He was worried about Frances. He'd almost lost her last year in Saddam Hussein's desert camp outside Baghdad. But this time the situation was worse, because Yernin was not some fanatic Arab on a jihad. He was an expert killer, and extremely well motivated.

About halfway, Lane pulled into a parking area overlooking the ocean. He took his gun out of the laptop, loaded it, checked the action, then got out of the car and lit a cigarette.

He was too keyed up. It was something that Yernin would count on. A man distracted by fear was apt to make mistakes, and Yernin had struck at Lane's core. But Frances was a trained intelligence officer. She was in trouble now, but she wasn't some damsel in distress. Given half a chance, a slightest opening, she would come down on Yernin like a ton of bricks. Or at least try to.

He supposed it was this last thought that had him the most worried. Frances was good, but Yernin was better, because where she might hesitate for just a fraction of a second to pull the trigger, he wouldn't.

Back at the car he pulled out the road map Hertz had supplied. In addition to the main coastal highway that ran the entire length of Morocco to its southern border with Mauritania there were numerous unpaved roads that closely followed the shore. More than a third of that distance was through the Western Sahara, a territory that Morocco oversaw. The vast wasteland was sparsely populated, and there were long stretches of totally uninhabited coastline.

Lane looked up. A perfect place for the submarine to put in. And a perfect place for Yernin to make his stand.

10

RABAT, MOROCCO

Lane circled the park, passing the Hotel Royal twice, looking for any sign that Yernin was waiting for him. He was certain that the man wouldn't dare remain in the city with Frances held captive. Too many things could go wrong to attract the attention of the police. But once again Lane felt that he couldn't afford to underestimate the man, even if it did slow him down.

Satisfied that the street was clear, Lane parked in front of the hotel and went in. The lobby was deserted. A sleepy clerk came out of the back.

"Good evening, sir," he said. He was an older man with gray hair, and glasses perched on the end of his nose.

"Is there a message for Bill Lane?"

The clerk thought for several seconds, shaking his head and scratching his chin as if he were trying to remember.

Lane laid a ten-pound note on the counter.

"I believe there is a message after all, Mr. Lane," the clerk said, taking the money. He got an envelope from a drawer beneath the counter and handed it across.

Yernin's message was specific. Lane was to show up at the main telephone building in Marrakesh at exactly 6:00 P.M. tomorrow where Yernin would phone him with the next set of instructions.

The clerk was looking at him.

"When was this delivered?" Lane asked.

"I don't know, sir. Sometime before I came on at six."

"How far is it to Marrakesh?"

"By train?"

"I'm driving."

The clerk shrugged. "Tonight, three hours. In the day, maybe four or five hours. I wouldn't recommend travel at night."

Lane read the note again. Something niggled at the back of his mind. Yernin was going to make him run around Morocco, gradually working south until the submarine showed up. The delay would give him plenty of time to set his trap. He suddenly had it.

"Do you have a room for the night? Something with a bath and a telephone? I need to make an international call."

"Yes, of course, sir."

"I want a bottle of good cognac and something to eat sent up."

"I'm sorry, everything is closed at this hour."

Lane laid a one-hundred-pound note on the counter. "Make it a good cognac."

The clerk suddenly smiled. "I know just what you need, sir."

Lane got his bag from the Toyota and went upstairs to a surprisingly spacious and clean room overlooking the park. He opened the window to catch the cool evening breeze, then telephoned the U.S. embassy in London. After a delay of several minutes Hughes came on the line.

"Our friends are screaming bloody murder."

"Do they know where I am?" Lane asked.

"Not yet. How are you?"

"I'm okay. But they're here all right. He wants me to come to Marrakesh tomorrow for the next installment. But it just struck me to find out how they got here. And when."

"Probably not on a commercial flight," Hughes said. "A private jet, something capable of flying that distance."

"Check with the airport on Guernsey. The airplane Yernin used to come here is probably the same one they used to get back and forth from St. Peter Port."

"Where can I reach you?"

Lane told him.

"This might take a couple of hours, especially with all the hell the British are raising with Garza. Be a good time for you to catch a couple of hours' sleep, William."

"I will. But hurry—once he's in place the advantage will be his again."

11

LONDON

It was actually after seven in the morning before Hughes was able to find the information, and telephone Lane at the hotel in Rabat from a pay phone a half block from the embassy. "It's a Gulfstream, registered to International Investments, Limited, St. Peter Port," he said. He gave Lane the tail number. "Left from Exeter, and landed at Rabat International at nine-seventeen local yesterday morning. They have a twenty-two-hour head start."

"What about the passengers and crew?"

"It wasn't a commercial flight, so they won't have that record. But the airplane is apparently still parked at the airport."

"Good work, Tommy."

"I'd like to call the CIA's chief of station in Rabat."

"No," Lane said sharply. He was still clearing the cobwebs from his brain. After he'd eaten he'd fallen asleep and hadn't stirred until Hughes called. "But if you haven't heard from me by this time tomorrow morning, you can call out the marines."

"Do you want me to come over there?"

"This is my fight," Lane said. "I need you to back-stop in case anything goes wrong."

"Hell," Hughes said.

"What's wrong, Tommy?"

"Brad Morgan and his merry band from Nottingham are here. Gotta go. Good luck, William."

12

RABAT, MOROCCO

The Gulfstream jet was parked on the apron outside the private aviation terminal when Lane showed up and pulled into a visitor's slot. The wheels were chocked and sunscreens covered the windshield and cabin windows.

Frances had been here yesterday. Someone had seen her with Yernin, the pilot, and possibly one or two other crew.

The morning was cool and gray. The North Atlantic front that had been stalled over the region for the past week showed no signs of moving out, and it deepened Lane's mood. Perfect weather for the submarine to sneak in on the surface, and get back out undetected by satellite.

He went into the terminal, where two men dressed in

jumpsuits were drinking tea behind the service counter while they watched CNN on a small television set. The dayroom and cafeteria were empty. They looked up.

"Good morning," Lane said.

"Good morning, sir," the taller of the two said.

"Some friends of mine came in on that Gulfstream yesterday morning. Did they leave a message for me? My name is Lane."

"No, sir, no messages."

"Damn," Lane said. "I was supposed to meet them and my sister, but I'm late. She was with them wasn't she?"

"There was a woman with them."

Lane forced a smile. "We were supposed to get together. Did the Rolls pick them up?"

The taller one shook his head. "No, sir. They rented a car after they cleared customs."

"But they left no message for me?"

"No, sir."

Lane shook his head in frustration. "Thanks for your help anyway. If they should call back, tell them I was here, would you?"

The taller one nodded.

"What sort of car did they rent?"

"A Rover."

"Dark blue?"

"No, sir. White."

"Thanks," Lane said, and he left the terminal, got in his car, and headed toward the coast road twenty-four hours behind them. But he had until six this evening before Yernin would realize that the rules had been changed.

13

ON THE COAST
WESTERN SAHARA

It was six o'clock in the evening and from his vantage point in the phosphate loading complex south of the sleepy town of La'youn, Yernin had been watching the comings and goings at the boarded-up facility manager's house. The Cuban team was in place, and they weren't doing much to hide their presence, though their vehicles were parked out of sight somewhere. But stealth wasn't really necessary. This section of coast was utterly deserted, except for an occasional truck or bus up on the highway a couple of kilometers away.

He put his binoculars down, and went back to where Nikitin was watching Frances. They'd picked up a few supplies on the way down, but the trip had been grueling, and fresh water was a problem, so they had to conserve.

"Any sign of the submarine?" Nikitin asked hopefully.

"Not yet," Yernin said.

They had snuck in without announcing their presence to the Cuban team, and had set up camp in a long gallery that looked down on the cavernous hoppers and conveyers that took the phosphate to the end of the kilometer-long dock where ships had once come to load. All the machinery was rusted, and a thick layer of white phosphate dust covered everything, getting into their clothes, into their nostrils and the backs of their throats. It did not bother Yernin, but Frances was having a hard time of it. She sat propped up against a steel support column.

"Can I have some water?" she croaked. Her lips were dry and cracked.

Yernin stared at her for several long seconds. It would be simpler to put a bullet in her brain right now. But he wanted to wait for Lane. He wanted to see the look in the bastard's eyes when his woman was killed. It would be the last thing Lane ever saw.

He gave Nikitin a nod. The pilot handed a plastic jug of water to Frances and she took it greedily.

Yernin checked his watch again. It was 6:10 P.M. He walked back to the broken windows and entered the number for the Marrakesh telephone exchange in his satellite phone.

The operator answered in *Darija*—Moroccan Arabic.

"I would like an English operator please," Yernin said.

"I can assist you," the woman said, switching to English.

"I have a call for William Lane. He should be there."

"One moment, please."

Frances was staring at him, and he turned back to look at her. He could see that hearing Lane's name had bolstered her spirits.

"I'm sorry, sir. There is no gentleman by that name here," the operator said.

"Are you certain?"

"Quite certain, sir."

A black rage threatened to engulf Yernin. With great effort, he said, "Thank you," and broke the connection. Then he called the hotel in Rabat.

"Hotel Royal."

"I left a message for Mr. Lane yesterday morning. Has he picked it up?"

"Yes, sir," the clerk said.

"When?"

"About this time last night."

Yernin broke the connection, pocketed the telephone, and for a moment toyed with the detonator which would fire the Semtex still taped to Frances's thigh. But then he picked up the binoculars again and trained them on the manager's house while he thought about this latest development.

14

ON THE COASTAL HIGHWAY

At six-thirty, Lane was parked at the side of the highway above the abandoned phosphate complex. It was already starting to get dark, and for as far as he could see in any direction there were no lights.

He'd driven hard through the morning and early afternoon, to get as far south as soon as possible. But once he crossed the border with Western Sahara, he'd slowed down, stopping from time to time at the occasional service station in the small towns to ask if anyone had seen the white Rover. No one had.

On the assumption that Yernin had passed this way to rendezvous with the submarine at some remote beach location, and that he would make it simple to find, Lane passed over everything but the obvious. He concentrated his search along the deserted stretches between towns, but as it neared six, when Yernin was supposed to call him in Marrakesh, he began to believe that he wasn't going to get lucky this time, and that he had made a bad decision.

But forty-five minutes ago he'd hit pay dirt in the town of La'youn, where the attendant at the Shell station remembered them. Two men and a woman. They bought food and water. The attendant was sure he remembered correctly because they'd only bought a few liters of gasoline, as if they weren't planning on going much farther.

Fifty miles south he'd spotted the weathered sign for the phosphate complex.

He got out of the car and walked down to the steel barrier blocking the rutted dirt road. The gate was held in place by a heavy padlock and chain, but the chain had been cut and then draped back over the shackle. At least one vehicle had come through here recently. The tire tracks hadn't filled in with blowing sand yet.

Lane ducked under the barrier and, taking out his pistol, hurried a hundred yards to where the road disappeared over the crest of a low hill. Near the top he crouched down, and then crawled the last few yards.

The phosphate loading complex was spread over a couple of hundred acres along the coast. A very long loading dock jutted out into the Atlantic, headed by three large corrugated-iron buildings, the largest of which was several stories tall. One huge pile of phosphate was still in place ready to be shipped, but the other storage areas were empty. To the south of the processing and loading buildings were what appeared to be garages and maintenance facilities, an office, and a couple of houses. Everything was ramshackle, rusted and falling down, long unused.

This was a perfect place for the submarine to land. There would be plenty of water at the end of the dock, and no prying eyes.

The problem was that Yernin knew that Lane wasn't at the Marrakesh telephone exchange. How much would he have guessed from that?

Lane rose up a little to get a better look at the maintenance buildings, then dropped back down. An entire army could be hidden down there, and he was going to have to figure a way of finding out.

15

THE PHOSPHATE FACILITY

"Got you," Yernin said. He was impressed despite himself.

He lowered the binoculars and hurried back to the gallery at the oceanside of the loading facility, where Nikitin and Frances waited.

"He's here. Keep a close eye on her."

Frances sat up, the lethargy immediately dropping away from her as if she'd jumped into a cold pool. "Bill is here?"

Yernin grabbed a one-pound brick of Semtex and a pencil fuse from one of his packs. "I have to leave for a few minutes. Watch her closely. I don't want her to warn him."

Nikitin nodded nervously. "It's going to be all right, isn't it, sir? The submarine is going to come?"

"It's going to be more than all right if you keep your head."

Frances sat back. "No it's not," she said, smiling. "Neither of you will leave here alive."

"Shut up, bitch," Nikitin shouted.

She laughed. "Why don't you take that gun and shoot yourself in the head, and get it over with. It'd be easier that way."

Nikitin grabbed his pistol and pointed it at her with shaking hands.

"Yakov," Yernin said softly.

Nikitin looked over at him.

"I need her."

Nikitin nodded after a second, and Frances laughed out loud as Yernin turned and hurried downstairs.

The white Rover was parked just inside the loading facility. Yernin jammed the block of Semtex beneath the driver's seat, then drove around to the side of the building and parked in plain sight of the access road that led to the crest of the hill where he'd spotted Lane.

Leaving the engine running, he got out of the car and inserted the fuse on zero delay into the mass of plastique. Whoever sat in the passenger seat would set off the explosive. The car was bait, and the plastique was insurance.

He'd planned the confrontation for sometime in the early-morning hours. But he was glad Lane was already here. There would be no more waiting. Though how Lane had come this far, this fast, was vexing and just a little worrisome.

Without looking toward the hill, Yernin went back inside the loading complex to arrange the next element of his trap.

16

ON THE DIRT ROAD

The first question was answered. Yernin was here, and in response to his telephone call to Marrakesh he was apparently getting ready to move out. But that didn't make sense. He wouldn't risk missing the submarine.

Keeping low, Lane studied the upper stories of the building that Yernin had come out of. Most of the windows were broken or missing and one section of the corrugated roof had collapsed. There were plenty of hiding places, plenty of places to set a trap. And, Lane thought, plenty of places for a man positioned with a pair of binoculars to see someone crouched up here on the road.

He moved out of sight, then jumped up and ran back to the highway, the last of the daylight fading. When the sun went down it turned dark very fast this far south. There was little twilight on the southern deserts.

Whether Yernin was getting ready to leave or was setting a trap, his attention needed to be diverted right now.

Lane removed the chain from the barrier and swung the gate out of the way. Up at the car, he took the extra magazine of ammunition from his laptop and pocketed it. Next he got a couple of long-sleeve dress shirts out of his overnight bag and, making sure that no one was coming from either direction on the highway, drove down onto the dirt road and headed toward the crest of the hill, the headlights off.

From the top of the hill the road ran absolutely straight down to the weigh station, then directly to where Yernin's car was parked.

Just below the crest, Lane stopped, put the Toyota into the low range of the four-wheel drive, put it in park, and lowered the windows on the driver's and passenger's sides. He pulled the dome-light lens free and removed the lightbulb, then got out and raced up to the top of the hill.

Dropping down into the ditch beside the road, he crawled the last few yards to the top, just far enough so that he could see that Yernin's car was still parked beside the loading complex.

It was very dark now, the Atlantic Ocean nothing but an empty black hole. But Yernin had apparently left his door ajar because the interior lights were on. Lane had to smile. Yernin was intelligent, highly trained, and ruthless, but he wasn't very subtle.

Back at the Toyota, Lane made certain that the car was lined up perfectly with the road and that its front wheels were straight, then tied the steering wheel to the armrests in both doors with his knotted-up dress shirts so that it could not turn.

Reaching through the open window, he switched on the headlights and pulled the gearshift lever into drive, then jumped clear as the Rover ground slowly up the hill.

Before it disappeared over the top, Lane was already racing to the north behind the sand dunes that separated a low swale from the phosphate complex and loading dock.

17

THE PHOSPHATE FACILITY

Yernin finished tying Frances spread-eagled across the front bumper of the Rover when headlights flashed from over the top of the hill.

"It's all over for you now, you bloody bastard." She laughed.

He hastily slapped a long piece of duct tape across her mouth. "Be glad I'm not taping your nose as well," he said, and he stepped back around the corner into the protection of the loading complex.

It wasn't supposed to be happening this way. Was Lane some kind of a fool charging in like this?

Nikitin came to the edge of the gallery three stories

above. "He's coming down the hill!" he called excitedly.

"Is there any sign of the Cubans?" Yernin demanded urgently. From this vantage point he could not see the manager's house.

"Not yet. But they're bound to see the lights."

This was all wrong. For the first time in his life Yernin was beginning to feel fear. He'd come up against Lane too many times before not to be concerned. The man didn't fight by the rules.

"What do you want me to do?" Nikitin called.

"Stay up there. If you get a clear shot take it."

"I thought you wanted to wait until he saw the woman."

"Just kill him if you get the chance!" Yernin shouted.

At that moment the submarine's horn blared from the end of the dock lost in the darkness a kilometer away.

18

THE PHOSPHATE FACILITY

Lane approached from the north, keeping the loading complex buildings between himself and Yernin's car. From where he crouched in the tall beach grasses he could see his Toyota slowly grinding down the hill, its headlights flashing on the buildings.

The submarine horn caught him completely off guard.

He jumped up and raced across the last fifty yards to the main building as the rattle of automatic weapons fire came from somewhere south of the dock. Probably from the maintenance garages or houses.

Someone was shooting at his car, which meant their attention was diverted now. Nobody would be watching this side of the complex.

He reached a large opening in the side of the building and ducked beneath the machinery that was supported by a jungle of steel posts and girders.

Moving from column to column he passed directly under the main conveyor system. The Toyota's headlights bounced crazily through a gap in the far wall, casting shadows through the machinery.

He caught sight of Yernin's Rover through the opening about twenty yards away. Someone or something was crouched in front of the car but he couldn't quite make it out. He started to edge forward when the Toyota exploded in a bright ball of flames, and the automatic weapons fire immediately ceased.

Lane sprinted to the next column, then pulled up short. In the sudden light from the burning Toyota he recognized who it was in front of Yernin's car, and his heart went into his throat.

It was Frannie. He could see that she'd been tied to the front bumper. Yernin was using her as bait, which meant he was somewhere very close.

Lane thumbed the Beretta's safety catch off and moved carefully to the next column.

There was a great deal of commotion on the far side of the complex. But Lane concentrated on the shadows between his position and Frannie.

Something moved on the gallery above, and Lane held perfectly still, his eyes searching the deeper shadows.

"He's dead," someone called from above.

There was no answer.

"The submarine is here, sir. Let's go with the Cubans. Lane is dead."

"He wasn't in the car, you fool!" Yernin answered from directly ahead, and very close.

Lane raised his pistol in the general direction of Yernin's voice. *"That's right, Vasha,"* he said softly in Russian. *"I've come to make a trade."*

19

THE PHOSPHATE FACILITY

Hearing Lane's voice in the darkness was the biggest shock of Yernin's life. Once again a blackness threatened to engulf him, blot out all sanity and reason. And once again by sheer dint of will, and hatred, Yernin pulled himself back from the brink.

"I have nothing to trade with you," he said. He took the detonator from his pocket.

"You know what I'm talking about."

"If I went to cut her loose, you'd shoot me," Yernin said. He edged around a support column so that he had a better line of sight to Frances, and a clear line of fire to where he estimated Lane was hiding.

"Send your pilot down, I have no reason to kill him. When she's clear, he can go to the sub, and it'll just be you and me."

"She can take my car, I'll have no further use for it. Is that what you're thinking?"

"No," Lane said. "She can leave on foot. No doubt your car is booby-trapped."

Yernin forced a laugh. "You're a very smart man, Lane. But you're forgetting something."

"What?"

"I want the pleasure of you witnessing your woman's death."

"Shoot her and I'll see the muzzle flash from your gun. The instant you fire, you're a dead man."

"Who said anything about shooting her?" Yernin said. He pushed the detonator button.

A bright flash from the radio-controlled detonator fuse came from above on the gallery, and Nikitin screamed.

20

THE PHOSPHATE FACILITY

Lane rushed forward. He pulled off two snap shots toward the gallery, and Nikitin pitched forward over the edge.

Still moving, he switched aim to where Yernin was raising his pistol toward Frances, his figure silhouetted in the light from the burning Toyota.

Lane fired, knocking Yernin off balance so that his shot went wild, missing Frances. Then he disappeared into the darkness, and Lane pulled up behind a steel column a few feet from where Nikitin's body lay in a heap.

"That was really clever of her," Yernin called softly from the darkness. "Putting the fuse in poor Yakov's pocket."

"Now it's just you and me, if you're man enough, which I doubt."

"You're forgetting the Cuban sailors. And my friends aboard the submarine."

"Then you *are* a coward."

Yernin fired from somewhere to Lane's right, and Frances cried out in pain.

Lane fired back, but a second later Yernin fired again, this time from farther back in the complex, and again Frances cried out.

Lane sprinted around the column directly toward Frances, trying to put himself between her and Yernin, as he fired two more shots over his shoulder.

Yernin fired back, the shot catching Lane in the fleshy part of his right thigh, knocking him down, so that Yernin's second shot went wild.

Lane fired three shots in rapid succession back into the darkness. The Beretta's slide locked open after the third, the gun empty.

He looked up into Frannie's eyes as he ejected the spent magazine, fumbled a new one from his pocket, slammed it home, and cycled a round into the chamber. She was ten feet away, and he could see a spreading stain of blood on her left leg, and at her left side just below her armpit. She was obviously in a great deal of pain.

Lane fired three more shots over his shoulder, and scrambled out of the building to Frannie's side, his right leg all but useless. He half expected to get a bullet in the back of the head.

A dozen men were racing across the complex from the manager's house, and at least that many were moving out on the dock toward the submarine.

Lane pulled the tape from Frances's mouth, and before she could utter a sound he frantically motioned for her to keep quiet.

He untied her arms from the Rover's bumper, then, keeping low, dragged her back inside the building, mindful of the excruciating pain he was causing both of them. But she didn't cry out.

"Stay here," he whispered. He darted to Nikitin's body, took the big Makarov automatic from his lifeless grasp, scrambled back to where Frances was propped against the corrugated-iron wall, and handed it to her.

"He's insane," she said through clenched teeth. "We've got to get out of here."

"I'm not leaving without him."

"Bloody hell. Listen, William, their submarine is here. They're not going to fool around chasing us through the desert."

The Cubans were close. He looked into her eyes. There was so much he wanted to tell her, but there was no time.

"All right, go," she said, reaching her own decision. "I'll hold them off from here for as long as I can."

"I love you, Frannie."

"I know. So kill the bloody bastard for the both of us!"

21

THE PHOSPHATE FACILITY

A fragment from a ricocheting bullet had struck Yernin in the neck, and the wound was bleeding profusely, though there was little or no pain, and he didn't think a major blood vessel had been severed.

He climbed up the ladder to the third-floor gallery and made his way to where he'd left his pack.

He'd hit the woman twice, and he'd seen Lane go down, but he didn't think either of them was dead. Not yet, he told himself, his head pounding. Not yet.

He took two bricks of plastique and two pencil fuses

from his pack, and hurried noiselessly to the end of the gallery, from where he could look down at the Rover, and the dozen or so Cubans closing in.

The woman was gone.

22

THE PHOSPHATE FACILITY

Nikitin hadn't fired a shot, so Frances figured there were nine rounds in the Makarov. She pulled herself into position behind a steel support column from where she could see the sailors racing over from the far side of the complex. The nearest of them was less than twenty yards away. She switched the safety catch off, took aim on the lead man, and squeezed off one shot. He went down. Before the others could react, she fired two more shots, hitting two more men; then she ducked back and hunched down as the side of the building was raked by automatic weapons fire.

23

Lane reached the top of the ladder and painfully hauled himself over the edge onto the gallery in time to see Yernin thirty feet away start to raise something over his head.

"Don't," Lane shouted, and he fired three shots from an awkward prone position, at least one of which hit Yernin, who fell back into the shadows.

There was a lull in the firing below.

"Ever the resourceful all-American Boy Scout," Yernin called softly. "But you and your woman aren't getting out of this one alive."

"Neither are you," Lane said, and he fired anther shot, then crawled behind the center loading hopper.

The silence outside was ominous. He wanted to call to Frances to find out if she was okay, but he didn't want her to reveal her position to Yernin.

"Even you can't beat sixty-to-one odds."

"I don't care about the odds," Lane said. "It's only us. Unless, of course, you need your friends to help you."

"I've never needed or wanted their interference. Without them I would have killed you much sooner,"

"Wishful thinking," Lane said. He moved to the corner and looked for a way to get to the top of the hopper. But the sloping sides were smooth.

"I have only one regret," Yernin called.

Someone was talking on a radio outside. Lane could hear the squawk, but not the words.

"What's that, Vasha? That you were ever born?" There was a ladder at the back of the hopper.

"That you won't get to see your woman die after all."

Lane started toward the ladder, but something in Yernin's voice, in its self-assured tone, made him turn back in time to see an object about the size of a book sailing his way.

Semtex, the thought crystallized in Lane's head.

Mindless of his injuries, Lane jumped up and batted the brick over the edge like a volleyball.

He leaped back behind the hopper as a white flash and tremendous explosion lifted the floor of the gallery by five feet. Almost immediately it buckled and started to slope away, the twenty-foot-tall hopper slowly falling on top of the conveyor system, which itself had been transformed into nothing but a mass of twisted steel rails, pipes, and girders, all collapsing toward the floor of the complex thirty feet below.

Lane's left foot caught the edge of a steel plate, and he pushed away from the hopper and dragged himself up onto a maintenance catwalk that ran along the row of support columns unaffected by the blast.

24

THE PHOSPHATE FACILITY

When the Semtex blew, Frances burrowed into a corner beneath a pair of intersecting support beams, and as the rusted machinery and twisted girders fell all round her, she buried her head in her arms.

After ten seconds the terrible din finally stopped, and a deathly silence fell over the entire loading complex.

From where she crouched unharmed she could see outside through a five-foot-long rent in the corrugated-iron wall. The Cubans had pulled back, taking their dead and wounded with them. One of them held a walkie-talkie to his ear. As she watched, he signaled for his men to head down to the dock, and within minutes they were gone.

25

THE PHOSPHATE FACILITY

After the explosion, his ears still ringing, Lane worked his way to the end of the catwalk to a spot above where Yernin had been standing. But the gallery was gone, collapsed in a tangled heap of metal on the main floor below. Yernin was dead, buried beneath tons of machinery.

A portion of the wall was gone, and from his perch he could see that the Cuban team had left. Probably down to the submarine.

The white Rover was untouched, except for a starred windshield, but all that remained of the Toyota was the smoldering burned-out hulk of the body.

"Frannie," Lane called down into the darkness, afraid of what he would hear, or wouldn't hear.

"William?" she called back, her voice surprisingly strong.

"Thank God," Lane muttered. "Are you all right?"

"Bloody hell, no I am not all right!" she shouted.

"My hair's a mess, I need a bath, and my makeup's a wreck. On top of that I think I peed myself."

Lane laughed. "If we're going to get married, you're going to have to learn to watch your language."

"Balls!"

"Hold on, I'm on my way down," Lane said. He safetied his Beretta, stuck it in his belt at the small of his back, and crawled a hundred feet back along the catwalk until he found a ladder that was still intact.

His leg had stiffened up, and pain came at him in throbbing waves like a gigantic toothache. At the bottom he had to pick his way through the wreckage, careful not to topple several pieces of machinery lying precariously balanced on their sides.

Frances, covered in blood, was calmly leaning back against a steel support column in the corner, the Makarov in her lap. She was in terrible pain, but her face lit up when she saw him.

"I knew you'd come," she said.

He knelt in front of her. "You were keeping some questionable company. I had to break it up to save our relationship. Tommy would never have forgiven me."

A look of alarm suddenly came into her eyes, and her lips compressed. "It's him," she mouthed the words. She picked up the Makarov, her movements hidden by Lane's body.

"Don't miss," he whispered, and he rolled left, snatching his own pistol out of his belt and thumbing the safety off.

Frances fired one shot, and Yernin grunted in pain. She pulled the trigger a second time but nothing happened—the gun was empty.

"Lane!" Yernin shouted.

Lane had only an instant to take aim at the dark apparition standing ten feet away, a brick of Semtex in one hand, a pencil fuse in the other, before he fired, hitting the assassin in the chest.

Yernin was shoved backward off his feet.

Lane scrambled up and went over to him.

Yernin was still alive, trying to insert the fuse into the Semtex, when he looked up. *"Yeb vas,"* he said, resigned.

Lane shot him in the heart.

26

THE PHOSPHATE FACILITY

It was after nine by the time Lane managed to get Frances over to the manager's house, and bind up her wounds and his own with things the Cuban team had left behind.

He also found them something to eat, and a couple of warm beers.

Afterward he hobbled down to the end of the long dock to make sure that the submarine had really gone, then went back to the loading complex, where he took the olive drab satchel from Yernin's body and went through its contents.

Among other things he found two electronic devices, one the size of a credit card, the other about the size of a cigarette pack with an extendable antenna.

He studied this second device for a long time, and when he finally raised his eyes, there was a look of satisfaction on his face.

He went back to the house, where Frances was anxiously waiting for him.

"Are they gone?" she asked.

Lane nodded. "We're finally alone."

"It's going to be a long walk back to Rabat unless you can disconnect the booby trap in the Rover."

"Why drive when we can fly?" Lane asked, taking Yernin's satellite phone from the pack.

She shook her head. "I almost forgot about that."

Lane entered the number for the U.S. embassy in London. This time he got through to Hughes almost immediately.

"How about giving an old friend and his fiancée a lift?"

"My God," Hughes said.

"Nope, just us. And if you can get somebody in Sixth Fleet to listen to you, tell them that the submarine left here about two hours ago. If they're on the ball they might be able to catch them."

"Where are you, William? Are you all right? What about Yernin?"

Lane looked over at Frances and smiled, then answered Hughes's questions in reverse order.

PART FIFTEEN

1

ABOARD 283

Maslennikov left the conn and headed forward to the officers' wardroom after making sure that his crew was settled down with the Cubans, and that sonar and radar continued to be clear. They ran on the surface at their best speed of fourteen knots on a course slightly south of west. In a few hours they would cross the tropic of Cancer. It was every Russian's desire to be warm year-round. Nobody liked snow, especially not peasants, the stock from which he'd come.

Ortega was seated with Cuban navy captain Raul Gomez across the small table from Lubiako and Kovrygin. They glared at each other, and when Maslennikov came in they looked up.

"Is everything in order?" Lubiako asked.

"Yes," Maslennikov said. He poured a glass of tea and settled down next to Kovrygin. "Have you four worked out a duty and training schedule?"

"*Nyet,*" Lubiako replied sharply. "They think they own the boat."

"We do," Ortega said mildly. Now that his people were aboard he was self-assured.

"Not yet, Colonel," Maslennikov contradicted him. "We've not received our final payment."

"You'll be paid when we arrive. That was the agreement."

"Perhaps the situation has changed."

"Perhaps it hasn't," Ortega said dangerously. "We

have lived up to our part of the bargain, I suggest you live up to yours.''

''There is still more than six thousand kilometers of open Atlantic to cross before—''

''We can handle it,'' Captain Gomez interrupted. Like some of the other Cubans, he was slender, dark, and handsome. His eyes were full of passion.

Maslennikov eyed him with distaste. ''Are you a trained submariner?''

''*Sí.*''

''Have you driven a boat across an ocean ?''

''No, but I am trained,'' answered Gomez without dropping his gaze. He was a proud man.

''We can manage,'' Ortega said. ''Certainly better than your star agent managed.''

Gomez smirked. ''If he hadn't sneaked into the phosphate factory without telling us, we could have helped him. As a result he's dead.''

''You didn't see the body,'' Maslennikov retorted sharply. The victory was bittersweet. In some ways Yernin had been like a son.

''No need. Nobody could have lived through that explosion. The entire conveyor building collapsed on itself. Whoever was inside was killed.'' Gomez gave them a hard look. ''Two of my men were shot to death, and one seriously wounded. Trust me, if I thought there was any chance that someone had survived, I would have gone in and killed them myself.''

· ''Very well.'' He called back to engineering on the growler phone. ''This is Maslennikov. How's it going back there, Eduard?''

''They haven't screwed anything up yet, Captain. But they're all over the place like a bunch of monkeys.''

''I want you to clear out of there. Take your crew with you.''

''Mother of God.''

''It's their boat now, let's let them handle it.''

The chief engineer laughed. "Our life rafts are in good shape. And we can use some time off."

"Good man," Maslennikov said. He hung up, and looked at Gomez. "Two-eighty-three is your boat, Captain. As soon as you're ready you may take the conn, and replace my crew with yours."

Gomez got to his feet. "I'll assume command now."

"By all means," Maslennikov said, smiling faintly. "If you have trouble with the Russian labels on the controls, my men will be happy to help."

"It won't be necessary," Gomez said contemptuously. "Count on it."

2

THE PHOSPHATE FACILITY

Lane found a stick to use as a cane, and hobbled painfully back to the destroyed loading building. The CIA's Rabat station had been notified, but it would be several hours before they could get down here. In the meantime Frances was sleeping at the manager's house.

The Rover had finally run out of gas and stalled. Lane found the brick of Semtex beneath the driver's seat, and carefully eased the pencil timer out and tossed it aside. It was one terrible legacy that Yernin would not leave behind.

He turned toward the opening into the building, hesitated a moment, then limped inside. He was on the last dregs of his energy.

Yernin lay half propped up against the piece of twisted machinery ten feet from where he'd fallen. He was dead now, but somehow he had managed to survive long enough to get within a couple of feet of the brick of Semtex he'd dropped.

Lane studied the assassin's face, twisted permanently into a grimace of pain and hate. After all that had happened over the past year, and especially these past weeks, Lane realized that he'd never really had Yernin's measure. He had badly underestimated the man. And it was a mistake that had cost a lot of good people their lives. A mistake he vowed never to make again.

He took out his Beretta and fired his last bullet into Yernin's forehead; then he turned and walked back outside into the clean night air.

3

LONDON

Hughes finally got through to Ben Lewis at the National Security Agency in Fort Meade, and quickly explained the situation to him.

"Where are they now?" Lewis asked.

"Still at the phosphate docks. We have somebody on the way down to get them. Apparently they were both shot up pretty badly, so we're bringing them here first. Point is, I'm under house arrest, and as soon as William arrives the British are going to arrest him. In the meantime the submarine is in the open Atlantic heading your way."

"It's not good enough. We still need proof. Has anyone actually seen the submarine?"

"One very angry French smuggler by the name of St.

Germaine. The British found him hiding on Sark Island. The *Charisma* ran him down and left him for dead, but he saw everything.''

''We'll turn this over to Sixth Fleet.''

''I already checked with them. They only have two ships anywhere near, and by the time they get into position it's even money if they'll find the sub. It might be an old boat, but it's being run by a handpicked crew. Maslennikov was one of the best.''

''All right, Tom. I'll take this upstairs and make sure it gets over to Newby.''

''To the president,'' Hughes said. ''We can't afford to play around.''

''I'll see what I can do,'' Lewis said. ''Oh, send them to Ramstein, our people can patch them up there. Won't do us any good if Lane is sitting in a British jail.''

Hughes chuckled. ''The aircrew has orders to develop engine trouble. They'll have to divert to Germany.''

''Yeah, I know,'' Lewis said, and he hung up.

--- 4 ---

RAMSTEIN AIR FORCE BASE GERMANY

Lane and Frances were stabilized and given painkillers before they were loaded aboard a CIA International Air America Learjet and flown out. But he was aware enough to recognize the base and Mario Garza waiting on the tarmac when they landed.

''They let you out of London on good behavior?'' Lane asked, his voice slurred.

"Something like that. But it was Tom Hughes's doing. The man's a pirate."

"Make sure Frannie's okay."

"Top priority," Garza said. "And as soon as they dig the bullets out of your hides and sew you up, we have a few thousand questions for both of you."

———— **5** ————

ABOARD 283

Someone was at the door to his cabin, and Maslennikov woke with a start, his heart pounding. "Come," he said softly. He reached up and switched on the dim red battle lamp.

The sonar officer, Vladimir Papyrin, slipped in. He was under stress, his Adam's apple bouncing nervously. "Sorry to bother you like this, Captain, but I think we have a problem."

"Have you talked to Captain Lubiako?"

"*Nyet*. I think the Cubans respect you more."

Maslennikov checked his watch. It read noon, which meant it was probably closer to 10:00 A.M. local. "Okay, what is it?"

"We submerged right after they took over, but it was too soon, our batteries weren't fully charged. Petr says we can't hold out much longer."

"It's their boat, Vladi. They'll surface when they realize what's going on."

Papyrin shook his head. "We can't."

"Why?"

"I was in sonar. To see how it was going. But they

kicked me out. They're all pissing in their pants back there because they don't know what to do.''

"Do we have a target?"

"Two of them. From what I saw I'm guessing they're frigates. Knox class, maybe."

"American ASW ships. Looking for us?"

"I think so, Captain."

Maslennikov got up and pulled on his shoes. "How close are they?"

"Fifteen thousand meters, maybe farther."

"They don't have us yet?"

"No, sir. But the range on one of them was closing."

"Ask Captain Lubiako to meet me in the conn," Maslennikov said. "You come too, but don't tell anyone else."

"Yes, sir," Papyrin said, and he left.

Maslennikov took his pistol from a locker, stuffed it in his belt beneath his sweater, and went aft to the control room.

Gomez was standing by the sonar compartment, a frightened look on his face. "What are you doing here? We're busy now."

"Not busy enough, unless you mean to get us all killed," Maslennikov said. He pushed past the Cuban and looked over the shoulder of the young sonar operator. "What designation have you given your targets, son?"

The sonar operator looked up, confused. "I haven't, I'm still trying to identify them."

"They're probably American Knox-class frigates, and they're looking for us." Maslennikov reached past the young man and switched on the tape unit. "We'll start recording their tracks now. First thing is to develop an accurate range and bearing, so that we can tell if they are in an active search mode."

"How can you be sure, sir? They don't sound like anything I was taught."

"They're using a Prairie Masker System. It changes their acoustical signatures. You have to know what you're listening for."

Lubiako showed up, and Papyrin slipped into the seat next to the Cuban sonar operator, donned a headset, and began flipping switches.

Gomez tried to pull Maslennikov away, but Lubiako shoved the Cuban roughly aside.

"You can have your toy back when we get you out of this mess. In the meantime, mind your manners or I'll start breaking body parts."

Ortega said something in Spanish, and Gomez backed off, a look of hate mixed with fear on his face.

"Definitely American Knox-class frigates," Papyrin said. "Sierra one, range twelve thousand five hundred meters and closing, bearing one-seven-eight. Sierra two, range sixteen thousand four hundred meters, steady, crossing starboard to port, bearing one-five-six."

"Our batteries are at fifteen percent," Lubiako reported from the conn.

"Can we sneak away from them?" Ortega asked.

"They're too close, and we don't have the battery power," Maslennikov said. "Your people saw to that by submerging last night when it wasn't necessary."

Although they hadn't been told of the situation, some of the other Ukrainian crew had drifted back. "We have a sharp thermocline at six hundred meters, Captain," said diving officer Yuri Bykov. "Recommend we dive under it and stay put."

A look passed between Lubiako and Maslennikov.

"Make your depth six-three-zero meters, but bring us down slowly," Lubiako ordered. "Rig for silent running."

"We're going to hide like frightened schoolchildren?" Gomez demanded.

"If this officer speaks again, bind and gag him," Maslennikov said. "But if he keeps his mouth shut, and his eyes and ears open, he might learn something. If we survive."

6

FF1065 *STEIN*

On the Knox-class frigate *Stein*, Commander Richard Gladen was seated on the bridge, his XO, Lieutenant Commander Don Magnuson, studying the choppy seas ahead through binoculars. Their twin, the *Marvin Shields*, was about three miles off their port quarter on a zigzag search-and-find pattern.

The growler phone buzzed and Gladen picked it up. "This is the captain."

"CIC. We've lost the possible target designated Sierra three-zero-one."

"What was its last estimated position?"

"About twelve thousand yards, bearing zero-zero-five."

"Talk to me, Max. Could we have picked up another biologic?" the captain asked.

"It's possible, Skipper. Whatever it was, it was quiet and deep."

Gladen detected a slight note of hesitation in his combat information officer's voice. "And?" he prompted.

"I was just thinking that we're looking in the wrong place," Lieutenant Max Schober said. "They had at least nine hours of darkness to run at maximum speed on the surface before they would have submerged at dawn. There's some traffic around the Canary Islands that they'd want to avoid. That would put them fifty miles west of here.''

''That's a good point,'' Gladen said. ''We'll stay on this course and pattern until we pass their last possible position. If we don't find anything, we'll follow your suggestion.''

''Yes, sir.''

Gladen hung up the phone and turned to his XO. ''Tell the *Marvin Shields* that we've lost sonar contact, but we're going to continue on this pattern for a little bit yet.''

''Another biologic?'' Magnuson said. Since passing through the Strait of Gibraltar at the start of their exercise last week their sonars had detected a lot of whale activity. It was the time of year when the animals headed south.

Gladen shrugged. ''Unknown. But Max thinks that we're looking in the wrong place. The sub should be another fifty miles west by now.''

''He's probably right,'' Magnuson said.

7

ABOARD 283

Papyrin held the earphones tightly to his ears, his face a mask of concentration. Beneath the thermocline the submarine's passive sonar was just as useless as the sonar equipment the surface ships were using. But the frigates were making a lot of noise, which Papyrin was listening to.

"Sierra one has passed overhead," he whispered. "Sierra two is coming up now. I can't tell the distance, but it's close."

The submarine was deathly still; even the air-circulating fans had been turned low, and all nonessential equipment had been switched off not only to avoid making any noise, but to conserve their dwindling battery power.

"It's coming closer," Papyrin said.

"Why can't we hear anything?" Gomez asked, but he shut up when Ortega glared at him.

The air was getting warm and stale. Maslennikov took off his sweater, and Ortega glanced at the pistol in his belt. Their eyes met, and Maslennikov shrugged.

"Now," Papyrin whispered.

Everyone in the control room instinctively looked up at the overhead. Some of them held their breath.

Papyrin turned to Maslennikov after another minute, and grinned. "It's fading," he said. "Definitely fading."

"Stay with them. They might turn back," Maslennikov said.

Papyrin shook his head. "The screw noises are increasing," he said. He held the earphones closer. "They're accelerating. They've found nothing and they're leaving."

Ortega and the others breathed a sigh of relief.

"We'll wait a half hour, then resume our course," Gomez said.

"On the contrary," Maslennikov said. "We'll turn right ninety degrees and continue submerged until our batteries are nearly drained, and then we'll come to snorkel depth and start the auxiliary generators."

"That's the wrong direction," Gomez argued.

"They haven't given up, you fool," Lubiako said.

"They're just leapfrogging ahead where they'll wait for us to catch up."

"Then they know where we're heading," Ortega said, concerned.

"It's possible," Maslennikov agreed.

"Bill Lane."

Maslennikov nodded tightly. "We're not out of the birches yet."

8

FF1065 *STEIN*

Three hours later the *Stein*'s LAMPS-I ASW helicopter touched down on the landing pad at the stern of the frigate, its rotors spooling down as the deck crew scrambled to secure it.

"Nada," Executive Officer Magnuson said.

"It's a big ocean, Don," Captain Gladen said. "We'll stay on this pattern until dark, and if we come up empty-handed we'll secure from the mission. Then it'll be up to the guys at the other end."

"I would have liked to have nailed them out here."

Gladen nodded. "Me too."

RAMSTEIN AIR FORCE BASE HOSPITAL

When Lane came around it was dark in his room and he was alone. He could see through the partially open blinds that it was night, but which night and how long he'd been out he had no way of knowing.

His entire body was a mass of pain and his muscles were stiff from the shock of several bullet wounds, the effects of the explosion including several cracked ribs, the operations, and the tight bandages around his leg and torso.

He sat up and removed the IV drip connected to his left hand, then reached over and shut off the monitor and pulled the monitor lead from his chest. He threw back the covers and slowly got out of bed. He was light-headed, and had to catch himself from falling, and hold for a moment until he regained his balance. His leg was throbbing and the broken ribs made breathing painful.

At the door he looked down the corridor. A nurse, her back to him, was talking on a telephone at the counter.

He hobbled next door and looked inside. A young black man was watching television. Lane crossed the hall and looked in. Frances, lying propped up in bed, was sleeping. Her left leg, in a cast, was elevated.

He pulled a chair over and sat down beside her. A few seconds later her eyes opened, and when she saw him, her face lit up.

"Hi, Frannie, how are you feeling?"

"Better," she said softly. "How about you? They said you'd lost a lot of blood."

"I'll probably live, much to the dismay of half the population of Whitehall."

She smiled, and touched his face. Then she turned serious. "Is he really dead?"

"He's dead. I made sure of it."

She smiled again. "Tom is here, and so is Brad. He wanted the doctor to give you something to make you wake up, and Tom practically took his head off." She laughed. "You have a good friend there."

"*We* have a good friend. He's going to be my best man at our wedding."

Her eyes clouded. "I have to go back and answer questions, and charges."

"That won't be forever. When it's done we'll be together."

"I don't know how."

"We'll work it out, Frannie. Trust me."

A nurse appeared in the doorway. "Here you are," she said sternly. "We're going back to bed."

Lane grinned at her. "Thanks for the offer, but no thanks. What you're going to do, however, is find us a couple of fillets, rare, some pommes Parisienne, a small salad, vinaigrette, and a good bottle of"—he looked at Frances—"Merlot?"

She nodded.

"And if the wine hasn't had time to breathe, we'll send it back. Now scoot."

After a string of doctors and nurses had trooped through, Hughes, Morgan, and Garza were finally allowed in, followed by a nurse's aide pushing a large silver serving cart. It was ten o'clock at night. She shoved past a scowling Morgan and set up the dinners and bottle of wine on the wheeled bed tray. She set a small vase with a single flower on the tray, then shook her head.

"You must have some pull, Mr. Lane," she said, and she left.

"This is beyond all reason," Morgan grumbled.

"Shut up, Bradley," Frances said.

Lane poured wine for them, and he and Frances clicked glasses.

"How do you feel, William?" Hughes asked.

"Hungry, but I'm going to fix that now," he said, and took a drink. "Passable," he said. "Have they found the sub?"

"No, but a half dozen ships from the Second Fleet and a few from the Coast Guard's Key West station are waiting for them. Havana is all but blockaded. When they try to get in we'll have them."

"The media must be having a field day."

Hughes shook his head. "It's all hush-hush, and so far there've been no leaks. We're out there on a joint navy–Coast Guard training mission."

"With live ammunition," Lane said.

"Mrs. Houlten is dead, doesn't that mean anything to you?" Morgan demanded. "Especially you, Frances?"

"It means a great deal to me," said Lane seriously. "The man who killed her is dead."

"No he's not. He's sitting here drinking a glass of wine like the irresponsible playboy he is." Morgan pointed a finger at him. "You didn't pull the trigger, but you might as well have."

Frances threw her wineglass at him, hitting him in the face, and breaking it. A small cut opened on the bridge of his nose.

"Get out of here, you whining bloody bastard!" she cried. "If I had a gun I'd shoot you myself and put you out of your misery."

Morgan stood rooted to his spot, stunned, his mouth open, wine and blood dripping from his face.

"Go!" Frances screeched. She reached for the wine bottle, but Lane stopped her.

"The Merlot isn't that bad," he said gently.

Morgan backed up, his hand going to the cut. He looked amazed, and hurt, but the anger was gone for the moment. "You have to come back to London."

"Yes, as soon as I'm released from the hospital."

"You'll face charges—"

"Yes, I know that. But so will you."

"For what?" Morgan blustered.

"Malfeasance for starters," Frances said calmly, her own anger dissipated.

"That's nonsense."

"It was you who ordered the Yard away from my house. And it was you who withheld the information I'd discovered about Sark Island." She looked at Lane and smiled sadly. "I'm sure I can come up with some other charges. We'll see." She turned back to Morgan. "Get out of here, Brad. Go home, and I'll be along in due time."

"Well," Hughes said after Morgan left. "Why don't we leave you to your dinner. We'll come back in the morning."

"Good thinking, Tommy," Lane said.

"I'll just see about getting you another wineglass."

"It's not necessary, Tom," Frances said. "We'll manage with one."

Lane left Frances's room after midnight. She was sound asleep and he could barely keep his own eyes open. Just the effort of walking across the hall and having dinner had completely worn him down. He had no stamina.

Before he crawled back into his own bed, he went searching for his bloody, torn clothing and the satchel he'd taken from Yernin's body. It was all in the tiny closet next to the bathroom.

He took the electronic device with the extendable antenna from the satchel and looked at it. Yernin had evidently thought it was important enough to pull out of the rubble after the explosion. It, the small detonator for the pencil fuses, and his satellite telephone were the three items he'd valued almost as much as his own life.

Yernin had had a plan. One last thing he'd meant to do before he disappeared somewhere on his own. Lane didn't think the assassin meant to board the submarine and sail with it to Cuba. Yernin had been a loner.

Lane looked up, his eyes narrowed in concentration. It would take the submarine three weeks to cross the Atlantic. And when it got there, Havana would be blockaded.

He put the device back in the satchel, then got into bed, and was asleep the moment his head hit the pillow.

PART SIXTEEN

1

Tom Hughes was working at his desk when Lane, dressed in a dove gray Armani suit, Hermès tie, and Gucci loafers, leaned against the doorframe. "I heard that you've complained for three weeks straight about the workload, so I convinced Ben to let me come back."

Hughes looked up and smiled warmly. "You didn't come back from the Farm just to see me. You must have heard from Frances."

Lane grinned. "I never could lie to you." He still used a cane. He limped to a chair, sat down, and put his bad leg up. "She's coming over on the Concorde the day after tomorrow."

"She's been cleared?"

"Evidently. But she was mysterious about it. Something about the prime minister apologizing, and he's in complete agreement with the president. Do you know what she's talking about?"

Hughes shook his head. "What about Brad Morgan?"

"Early retirement. Nobody wanted to drag him or the SIS through the mud. But Frannie quit the Service too."

"A waste of good talent, but the Service always was an old boys' club. Not enough women to give them insight."

"That's what I told her."

"What'd she say?"

Lane laughed. "She called me a chauvinist pig, and as I recall, I think you were included in that class. She said that since I wasn't going to quit and move in with her, she'd have to take the bull by the horns and move in with me."

"Then we better keep this from Moira," Hughes said seriously. "She doesn't condone people living in sin."

"It won't be for long, providing you and Moira are still willing to stand up for us."

"Gad," Hughes said. "I'll be financially ruined. Do you have any idea what it'll cost to outfit my wife and six daughters in new dresses? Not to mention shoes, purses, and panty hose?"

"Maybe Ben will give you a raise."

Hughes looked at him appraisingly. "You're back because of two-eighty-three."

"I haven't heard a thing. Where is it?"

"It hasn't shown up yet. Maybe it was never headed for Cuba in the first place. Or maybe there was an accident—it's an old boat."

"With one of the best submarine crews in the world," Lane said absently, his mind elsewhere. He got up without a word and went across to the crisis center, the big screen that dominated the far wall blank.

Hughes followed him over. "It's up to the navy and Coast Guard. They're not going to let it reach Havana."

Lane limped down to one of the control consoles, put his cane aside, and brought up a Robinson projection of the Western Hemisphere on the screen. Using a light pencil he drew a course on the big screen from Western Sahara straight across the Atlantic, through the Windward Passage between Haiti and the eastern tip of Cuba, then up the north coast to Havana.

"This is what the navy is expecting," Lane said.

"It's the easiest route," Hughes said. "The logical route."

"Maslennikov knows that," Lane said. He redrew the course, this time bringing the submarine into the Caribbean through the Mona Passage four hundred miles farther east, between the Dominican Republic and Puerto Rico.

"They'd still have to double back and take the Windward Passage north, right past Guantánamo Bay."

"If they were headed for Havana," Lane said. He drew a course directly for the city of Santiago de Cuba, about fifty miles west of Guantánamo.

"How about that," Hughes said softly. "If they have the subsea-launched missiles, our base would be in easy reach."

Lane was staring at the screen. "Get Ben down here. We're going to need a ride down there this morning."

"Turn it over to the navy," Hughes said.

"Too late, Tommy. They're probably already in position. But I can stop them."

Hughes shook his head. "Why did I think you were going to say something like that?"

2

ABOARD 283

Nearly everyone aboard the submarine was sick now as Lubiako left Maslennikov's cabin and went aft to the control center. They were nauseous all the time, and the boat stank of vomit.

Gomez was at the periscope, the Cuban crew back in control.

"Are we in position?" Lubiako asked.

Gomez, his eyes red, his face pale, looked at him and nodded. "How is Captain Maslennikov?"

"He's dead."

"As we all will be very soon," Gomez said, resigned. "You should have warned us about the radiation."

"It wouldn't have made any difference," Lubiako said. He looked through the periscope. The entrance to Guantánamo Bay was about five kilometers directly ahead. In the distance a helicopter was headed out to sea, slightly west of them. He straightened up. "This is why you wanted the boat?"

"We weren't going to attack so soon. Maybe next month, but now is just as good a time as any."

"There's a helicopter up there. Probably looking for us."

"I saw it. But they're too late." He turned to his weapons control officer. "Are we ready on tubes one and two?"

"*Sí*," the young man answered weakly.

"Where's Colonel Ortega?"

"In his bunk, but he approves," Gomez said. "Surface the boat," he told the diving officer. "Once we're on top you may fire the missiles."

"Why let them know that we're here?" Lubiako asked, though he really didn't care.

"So that the bastards will know what happened to them," Gomez said, as the submarine's bow tilted upward.

3

ABOVE GUANTÁNAMO BAY

Aboard the Sikorsky SH-60F LAMPS III helicopter, Lane was at the open hatch; Hughes was back at the marine base to act as liaison with two navy ASW frigates heading around the eastern tip of the island. The copilot was the first to spot two-eighty-three.

"Jesus. I have a submarine surfacing about nine o'clock."

The pilot hauled the ASW helicopter around in an extremely tight turn to the east, and Lane had to brace himself to keep from being banged around.

He could hear all their communications through his helmet headset.

"Home Plate, this is Babe Ruth, we have a positive contact on a Romeo-class submarine," the pilot radioed his ship. He gave a grid reference.

"Roger, Babe Ruth. You're authorized to find a firing solution and arm your weapons."

"Roger."

The helicopter carried two Mk 46 torpedoes in addition to an array of submarine detectors.

Lane keyed his mike. "Lieutenant, I want you to make a pass directly over the sub before you drop your torpedoes."

"We're not going to parley with them, Mr. Lane."

"They're not here to talk either. Just get me close and I'll save us all some time and trouble."

"Babe Ruth, this is Home Plate, you have authorization to release your weapons."

"Roger, Home Plate. Mr. Lane wants us to make a pass over the target first."

"Stand by."

Lane took out the electronic device he'd got from Yernin's satchel, extended the antenna, and turned it on. The electronics officer seated at his console was looking at Lane.

"Babe Ruth, Home Plate. Go ahead and do it, Scotty, but do it smartly."

"Roger," the pilot said, and he headed directly for the submarine, still a half mile out. "Mr. Lane, are they getting ready to attack Guantánamo?"

"You can count on it," Lane said.

"If they already loaded their missiles, and have firing solutions, we're running real short on time."

"Steady," Lane said. "Just one pass."

The pilot said nothing, but the helicopter did not deviate from its course directly toward the submarine.

At the last instant, the submarine directly below them, Lane pushed the start button on the electronic device.

For a moment nothing seemed to happen, but then three geysers of water boiled to the surface along the length of the sub, followed a second later by a huge explosion that lifted the boat almost completely out of the water.

"Holy shit," the copilot said.

The pilot peeled off to the south. "Home Plate, we have a major event here. The submarine just exploded."

"Did you fire at it?"

"Negative," the pilot radioed, and they came around in a gut-wrenching turn, then pulled up sharply into a hover about two hundred yards away.

Two-eighty-three was laid over nearly sixty degrees on her starboard side, two-thirds of the bottom of her hull blown away. Machinery and men were caught in a mad jumble as the boat went down like a stone.

Within seconds it was over; an oil slick, pieces of flotsam, and a dozen or more bodies were all that was left on the surface.

"What the hell happened, Mr. Lane?" the pilot demanded.

Lane tossed the detonator out the hatch. "I just delivered a message from a guy I used to know," he said. He sat back in his seat, closed his eyes, and thought about where he was going to take Frances for dinner tomorrow night.

—————— **4** ——————

THE WHITE HOUSE

Hughes was delayed coming back from Dulles with Frances, so Lane had to go alone to the White House. When the president called for a meeting it was best not to be late.

The president's national security adviser, Leslie Newby, was waiting in the hall. "Here you are finally," he said.

"Am I late?" Lane asked.

"No, but the president's schedule is extremely tight this afternoon, and he wants to get you started as soon as possible."

"Started with what?" Lane asked, following Newby back to the Oval Office, but there was no answer.

Frances and Hughes were seated on the couch across from National Security Agency director Tom Roswell and President Reasoner.

Frances smiled sweetly.

"Welcome back, Bill," the president said. "Once again you've done a hell of a job for us."

"Thank you, sir," Lane said, and he and Newby sat down. Both Frances and Hughes were grinning like Cheshire cats.

"How are you feeling?"

"Just fine, Mr. President. But I have to admit I'm a little puzzled right now."

The president chuckled. "I imagine you are. Sorry to go behind your back like this, but I wanted the issue with Yernin and the submarine to be resolved first, and then I wanted the prime minister's complete understanding and agreement. All of that has been accomplished."

"I, for one, am going to miss them," Roswell said. "A sentiment shared by Commander Shipley's people."

"But you agree with the need," the president said.

Roswell nodded begrudgingly. "Yes, Mr. President."

"Then it comes down to Bill accepting the job."

"What job is that, Mr. President?" Lane asked, completely mystified.

"Before the Office of Strategic Services was formed because of World War II, President Roosevelt understood that the country needed an effective intelligence-gathering agency that could go anywhere and do just about anything on a moment's notice. So he formed what he called The Room. Mostly businessmen who traveled abroad, who would keep their eyes and ears open, and report back to him when they came home.

"Our problem these days is that we're top-heavy with intelligence agencies—the CIA, the NSA, the National Reconnaissance Office, the State Department's intelligence unit, the military intelligence sections. The list is nearly endless, as are their bureaucracies. What's needed is a special unit, a small task force. A troubleshooting unit that can keep on top of troubling situations here as well as abroad."

Newby started to say something, but the president waved him off.

"I don't mean places like Bosnia or Zaire, I mean situations like what occurred last year in the Persian Gulf because of Yernin, and again most recently off Cuba. In both instances without Bill Lane's fast work, the NSA and CIA would have acted too slowly."

"I don't know what to say, Mr. President," Lane said.

"We'll keep it small, no top-heavy bureaucracy. It'll be jointly staffed between our intelligence agencies and those of Great Britain. You and Commander Shipley would direct the unit, and you would report only to me and the prime minister."

Lane looked over at Frances.

"We'd be together," she said.

"I understand congratulations are in order," the president said. "I hope you'll invite me and Mrs. Reasoner to your wedding."

"By all means, Mr. President," Frances answered for them.

"When would we start?" Lane asked.

"Immediately."

"What about a budget?"

"Unlimited, within reason of course. Leslie will coordinate with London and set it for you."

"Offices?"

"Wherever you and Commander Shipley want. I would suggest offices here and in London. It would entail a certain amount of travel, but you'd both be closer to your resources."

"What have you decided to call this unit, Mr. President?" Lane asked.

President Reasoner smiled. "If you'll permit me a bit of historical vanity, I'd like to call it The Room."

Lane had to laugh. "I can hardly say no to my president," he said.

"Or I my prime minister," Frances said. "But we'll need time for our honeymoon."

"Indeed," the president said. "But don't take too long, because there are a half dozen extremely urgent items already on the table for you."

"In the meantime I'll get everything set up at this end," Hughes said. "Because somebody will have to keep you two on the straight and narrow."

"I couldn't think of anybody better to do it," Lane said.

"Ditto, as you Yanks say," Frances added. "But that means you're going to have to agree with me every now and then."

"I couldn't imagine anything easier," Hughes said, "or more delightful."